Savannah Martin has always been a good girl, doing what was expected and fully expecting life to fall into place in its turn. But when her perfect husband turns out to be a lying, cheating slimeball - and bad in bed to boot - Savannah kicks the jerk to the curb and embarks on life on her own terms. With a new apartment, a new career, and a brand new outlook on life, she's all set to take the world by storm.

If only the world would stop throwing her curveballs...

When Savannah wakes up alone on what is supposed to be her wedding day, she isn't sure what to think. Did her fiancé—bad-boy TBI agent Rafe Collier—decide he couldn't face being shackled to one woman for the rest of his life... or is something more sinister going on?

Savannah's mother Margaret Anne, in Nashville for the nuptials, is certain she knows the truth: her future son-in-law has always been an ill-bred cad, and leaving his pregnant girlfriend practically at the altar clinches it. But the people who know Rafe aren't so sure. Wendell Craig with the TBI and Tamara Grimaldi with the Metro Nashville PD suspect foul play, and set out to prove it.

Shortly, a dead woman turns up in Savannah's house. Rafe's son David goes missing from church camp on the Cumberland Plateau. And a shadowy figure from Rafe's past is stalking them all—a knife-wielding serial killer who likes to hurt women, and who has a score to settle.

Now Savannah must solve the murder, find David, and avoid getting herself killed... or she can kiss her happy ending—and Rafe—goodbye.

Unfinished Business

Jenna Bennett

Magpie Ink

One

I woke up alone on what should have been my wedding day.

That might not strike you as unusual for a bride, but I was living in sin with my husband-to-be, and it was quite a while since I'd woken up alone in bed. Usually I woke up with Rafe's arm around me, his hand splayed protectively over my stomach, and his nose buried in my hair.

Today, his side of the bed was empty and cold.

Under normal circumstances, I might have reasoned he'd just gone to work. But it was a Saturday, and he'd taken the day off from working out to get married, so he wasn't on the clock.

And it was almost nine o'clock. He's usually an early riser. I'm not, since I'm four months pregnant and spend much of my time feeling like I've been bitten by the tsetse fly. But at this point of the morning, and especially given today's agenda, I would have expected him to have woken me.

I spent a few moments listening to the sounds of the house. It was June, and approaching ninety-five degrees outside, so the A/C was pumping cold air through the vents. The system hummed. Other things hummed, too. Electrical things. Things like the refrigerator downstairs, and the TV and computer, even when they weren't in use. It's never entirely silent anymore unless the electricity goes out.

But while I could hear electrical humming, and birds singing outside, and the sound of a lawnmower somewhere in the neighborhood, I couldn't hear any sounds of activity inside the house. If Rafe was up, and downstairs, he was being very quiet.

I swung my legs over the edge of the bed. The hardwood floors were cold from the air conditioning as I padded toward the door. "Rafe?"

There was no answer from downstairs. I grabbed a robe from behind the door and shrugged into it as I walked across the landing to the stairs. I didn't think anyone was in the house, but I'm still well-bred enough that I don't wander around in the altogether with my breasts and pregnant stomach on display. You never know when someone might be standing on the porch with his nose pressed to one of the windows.

No one was. The foyer downstairs was deserted, and the porch and yard were empty. I padded down the hallway to the kitchen, glancing left and right as I went.

The first room on the right was the library, where—ten months ago—Rafe and I had discovered Brenda Puckett's butchered body lying in front of the fireplace. We hadn't been living here then, of course. The house had belonged to Rafe's grandmother, and Brenda Puckett was a realtor colleague of mine, who was trying to sell it.

There was no one in the library now. Ditto for the parlor and the dining room. I ended up in the kitchen, at the back of the house, and looked around.

The first time I'd walked in here, the second week of August last year, it had had avocado green appliances and a cracked and peeling linoleum floor. Now it was gorgeous, with new cabinets, hardwoods, and stainless steel appliances. The baby I was carrying had been conceived on the table that stood in the middle of the room.

Though gorgeous, the kitchen was empty. I walked around, peering at the table, the counters, and the refrigerator, but Rafe had not left a note.

My phone was upstairs by the bed, charging, but he hadn't called, either. Or texted me. If he had, I would have woken up.

I padded back upstairs to put on clothes and brush my teeth. That done, I tried calling him. The phone rang twice, three times, and then went to voicemail. "This is Rafe. You know what to do."

"It's me," I said. "Nine o'clock on Saturday. You're not home. Call me when you get this, please."

And then I went back downstairs and ate breakfast—bagel with cream cheese and chives, my go-to craving throughout the pregnancy—while I waited for him to call back.

The logical part of my brain tried to convince the other parts that he was probably just at the gym. He'd woken up early—a little nervous about what would happen today, maybe—and had decided to get in an early workout, to take his mind off the fact that in six hours, he'd have shackled himself hand and foot to the same woman for the rest of his natural life.

It made sense, and I wouldn't blame him. Getting married can be scary, especially when it's your first time. I'd been through it once already, and knew I wasn't making the same mistake again. But Rafe had never done this before, and it was natural that he'd be a bit worried.

I would have thought he'd be home again by now, though. We weren't planning a big ceremony, just a quick stop at the county clerk's office. My first wedding, to Bradley Ferguson when I was twenty-three, had taken place at the church where I'd been christened as a baby, in Sweetwater, Tennessee, an hour, hour and fifteen, south of Nashville.

But while Rafe was also from Sweetwater, I knew he hadn't wanted to get married there. He never goes back to Sweetwater if he can help it.

No, we were going to the courthouse, and my brother and sister were driving up from Sweetwater to witness the ceremony along with our friend, Metro Nashville Homicide Detective Tamara Grimaldi, and Rafe's boss at the Tennessee Bureau of Investigations, Wendell Craig.

It was going to be an intimate occasion, to put it mildly.

Was it possible that he and Wendell had gone out for breakfast before the big occasion? Or had just kept partying through the night?

They'd been out together yesterday. Rafe hadn't wanted a bachelor party—nor did he have many friends he could invite to one, after spending ten years undercover for the TBI. The friends he'd made during those years were mostly in jail, and wouldn't wish him well if they'd known about the nuptials. But he and Wendell and the rookies Rafe was training to be agents, had gone out for a beer after work yesterday, to celebrate Rafe's last night of freedom.

Which was ridiculous, if you ask me, because I certainly wasn't going to stop him from going out for a beer with the guys after we got married.

But at any rate, he'd been out last night.

And now here I was. Alone, on my wedding day.

I pulled the phone over and dialed Wendell's number.

Back in the day, when Rafe was undercover, Wendell had been his handler, and Wendell's phone had been the only way I had of getting in touch with Rafe. I'd call Wendell, Wendell would tell Rafe, and Rafe would call me. For a couple of months, whenever I'd call, Wendell would tell me I'd reached a car lot, or a grocery store, or a pool hall.

Those days were over. Now he simply said, "Craig."

"This is Savannah Martin," I said. And just in case he didn't remember me, I added, "Rafe's girlfriend."

"I know who you are, Savannah." He sounded amused. "You getting ready for your big day?"

"I would be," I told him, "if I could find the groom."

There was a beat of silence.

"He wasn't here when I woke up. I thought maybe..." I trailed off.

"No," Wendell said, and I could hear the tension in his voice, just as I could hear him try to sound calm so I wouldn't notice. "Last time I saw Rafe was last night around eleven. He was going home."

"I'm not sure whether he got here or not. I sleep like the dead these days. But I didn't see him." And I was surprised he hadn't woken me up, if he'd been home. "He hasn't been in touch with you?"

"No," Wendell said grimly. "Are you sure he isn't just at the gym? Working off some nerves?"

"He might be. And if he is, he'll call me back soon. But he isn't here. I thought maybe the two of you had decided to go out to breakfast or something."

"No," Wendell said. "I wasn't planning to see him—see either of you—until I got to the courthouse at eleven."

The courthouse at eleven.

Right.

My brother and sister were driving up from Sweetwater for this. They were planning to meet us there. I should call them and tell them the groom was missing.

"Thanks," I told Wendell. "If you hear from him, tell him to get in touch with me, OK?"

Wendell said he would. "And when he comes back, let me know."

"I will," I said. "I'm sure he's just somewhere, doing something."

Wendell agreed that Rafe was undoubtedly somewhere, doing something. "I'll give the boys a call, see if any of them have spoken to him. And just let me know when he gets there."

I promised I would, and hung up. And tried Rafe's phone again. There was no answer this time, either.

My next call was to my brother, Dixon Calvert Martin—Dix to his friends and family. All except Mother, who calls him by his full name.

The phone rang a couple of times, and then my brother's voice came on. "I'm on my way, sis."

"Oh," I said. "Here?"

"Where else?" There was a pause while I heard murmurs in the background, and then he added, "You haven't changed your mind, have you?"

"No," I said. "Of course not."

"Of course not," Dix repeated, either to me or to someone who was there with him.

"Are you in the car?"

"Just leaving Sweetwater," Dix confirmed. "I dropped off the kids with Jonathan, and now we're on our way."

"You and Catherine?"

Catherine is my older sister. Our older sister, I should say. Jonathan's wife. She's a couple of years older than Dix, who's a couple of years older than me.

"And Mother," Dix said.

Mother?

My mother—our mother—was coming to see me get married?

Why, for heaven's sake? She can't stand Rafe. In fact, if she heard that he was gone, she'd no doubt consider it divine intervention and a personal victory.

Dix didn't say anything—I guess he couldn't, with Mother right there—and eventually I got my voice to cooperate again. "Maybe you should stop somewhere for breakfast. Or lunch." No, too early for lunch. "Brunch," I corrected. "Or coffee."

"Why?"

I told him.

"What?" Dix said.

"You heard me. I don't know where Rafe is. That's why I'm calling. I wanted to know whether you'd heard from my boyfriend."

"No," Dix said, his voice tight, "not today."

"Anytime recently? Do you have any idea what he's doing this morning?"

"None," Dix said.

No. "He's probably just somewhere, doing something. Working out, or buying champagne, or... or something."

"Sure," Dix said. "Have you checked with Tamara?"

I shook my head, even though he couldn't see me. "She's next. I spoke to Wendell, Rafe's boss at the TBI. He hasn't seen Rafe since last night."

"Call Tamara," Dix said. "Then call me back."

I said I would. I was just about to hang up when he added, "Savannah?"

"What?"

"Don't worry. I'm sure everything's fine."

"Sure," I said, without believing it. "Thanks, Dix. I'll call Detective Grimaldi and get back to you."

"OK," Dix said. "We'll see you at the courthouse at eleven."

"I'll be there," I said. "And I'm serious, Dix. Stop for coffee or something. If you don't, you'll be there too early."

"Just call Tamara and get back to me." He hung up before I could say anything else.

I dialed again.

The first time I met Detective Tamara Grimaldi was the day Brenda Puckett died. After Rafe and I found the body, I'd asked Rafe to call 911—as any law-abiding citizen would—and Grimaldi caught the case.

It wasn't what you'd call an auspicious beginning. She didn't like me, and the feeling was mutual. I found her intimidating, and she found me annoying. She didn't suspect me of murder, though. That honor was reserved for Rafe. It wasn't until Grimaldi learned that he was deep undercover for the TBI, that she stopped suspecting him of various things that happened.

Over time, our relationship had developed into a friendship. The detective still intimidated me, and I think she probably still thought I was annoying, but we got along well enough. She and Rafe had worked together on more than one occasion, and since Sheila died and Grimaldi solved that case too—with a little help from yours truly—Grimaldi and Dix had developed a relationship of their own, one I wasn't sure Mother knew about.

To be honest, I wasn't entirely sure what kind of relationship it was myself either. It was more than friendship, but maybe not quite a romance yet. At any rate, I didn't think they were sleeping together. If they were, they were keeping it very quiet. So quiet that I hadn't seen any of the usual signs.

The detective had the day off, too. Not because of the wedding, but just because it worked out that way. She was on call on weekends a lot of the time, and when she had a case, she worked pretty much 24/7 until it was solved, but we'd lucked out, and decided to get married on a day when someone else was on call and Grimaldi had been available.

As a result, I called her cell phone, and caught her at home. "Detective."

"Ms.... Savannah."

Neither of us has quite gotten the hang of this new relationship. I'm still more comfortable addressing her by her title, and she's struggling to overcome her aversion to using my first name.

"Have you heard from Rafe today?"

There's no point in beating around the bush with the detective. She doesn't appreciate it, and anyway, it was a waste of time.

"No," Grimaldi said. "What happened?"

"I don't know that anything did. But I woke up this morning and he wasn't there. His side of the bed looks like it wasn't slept in."

Grimaldi didn't answer.

"I spoke to Wendell Craig. He and Rafe and the rookies were out drinking beer last night. Their version of a bachelor party. Wendell said Rafe headed home around eleven."

"Did he get there?" Grimaldi asked.

"I didn't see him. You know— Well, maybe you don't, but I sleep all the time. Like the dead. Once I'm down for the night, I'm not easy to wake. So he could have come home without me realizing it. But if he did, he didn't talk to me. And the blankets were still smooth this morning."

"Was he riding the bike?" Grimaldi asked.

"When he went to work yesterday morning he was. That's the last time I saw him. We spoke later, but he went out directly from work. I assume he still had the bike last night. He wouldn't have drunk enough that it was a problem for him to drive."

"No," Grimaldi said, "I'm sure he wouldn't."

There was a moment's pause.

"I assume you've checked with the hospitals?"

God. "No." My voice shook, and I tried to firm it. "I haven't. I'll do that next."

"Leave it to me," Grimaldi said. "You have a wedding to get ready for."

"Without the groom?"

"He won't leave you standing at the altar," Grimaldi said firmly. Just as I was starting to feel better, she added, "Not if he can help it."

"What if he can't help it?"

"Then we'll find him," Grimaldi said, "and figure it out."

I didn't answer. Couldn't. She continued, "He loves you, Savannah. Maybe he's just planning a surprise for you. The best thing you can do is get dressed and ready and over to the courthouse."

Maybe. And because I really wanted to believe she was right, I said, "You'll be there, right?"

"Of course."

"Dix is on his way. I just spoke to him."

Grimaldi didn't answer. She usually doesn't when I bring up Dix's name. I think she thinks I'm fishing.

"He's bringing Catherine," I added. "And Mother."

That got a response. "Your mother's coming?"

"So it seems. It shocked me, too. I mean, you know how she feels about Rafe. Why would she want to watch me marry him? Nothing would make her happier than if I changed my mind and said 'I don't' when the preacher asked if I take this man."

"Maybe she's hoping you will?"

"Maybe." Or maybe she was hoping he wouldn't show up. If so, it looked like she might get her wish.

"Go get ready," Grimaldi told me. "I'll see you at the courthouse at eleven."

"I'll be there. And if you hear anything before then—"

"I'll call you. Of course."

"Thank you," I said.

"Don't mention it," Grimaldi answered. "He'll be there, Savannah."

"I hope you're right," I told her, and went to get ready to get married.

Two

I had bought a new dress for the occasion.

It wasn't a white gown. I'd had the white gown once before, and wearing it a second time would be tacky. Also, I was starting to become visibly pregnant, and showing up to your own wedding in a white gown when you're visibly pregnant is also tacky. And since we were just going to the courthouse, a gown would be out of place anyway.

So the dress was sort of off-white, an oystery color, with an empire waist and an interesting neckline that drew the eye away from my stomach. Or so the sales clerk at the pregnancy store had assured me. There hadn't been anything wrong with my breasts before, but they'd gotten bigger in the past few weeks. The dress made the most of them, albeit not in a tacky way. Of course not. It was a very tasteful dress, one I could wear for the rest of the pregnancy too, whenever I had to go to a semi-formal occasion.

I put it on, and did my hair and makeup just as if I weren't afraid I'd get left at the altar. Rafe would be there at the courthouse to meet me. I had no idea where he was or what he was doing, and why he wasn't here this morning, but he would be there at eleven.

His suit, the one he had planned to wear, was still in the closet.

Should I bring it with me? If... *when* he showed up, he could go into a bathroom and change.

Or would it be better to leave it here? In case he came looking for it?

If he didn't—if he showed up at the courthouse in the jeans and T-shirt he'd left in yesterday morning—I'd still marry him. I didn't care about that. Mother would, of course, but I didn't.

I decided to leave the suit. And since it was ten-thirty, I made my way downstairs and out the door to the Volvo that was the only thing—in addition to some bad memories and a nice monetary settlement—I had kept from my first marriage.

The Volvo was parked where I'd left it, in the circular driveway in front of the house. There was no sign of Rafe's Harley-Davidson, which is usually parked nearby. We'd been talking about putting up a garage, or maybe a carport, since both of our vehicles would benefit from being under a roof in inclement weather, but with the baby coming, we expected money to be tight, and so we'd decided to defer the building until some other time.

The house we lived in used to belong to Rafe's grandmother, Tondalia Jenkins. I guess it still did, but she wasn't able to live here anymore. She went in and out of reality, never sure whether Rafe was himself or his father Tyrell. As for me, I was either myself, or I was Rafe's mother LaDonna. The pregnancy had made the poor old lady even more confused, since LaDonna had been pregnant too, with Rafe, when her father, Old Jim Collier, had gunned Tyrell down.

It's a long story, and the bottom line is that Mrs. J is living in a home where there are people who know how to take care of her. She wandered off and got lost a lot when she was living at home, so we needed a safe place for her. And she seems to like it there. It's nice and clean, the staff cooks for her and makes sure she has clean clothes to wear and that her hair is washed, and she's made friends she can talk to. We go to visit her regularly, and Rafe has brought David by to see her, as well, although that tends to make her even more certain that Rafe is Tyrell, because she can't wrap her brain around the fact that Rafe is her grandson and David her great-grand.

David.

If Rafe had decided to leave town—to leave me—because he

didn't want to get married, he might have called his son to explain and to say goodbye. They hadn't known of the other's existence for very long, but in the time since the discovery, they've gotten to know one another. If he was leaving, I had to believe Rafe would let David know. Even if he couldn't face me, he'd tell his son what was going on.

I got into the car, but instead of cranking the key over in the ignition, I pulled out the phone and dialed. It rang twice, and then was answered. "Hello?"

"Ginny?" I said. "This is Savannah Martin."

"Savannah!" David's adoptive mother sounded delighted to hear from me. "How are you? This is the big day, isn't it?"

"It was," I said, "until Rafe turned up missing."

"Missing?" I could hear the need to protect her son loud and clear in her voice.

David had been born when Rafe was eighteen and in prison. His mother had been a seventeen-year-old high school girl in Columbia, Tennessee, who had been made to give the baby up for adoption by her weirdly fundamentalist father. Virginia and Sam Flannery were David's adoptive parents. Like Rafe and Elspeth, they were a mixed race couple—not that Rafe and Elspeth had ever been a couple—and they'd been delighted to find a mixed race baby they could call their own. When Rafe turned up in their lives last year, they'd been terrified that he was going to take David away from them. Since then, things had mellowed out considerably. Rafe had made no move whatsoever to claim custody of David, and by now, Ginny was probably just worried about David's feelings when he learned his biological father was in the wind.

"Maybe not missing," I said. "I don't know that he's missing. He's just not here. He went out with a couple of guys from work last night, and they said he went home at eleven. But I'm not sure he ever got here."

"That doesn't sound good," Ginny said.

No, it didn't. "I thought maybe—if he'd decided to leave—he would have contacted David to tell him."

"If he has, David hasn't mentioned it," Ginny said. "But he's not home this week. He's at church camp."

"Where?" Was there a chance Rafe had gone there?

"The Cumberland Plateau," Ginny said. "An hour and a little more from here. Cabins, an archery range, zip-lines, the lake..."

"What's the name of it?"

She told me, and I scribbled the name on the back of a business card I found in the console. "Thanks. Would you mind giving David a call and asking him whether he's seen or heard from his... from Rafe?"

"I can't," Ginny said. "The kids call home at night. The rest of the time it's a no-technology zone. But I'll see if I can get hold of one of the counselors."

"Thank you."

There was a moment of silence.

"I'm sure he's fine, Savannah," Ginny said. "You know he can take care of himself."

I did know that. He survived two years in prison and ten years undercover, not to mention everything his grandfather dished out while he was a kid—and there was no love lost between Old Jim Collier and the good for nothing, colored boy his daughter had spawned. But that didn't mean something couldn't have happened to him now. He was adept at self-preservation, but no one can be vigilant every moment of every day. And Rafe is just as mortal as the rest of us, if a bit harder to kill.

"I should go," I said. "To the courthouse. My brother and sister," and mother, for my sins, "are on their way there."

"Let me know how it goes," Ginny told me. "I'll call you after I speak to the counselor. Or after I speak to David."

I thanked her again, and hung up. And this time I really did turn the key in the ignition and navigate the Volvo down the graveled driveway to the street.

I was late, of course. To my own wedding ceremony. By the time I walked into the waiting room at the courthouse, my siblings and my mother, as well as Tamara Grimaldi, were already present.

Rafe was not. Nor was Wendell Craig.

Ginny had called me back while I was driving, to tell me that while she had managed to get in touch with one of her son's camp counselors, David himself had been unavailable, on a half-day hike. He wasn't expected back until the afternoon. At that point, the counselor would ascertain whether David had heard from his biological father, but until then, there was nothing they could do to help, since cell phone coverage was non-existent out there in the middle of nowhere where the kids were.

It sounded dangerous to me—a couple dozen kids in the wilderness with no way to contact anyone in the event something went wrong—but what do I know?

"I have to ask, Savannah," Ginny had said. "Please don't take this the wrong way, but I have to know."

"Sure." My hands were sweaty on the steering wheel, in spite of the icy air pumping from the vents.

"Is there... I'm sure there isn't, but is there any chance he'll go to the camp and take David?"

I blinked. Opened my mouth, and found I had no words. Nor any voice to speak them. I closed my mouth and tried again. "Take him?"

"You know," Ginny said. "If he's decided to leave, maybe he wants to take David with him."

I blinked again. And swallowed. "No," I managed eventually. "I don't think you have to worry about that."

If he had decided to leave, it was because he didn't want to be tied down with a wife and a kid. He wouldn't bring his other kid along. Especially as he had to know he'd be committing a crime if he did. He had no legal rights where David were concerned. Ginny and Sam were David's legal guardians. Rafe was just the man who had donated the sperm.

Ginny sounded like she wasn't sure whether she could be relieved and whether she could believe me. "Are you sure?"

"Positive," I said. "He wouldn't do that."

"I hope you're right," Ginny told me. "Either way I've put the camp counselors on alert. If he shows up there, they'll call the police."

My breath went again, and for a moment I couldn't speak. "That's a little drastic, don't you think?" Rafe wasn't a threat to anyone. Least of all David.

"He's my child," Ginny told me, in a voice that was turning shrill. "If anyone tries to take him away from me, it'll be over my dead body."

I forced myself to sound calm. "Rafe wouldn't take David away from you. Not like this. If he wanted custody, he'd fight you in court."

Ginny didn't answer that, and I guess maybe, in playing it back, it wasn't very comforting.

"And he's not going to do anything illegal. He's a TBI agent." As well as a convicted felon. Which wouldn't look good if someone suspected he was trying to take David. "He isn't stupid."

"I hope you're right, Savannah," Ginny told me, "because if he comes anywhere near David, I'm having him arrested."

She didn't wait for me to answer, just hung up in my ear.

My hands were still shaking when I walked into the waiting room of the courthouse and found my family and Tamara Grimaldi there. The detective was talking to Dix, but looked up when I came in. A second later she was on her way across the floor toward me. I'm not sure she even excused herself.

"Savannah!"

"Detective," I managed.

She took my arm. I guess I must look like I was about to drop. I felt like I was about to drop.

"What is it? Have you heard something?"

"No." I shook my head. "Not from Rafe. I just spoke to Ginny Flannery. David's mother. Adoptive mother."

Grimaldi nodded.

"David's away at church camp. Somewhere on the Cumberland Plateau. She said if Rafe goes anywhere near him, she'll have him arrested."

"She can't do that," Grimaldi said.

"Are you sure?"

Grimaldi nodded. "Not without a restraining order. And for that, she'd have to prove cause. Which she can't. Besides, it takes time."

I shuddered. "I hope you're right. Because she sounded serious."

Grimaldi rubbed her hand up and down my arm. I was cold, in spite of the heat outside and having had to walk through it to get inside. "Do you think he'll go out there?"

"I have no idea what he'll do," I told her, skirting hysteria, "because I have no idea what's going on. I don't know if he's dead in a ditch, or in a hospital bed somewhere with amnesia, or halfway to Montana by now."

"Montana?"

"It's where people hide, isn't it?" All those woods and wide open spaces.

"Oh," Grimaldi said dryly, "I think your boyfriend would have more sense than to try to blend in somewhere like Montana."

Maybe so. Come to think of it, those woods and wide open spaces hide a lot of militia and white supremacists, and those kinds of people likely wouldn't appreciate my mixed-race boyfriend. Even if he could handle weapons with the best of them.

"Alabama, then. Or Texas. Just as long as he's not dead."

"He isn't in the morgue," Grimaldi said. "And he isn't in the hospital."

"Doesn't mean he couldn't be dead in a ditch and nobody's found him yet."

"He was carousing at Gabe's Bar last night," Grimaldi said. "I checked with Mr. Craig. There aren't any ditches between there and where you live. Or at least none where a dead body could lie for hours without someone taking notice."

Comforting. Not.

I had my mouth open to ask whether she'd checked if he was in jail... but by now Mother had made her way over to us. "Darling." She gave me a tight smile.

"Mother." I forced one of my own, and leaned in to give her an air kiss in the neighborhood of her cheek. "Thank you for coming." *But you shouldn't have.*

"Of course, darling." She looked around. "I don't see Rafael."

"That's because he isn't here," I said, with a glare at Dix, who obviously hadn't told her that my husband-to-be was nowhere to be found this morning.

Coward, I mouthed. Dix shrugged and spread his hands, as if to say that I would have done the same thing. And since he was most likely right—I wouldn't have said anything, either—there wasn't much more I could do.

"What's going on?" Mother asked, a delicate wrinkle between her brows. She's in her late fifties, but looks ten years younger, and she'd obviously gone out of her way to make herself presentable this morning. Under other circumstances I would have been grateful, but at the moment I just wished her far, far away.

"We don't know yet. He didn't come home last night."

"Oh, dear," Mother said, pressing her lips together. I'm not sure whether she was suppressing a smile or she actually was sympathetic.

I narrowed my eyes. "Did you have something to do with this?"

"Me?" She sounded sincerely shocked, and a bit offended that I'd ask. "Darling, why would you suggest such a thing?"

"Because you hate Rafe," I said, "and I'm sure nothing would make you happier than if I didn't marry him."

Mother squirmed like a five-year-old on an anthill, but didn't deny it. Not the marriage part. Instead she said, "That's silly, darling. Of course I don't hate him."

"Your nostrils twitch every time you get close to him. Like he smells bad." And he doesn't.

Mother had no answer for that. "How would I be able to ensure that Rafael didn't come home last night?" she asked instead, reasonably. "Surely you're not suggesting that I drove to Nashville last night and spiked his drink?"

Hah! I put my hands on my hips. "How did you know he was drinking last night?"

"I assumed," Mother said coldly. "He seems the type."

"It was the night before his wedding! The guys were throwing him a bachelor party." Sort of.

Mother sniffed. "So where is he?"

I felt some of the air go out of me. "I don't know. And I wasn't suggesting that you'd driven to Nashville and spiked his drink. I thought you might have hired someone to take him out."

"Darling," Mother said, shaking her head.

"Well, it isn't like it hasn't happened before! You don't have to act like it's unheard of."

"I would never consider doing such a thing," my mother said.

No, she wouldn't. And if I'd been thinking clearly, I wouldn't have suggested it. She wouldn't have done anything illegal. If my mother wanted to get rid of my unsuitable suitor, she was much more likely to do it the old-fashioned way. "You didn't offer him money to disappear," I asked suspiciously, "did you?"

"No," Mother said. "Really, Savannah. If you want to throw

your life away on a man who isn't worthy of you, that's your business. I drove up here to support you, but now I'm thinking that perhaps I shouldn't have bothered."

She glanced around for Dix, as if thinking she'd just have him turn around and drive the hour-and-a-bit-more back to Sweetwater again.

"I'm sorry," I said, since she'd gotten dressed up and had made the drive up here to attend my wedding, even to a man she wished I wouldn't marry. "I shouldn't have said those things."

"No, darling," Mother said, "you shouldn't."

I said I was sorry! trembled on my tongue, but I bit it back. "I'm sorry," I said instead, humbly. "I'm just worried."

"Of course, darling." She patted my hand. "I'm sure he'll turn up in his own time."

I wished I could believe that, but I honestly wasn't sure. Part of me was certain he'd run away, that the prospect of tying himself to one woman and a baby for the rest of his life had finally caught up to him, on the night before the wedding. The other part skirted very delicately around the other possibilities, since they were even worse. I loved him. I wanted to spend my life with him, raising our child. But between that and knowing he was dead in a ditch somewhere, I'd rather have him alive and well and somewhere else. If he didn't want to marry me, he didn't have to. I wanted that, but I wasn't going to force him.

Did he feel like I was forcing him?

I'd tried very hard not to, but maybe I hadn't succeeded?

"There's Mr. Craig," Tamara Grimaldi's voice said, and woke me from my reverie. The interruption wasn't unwelcome, and not just because I hoped that Wendell would have some news. My own thoughts weren't very good company just then.

However, if he had news, it wasn't good news. His face was grim as he strode across the floor to us. By now, Dix and Catherine had joined us too, and we were all standing in a huddle. I had my brother and Tamara Grimaldi on one side of me, and mother and Catherine on the other. A bit hysterically, I reasoned that if I fainted, I'd have to drop right, since Mother and Catherine couldn't be counted on to catch me, while Grimaldi and Dix could.

Grimaldi, at least, had good reflexes.

"I'm sorry," were the first words out of Wendell's mouth, and I felt my head go light. "I don't have anything new to tell you."

So no news. And now I realized what that old chestnut 'No news is good news,' meant. Right then, no news was *so* much better than bad news.

"I contacted the boys and asked them if any of them had heard from him since last night," Wendell continued, "and no one had. Two of them were at the bureau this morning, sparring. They knew Rafe wasn't gonna be there, so they'd arranged to work out with each other instead. Number three was sleeping in."

So he hadn't shown up for work. I wondered whether that was significant, or just a result of his boss—Rafe—not being on the clock today. Likely it was just the latter, and nothing suspicious at all. Although I kept it in reserve in case Rafe hadn't left of his own free will, and one of the rookies had something to do with it.

"I asked around," Wendell added, "and nobody knows nothing. Nobody expected him this morning, since he had the day off."

"Did... um..." I cleared my throat and tried again, "did anyone mention whether he'd said anything about cold feet?"

Wendell blinked. He's an older, grizzled, black man with a military haircut, who's been working in law enforcement for a very long time. He was Rafe's handler during the ten years Rafe spent undercover, trying to infiltrate the biggest SATG—South American Theft Gang—in the Southeast, and I imagine he's seen a lot in his years. Whenever I've had dealings with him, he's always been supremely poker-faced. This was the first time he'd shown any kind of unexpected emotion, and although it was nice to know that he could, I wasn't entirely happy about it.

"No," he said eventually. "And I didn't ask. Didn't think to."

"He hasn't mentioned anything to you?"

"About cold feet?" Wendell shook his head. "No."

Good to know.

And on the other hand, not so good to know, because if he hadn't suddenly developed cold feet and run away, something was wrong.

"Thanks," I said, trying not to think about it.

Wendell nodded and checked his watch. "It's eleven-thirty."

Yes, thank you for pointing that out. "It doesn't look like he's coming," I said, and tried to keep my voice steady.

Mother murmured something. I didn't hear it, and elected not to ask what it was.

"We can wait a bit longer," Catherine said, with a glance at her own watch.

I shook my head. "There's really no point. If he was going to come, he'd have been here by now." He would have been in bed this morning, too.

I swallowed the lump in my throat. "I'm afraid the wedding's off."

Three

"How about some lunch before we drive back to Sweetwater?" Catherine asked brightly.

For the first few seconds after my pronouncement, everyone had just stood there in glum silence.

All right, the silence may have been a happy one on Mother's part, but she managed to keep from jumping up and down with glee. The three inch heels on her shoes may have had something to do with that. Or maybe it was just good manners, which she has in spades.

At any rate, when Catherine asked her question, Mother was the first to recover. "What a lovely idea," she said warmly. "I've heard good things about the Germantown Café. And it's nearby, isn't it?"

It was. Half a mile as the crow flew, straight up Fourth Avenue from the courthouse garage.

"If y'all don't mind," Wendell said, "I think I'm gonna pass."

I turned to him. Far be it from me to question why anyone would choose not to have lunch with my mother, but I felt I had to ask. "Are you sure? You're welcome to join us."

He shook his head. "I'm gonna go back to the bureau. If the boy's missing, the brass is gonna wanna know about it."

I would imagine so. "You'll let me know if you hear anything, right?"

"Course," Wendell said. "Hang in there. He can take care of himself. I'm sure he's fine."

I wasn't, but it was nice of him to try to reassure me. "I'll let you know if he gets in touch," I said, "although it's more likely he'll get in touch with you than me."

"Depends on what's going on," Wendell said. He nodded to my mother and sister. "Nice to meet y'all." To Tamara Grimaldi he said, "I'll be in touch."

She nodded. "Missing persons isn't my jurisdiction—and we'll hope my jurisdiction won't be needed for this—but if there's anything the MNPD can do to help, please don't hesitate to ask."

Wendell promised he wouldn't, and took himself off.

"You're coming with us," I asked Grimaldi, "aren't you?"

She didn't glance at Dix, nor he at her, but I could feel the connection anyway. I wondered if Mother could. "If you don't mind."

"No." I shook my head. "I don't mind at all. I'd like you to come. Please."

Of all of us, and with the exception of me, she knew Rafe the best. In some ways she probably knew him better than I did, since they had the law enforcement background in common. When we got to the Germantown Café, I already knew Grimaldi would take a seat with her back to the wall and her eye on the door, just as Rafe would. She understood him on an elementary level that I'm not sure I did, or ever would.

Besides, she was a cop. And you never know when a cop might come in handy. Especially when someone didn't show up for his own wedding.

So we sorted ourselves into three cars—Mother with Dix and Catherine with me, Grimaldi on her own in her police issued sedan—and drove the half a dozen blocks to Germantown.

It's a formerly industrial area just north of downtown. A hundred years ago it was Nashville's meatpacking district. Now it's a hip and happening urban neighborhood in the downtown core, with the hip and happening bars and restaurants to go with it, and a view of the Nashville skyline and the state capitol. It was also the neighborhood where my ex-husband Bradley worked up until he was arrested a few months ago.

Indeed, when I walked through the door of the Germantown Café, the first person I saw was Diana Morton, one of the partners at Bradley's former law firm, at a table against the back wall, in conversation with a good-looking dark-haired man in his early thirties.

Diana, for your information, is a cool blonde in her forties, and as far as I know, she's happily married. Yet here she was, having a tête-à-tête with a good-looking—*extremely* good-looking—younger man.

Of course, that was her business. I wasn't even sure she'd recognize me. I'd only met her a few times during the two years I'd been married to Bradley, and it must have been four or five years ago now. I did know I had no desire to talk to her. So I pretended I had no idea who she was, and sat down with my back to her, at a table by the window, on the opposite side of the room. Mother sat down across the table, with Catherine next to her, and Dix bowed Tamara Grimaldi into the seat next to me, leaving himself the chair that had been hastily added to the short end of a four-top table.

"So," my brother said, making himself comfortable—and I'm sure his knee was touching Grimaldi's under the table, "now what?"

It was a good question. I could go home—to Rafe's house, where I had no business being without Rafe—and curl up in a corner and cry. It was what I wanted to do.

Or I could eat too much food to try to fill that gaping hole in my stomach—and for once, it had nothing to do with the pregnancy. Then I'd get sick, and I'd have a legitimate reason for curling up in a corner wanting to cry.

No, scratch that. Having my boyfriend go missing on our wedding day was reason enough. I didn't need another.

Of course, if I started putting everything in sight in my mouth, Mother would have something to say about it. I couldn't help it that my waistline was expanding, but she'd remind me that whatever pounds I put on now, were extra pounds I'd have to take off again after the baby came.

God forbid I ended up a size bigger after having a baby.

Or I could pull myself together and try to figure out what was going on.

While I'd been weighing the options, Mother had spoken. "It's obvious," she said. We all turned to look at her, and without missing a beat, she added, "She'll have to come back to Sweetwater with us. She can't stay here, in *his* house, after being practically left at the alter."

She turned to me. "You don't have your rental apartment anymore, do you, darling?"

"No," I said. "I gave that up after the prostitute was murdered in my bed last month."

There was a moment of silence. Not even Mother wanted to touch that one. And in justice to her, it was a tough act to follow. Also, it was true. A prostitute had been murdered in what used to be my bed, and I'd stopped renting the place out after that, and had handed the keys back and let the lease lapse with a month to go. So Mother was technically right: I had nowhere else to go. Just Rafe's house and the ancestral mansion in Sweetwater. An ancestral mansion I hadn't returned to after Bradley and I divorced, much to Mother's annoyance.

However, if I hadn't scurried home with my tail between my legs when my marriage fell apart, I wasn't about to do it now.

In the silence following my prostitute remark, the scuff of a foot sounded next to the table. The waitress stood there, eyes wide. "Um..." she said. "I'm sorry, I couldn't help overhear what you were saying."

I smiled magnanimously. "No worries. These things happen."

I was referring to people overhearing what other people were saying when those other people were talking in a public place, but she must have thought I was referring to prostitutes turning up dead in people's beds, because she gulped.

"Take your time," Dix said kindly, while Mother sniffed. Grimaldi hid a smile.

The waitress took a breath and closed her eyes for a second. "Welcome to the Germantown Café," she said when she'd opened them again, with a passable, clearly fake smile. "Can I start you off with something to drink?"

I wanted to order wine, but of course I couldn't. "Sweet tea, please. Extra sugar." For the shock.

Mother frowned, but placed her order too. The others did the same, and the waitress wandered off, I'm sure to share with her brethren what she'd overheard us talking about.

"We should take a look at the menus," I said and opened mine. "And be ready to order when she comes back."

Since it was a reasonable suggestion, the others followed suit. For a couple of minutes, all was peaceful and calm. Then Mother closed her menu and opened her mouth. "You can't mean you'll consider staying here, Savannah."

"You can mean you expect me to leave," I shot back. "It's only been a few hours. And we don't know where Rafe is. He could walk in the door at any moment."

I glanced at it. Nobody walked in, although Diana Morton's companion was on his way in that direction. I guess their meeting was over. As he passed our table, he slowed down and then came to a stop. "Slacking?" he asked Grimaldi.

Up close he was even more gorgeous than from a distance, and I could feel Dix bristle. There's nothing wrong with the way my brother looks—like me, he takes after Mother's people, the Georgia Calverts. We're all tallish, blue-eyed, and fair of hair and complexion. Catherine, on the other hand, takes after our father's family, and is shorter, rounder, and darker.

However, Dix was no match for the guy currently grinning down at Grimaldi. And while I love Rafe, and remain quite convinced that he's the most gorgeous man in Nashville, this guy ran a close second. Like Rafe he was dark, with black hair and melting brown eyes, high cheekbones and the kind of eyelashes women dream about. Unlike Rafe, who prefers to dress casually in jeans and T-shirts, the newcomer was decked out in a killer suit that I'm sure had cost as much as Rafe's entire wardrobe, and a gorgeous silk shirt. Mother clearly approved, because she shot me a look that said, *"See? This is what you could have ended up with if you hadn't hitched your star to a loser who couldn't even bother to show up for his own nuptials."*

"Maid of honor at a wedding," Grimaldi said.

"Congratulations." He had obviously picked me out as the bride, because he transferred the grin to me. Not surprisingly, since I was the one in the semi-white dress. Mother was wearing blue and Catherine pink, while Grimaldi had jazzed up her usual dark suit with a turquoise shirt.

"And you must be the lucky guy," he told Dix. "Congratulations." He held out a hand.

"I'm the brother of the bride," Dix answered, but took it anyway. "Dix Martin."

"Jaime Mendoza." They shook, and if Dix tried to crush bones, Mendoza gave no sign of it. Dix was either behaving himself, or Mendoza was made of sterner stuff.

"The groom didn't bother to show up," Mother said. "I don't suppose you'd want to marry my daughter?"

Mendoza's dimples deepened.

"Mother!" I exclaimed, somewhere between shocked and embarrassed and furious, at the same time as Mendoza said, his face solemn but his eyes twinkling, "While I appreciate the offer, ma'am, I'm not entirely divorced yet. I figure I'll better wait until it's official. No offense." He winked at me.

"None taken," I said. "Sorry."

He just shook his head, and turned back to Grimaldi. "See you around, Detective."

"Likewise," Grimaldi said. "Be careful out there."

"Always." He bathed us all in the glow of that thousand-watt smile. "Nice to meet you all. Have a nice day."

And then he headed for the door. I barely waited until he was out of earshot before I turned on Mother—and I do mean *on*. "How could you ask him that?! He's a stranger! He doesn't need to know that my fiancé didn't show up to the wedding. And besides, I don't want to marry him. I want to marry Rafe."

"It seems," Mother said, her lips tight, "that Rafael doesn't want to marry you."

"You don't know that!" My fingernails dug divots into my palms because I was curling my fists so tight. The tiny pinpoints of pain kept me from launching myself across the table and going for her throat. "It's only been a few hours. He could have gotten caught up in something. Or he could be hurt. He could be dead. He could be in terrible trouble, and we're sitting here waiting to eat while you ask a perfect stranger if he'd like to take your pregnant daughter off your hands! I'm surprised he didn't run screaming out of the restaurant!"

"Inside voice, darling," Mother reminded me, with a glance around to make sure no one else was listening.

"I don't care about my inside voice!" I shrieked, just as Diana Morton walked by. She sent me a startled look, and then did a double take, as if she thought she recognized me. She hesitated for a second, but then she moved on. No doubt she realized that now wasn't a good time to ask me if I was Bradley Ferguson's ex-wife.

On the heels of Diana came the waitress, who by now looked acutely uncomfortable, like she wished she'd called in sick and stayed in bed today. I wished I could go back to bed, too, and pull the covers over my head, and wake up tomorrow with this all having been a horrible dream.

But of course I couldn't. And with Mother on the opposite side of the table, I had to keep a stiff upper lip. "I'd like a Grilled Chicken Caesar Salad," I told the waitress as she put my iced tea on the table. "With extra cheese."

Mother gave me a look across the table, and I added, "Dairy is good for the baby."

She had no answer to that, just turned to the waitress and ordered a Cobb salad of her own. Catherine followed suit—we've both been brought up by the same standards of eating—while Dix wanted a turkey sandwich on wheat with a side of coleslaw. Grimaldi, bless her heart, bucked the system and asked for a blue cheese burger with extra bacon and a side of onion rings.

Mother sniffed.

"I love you," I told Grimaldi.

She stared at me for a second, and then she grinned. "Thanks. But I'm not marrying you."

"I don't love you that much. Besides, I haven't given up on Rafe yet."

"No," Grimaldi said, "don't do that. He'll be back."

"I hope you're right," I said.

Grimaldi had her mouth open—probably to tell me that she was always right—but her cell phone rang, and she excused herself to answer it.

As she walked toward the back of the restaurant, phone at her ear, I turned to Dix. "I love her."

He nodded. "I know. I heard you."

"You should marry her. Since I can't."

Dix blushed.

"I know it hasn't been very long since Sheila died. But Grimaldi's great. And I'm not just saying that because she believes Rafe is coming back. She bought your daughters Police Barbies for Christmas!"

"Darling..." Mother protested weakly. "Dixon can't marry Detective Grimaldi. They barely know one another."

I opened my mouth. And I wouldn't have said that they obviously knew each other a lot better than Mother realized. I really wouldn't have. But Dix must have thought I was going to, because he interrupted. "We all believe Collier is coming back, Savannah."

"Mother doesn't," I said. "She believes he ran off and left me, so she has to marry me off to someone else. Like a man I've never laid eyes on before. Dix knows Detective Grimaldi better than I know Detective Mendoza, Mother. And you asked him if he wanted to marry me!"

Mother pressed her lips together. "He seemed like a nice man," she said. "Handsome, well-dressed, gainfully employed..."

"Rafe is gainfully employed!"

"But he isn't here," Mother said, "is he?"

No, he wasn't. And there was absolutely nothing I could do about it. Launching myself across the table to strangle my mother would have felt good, but wasn't a good idea either, especially with a homicide detective in the party.

And speaking of which... Grimaldi came back to the table and sat down.

"What happened?" I asked. "Did you get called in to work?"

She shook her head. "The call was about Mr. Collier."

"About Rafe?"

She nodded. "Wilson County reported a John Doe this morning."

"A John Doe?" Mother asked, while I could feel all the blood drain out of my head. Wilson County is just east of Davidson, and Davidson County is Metro Nashville. Wilson County is close, in other words. Twenty minutes, maybe a half hour. And a John Doe...

"Unidentified male DB," Grimaldi said. And added before Mother could ask, "Dead body."

"Oh, dear." Mother glanced at me. I lifted my glass of sweet tea—my hand was shaking, so the ice cubes clicked together—and took a healthy swig. I didn't think we were talking about Rafe—surely, if we were, the detective wouldn't drag out the news like this? Unless maybe she thought she needed to work up to it—but I wasn't a hundred percent certain.

"The general description matched," Grimaldi said. "So I sent over a picture and was told it might be him."

Oh, God.

"But I wanted to be sure before I said anything. So I told Spicer and Truman to drive out there to see if they could make an identification. Since they know Mr. Collier."

I nodded. Lyle Spicer and George Truman are two police officers who work the neighborhood where Rafe and I live. When we'd stumbled over Brenda Puckett's body in Rafe's grandmother's house last year—before we knew Mrs. Jenkins was Rafe's grandmother—when we'd called 911, Spicer and Truman showed up. And that wasn't the last time I'd seen them. They crop up in my life on a regular basis. The last time was just a few weeks ago, after the aforementioned prostitute had been strangled in my old apartment. They'd gone door to door in the complex, knocking on doors, to see whether any of my neighbors knew anything. And they'd caught me breaking and entering before, as well as making out with Rafe on a street corner.

Hell—I mean, heck—they'd hauled Rafe in for questioning more than once last fall.

Yes, Spicer and Truman knew Rafe well enough to be able to identify him. If there was enough left to identify.

"The sheriff out there must be old school," Grimaldi said with a grimace. "The type who thinks they all look alike. Truman said there wasn't much resemblance, really."

"So it wasn't Rafe."

She shook her head. "I didn't want to tell you about it before I knew for sure."

"I appreciate it." And I did. If she'd told me this two hours ago, I'd have been a nervous wreck this whole time.

Hell—heck—I would have insisted on going to Wilson County to do the identification myself.

No, much better to learn this way that some other wife or girlfriend, mother or sister, had lost a loved one. But it wasn't me.

"Thank you," I told Grimaldi.

She shook her head. "Don't mention it."

"Tell Spicer and Truman thanks, too."

She nodded. "We'll find him, Savannah."

"I know," I said. But what I thought was, would we find him alive or dead? And would we find him soon? Because as of right now—I checked my watch—it had been just over three hours since I'd woken up and realized he was gone. If I had to go through the rest of the day, and tomorrow, and the weekend, and next week, or next month, like this, I wasn't sure how I'd be able to stand it.

Four

"We should think about getting home," Catherine said apologetically after the food had been served and consumed, mostly in silence. "I'm sorry, Savannah. But it's over an hour's drive. And Jonathan's been home alone with all five kids since we left."

I nodded. "Of course." She had a husband and children to take care of at home, and there was nothing she could do here. Except hold my hand, but while that might make me feel better for the time it lasted, it wouldn't actually help me figure out what was going on. "There's nothing any of you can do. You might as well go home."

There was a moment's pause. Then—

"I'm not leaving," Dix said.

Catherine stared at him. "You drove us here!"

"Call your husband," Dix said. "Have him come pick you up. And take Mother home while you're at it. Will you keep my girls for a day or two?"

Catherine blinked at him. Then she said, "Of course."

"I don't know that there's anything I can do here," Dix said. "But I want to be on hand, just in case."

He didn't say in case of what, but I could guess. In case the body in Wilson County turned out to be Rafe after all, and I had a nervous breakdown when I heard the news. Or if not that body, then another.

"You don't have to," I told him. "There really isn't much anyone can do, and you have responsibilities in Sweetwater. And I don't need my hand held while I wait to find out whether Rafe is dead or alive."

I'd need someone's shoulder to cry on if it turned out that he was dead, but that was a worry for later. For right now, I was still waiting, and still keeping my hopes up, and Dix had better things to do than sit around and hold my hand.

Just as I had better things to do than sit around and have my hand held.

"Why don't you call Jonathan?" I told Catherine. "It's only an hour's drive. Although the car might be a bit crowded, with five kids in the back." And three adults in the front.

They did have a minivan, so their three and Dix's two would fit in the back. Catherine often takes care of Dix's girls, since the two of them and Catherine's daughter Annie are good friends. At the time when Sheila was murdered and Dix was grieving, it was Catherine who kept Abigail and Hannah going and distracted.

"Why don't you give him the address to the house?" I added. "We can't stay here. And I want to see whether Rafe has turned up. You can see the place. You've never been there, right?"

Catherine shook her head, the phone already at her ear. "Hi, honey," she said as Jonathan picked up on the other end.

"You don't mind," I asked Dix, "do you? You have been there before."

He nodded. "No, I don't mind. I want to see if Collier's turned up, too. And if he has, I want to punch him for making you worry like this."

"That wouldn't go over well," I said, while across the table, Catherine continued to murmur into her phone. "He hits back."

Only if he's able to, hung in the air. Nobody said it.

"What about you?" I asked Grimaldi. "Do you want to come back to the house with us?"

She shook her head. "I've got the day off. I'm going to hook up with Spicer and Truman and ride along. See what the three of us can get up to. I'll let you know if we learn anything."

"That's a hell..." Rafe was obviously rubbing off on me. I shot a guilty look in Mother's direction and amended, " —a heck of a way to spend your day off."

"Your boyfriend's missing," Grimaldi said, as if I needed reminding. "I want to be available if Mr. Craig asks the MNPD to do something. And I'm not going to spend my day on the couch relaxing when I know a fellow law-enforcement officer might be in trouble. Let alone a friend."

"Thank you."

"Don't mention it," Grimaldi said. "I'll let you know if I hear anything. You do the same."

I promised I would, and she left, with a nod at Dix and a polite, "Safe travels," to Mother. Catherine was still on the phone, but winding down. "What's the address?" she asked me, as Grimaldi walked away.

I gave it to her, and listened as she repeated it to Jonathan.

"Potsdam. P-O-T-S-D-A-M. Yes, like the town in Germany. One-zero-one." She shook her head. "No, I don't know where it is. I've never been there."

"East Nashville," I said.

Catherine glanced at me. "Just put it in the GPS, Jonathan. Are you leaving now?"

Jonathan quacked, and Catherine nodded. "I'll see you then. Drive carefully." She dropped the phone in her purse. "He's on his way."

"I guess we should adjourn to the house." I glanced at Dix. "Do you remember how to get there?"

"I'll follow you." He got to his feet. "We parked in the same lot."

We had. And ten minutes later, we were behind the wheels of our respective cars and traveling across the Jefferson Street Bridge, with the Nashville skyline on our right and the Cumberland River below.

"Is this where Sheila drowned?" Catherine asked, with a glance at the muddy water below the bridge.

I shook my head. "It was the same river, but we're north of

downtown right now. Sheila went in on the south side, five miles or so from here."

Catherine nodded. She was silent for a minute, until we'd gotten across the bridge and down onto solid ground again, and then she said. "I don't mean to upset you, Savannah."

But she was going to anyway? "Sure," I said.

She grimaced. "I'm sorry. But I know you're stronger than Mother... than any of us ever give you credit for."

"Thank you." That was nice of her to say, and under different circumstances, I'm sure I would be quite touched by it. But at the moment I didn't feel very strong at all. And it wasn't like I didn't already know what her question was going to be, or what the answer was.

And here it came, just as expected.

"Are you sure Rafe is still alive? I mean... Mother seems sure he ran off because he didn't want to get married. But he always seemed committed to me. To you, I mean. He seemed committed to you. To me."

"I thought he was," I said. "I still don't know that he wasn't. Isn't. I mean... I'd like to think something or someone is preventing him from coming home. That he didn't just leave."

Although... No, actually. I didn't want to think that at all.

"What I mean is, I don't want to believe he just left. It's easier to believe that something happened to him. Even if I don't really want to believe that, either."

"Of course not," Catherine said. "Because if he wants to come home, but can't, he's either hurt, or—"

Or dead. Right.

"So I guess I'd really rather believe he ran away. At least that way he's safe, and not hurt."

Catherine nodded.

"But I'm not sure what to think. I thought he loved me. There was nothing he said or did that made me think otherwise."

I signaled to take a right onto Dresden. Behind me, Dix did

the same thing. I wondered what he and Mother were talking about, and whether their conversation was as uncomfortable as this one.

Most likely they were saying much the same things we were, with Mother insisting that Rafe had to have left of his own free will, because he was a rolling stone that wouldn't want to be tied down. Meanwhile, Dix probably—hopefully—came down on the side of hoping—or fearing—that someone or something had prevented Rafe from getting to his own wedding.

"It's not like he had to run away, you know," I told Catherine. "If he'd come to me and said, 'I'm not ready for this; can we put it off awhile?' it's not like I would have said no."

Catherine shook her head.

"I'm not desperate to get married again. Mother's concerned about the baby being born out of wedlock, but I'm not. Rafe was born out of wedlock, and he turned out OK. It's not the end of the world anymore. Single women have children all the time. People live together for years without getting married. And I would rather live in sin for the rest of my life than scare Rafe away because he thinks he has to marry me and doesn't want to."

Catherine nodded.

Potsdam Street was coming up on the left, and I switched on my turn signal. On our right was the Milton House, the horrible institution where Brenda Puckett had stuck Rafe's grandmother after she—Brenda—had cheated Mrs. Jenkins out of her home. The first thing Rafe did once he could prove that he was Mrs. J's grandson and next of kin, had been to get her out of there.

God, if he didn't come back, I'd have to tell her he was gone. She'd already had to live with the death of her son. Now I might have to add a dead grandson to the mix. And with her habitual confusion, she might not realize Rafe was her grandson, but might think she'd lost Tyrell all over again.

"This is a nightmare," I said.

"Tell me about it," Catherine answered. "You live *here*?"

I looked around. Last August, when I'd driven over to this part of town from the real estate office, to let Rafe into the house that turned out to be Mrs. J's, I'd been worried about venturing into what was generally considered to be a sketchy neighborhood. And the sight of Rafe, astride his big, black Harley-Davidson, with muscles bulging and eyes hidden behind a pair of dark sunglasses, hadn't been reassuring. Sure, he'd taken my breath away. It had been instant, if unwilling, attraction. But he'd looked like someone I should stay far, far away from, no matter how gorgeous he was. And then, of course, I'd realized who he was, and how much more I needed to stay away from him. And then there'd been the bloody corpse inside the house...

However, since then I'd become inured to the area. Sure, there were still drug deals going down on the corners, and most of the residents came from a lower socio-economic bracket than the one I'd grown up in. The crime rates were a bit higher than across the parkway, in the 'nicer' parts of East Nashville. But things were looking better all the time. Our house had been renovated. A couple of others had followed suit. A few brave pioneers had moved in. And a real estate developer had bought some of the empty lots and a few small crackerbox houses, and had knocked down the houses and built new, bigger homes on the land. We were halfway to gentrified. Or at least a few steps along the way.

But to Catherine, who hadn't been here before, and who was used to her safe subdivision and charming, quaint old town, I could well imagine it looked like something out of a scary movie.

"It's not as bad as it used to be," I told her, while I wondered what was going on in the other car. Dix had been to the house before, and hadn't seemed concerned, but Mother was surely aghast at the depths to which her youngest daughter had descended. This was likely to make her even more determined to talk me into coming back to Sweetwater with her.

Although with Dix in the house, she might concede that I'd be safe.

Unless Dix was planning to scurry off to Tamara Grimaldi's house as soon as Mother's back was turned...

"Wow," Catherine said. She was peering out the front window. "That's quite a house!"

"Which?"

"That one." She pointed. "The brick Victorian, with the round tower on the corner."

"That's my house," I said, and turned into the circular driveway. Crunching across the gravel with someone who had never been here before, brought back memories of the first time I'd driven up to the house, on the first Saturday in August last year.

It had been hot then, too. I'd been nervous about venturing into the 'bad' part of town. And Rafe had been in the driveway, scaring me and attracting me in about equal measure. And that was before I realized who he was: my hometown bad-boy, the one whose mother had been held up as an example of what not to do.

The house itself had looked considerably worse than it did now. The bones had been there—a three-story brick Victorian, 1880s, with a round tower on one of the corners—but it had been rundown and derelict, like no one had done any work to it in thirty years.

Which was about the time that had passed since Tyrell was shot, so probably a fairly accurate estimate.

The brick had been crumbling and there'd been ivy climbing the walls. Several of the windows had been broken and they'd all been dirty. The porch had been missing some of the ornate gingerbread trim, while the floorboards had looked as if they were thinking of breaking at any moment, and dumping whoever stepped on them into the no-man's-land underneath. There were missing roof tiles, and waist high weeds all over the backyard.

I could go on, but I won't. Rafe had done a heroic job after he took over, in making the house look better. And on a limited budget, since undercover work for the TBI doesn't exactly fill the coffers with a whole lot of gold. But the grass was cut and the ivy gone. The brick had been tuck-pointed and the broken windows replaced. I cleaned them regularly, at least on the inside. The roof had been replaced, and so had the rotten floorboards. And inside, there were refinished wood floors, gleaming woodwork, and fresh paint.

It was a beautiful, one-of-a-kind house. The neighborhood might still leave something to be desired, but the house itself shouldn't scare anyone off.

I stopped the Volvo at the foot of the stairs and cut the engine. Catherine and I got out. Meanwhile, Dix pulled to a stop behind us, and he and Mother did the same.

The driveway was empty other than our two cars. Rafe's motorcycle hadn't magically reappeared while I was gone. I hadn't really expected it to, but it was still disappointing.

I waited a second for Mother to make a comment about the neighborhood or the property. When she didn't—reserving judgment until she'd seen the interior, no doubt—I headed up the stairs to the porch. "Come on."

Down on the street, a souped-up brown Buick rolled by, blasting rap music loud enough to shake our eardrums. The same thing had happened back in August—with a green Dodge, and a sullen-faced young black man who had scowled at us through the window. It had made me nervous. Now I just lifted a hand to greet the kid who lived in the house two doors up. He was nineteen, answered to Malcolm, and worked at the gas station on the corner of Dickerson and Dresden.

He gave me a toot of the horn in return, and rolled off down the street. Going to work, no doubt.

Mother watched the byplay with a tiny wrinkle between her

brows, but she didn't say anything. Just waited on the porch until I'd opened the three locks on the front door—Rafe agreed to let me live with him, but he'd insisted on taking precautions, especially after I got pregnant—and disarmed the shrieking alarm system.

"Come on in."

I waited until they'd filed past me into the foyer, and then I closed and locked the door behind them. I was no longer uncomfortable being here by myself, but it never hurts to be careful.

"So you live here," Mother said after a moment.

I nodded, resisting the temptation to ask whether she really thought I'd take her—take all of them—into someone else's house.

Of course, I could have. Quite easily. I still had my real estate license, and with it, access to every house for sale in Davidson County. But that would have been dishonest. And anyway, I liked my house.

Rafe's house.

Mrs. Jenkins's house.

Whatever.

"It's gorgeous," Catherine said, looking around. "The woodwork... it's original, isn't it?"

I nodded. "1880s. Never been painted. Everything here is original. Except the kitchen. And the bathrooms. We... Rafe kept the original clawfoot tubs, but everything is updated."

Catherine nodded. "I love an old house."

I do, too.

"Although it's nice when everything works the way it should." She smiled.

I smiled back. "Old houses sometimes have quirks. For instance, it takes a minute to get the hot water upstairs, through all the pipes. But it's worth it."

Catherine nodded. And looked around, enviously. Like Dix,

she lives in a new subdivision home in Sweetwater. And while it's very pretty, and spacious, and well-insulated, and has a garden tub and a walk-in closet and a media room above the front-loading garage, it does lack some of the charm of a genuinely old house.

Of course, it does make up for it in convenience. But I wouldn't want to trade.

"Will you give us the tour?"

"Sure." I put my bag down on the bench in the foyer. "Down this way are the formal rooms and the kitchen."

We made our way down the same hall I had walked barefoot this morning, our heels clicking on the hardwood floors. "Library, parlor, dining room, kitchen."

"Nice," Catherine said, looking around with approval.

"Thank you." I took another look around myself, just in case I had missed a note from Rafe the first time. Or just in case one had appeared in the time since.

It hadn't.

"The library is where your colleague was murdered," Mother asked, "isn't it?"

I nodded. "She doesn't haunt the place, though. And the bloodstains came out of the floor. Unlike in the ghost stories Dix used to tell me."

Dix grinned. Mother shuddered delicately.

"The second floor is all bedrooms and baths." We went back down the hall and up the staircase to the second floor. "Our room." I opened the door to the room I shared with Rafe. The bed was still unmade, since I hadn't taken the time to fuss with it before I left.

"Mrs. J's room." Pale lavender, across the hall. When I first saw the house last August, there'd been an old, soiled mattress in this room, that housed a family of mice.

Rafe had told me they were rats, but I prefer to think he was just yanking my chain. We didn't know each other very well then. Anyway, the mattress and rodents were long gone.

"This one used to be Marquita Johnson's room." I pushed open the door to the third bedroom. Yellow, with a brass bed. "Now it's just another guestroom, I guess."

"The nurse," Mother said.

I nodded. "Her husband—ex-husband—works with Bob Satterfield." Bob is Mother's gentleman friend, and also the Sweetwater sheriff. "Rafe hired her to take care of Mrs. Jenkins. We took a casserole to Cletus's house after she died, remember?"

Mother nodded. She hadn't wanted to go, but I had made her. Both because I felt guilty—I hadn't liked Marquita, and she hadn't liked me—and because I thought there was a chance Cletus, her ex-husband, might have killed her. Another long story.

"This one," I pushed open the last bedroom door, "will become the nursery."

Or at least that had been the plan before today. Before my boyfriend, the father of my baby, and the person whose house I lived in, had vanished without a trace.

There was a moment's pause. Then—

"Would you like for us to help you look around?" Catherine said. "We don't have anything else to do until Jonathan gets here."

Dix rolled his eyes at her. "He isn't hiding in a closet, Cat."

"I know that," Catherine said. "But maybe there's a clue here to where he's gone or what happened." She turned to me. "Did you check?"

I shook my head.

"Did you at least look in his closet to see whether he packed a bag?"

"No," I admitted. "All I thought to look for, was a note. And his suit. The one he was getting married in. It's still here. I was wondering whether to take it with me to the courthouse or leave it, in case he came back."

"Let's look now." Catherine set out, briskly, for the master bedroom, and pushed open the closet doors. "Can you tell if anything's missing?"

I peered in. "Not that I can see. But most of Rafe's clothes are in the bureau. He doesn't wear suits and ties very often."

"Then look there," Catherine ordered.

"Yes, ma'am." I crossed to the bureau and pulled out one of Rafe's drawers. (I have three, he has two.)

The scent of him rose and smacked me across the face, spicy and masculine, and I sucked in a breath.

Catherine was next to me immediately, with an arm around my waist. "What is it? What happened?"

"Nothing." I bit my lip against the tears crowding my eyes. "It just... the clothes smell like him."

Catherine didn't have anything to say to that. Or if she did, she didn't bother. Instead, she just wrapped the other arm around me, and let me cry on her shoulder while Dix awkwardly patted my back.

Five

Catherine left thirty minutes later. Jonathan pulled up in the driveway and honked the horn. "Sorry, Savannah," he said when I opened the door, "but if I let the kids out of the car, I'll never get them back in."

I nodded. "Thanks for coming."

"It's no problem," Jonathan said, nodding to Dix, who had followed me out on the porch to see his girls. "We'll take care of them until you come home."

"I'll be back tomorrow," Dix told him, moving down the stairs. "And I'll keep you up to date by phone."

"I appreciate it." Jonathan's attention moved past us to the door. "Are they coming?"

"Probably just visiting the powder room before getting in the car. I'll check." I left the two men outside with the kids, and went back through the door to see what was keeping Mother and Catherine.

I didn't have to look far. They were in the kitchen, arguing, their voices carrying down the hallway to the foyer. Their very polite voices, since we'd all been taught that yelling is unladylike.

"I'm not sure that's a good idea," Catherine was saying as I headed down the hallway.

"She can't deal with this alone," Mother answered.

"She won't be alone. Dix is staying, and she has friends here. Including the police detective."

"That's not the same as family," Mother said.

"Dix is family," Catherine told her.

"Dixon is a man," Mother answered, and of course there was nothing Catherine could say to that. And at any rate, I had reached the kitchen by then, and stopped in the doorway to look from one to the other of them.

"Jonathan's outside, waiting. With all the kids. And they're getting impatient. What's the problem?"

"Mother won't leave," Catherine said.

I turned to Mother, who said, "You can't deal with this alone."

"I'm not alone," I said. "Dix will be here. And Grimaldi will call. And Wendell. And I have friends at work." Sort of. "And neighbors."

"That's not the same as having family around," Mother said.

No. But— "No offense, but I'm used to not having family around. I've been living in Nashville for almost seven years. I got through divorcing Bradley on my own."

"You haven't dealt with this situation before," Mother said.

Well, no.

Then again, I sort of had. Or something similar. "I spent most of October and November not knowing whether Rafe was alive or dead, and whether he'd come back or stay gone forever. I was pregnant then, too. It's been a while since I had to deal with it, but I'm sure it'll come back to me."

"Don't be facetious, darling," Mother said.

"I'm not. I'll be fine. I don't need you to stay."

"I'm sure you don't," Mother said, sounding very sure I did, "but my mind is made up."

"You didn't bring a change of clothes."

"Nor did Dixon," Mother said. "I'm sure I can find something of yours to wear."

Maybe, although she's a few inches shorter and a bit skinnier than I am. Especially right now.

And I guess Dix would have to raid Rafe's closet. He was at least three inches shorter than Rafe, and rather less muscular—being a lawyer instead of an undercover TBI agent—but I was sure I could dig up something he could wear. Worst case scenario, we'd stop by the nearest Target or Walmart and buy him a pair of jeans that fit, some underwear, and a pair of cheap loafers. It wouldn't hurt him—wouldn't hurt either of them—to rough it for a couple of days.

But while I didn't mind Dix sticking around—my brother and I have always gotten along well, being close in age—there was no part of me that wanted to put up with Mother. The situation I was in was already difficult enough. And she hated Rafe. The last thing I needed was someone breathing down my neck, telling me every hour that he'd run away rather than marry me. It was hard enough to convince myself that he hadn't without her help.

"You'd really be more comfortable at home," I said. "And don't you and Bob have plans tonight?"

They usually did. Dinner at the Wayside Inn, the nicest restaurant in Sweetwater. Followed by, I'm sure, something I didn't want to think too closely about.

"Bob will understand," Mother said firmly.

"You'd have to stay here. In this house. With just me and Dix for protection."

And how would Dix feel about this? He might be planning to spend the night with Grimaldi. But with Mother bunking across the hall, he wouldn't be able to leave. And no way was he going to explain to her that he'd figured on spending the night with a woman. Mother would have a fit.

"Are you sure you're comfortable with that?" I added, a touch desperate. "The neighborhood isn't what you're used to."

"If Dixon is here," Mother said, "I'm sure I'll be fine."

If Dixon was here. *Right.*

Outside, Jonathan leaned on the car horn. Catherine made a face. "I have to go."

"Go," Mother said. "I'll be fine here. I'll drive down with your brother tomorrow. Or the next day. Whenever it's time for him to go back."

"Are you sure?" Catherine moved a few steps closer to the door.

"Positive," Mother said, waving her off. "Go, before your husband leaves without you."

"He won't leave without me," Catherine said. "Not after driving all the way here." But she went anyway, practically running down the hallway.

Mother and I looked at one another.

"After you," she said.

"I think you're going to regret this," I told her, and went. Behind me, I heard the clicking of her heels.

Outside, Catherine was already in the minivan when I got there. I sidled up to Dix and spoke softly. "Mother decided to stay."

He nodded without looking at me. "Catherine told me."

"Sorry if that upsets your plans for the evening."

He shook his head. "I wasn't going anywhere."

"Good. Because I'm not dealing with her on my own."

"I wouldn't expect you to," Dix said. "Maybe we can play charades."

Mother reached the porch and I told him, "We usually just sit and count the gunshots. And do shots of Tequila"

Nobody said anything.

"Are you sure you won't change your mind?" Catherine asked Mother. "It isn't too late."

Mother shook her head. "My daughter needs me."

"Like a rash," Dix muttered.

Indeed.

"Last chance," I said, as Jonathan put the minivan in gear.

"Goodness, darling," Mother told me. "The way you're talking, one might almost think you don't want me to stay."

And one would assume correctly. But since I wasn't quite at the point where I was willing to say that, out loud, to my mother, I just forced a smile. "Drive safely."

Jonathan nodded. "Call me," Catherine said. "Let me know what happens." Her voice got progressively louder as the car rolled away from the steps. "Don't forget!"

I lifted a hand. We stood there and waited until the minivan had taken a right on Potsdam and disappeared down the street, and then I turned and headed back inside the house. "I'm going to change."

"Of course, darling," Mother said sympathetically.

"It's a long drive to Peaceful Pines. I might as well be comfortable." I headed up the stairs.

"What's Peaceful Pines?" Dix called after me.

I stopped halfway up to look back at him. "Church camp. Somewhere on the Cumberland Plateau. Ginny said it was at least an hour from here. Rafe's son David is there. I want to talk to him. See if Rafe has been in touch. See whether he has mentioned anything about... anything."

There was a moment's pause. I waited to see if anyone had anything to say. When they didn't, I added, "I'll be back downstairs in a couple of minutes. If you want to change out of what you're wearing, now's the time."

And then I continued up the stairs to do my own changing. I'd been wearing this wedding dress for long enough. It was time to get down to business.

Twenty minutes later we were on our way out of Nashville, toward the Cumberland Plateau. Dix had keyed the coordinates for the camp into his GPS, and we were making good time. It was a Saturday, traffic was light, and Dix's SUV was purring along. Dix was driving, and Mother sat in the front seat, which left me to lounge in the back. Abigail and Hannah were both still in booster seats, and my derriere is too big to fit in one of those, so I'd had to unhook one and shove it down on the floor, between the back of Dix's seat and the backseat, to have room.

In six months or so, I'd be driving around with a baby seat in the back of my own car. With a baby in it.

Would that baby have a father? One who was part of its life? Or would its only knowledge of its father be in the stories I told and the few—very few—pictures I had?

I took the thought out and looked at it. Sideways at first, and then straight on.

Rafe was gone. Whether willingly or unwillingly I had no idea yet. If he'd developed cold feet, he'd shown no sign of it to me, but then he'd undoubtedly make sure he didn't. Wouldn't want me to know he'd changed his mind. That he couldn't be who I wanted him to be. A good husband and father.

If that's what had happened, I could even understand it, to a degree. He'd grown up fatherless, with a grandfather who'd liked nothing better than to knock him—and his mother—around. He had no frame of reference for what a good father should look like, and although I believed, with everything I had, that he would fall in love with our baby and become a great father, he might not believe it. He might worry about his abilities in that regard. That might be why he'd never even considered asking for custody—even joint custody—of David. Until last year, he hadn't known about David's existence. Hadn't known he had a son. He had every right, legally and morally, to insist on a chance to be that son's father.

But he hadn't. And I'd never asked why. I had assumed I knew. David was happy and healthy and well-loved. He had parents who adored him, who would be devastated to lose him. They were the only parents he'd ever known. He'd enjoyed getting to know Rafe, but Sam was still his dad, and Ginny was his mom. He'd be devastated to lose them, too.

I had assumed that was why Rafe hadn't made anything of it. Because of what was best for David. But maybe he'd been worried about his own abilities to be a father, as well? It's one thing to make friends with his kid while someone else has all the difficult responsibilities of parenting, but something else entirely to be a full-time father.

With our baby, he couldn't leave the parenting to someone else. Not unless he left.

My stomach roiled unpleasantly, and I put a hand to it. Dix glanced at me in the rearview mirror, as if he could sense what was going on. "Are you feeling all right, Savannah?"

"A little nauseous," I admitted.

"D'you need me to pull over? Get you a ginger ale, or something? There's an exit coming up, with a couple of gas stations."

"I think I'm OK." It wasn't morning sickness. Or afternoon sickness. Just a result of what I was thinking. Ginger ale wasn't going to help that. "I'll let you know."

Dix nodded.

"Would you like to sit up front?" Mother asked, martyr-like. "I can sit in the back."

Oh, sure. Just my mother, her Manolos, and the booster seats. I'd never hear the end of that.

"I'm all right," I said. "I'll let you know."

She nodded and faced front. No doubt praying that I wouldn't.

The car kept going.

"I'm going to take a nap," I said, and closed my eyes.

"I'll wake you when we get there," Dix answered, sounding relieved.

"Probably do her good," Mother murmured. I slitted my eyes open and saw that Dix nodded. And then I closed them again.

I don't think I actually slept much, but I went into a sort of half-awake state where my thoughts weren't so loud and turned into freaky half-asleep daydreams mixed with memories instead. Rafe was facing off against Hector Gonzales, who had a knife and wasn't afraid to use it, while I was tied to a chair unable to do anything to help. Rafe was slumped on his bedroll in the trailer in the Bog, with Elspeth's dead body sprawled on the floor, and blood everywhere. Rafe was driving away, the taillight of his Harley-Davidson fading into the distance and then turning the corner at Fifth and Main, where I used to live.

Rafe was back, sitting on the edge of the bed in Mrs. Jenkins's house at Potsdam Street, his hand warm and rough as he stroked my shoulder and arm.

"Rise and shine, Goldilocks."

I jerked awake and looked around. His voice had been so real that for a second, it was like he should be there. But I was still in the car, and there was no Rafe. Just Mother and Dix.

"We're here," my brother added.

I sat up and looked out the window. Yes, we were. The car was parked in a clearing surrounded by tall pine trees. In the distance, between the trunks of the trees, I could see blinking water where the sun struck it. A dozen small log cabins were spaced out on the hillside down toward the water. A sign above the door of the nearest cabin said 'office.'

"We're here," I said.

Dix nodded. "That's what I said."

"Sorry." I rubbed my eyes. Carefully, so I wouldn't smudge the makeup any worse than I figured it already was. "I guess I fell asleep."

"Guess so." Dix opened his door. "Stay there. I'll come around and haul you out."

I nodded.

But of course he stopped and helped Mother first, as a dutiful son should. By the time he got to me, I'd already opened my own door and swung my legs out.

"Watch your head," Dix said, and took my hand. "Come on." He pulled me out of the car and supported me for a second. "OK?"

I nodded. "Bad dreams."

"Sorry." He gave my arm a squeeze. "We'll figure it out."

I nodded. Yes, we would. One way or another. But that didn't mean my life would ever be the same again.

I had changed into a comfortable cotton sundress and a pair of sandals before we left Mrs. Jenkins's house. Dix had had the good sense to leave his suit jacket behind, and to remove his tie and roll his sleeves up to the elbows. Mother, meanwhile, was still dressed in her three inch heels, her pencil skirt, and her silk blouse. She looked ridiculous balancing on the rough grass, surrounded by the pine trees and silence.

"Why don't you stay in the car?" I suggested. "Dix can leave the air conditioning running. It's hot out here."

Mother shook her head. "I'll be fine once we get inside."

I doubted it—from what I could tell, there was no A/C in the cabins, not even the office one—but she was a grownup, after all. She could make up her own mind.

"Then let's go see whether David's back from his hike and whether we can convince someone to let us talk to him for a minute."

I headed for the open door to the cabin without waiting for an answer. Dix offered Mother his arm, and they followed.

It was just as hot inside the office as I had anticipated. The front door stood open, and so did a back window. An oscillating fan moved the air around. But all that did, was create a breeze. The breeze was still above ninety degrees. The college-age girl who was sitting behind the desk tapping on a computer keyboard had perspiration beading at her temples and at the hollow of her throat. Any makeup she had started the day with—if any—had evaporated in the heat and humidity.

When we walked in, she looked up. "Can I help you?"

Blue eyes moved from me to Dix to Mother.

"I'm Savannah Martin," I said. "I was hoping for a chance to talk to David Flannery."

Those blue eyes shuttered. "I'm afraid there's nobody here by that name."

"I spoke to his mother," I said. "Ginny said he was here."

She hesitated.

"She said he was on a hike this morning, but that he'd be back by this afternoon. And it's late afternoon now."

"I'm afraid..."

"She said she'd told you to call the police if David's biological father showed up and tried to take him. Does any of us look like David's biological father to you?"

"No..."

"David's biological father is missing," I said. "He should have been at the courthouse at eleven today to get married. He should have married *me*."

Her eyes went from suspicious to sympathetic, and then horrified. "He left you at the altar?"

"There's no altar at the courthouse. But yes, basically he did. I'd like to know whether he said anything to David about leaving. If he didn't, it's possible something bad has happened to him."

She hesitated.

"All we want to do is talk," Dix said and stepped up next to me. He put one of his business cards on the desk. "I'm an attorney. I assure you we have no plans of absconding with the boy."

The girl pursed her lips. "Are you David's biological mother?" she asked me.

I shook my head. "David's mother's dead. She died last fall." In that shootout in the Colliers' trailer in the Bog I'd been having nightmares about on the trip here. Rafe had been shot, too, although not as badly. And the next day was when Dix and I had first discovered David's existence, when my brother, Elspeth's attorney, had gone over to her house to start the process of handling the estate.

And incidentally, if Elspeth hadn't gotten herself shot, she would have been in prison now. For a couple of counts of murder and attempted murder. One of those attempted murders had been of me, although I wasn't too upset over it anymore, since the reason she'd died was because she'd refused to move from in front of Rafe, who was the man with the gun's real target.

"David knows me, though," I added. "And you are, of course, welcome to stay while we talk to him. We don't have anything to hide."

There was another pause. Then— "Wait here." She got up from the desk and brushed past us and outside.

"Looks like she might be getting him," Dix said.

"Or like she wants to call the police from a different phone." I shook my head. "It's ridiculous of Ginny to be so nervous. Nobody's going to take David. I just want to talk to him. And if Rafe were to show up, he wouldn't take David, either. He'd probably just want to say goodbye."

Neither Dix nor Mother had anything to say to that, so we ended up waiting in silence for the camp counselor to come back.

When she did, she was trailed by two male persons. One was roughly the size of a refrigerator—six feet tall and built like a linebacker. The other was a boy with Rafe's eyes and Rafe's nose and Rafe's smile.

"Savannah!" He grinned, looking so much like his father that it hurt. "Is my dad here, too?" He looked around.

I forced a smile. "I'm afraid not. This is my mother, and my brother Dix."

David gave them each a curious look. "Hi," he said politely.

Dix nodded. Mother just stared at him, with a funny expression on her face.

I turned back to David. "Have you spoken to your... to Rafe recently?"

It was David's turn to look confused. "Not since I got here last Saturday."

"When was the last time you saw him?"

"The week before that," David said promptly. "We went to a baseball game. Remember?"

I did. I'd spent the evening at home, in the air conditioned comfort of my bed, reading a book. I'd fallen asleep before Rafe got there, and he'd woken me up when he got home to make love.

"Did he..." I hesitated, "say anything?"

"He said lots of things," David said. He tilted his head. "What's going on?"

When I didn't answer immediately, he added, "You can tell me. I'm mature for my age. My mom says so."

I smiled. "I'm sure you are. It's just that I don't know what's going on. I was hoping you did."

"No," David said and shook his head. "What are you talking about?"

I took a breath. "Rafe and I were supposed to get married today. Did he tell you that?"

"Yeah." He nodded. "That's cool. I get two mothers and two fathers."

"Last night, he and a couple of the guys he works with went out for a beer after work. To celebrate and... stuff."

David grinned. "You mean, like a bachelor party? With strippers and stuff?"

"No!" *God, no.* Was he even supposed to know about strippers at his age?

Dix hid a grin, not very successfully. "No strippers," he told David. "Just a couple of guys drinking beer and shooting pool and hanging out."

David nodded. "That's cool."

"I'm sure it was. But Col... your dad didn't come home afterwards."

David's face immediately sobered.

"We thought maybe he'd mentioned something to you about going away," I said.

He shook his head.

"Nothing?"

"No. He said after getting married, you were going away for the weekend, but that he'd be back next week. We're going to another game." For a second, his face crumpled. "Or we were."

For a second, my face crumpled too. If Rafe had done this on purpose, then damn him. Bad enough that he'd disappointed me, but there was no excuse for disappointing his son.

But he hadn't done this. He couldn't have done this. The man I knew would not tell his son that he'd be back to take him to another baseball game, and then leave.

"You haven't heard from him since you got here?" Dix asked.

David shook his head. "This is a no-tech zone." He made a face. "I only get my phone at night, when I have to call my mom. But he hasn't called."

"And you haven't seen him?"

"No. You think he'll show up here?" He looked around, as if hoping to see Rafe lurking behind the nearest pine. I looked around too, automatically. There was no Rafe, of course.

"I doubt it," I said. "But if he does, I'd appreciate it if you'd let me know."

"Sure." David nodded. "I'm sorry, Savannah."

"I am, too," I said. "I'll let you know how it goes, OK?"

He nodded. "OK." After a second, he surprised me—and maybe himself—by giving me an awkward hug. I hugged him back, my stomach—round and hard—between us. When he stepped back, there were tears in my eyes, and I think they may have been in his, too.

He turned away without a word, bodyguard on his heels. If Rafe showed up and tried to abduct David by force—something he'd never, ever do—he might have a hard time getting through the refrigerator.

"Thank you," Dix told the camp counselor, while I was still clearing my throat. "We appreciate it."

She nodded. "Is he in danger?"

"I don't imagine so," Dix said easily. "We're not concerned about David's safety at this time. We're trying to track down his father, and thought David might know something. That's all. But I'm sure you always take precautions."

She sniffed, offended at the suggestion that they might not. "Of course."

"Will you call me if someone else shows up asking for David?"

The counselor said she would, obviously taken in by Dix's professional demeanor and business card, and on that note, we took our leave.

Six

"So that's Rafael's child," Mother said when we were back in the car and bumping our way along the rutted dirt track from the camp up to the main road.

From her tone of voice—flat—it was impossible to guess what was behind the question. She had to be thinking something, but I was damned—darned—if I knew what it was.

So I did the only thing I could do, and told the truth. "Yes. That's David. Rafe's son."

"And Elspeth Caulfield's," Dix added.

Mother glanced at him. "The woman who died last fall."

"After shooting Marquita and Yvonne McCoy and trying to kill me," I said. "Yes."

Mother was silent for a few seconds. "Your child will look like that," she said.

Again, there was no clue in her tone to what she was thinking, so I didn't know whether to bristle or not. I wanted to bristle—because I assumed she was being critical—but I forced myself to sound calm. "I'm sure he will. Or she. Whenever we find out the gender."

Mother didn't say anything.

"For what it's worth," I added, "I think David's quite a handsome boy. He looks a lot like Rafe did at that age." Or so I assumed. I hadn't had much to do with him until I started high school at fourteen. And he was seventeen by then. But David looks a lot like I imagine Rafe did when he was a boy. "Only better fed with nicer clothes and fewer bruises."

Mother chose not to respond to that one. "He seems like a nice boy," she said instead, primly.

"As far as I know he is. His parents are nice people, who love him a lot. They live in a big house in West Meade, and he goes to private school. And obviously he goes to church, if he's spending part of the summer at a church camp."

Mother nodded.

"From everything I've seen, he's a great kid. I hope mine turns out as well."

Mother might have said something to that—I'm not sure—but that's when the phone rang. We'd just reached the main road, and Dix turned the nose of the car back toward Nashville. I fished the phone out of my bag and put it to my ear. "Hello?"

"Ms.... Savannah," Tamara Grimaldi said.

"Detective." My heart started beating faster. It couldn't be good news. If she'd found him, that'd be the first words out of her mouth.

"I hooked up with Spicer and Truman when they came back to town. We've been driving around."

"OK," I said.

"We stopped by Gabe's Bar, to take a look around, once they opened."

"OK."

"Have you ever been here?"

I hadn't. Rafe is willing to expand my horizons to a certain degree, but not to that one. "I know where it is. And what it looks like." A dive up on Trinity Lane, near the interstate.

"There's an old shed at the back of the parking lot. They keep drums of cooking oil and grease in it."

"I've seen it," I said. "Driving by." A small structure even more dilapidated than the cinderblock building that houses the bar itself.

"Truman decided to check inside, and found your boyfriend's bike in there."

"Inside the shed?"

"Yes," Grimaldi said.

"Rafe's bike?"

"I ran the registration. It matched."

Then yes, it was Rafe's bike. "What was it doing there?"

"As far as we could tell," Grimaldi said, "not a blessed thing. Track with me, Ms.... Savannah. Why would your boyfriend leave his bike inside a shed at Gabe's?"

"He wouldn't," I said. "He loved..." *Gah!* "He loves that bike. If he was planning to run away, he'd ride away on it. If he was running away with someone else—"

And wasn't that a new and disturbing thought I hadn't had yet?

"—I still don't think he'd have left it there. He would have taken it home, or somewhere else where it would be safe, first. But he wouldn't leave his bike in the parking lot of a bar in a not-so-nice part of town."

I could feel Grimaldi nod, even if I couldn't see her. "That's my thinking, too."

"Is it possible that one of the staff put the bike in the shed? That it was left in the lot after closing, or something?"

"We'll ask," Grimaldi said, "but off-hand, it doesn't make sense. The staff wouldn't have moved it during business hours, since the owner might still be inside. And the bar's open until two. Mr. Craig said your boyfriend left at eleven, to go home. That must mean Mr. Craig was still inside the bar at that point. If he'd come out later and seen the bike in the lot, but no sign of Mr. Collier, don't you think he would have found that strange?"

Of course he would have. He was a trained agent of the TBI. It wasn't like he'd overlook or disregard something like that.

"Have you asked him?"

"I will," Grimaldi said. "I want to talk to the rookies, too."

"Can I come?"

She hesitated. "I suppose that might be OK. Under the circumstances."

"We're on our way back to town," I told her. "We drove out to Peaceful Pines to talk to David."

"Peaceful Pines?"

"The church camp where David is staying. He says he hasn't heard from or seen Rafe since last week." I bit my lip. "I think I just rocked his world. And not in a good way."

"If you told him his biological father is missing, I'm sure you did," Grimaldi agreed, but without censure in her voice. "He didn't know anything?"

"He said he didn't. I believed him."

In the front seat, Dix nodded.

"He promised he'd let us know if he sees or hears from Rafe," I added. "The camp counselor said the same thing. Dix left them his card. And David has what looks like a bodyguard. He's almost as tall as Rafe and twice as broad."

"Good," Grimaldi said. "I doubt the boy's in any danger, but why take chances?"

Why, indeed?

"When are you planning to talk to Wendell and the rookies? Are you sure it'll be OK if I'm there?"

"If I say it's OK," Grimaldi said, "then it's OK. How about six-thirty? That'll give them all time to get there."

I glanced at the dashboard clock. "We can make that. At the TBI?"

"That seems easiest," Grimaldi said.

"Do you need me to come to Gabe's for anything?"

"No," Grimaldi said. "Spicer and Truman will talk to the staff about the bike, just in case one of them did move it inside the shed. And I've arranged for a flatbed truck. We need to examine the bike for fingerprints. See if we can get some idea who put it in the shed. If it wasn't one of the staff."

"Thank you."

"Don't thank me," Grimaldi said. "I'm doing my job."

"Thanks for doing your job well."

She didn't respond to that. "I'll see you at six-thirty at the TBI. Call me if anything happens before then."

I said I would. And added, before she could hang up, "I don't suppose you've checked whether anyone Rafe put away has been released in the last few days or weeks? He spent ten years undercover. He must have been responsible for sending a lot of people to prison. Some of them might hold a grudge."

"Oh," Grimaldi said, "I'm sure many of them do. And I'll do that. I know that anyone I was involved in arresting hasn't gone anywhere. After Mr. Lamont escaped this winter, I put the fear of God into everyone in the penal system. If anyone I've ever arrested so much as moves toward the exit, I hear about it. But if I wasn't involved in the case, I wouldn't necessarily know. So that's a good thought. I'll look into it."

"Thank you."

"I'll let you know what I find out." She hung up without giving me time to respond.

There was a moment of silence while I dropped the phone back into my bag. Then—

"The Harley?" Dix asked. He was watching me in the rearview mirror, with one eye on the road.

I nodded. "They found it in a shed behind the bar where Rafe was last night."

"That's not good," Dix said.

I shook my head. "It makes it less likely that he left of his own free will. He wouldn't just walk off and leave the Harley sitting there."

"Maybe he decided to hitchhike," Mother suggested, her tone of voice implying that he was the type of person who would.

"I suppose he might have," I agreed, more to work it through in my own head than because I believed it. "There's a truck stop half a mile down the road from Gabe's, on the other side of the interstate. He could have walked there and found a ride."

Mother nodded.

"But why would he? He had a vehicle of his own. And if he didn't want to ride the bike out of town, he could at least have driven to the truck stop. Why walk along the road for half a mile when he didn't have to? In the dark, with cars flying by, there was a good chance someone would run him down before he made it fifty feet down the road."

Mother had no answer for that.

"And if he was concerned enough for the bike to roll it into the shed, he would have been concerned enough not to leave it there at all. The TBI is only a five minute ride from Gabe's. The house is even less. And the bike would have been safer in either place."

"Perhaps he ran out of gas," Mother said.

Huh. I suppose he might have. Although if he was that low on fuel when he got to Gabe's, I would have expected him to take care of it before he went inside. He wouldn't want to deal with it at eleven o'clock at night.

But maybe someone siphoned off the gas while he was inside Gabe's. And when he came out, the bike wouldn't start. So he rolled it into the shed where it would be safe, until...

But no. If the gas tank was dry, he wouldn't have to worry about anyone stealing the bike. If it had started, Rafe would have left on it. And anyway, he wouldn't have started walking down the road. He'd have gone inside and asked Wendell or one of the rookies for a ride to the nearest gas station. These were TBI agents. They didn't take stupid chances. Or at least not those kinds of stupid chances. If someone had siphoned off the gas and left Rafe stranded, he would have wondered why. He certainly wouldn't have done something like start walking down the side of the road on his own in the dark.

Still, I'd make sure to ask Grimaldi to have the forensic techs check the tank. Just in case there was something to Mother's suggestion.

"Anything else?" Dix wanted to know.

I shook my head. "We're meeting Wendell and the rookies at the TBI at six-thirty. And Grimaldi's checking to see whether any of the people Rafe put in prison is newly released and looking for revenge."

Dix nodded.

"For now, I guess we just wait and see what happens."

"Easier said than done," Dix muttered, and that was certainly true. I settled back into the seat and watched the trees flash by outside the car, and thought unpleasant thoughts.

The Tennessee Bureau of Investigations is located in Inglewood, a mile or two north of Mrs. Jenkins's house. It's a big brick building with lots of windows, and a roof bristling with antennae. To get there, you have to drive up Gass Boulevard, past the medical examiner's office, which is always unpleasant. Not because there's anything to see. It's just a low-slung brick building with no identifying marks. Unless you happen to know what *Center for Forensic Medicine* means, it could be anything at all. But I've been there a couple of times, and neither were happy occasions. These days, I feel slightly sick just looking at the outside of the building.

Anyway, we passed the ME's office and crested the hill before pulling into the parking lot outside the TBI. Wendell had cleared us through, so all we had to do was show identification and turn our pockets and purses inside out, before we were allowed inside. Mother looked deeply perturbed at having a ham-fisted security guard pawing through her purse, but since Dix and I didn't complain, there wasn't anything she could say or do about it.

This trip had proven to be educational for my mother in a myriad of ways. I just hoped she was learning something from everything that had happened.

Grimaldi was already there when we arrived, and so were Wendell and the three rookies.

The boys looked about like I had expected. One black, one white, one Hispanic. All three were around twenty, and none of them looked like choir boys. If I'd met either in a dark alley—or for that matter on a deserted sidewalk in broad daylight—I'd have walked the other way, and fast.

"Jamal Atkins," Wendell said, nodding to the black kid. "Clayton Norris. José Garcia."

That last one sounded to me a lot like John Smith, but what do I know? "Nice to meet you."

The boys all nodded.

"I'm Rafe's girlfriend. This is my brother and my mother. They came up for the wedding that didn't happen."

Jamal opened his mouth. "That's bogus, man."

"No," I said. "It isn't bogus at all. He didn't show up."

Jamal refrained from rolling his eyes, but only barely. "That's what I'm saying, man."

Right. It was probably best not to point out that I wasn't a man. Clearly, I couldn't take anything Jamal said literally.

"Sorry," Clayton added, while José nodded.

They were about as different as they could be from one another. Jamal must be as tall as Rafe, and looked like he weighed thirty or forty pounds less. He was a beanpole of a kid, whose pants undoubtedly hung below his butt when he stood up. José was a fireplug: shorter than me, with a sullen pout and overdeveloped shoulders under a snug-fitting T-shirt. And Clayton looked like a skinhead, with fair hair buzzed short, a nose ring, and tattoos all up and down his arms.

Nobody in his right mind would have looked at either of them and thought 'undercover agent.' Which was the point, I guess.

"Now that we're here," Grimaldi said, "we can get started."

She went over everything she'd already told me on the phone, and ended with, "The techs did not find any usable fingerprints on the handles of the bike. Mr. Collier's are all over the bike, of course, but on the handle they're smudged. We're assuming someone else moved the bike into the shed."

She paused a moment to let that piece of information sink in before she continued. "At this point, we're trying to ascertain who that someone was, and when it happened. And of course what happened to Mr. Collier after he left the bar."

"I was already gone by then," José spoke up, with a glance at Wendell, maybe to make sure it was OK to speak. "I left first. Ten-thirty, maybe." He shrugged. "I live in Antioch. It's a long drive."

It was. Or at least a lot longer than Rafe's, who only had a few minutes to go to reach home.

"The rest of us stayed," Jamal offered. "Clay and I were playing pool. Rafe and Mr. Craig were talking. Then Rafe said he was gonna go, and Mr. Craig came to join us."

Clayton nodded. "We hung out until the game was over, and then we left, too. Twenty after, maybe?"

He glanced at the other two. Wendell and Jamal both nodded. "About that," Jamal said.

"Was there anything going on in the parking lot when you got outside?"

They all shook their heads. "We woulda stopped it," Jamal said, with a cocky grin.

"Was Mr. Collier's bike in the lot?"

They glanced at one another. "I didn't see it," Clayton said. Jamal shook his head.

"We got there at the same time," Wendell told us. "I parked in the slot next to him. When I came out to leave, the bike was gone. If it hadn't been, I woulda known something was wrong."

Grimaldi nodded. So did I. "And he didn't come back inside the bar? To say he had run out of gas, or anything?"

They all shook their heads.

"We didn't see him after he walked out," Jamal said. Clayton nodded.

Grimaldi turned to José. "You left earlier than the others. Where did you park relative to Mr. Collier's bike?"

"Couple spaces down," José said.

"Did you have to pass it to get to your own car?"

José nodded.

"Can you remember if it was there?"

José scrunched up his face. "Pretty sure. I mean, if it wasn't, I'da noticed, you know? Cause I knew Rafe was gonna need it to go home."

"Can you remember what it was parked next to?"

"Mr. Craig's ride," José said, glancing at Wendell. "Black Lincoln Town Car."

Wendell nodded. So did I. I'd taken a ride or two in that car last August. Although I hadn't realized it was Wendell's personal car that Rafe had borrowed.

"And on the other side?"

José scrunched up his face. "Van," he said. "Dark blue? A Chevy?"

"Windows?" Grimaldi asked.

José shook his head, his eyes still closed. Clayton and Jamal exchanged a glance and a smirk. "Cargo van," José said. "Maybe ten years old. Dirt on the bottom."

"License plate?"

"Dirty," José said. "I see a one, a N or a H. Eight, or could be a B."

"Does anyone else remember seeing the van?"

Everyone shook their heads. "It was gone when I came out," Wendell said. "Both the spaces next to my car were empty."

That seemed to take care of that, then.

"You want I should go run the plate?" he added.

"In a minute. I have a couple of questions about an old case first."

Wendell nodded. "How about you boys see what you can make of the cargo van? Run the partial, see what you come up with."

They all three nodded, and ambled out, arguing about who

should man the computer. Neither of them wanted to, it seemed. The last thing I heard before the door closed behind them was Jamal's voice. "Rock, paper, scissors?"

Wendell rolled his eyes. "They're good boys. And they'll make good agents. We just gotta knock some of the sass outta them first."

"They were helpful," I said, scooting my butt around on the hard chair. "Do you think José was right about the van? And the license plate?"

"The boy's got a damn near photographic memory," Wendell answered, "so yeah, likely he was. Good asset." He grinned.

Rafe's got a good memory for details, too. I'm sure you learn to cultivate one when your life might depend on it someday.

"I've been looking into prison releases," Grimaldi said, and put a file on the table. "Anything connected to Mr. Collier or Hector Gonzales. Anyone who might be holding a grudge."

Behind me, I could hear Mother whisper to Dix. "Who is Hector Gonzales?"

Wendell nodded. "He put away a lot of people. Some of'em are likely out by now, and could be looking for a bit of their own back."

"A criminal," Dix whispered back. "He ran a gang. One with cells all over the Southeast. Collier broke it up last year."

"I found four," Grimaldi said. "One was released two years ago, and has managed to keep his nose clean. Two were released last year, but one is back behind bars. And one was released last month."

Wendell reached for the folder.

"Why would anyone wait a year or more to come after Rafe?" I wanted to know. "He isn't hard to find. And last year he was still part of Hector's gang."

"That's why it may have taken someone all this time," Grimaldi explained. "Last year, he was still with the gang. Until we put it about that he died. That was September, wasn't it? Or

October?"

I nodded.

"By now, it's become common knowledge that not only isn't he dead, but he was an undercover informant all along. Someone who didn't suspect him a year ago might have learned better now."

True. "So who are these people?"

"That's the problem." Grimaldi sounded grumpy. "The one who's back in prison would have been my first choice. He has a violent background. The other two don't. They were just petty crooks who got swept up with the rest of the petty crooks while Collier worked his way toward the center of the gang. They served their year or two in prison for theft or possession of stolen property or whatever, and now they're staying mostly on the straight and narrow. One has a wife and a new baby and a job in a warehouse, and the other drives an eighteen-wheeler. He isn't even supposed to be in town this week."

"A couple of years in prison can change someone," I said. "Even if they weren't violent before, they could be now."

Grimaldi conceded my point.

"There's a truck stop just down the street from Gabe's. And there's certainly plenty of room in a semi-truck to tuck someone away."

"That's why I contacted the company he drives for. They checked the GPS on the truck and said it's in Kansas."

"A long-distance truck driver," Dix said, "could easily have made Kansas between now and last night at eleven."

Grimaldi nodded. "I have a call in to the Kansas State Police. They'll keep an eye out for the truck and pull him over if they see him. Just to make sure he's alone. And I sent Spicer and Truman to check out the warehouse where the second guy works. Just in case."

"What about the most recent guy?" I wanted to know. "The one who was released last month?"

He sounded like the best option to me. If nothing else, the timing worked. Because, yes, even if someone hadn't realized until Christmas that Rafe worked for the TBI, that was still six months ago. A long time to wait for revenge. And surely it doesn't take six months to figure out how to abduct someone?

"Eugenio Hernandez," Grimaldi said. "On the face of it, he seems unlikely. His arrest wasn't even related to the Gonzales investigation. He just happened to get himself caught with a prostitute."

"That doesn't sound like anything he could blame Rafe for," I said.

Grimaldi shook her head. "There's something weird about it, though. Hernandez spent several years in prison. Excessive for someone just picking up a hooker. Usually, paying for sex is a misdemeanor. I think it carries a maximum sentence of six months."

"The girl was underage," Wendell said, closing the folder and pushing it across the table. "Not much under—just a couple of months, if memory serves—but legally under eighteen. That ups the sentence to 1-6 years automatically. And he had a knife in the room. Hadn't used it on the girl, but it was there. That added some time, as well."

"You were involved in it?"

Wendell nodded. "Rafe called me and I called the cops. We had to keep it off the record at the TBI, so as not to spook the brass. Didn't want nobody thinking the boy was going soft, or that he was willing to throw the whole investigation over a streetwalker. But Hernandez was a predator. Little Ginger wasn't the first prostitute he picked up."

Little Ginger? My nose wrinkled involuntarily.

"So Rafe was worried about her?" I asked. "That's why he interfered?"

Wendell nodded. "But Hernandez said she'd told him she was legal, and she had the fake ID to back it up. We couldn't prove otherwise. And we couldn't find anyone else to testify against him. So we took what we could get, to get him off the streets for a while."

"Then I guess it's possible this guy figured out that he had Rafe to thank for sending him to jail, and he decided to get even?"

"Anything's possible," Wendell said, and on that note, the door opened again, and the boys filed back inside the room.

Seven

"No dice," Jamal announced. "There's no blue van with those letters and numbers in the license plate. In any order."

He put a piece of paper on the table.

"So either," Clayton added, "Einstein here don't remember as well as he thinks he does—"

José used his well-developed shoulder to knock him sideways. Clayton staggered.

"Boys," Wendell said.

"—or the owner of the blue van helped himself to someone else's license plate."

"Or the license plate expired," Grimaldi said. "While the owner of the car was in jail, for instance."

The boys exchanged a glance. "You got somebody in mind?" Jamal wanted to know.

"Go do another run on expired plates," Wendell told him. "See what you can come up with. And hurry."

"Yessir." They scrambled over one another to get back out the door, like a litter of puppies.

"They're cute," I told Wendell, with what felt like my first genuine smile of the day.

"They're a pain in my ass," he told me. "And in your boyfriend's." He scratched his head. "Course, *he* was a pain in my ass ten years ago, too. And he turned out all right."

Yes, he had. "I just hope he's OK," I said. "If someone took him—" and put him in a van, or a semi-truck, or a warehouse somewhere, "anything could have happened to him."

"He ain't easy to kill," Wendell said. "You know that."

I did know that. But he wasn't invincible. If someone had gotten the drop on him, he was just as mortal as the next guy. I'd seen him get shot, and I'd seen him get stabbed. And he bled, just like anyone else.

I pushed my chair away from the table. The legs moved across the floor with a screech. "Sorry. I just... I have to go."

Wendell didn't say a word about the break in my voice. "The boys and I'll keep trying to track down the blue van. If it don't show up in expired licenses, we'll go outside Davidson County to the rest of the state." He turned to Grimaldi. "You got the trucker and the warehouse under control?"

She nodded. "Eugenio Hernandez has an address listed with his parole officer. I didn't bother with it earlier, since I didn't think he was really a contender. And I don't guess there's much chance he's got Collier there, if he's got Collier at all. But someone should check. I can send Spicer and Truman, or..."

"The boys and I'll do it," Wendell said. "It'll give 'em something to do. Make 'em feel like they're contributing."

It seemed to me like they were already contributing. I wanted to contribute, too, although I knew that between them, the police and the TBI had the situation well in hand. "Can we come with you? And wait outside? Just in case?"

Wendell glanced at Grimaldi before answering. "Sure, darlin'. I don't think we'll find him there, but..."

"But just in case."

He nodded. "I'll go hustle the boys. Text me the address."

"We'll see ourselves out," Grimaldi said. "And meet you there." She gestured Dix and Mother toward the door. "Let's go."

"Do the two of you want to come with us?" she added when we were outside in the parking lot, standing between her police issued sedan and Dix's SUV. "I can take Savannah with me and bring her back if the two of you have had enough."

I could just imagine Dix's reaction to the suggestion that he should take Mother back to the house on Potsdam Street and stay with her while Grimaldi and I went looking for trouble.

"We'll come along, if you don't mind."

"I don't mind at all," Grimaldi said, "as long as you stay out of the way and let the TBI handle things."

Dix's voice was cool. "Of course, Detective."

"We'll stay in the car," I added. "I don't want to interfere. I just want to be there in case they find him."

"They won't find him," Grimaldi said. "If this is our guy, and I'm not sure it is, he won't be stupid enough to keep your boyfriend somewhere where we can find him this easily." She stalked toward her car.

"She didn't tell us where to go," Dix said, and opened his mouth to call after her.

I put a hand on his arm. "Let's just follow. She's upset. She feels guilty."

Dix glanced at me. "Why? She didn't do anything."

"It's part of the job," I explained. "Law enforcement. They feel guilty when bad things happen. Even if they know they can't be everywhere and do everything. They still feel they should have been there, then."

One of Rafe's rookies had been killed earlier this year, and I knew Rafe still blamed himself. I blamed myself, too, since it had been my ex-husband Manny Ortega had been following when he got shot. I knew it wasn't my fault, that it was the fault of the person who killed him, but I still felt responsible for Manny being in the wrong place at the wrong time. And if I felt that way, just imagine how Rafe felt, when it was he who had told Manny to be there.

"Just drive," I told Dix and crawled into the backseat. "If we're lucky, maybe we'll find him."

Dix muttered something—no doubt it was along the lines of what Grimaldi had said—but he didn't say it out loud. Mother prudently kept her mouth closed, as well, when she made her way into the front seat.

Eugenio Hernandez's address turned out to be a small tract house in the Woodbine area.

Woodbine is an older neighborhood southeast of downtown, but not as far south as, say, Antioch or Brentwood. And it's densely populated. The lots are all about forty feet wide, and there are houses on most of them. Not a great place to keep a hostage, in other words. Not unless Eugenio Hernandez had prepared himself with an underground, soundproof dungeon, and that was unlikely.

Grimaldi parked up the street a couple of houses. Dix rolled to a stop behind her sedan just as my phone rang. I pushed the button to answer the call. "Detective."

"It's the blue house on the other side of the street," Grimaldi said, her voice tinny through the speakerphone. "I don't see a car."

I didn't, either. There was a driveway from the street to the house, that ended in a carport. The carport's back wall was solid, so it wasn't possible to pull around behind the house. And both carport and driveway were empty.

I checked the surrounding driveways, as well. There was no blue van anywhere.

The house itself appeared to be deserted. The curtains were all closed, and the grass looked ankle high. The mailbox was open, with a pile of circulars hanging out.

"Here comes the TBI," Dix said, watching in the rearview mirror. I turned to look out the window as a white SUV with the TBI logo pulled into the driveway and stopped. Wendell slid out of the front seat along with Jamal, while José and Clayton extricated themselves from the back. All four of them congregated at the rear of the vehicle, out of sight of the house, where they strapped on Kevlar vests and pulled on SWAT jackets in spite of the heat. Each of them grabbed a gun and checked the magazine, and then they made their way up to the house. Wendell sent José and Clayton to slide along the wall in the front, while he and Jamal disappeared around the carport to the back. A few seconds later, Clayton and José vanished around the other corner, as well.

We sat and waited, with the car pumping out cold air. I could hear Grimaldi breathing through the phone, but she didn't say anything.

"You can come over to our car if you want," I offered. "We've room for one more." I'd just have to move the booster seat into the trunk.

"Thanks, but I'm fine here. I doubt we'll be here long."

My stomach growled, and Mother glanced at me over the seat. Bodily noises are unladylike, in case you wondered.

"I'm hungry," I said defensively.

"You can eat something," Grimaldi told me through the phone.

"I wasn't talking to you," I said. "I was talking to my mother."

"You're pregnant," Grimaldi told me. "Tell your mother you get to eat."

"You're on speaker. I think she heard you."

"Oh." She was silent for a moment. "Well, you can get something to eat after we're finished here."

"I can't wait," I told her honestly. "I know that's horrible, to think of food when my boyfriend—my fiancé, my baby's father—could be dead, but I'm starving."

"You're pregnant," Grimaldi said again, while Mother looked pained at my admission. "You have to eat. Not eating is bad for the baby."

"What kind of food do you want?"

She hesitated. I guess she was thinking she should just keep working instead of taking time out to eat. But then there was Dix. "We'd love it if you would join us, Detective," he said.

Mother looked less than delighted, of course, but then she always did.

"Let's talk about it later," Grimaldi said. "They're coming

back."

They were. All four of them, coming around the house. Alone, and sauntering, so obviously they hadn't found Rafe or Mr. Hernandez inside.

In front of us, Grimaldi exited her car. I scrambled out of the backseat of Dix's, and ran to catch up.

"Anything?"

Wendell shook his head. "Someone's been there recently. There's beer in the fridge and dirty dishes in the sink. But the towels are dry and nobody's taken out the trash for a couple days."

"Was there any clue at all that he knows who Rafe is or was targeting him?" I asked.

"None. He coulda gone out for a drink. He coulda gone out to find another hooker. He coulda driven to Panama City Beach for some sun and sand. There's just no telling."

"And no way to know whether he had anything to do with Rafe's disappearance."

"No," Wendell said. "Sorry." He holstered his gun, and the rookies followed suit.

"That was awesome," Jamal said. And added, "Not that we were looking for Rafe. Rafe's cool. I don't want nothing to happen to Rafe. But that was awesome!"

Clayton and José nodded. Wendell rolled his eyes. "Get in the car," he said. "She don't need to hear you three talking about how excited you are to be doing this. Show some respect."

"I just did," Jamal protested. "We're real sorry about Rafe, lady. We don't want nothing to happen to him. We'll keep looking till we find him."

Clayton and José nodded. Two pairs of brown and one pair of blue eyes gazed at me with patent sincerity.

"We can stake the place out tonight," José said. "See if dude comes home."

Wendell hesitated.

"Call it a training exercise," Clayton added.

The two pairs of brown and one blue transferred themselves to Wendell, who blinked and turned to Grimaldi.

The detective shrugged. "I was going to tell the south precinct to have whoever patrols this area drive by a couple times overnight, and call in if they see a light on or a car in the driveway. But if your boys want to practice, that's fine with me."

The boys turned back to Wendell for approval.

"Just make sure they don't shoot anybody," Grimaldi added. "We want him alive so we can talk to him."

The boys all nodded solemnly. "Let's go," Jamal told Wendell. "The sooner we get back, the sooner we can get back."

He signaled the others, and they all headed for the SUV. We watched as they started divesting themselves of guns and Kevlar vests.

"I'll let the south precinct know they're here," Grimaldi told Wendell. "That way, nobody'll try to arrest them."

He nodded. "I appreciate that. Can't have'em sitting out here in an official vehicle, so they'll either be in Clayton's Camaro, or Jamal's souped up Buick, or José's truck with the Virgin Mary in the rear window."

Grimaldi grinned. "Nobody's likely to think either of those is the TBI, anyway."

Wendell shook his head. "I'll be in touch. Let me know if—"

The rest of the sentence was cut off by the horn of the SUV. Guess Jamal was getting tired of waiting. Or one of the others was, and had instructed Jamal to honk the horn.

"Goddamn kids!" Wendell snarled and headed for the SUV.

Grimaldi turned to me. "FinBar?"

"That's fine. We'll see you there in about twenty minutes."

I headed back to Dix's SUV and told him where we were going.

"A sports bar?" Mother inquired, brows raised.

"You'll like it. I promise. It's right down the street from my office. Brenda Puckett used to take her sixteen-year-old daughter there."

She also used to take clients there for shady deals, but that was another story. And anyway, the FinBar was a very nice place, clean and full of ferns. Mother would like it.

And indeed, she looked around with approval when we walked in. At the ferns, and the clean floor, and the gleaming dark wood, and the brass. There were big flat-screen TVs on all the walls, but they only bothered you if you looked at them. And since one showed baseball and one sailing and one some sort of violent MMA fighting, I didn't think Mother would be interested. The last screen showed a bunch of people running around the wilderness with sheets of paper in their hands. It was either an episode of *The Great Race*, or that weird sport they call orienteering. But it wasn't violent, and there was no blood, so as far as I was concerned, that made it A-OK.

Grimaldi walked in a minute or two after we did, and joined us in a booth in the corner. "Sorry I'm late." She scooted in next to me, with her back to the wall. We'd taken the same positions we'd had for lunch, except Dix sat across from Grimaldi instead of at the end of the table. "Kansas State Police called"

"They found the truck?"

She nodded. "He was somewhere near Topeka when they pulled him over. Routine check, as far as he knows. The cab was empty, and so was the trailer. Sorry."

"It's OK," I said. I hadn't really expected Rafe to be trussed like a turkey, rolling around the cargo hold of an eighteen-wheeler on its way through the heartland. It would have been nice, but I hadn't expected it.

"Spicer and Truman are still going through the warehouse. It's a big place. And here's an interesting coincidence."

"What's that?"

"It used to belong to Julio Melendez," Grimaldi said. "I guess it still does. Anyway, Julio's still in prison. I checked. But a company called Ibarra Imports is renting it."

That *was* an interesting coincidence.

"Who's Julio Melendez?" Mother wanted to know.

I glanced at Grimaldi to see whether she wanted to respond, and when she didn't, I said, "He's someone who got swept up in my friend Lila's murder investigation last fall. Lila Vaughn, remember? The realtor who was strangled? The open house robberies?"

"Of course," Mother said, although I had no idea whether she actually remembered or not. It hadn't affected her personally. Not the way it had affected me. So there was no real reason she'd remember it.

"Julio Melendez's import/export business worked with Hector Gonzales and the open house robbers," including Rafe, "to store and move and sell the stolen goods. Julio was a suspect in Lila's rape and murder, and when Grimaldi found some of the stolen goods in his warehouse, she arrested him."

Grimaldi nodded.

"You're mentioning a lot of Spanish names," Mother said. "Melendez, Gonzales, Hernandez..."

"Hector Gonzales ran an SATG," Grimaldi explained. "A South American Theft Gang. Some of the members were black or white, but most were Hispanic. Interestingly, it wasn't until Mr. Collier 'died,'" she made quotation marks in the air around the word, "and took on the persona of Jorge Pena, that he was able to penetrate to the inner circle of the gang."

"Hector probably trusted his own kind more than anyone else," I said.

Grimaldi nodded. "Anyway, Julio Melendez is still behind bars. I double-checked. But our second suspect works for Ibarra Imports. In what used to be Julio's warehouse."

"Ibarra's another Spanish name," Dix said, "isn't it?"

Maybe it was. However— "Hector's organization is dead. Rafe cut its head off." Although that didn't mean someone couldn't be trying to start up another.

"There are plenty of SATGs around," Grimaldi said. "Most don't ever achieve the size or scope that Gonzales's organization did. It's probably another small outfit trying to get in on the action. Someone will take care of it."

Maybe José. Or Jamal or Clayton. "But it won't be Rafe."

Grimaldi shook her head. "By now, everyone knows who he is. He's out of the game."

And a good thing, too. Although being out of the game seemed to bring its share of dangers, as well.

"You do think we'll find him," I asked, "don't you?"

Grimaldi hesitated. I didn't like that.

"Alive?" I added.

Grimaldi glanced at the door. Then she glanced at Dix. Then she said, "I think we can assume he didn't leave by choice. Not without his mode of transportation. Not without letting someone know. If not you, then his boss. After more than ten years with the TBI, I don't think he'd just walk off the job without a word."

No. He cared more about Wendell than that. "You do realize you're not actually answering my question, right?"

"Yes," Grimaldi said. "And the truth is, I'm not sure whether we will or not. He's been in tough spots before, and he's always made it out alive. But it only takes once. And the fact that someone may have managed to grab him means that he could be dead already."

I nodded. I didn't like to hear it confirmed, but I knew it. "But you think there's a chance we'll find him alive?"

"With anyone else," Grimaldi said, "I'd say no. But I have a lot of respect for your boyfriend's ability to stay alive. So I'm not sure I'd give up hope just yet. I haven't."

I hadn't, either. "Thank you."

"Don't mention it," Grimaldi said, and looked around for the waitress.

We ended up staying at the FinBar until almost ten. By then, Spicer and Truman had finished their search of Julio Melendez's warehouse and come up empty, and had gone home to their respective beds and significant others. They'd be back at it tomorrow, Grimaldi assured me. The truck was making its way across Kansas toward the Colorado border with an ex-con at the wheel, but no Rafe onboard. And the TBI rookies, parked down the street from the house in Woodbine, reported no activity whatsoever at that location.

There was nothing going on at the house when we got there, either. Everything looked just as it had when we left. The Volvo was parked in the driveway. Rafe's Harley was still missing—obviously, since Grimaldi had arranged for it to be fingerprinted. I'd forgotten to ask when we could pick it up, but if Rafe didn't come back, it wasn't like I'd need it, was it? I enjoyed riding behind him—the vibrations were nice, and so was the flex of his muscles between my thighs—but I had no plans, nor any desire, to pilot the beast myself. Nor was it particularly safe for me, in my condition.

No one had called or emailed while we'd been out, and the mailbox was as empty as it had been last time I checked it: this afternoon before we got into Dix's SUV to make the drive out to Peaceful Pines.

We separated ourselves into rooms. I stayed in my usual bedroom, of course. Mother took Mrs. Jenkins's lavender room, and Dix Marquita Johnson's yellow one. I dug up extra toothbrushes from the linen closet and handed them out. Mother always told me to keep things like that on hand, just in case, and with her here, I was glad I had listened. If I hadn't been able to produce an unused, new, clean toothbrush, still in the plastic wrapper, she would have let me feel her disappointment.

They went into their respective rooms. A minute went by, and then I could hear murmurs from behind both doors. Mother was probably checking in with Bob Satterfield, telling him what was going on. And it was too late for Dix to be talking to the girls—he'd excused himself while we were sitting at the FinBar, to make a quick phone call to his daughters at bedtime—so now he was either talking to Catherine, telling her what the rest of the day had brought, or he had called Tamara Grimaldi for some pillow talk before bed. Or perhaps he was talking to Todd Satterfield, Bob's son and Dix's best friend since childhood.

But no, he wouldn't be that stupid, would he?

I could just imagine what Todd would make out of this situation. Like Mother, he'd be convinced that Rafe had walked away because he didn't want to be shackled with a wife and kid. The difference was, Todd would be determined to swoop in and safe the day, and would no doubt offer to marry me himself.

It wouldn't be the first time. He'd proposed before he went to college at eighteen. But since I'd been sixteen at the time, and still in high school, I'd laughed it off. He hadn't said anything more about it, and hadn't married either; not until I married Bradley Ferguson at twenty-three. That's when Todd found himself a wife, as well. A wife Mother swore he married because she reminded him of me.

And no sooner had I divorced Bradley, than Todd divorced Jolynn, as well.

He'd proposed to me again, last fall. With a diamond ring and everything. And he hadn't taken it well when I'd told him no, because I'd fallen in love with Rafe.

With Rafe out of the picture—maybe permanently—what were the chances that Todd would show up here tomorrow, bent on rescuing me?

It was hard to know whether I should laugh or cry. I compromised by turning on my side—stomach-sleeping was no longer an option—and burying my nose in Rafe's pillow. It smelled like him. I closed my eyes and inhaled deeply. If I concentrated, I could almost pretend he was here.

But maybe that wouldn't be a good idea. I might have to learn to live without him, and pretending he wasn't gone wasn't going to help with that.

The only redeeming aspect of the situation at the moment was that I was pregnant. I was carrying Rafe's baby, and if he never came back, at least I'd have that.

Although if I thought too hard about it, I'd probably come to the conclusion that no, that wasn't actually a good thing either, since I was—or at least might be—looking at becoming a single parent. But in this case the pregnancy worked in my favor. It had been a long day full of stress, worry, and a lot of activity. It was past my usual bedtime. I didn't have the chance to do much thinking, and just a small amount of crying, before I dropped off into exhausted sleep.

Eight

It was still dark when I woke up. Quite unusual these days, when—like this morning—I tended to sleep rather late unless someone took the trouble to shake me, or otherwise make sure I opened my eyes.

Yet there I was, wide awake in bed, eyes open, staring into the darkness. The illuminated numbers on the alarm clock announced that it was a quarter after two.

Water gurgled in the pipes, as if someone had flushed the toilet. There was a squeak of bedsprings from Dix's room, and a muffled noise. Maybe a snore or maybe just a grunt. Maybe a curse. I hadn't ever tried to sleep in Marquita's bed, so I had no idea how comfortable it was. Or how uncomfortable.

There were no sounds coming from Mrs. Jenkins's—Mother's—room.

Another side effect of the pregnancy was that I had to pee all the time. I'd had a lot to drink at the FinBar—sweet tea, I mean, not alcohol—and at a later hour than I usually drink. Now that I was awake, I could feel my bladder nudging me for relief. Maybe that's what had woken me.

I swung my feet over the edge of the bed and pushed myself up. And padded across the floor to the door, down the hallway, and into the bathroom. Where I took a seat on the toilet before I realized that the toilet wasn't actually running.

But water was still gurgling through the pipes.

Maybe Mother had woken up and gone downstairs for something? A glass of water from the kitchen?

Or maybe she was feeling unwell, and hadn't wanted to risk waking Dix or me with any unpleasant noises she might make. My mother is certainly well-bred enough to drag herself out of bed in the middle of the night to stagger down a flight of stairs in an unfamiliar house so no one else had to listen to her vomit. Or—God forbid—have diarrhea.

Maybe I'd better make my way down to the first floor, too, to see if there was anything I could do to help. It was something she ate, most likely. The food at the FinBar must have upset her delicate stomach. I can practically guarantee that my mother doesn't dine on hamburgers and French fries most of the time. Too much grease, too much fat.

I padded barefoot down the stairs, and tried not to think of doing the same thing yesterday morning, looking for Rafe. For a second, when I first opened my eyes, I'd forgotten that he was gone. Until I realized I was alone in bed, and remembered what had happened, and that Mother and Dix were across the hall. Or, as the case may be, in the bathroom on the first floor.

Downstairs was dark and quiet. The porch light was on, shining in through the window in the front door, laying an elongated, twisty rectangle on the floor. I glanced out, and saw the dark bulk of Dix's SUV and my Volvo in the driveway. Nothing was stirring outside, not even the wind.

From down the hall came a tiny sound, like a small trickle of water. Mother soaking a washcloth to wipe her face, maybe. I headed in that direction, my feet noiseless on the wood floor.

Most of the time, I don't have a problem living in the house where Brenda Puckett met a violent end. She doesn't haunt the place, and anyway, it looks and feels like a different house now. Whenever I start to think about it—about walking into the library and seeing her corpse sprawled there, in front of the fireplace, with her throat slit from ear to ear—I remind myself that a lot of good things have come from Brenda's death. Mrs. Jenkins got her house back, and found her grandson at the same time. Rafe found his grandmother, his only living relative. Or the only one he knew about at the time, anyway.

I found Rafe. And while it took me a while to admit—to

myself and to the world—that I wanted Rafe, that was a very, very good thing. I won't say that Brenda's death was worth it—that would be horribly cold-blooded of me—but I could still see the good that had happened as a result.

Anyway, being here doesn't usually bother me. But I'm not usually walking around alone in the middle of the night, either. I could feel goose bumps breaking out on my arms and my scalp. My hair prickled, and I made very sure not to glance into the library on my way past. Just in case.

The tiny splashes and tinkles continued from the half bath, along with some weird moans and grunts. Under other circumstances I might have been tempted to make fun of it, but I felt too sorry for Mother: she must really be feeling bad to make such very unladylike noises.

"Mother?" I reached for the doorknob. "Are you OK?"

I turned the knob and pulled the door open, squinting against the bright light. And fell back a step when I realized it wasn't Mother in the bathroom.

And then I saw the blood, and screamed.

Normally, Rafe would have caught me. This was obviously not normal, because I went staggering back, bounced off the wall, and sat down on the floor while he stood there. Vaguely, in the back of my head, I could hear sounds from upstairs: thuds and footsteps as Dix and Mother scrambled out of bed in response to my scream.

By the time they'd made it down to us, I had made it back up on my feet, and was standing there ineffectually wringing my hands and babbling.

"Oh, my God. What are you doing?"

It was a stupid question, and got the stupid answer it deserved.

"Washing up," Rafe said, with a bloody washcloth dangling from his fingers and a sink full of red water behind him. "Can't get into bed like this."

He looked and sounded perfectly lucid—apart from the bloody cuts scoring his chest like some crazy cross-stitch pattern, interspersed with small, irritated-looking red dots—but he obviously wasn't thinking straight.

"Have you lost your mind?" I demanded. "You can't get into bed at all. You have to go to the hospital!"

By now Mother and Dix had reached us, and I heard Dix's curse and Mother's sharp intake of breath. She fell back a step.

I couldn't blame her. Part of me wanted to wrap him in my arms and assure myself he was whole and here and solid and not just a figment of my imagination. The other part didn't even want to look at him.

I took a breath and tried to keep my voice even. "What happened? You look like you walked into a sausage slicer." Again and again and again.

His lips twisted. "It's just a scratch."

Sure. Try to be funny at a time like this. "This isn't a romance novel," I said crossly, "and you're not the stupid hero. It's not just a scratch. It's a lot of scratches, and some of them are probably going to need stitches."

Rafe looked down at his own chest, and nodded. "Prob'ly."

"Are you drunk?" Mother asked suspiciously, her nostrils twitching.

I turned on her. But before I could tell her to leave him alone—what if he was? Wasn't he entitled?—Dix spoke up. "If he isn't, he should be. D'you have any liquor in the house, sis?"

"Cabinet in the parlor," I said. "Next to the room where—"

"I'll find it." He was already moving. "Go get a glass," he told Mother. "Kitchen."

Mother's lips tightened, but she went. Padding barefoot down the hall with the hem of her borrowed nightgown dancing around her thighs.

Rafe watched her. "That's your mama," he told me.

"Yes, it is." I took the wet washcloth out of his hand and dropped it into the bloody water. "She came up for the wedding, and stayed."

I lifted a towel off the rack and began mopping his chest dry. Bright red blood stained the white terrycloth. "God, Rafe...!"

Looking at him hurt. And didn't hurt anywhere near as much as I was sure he must be hurting.

He didn't try to be funny this time. Just stood there while I wiped blood and water off his chest, looking down at me. "Sorry."

"It wasn't your fault." Clearly. Whatever had happened to him—whoever had done this, because it certainly hadn't been an accident—was responsible for his not being here this morning. Not he. "I'm just glad you're..."

I faltered on the next word. *OK* wasn't quite what I was looking for. He clearly wasn't OK. He wasn't fine. He was alive, and mostly whole, and here—but he wasn't OK. Not by a long shot.

"God." I blinked away the tears, but he must have seen them anyway. His hand came up to cup my cheek.

"Darlin'..."

"I thought you were gone," I told his chest, my hand closing tight on the towel. "I thought you didn't want to marry me. And then I was afraid that you hadn't left on your own. That you did want to marry me, but that something... or someone..."

His thumb stroked my cheek.

"I love you," I said, and this time I didn't care that the tears overflowed and ran down my cheeks. "I was so afraid you wouldn't come back."

"I'll always come back."

Sure. Except for the one time when he couldn't.

But that time wasn't this time. I squared my shoulders. "We have to get you to the hospital. Someone needs to look at this. Someone other than you and me. You'll need some stitches, and bandages, and... and something... on whatever these little marks are...”

“Cigarette burns,” Rafe said calmly, and reached out a hand for the bottle Dix was holding. “Thanks.”

Dix blinked, and handed it over. By the time Mother came back down the hallway with a squat glass in her hand, Rafe was already swigging scotch straight from the bottle.

“Better go get dressed,” I told Dix. “We have to take him to the hospital.”

“Shouldn’t we call 911?” Mother asked, as Dix headed down the hallway to the stairs.

“It’ll be quicker just to drive there. It isn’t far. And he’s not about to die.” Just in a lot of pain, I imagined. Hopefully the scotch would numb some of it, at least long enough for us to drive him to the emergency room where they’d get some real pain medicine into him. He’d need that, once they started working on closing up some of the deeper cuts. “He made it here. I’m sure he can make it for ten more minutes until we get to the hospital.”

Dix was already on his way up the stairs. Mother nodded and followed.

“I need to put on some clothes, too,” I told Rafe.

He nodded. “I’m just gonna sit down.”

And he did, right there in the hallway. Put his back against the wall and slid down until he was sitting on the floor, his legs stretched out in front of him and the bottle of scotch in his lap, with a hand wrapped around the neck.

I checked the wall, but there was no smear of blood left behind. The damage seemed to be to his front. That must mean something.

Like, the person who had done this to him, had wanted him to watch what was happening.

Nausea crawled up my throat, and I swallowed it ruthlessly. “I’ll be right back. Don’t go anywhere.”

"Don't think I could if I tried," Rafe said, his eyes closed and his eyelashes lying like fans against his cheeks. "Didn't think I was gonna make it here."

"Where..." I shook my head. "No, never mind. That doesn't matter now. We'll talk about it later. I'm going to go throw some clothes on. Then we'll go to the hospital. Two minutes."

He didn't even open his eyes when I walked away. He must be feeling awful. Usually he'd take the opportunity to look up my nightgown, if only because he knew doing it would make me blush.

By the time I reached the top of the stairs, Dix was already on his way back down, buttoning his shirt as he went.

"He's on the floor in the hallway," I said. "If you give me a minute, I'll help you get him up and in the car."

"Not sure you should be hauling him to his feet, in your condition." He brushed past me and headed down. "I can manage."

"Be careful with him," I threw after his back. "I'm not sure how much more he can handle."

"I imagine he'll handle whatever he has to handle," Dix answered, without pausing. I ducked into my own room, where I stripped off my nightgown and pulled on the same dress I'd worn yesterday afternoon. When I got back out into the hallway, Mother was also dressed, and coming out of Mrs. J's room.

She was pale, and looked a bit more rumpled than usual. Her clothes were wrinkled and her hair not quite its usual smooth cap. I might even go so far as to say there were bags under her eyes—although I wouldn't say it to her face.

"You don't have to come with us," I told her instead. "You can stay here, if you want. Try to get some more sleep."

Her voice was as crisp as ever. "No, thank you, darling. I would prefer not to be left alone in the middle of the night, in this neighborhood."

"Then let's go. I want to get him to a doctor as soon as

possible. He's lost enough blood already."

I headed down the stairs with Mother's heels click-click-clicking behind. Downstairs in the hallway, Dix had managed to get Rafe upright. His arm was draped over Dix's shoulders and the bottle of scotch was in his other hand.

"I think we can probably leave that here," I said, and reached for it.

Rafe twitched it out of my grasp and lifted it to his mouth for one more quick swallow before relinquishing it. Further proof, if I had needed it, that he was in a bad way. He's not in the habit of overindulging in anything stronger than beer, and only rarely overindulges in that.

I didn't comment, just handed the bottle to Mother and went to brace him on the other side. He was shivering. Cold or shock or pain, or a combination of all three.

"Do you want something more to wear?"

He shook his head. "It's warmer outside."

Yes, it was. Even in the middle of the night, it was above eighty out there. It was just in here that cold air blasted from the vents.

"No sense ruining another shirt."

I guess not. They'd have him out of it at the hospital, anyway. "Maybe they'll put you into one of those hospital gowns that leave your butt bare," I said optimistically.

"They can try," Rafe answered, and draped a heavy arm over my shoulders.

We lurched down the hallway and onto the porch. Mother scurried ahead to open the door of Dix's SUV.

"Let's put him in the back," I huffed as we made our slow way across the porch and down the steps. "I'll sit with him."

Dix nodded. "You go in first. I'll push and you pull."

Good idea.

It didn't quite come to that, though. I did get into the backseat first, but Rafe was able to crawl in after me with no pushing or pulling necessary. I thought about putting his head in my lap, so I could run my fingers through his (practically non-existent) hair, but in the end I figured he'd be just as comfortable sitting up.

We pulled up in front of the emergency entrance at Skyline Hospital less than ten minutes later.

Dix got out and opened the door for me. Meanwhile, Mother looked around. "Isn't this where—?"

"Yes." This was where I'd had my second miscarriage—the first had been while I'd been married to Bradley—last November. The hospital had notified Mother, as my next of kin, and she and everyone else had come rushing up to Nashville. She'd walked in on me holding Rafe's hand, trying to explain to him why I hadn't told him I was pregnant until I was almost three months along.

He'd walked out of the hospital thinking it was Todd's baby I'd lost, and I hadn't seen him for weeks after that.

I wondered whether he remembered it too... and then I realized that it was unlikely he remembered much of anything at the moment. He had other things on his mind. Like the fact that he was in pain, and a little bit drunk, and was in for some rather uncomfortable patching up.

"We have to call Grimaldi," I told Dix. "And Wendell. Tell him to call off the boys."

He nodded. "After we get him inside and know what's going on. It's the middle of the night."

It was. But I doubted either Grimaldi or Wendell were sleeping well. They'd want to know what was going on ASAP.

Nonetheless, my brother had a point. Rafe, and getting him cared for, had to be the number one priority. We—the cops and the TBI—could go after whoever had done this to him once we knew he was comfortable and safe.

So we hauled him out of the SUV and between us, managed to get him through the sliding doors and inside. The nurse at the desk looked up, and her mouth dropped open.

"*Madre de Dios*!" She crossed herself. "What happened?"

Nobody answered. First because we didn't really know, and second because I didn't think she actually expected an answer. She went into business mode, calling doctors and nurses to the front at warp speed. Less than a minute later, they had whisked Rafe onto a gurney and through the double doors into the hospital. "Someone will let you know when you can come in," one of the nurses told us over her shoulder just before the doors flapped shut behind them.

I looked at Dix. He looked at me. Then we both looked at Mother, who had surely gotten a bit more than she'd bargained for on this trip. She wasn't looking at either of us, but was still watching the door where Rafe and the doctor and nurses had disappeared.

"I'll take Wendell," I told Dix, "if you take Grimaldi."

He nodded, already reaching for his phone. I did the same, and dialed.

Wendell answered on the first ring, and sounded wide awake at this ungodly hour. "Savannah."

He didn't bother with the civilities, so I decided I wouldn't, either. "He's back," I said.

"In one piece?"

"Mostly. We're at Skyline Hospital."

"Twenty minutes," Wendell said and hung up.

OK, then. I turned to Dix, who was deep in conversation with Grimaldi. And then I turned to Mother, who was still standing there, watching the swinging doors with that tiny wrinkle between her brows. "We may as well sit down," I told her. "This could take a while."

She nodded. And walked over and sat, but without speaking a word.

I sat, too, and crossed one leg over the other. Over by the door, Dix was still talking to Grimaldi.

It was a fairly quiet evening in the ER. I'm sure they didn't get many of them, and honestly, I was a bit surprised, especially considering that it was a Saturday. Then again, Skyline isn't the most centrally located hospital in town. There was a gentleman snoring in a chair over by the wall—his head tipped back and his mouth open—and two black women with their heads together in a corner. Other than that, it was just us.

"Are you OK?" I asked Mother.

She glanced at me, and for a second, it was like she didn't know who I was. Like I were a stranger sitting across from her. Then her eyes cleared, and she smiled faintly. "Of course, darling. Why wouldn't I be?"

"I can't imagine," I said dryly. "I'm sure this happens all the time, that you have to rush someone to the hospital because he's been tortured by some drug lord or crime boss or kingpin or whatnot."

"Is that what happened?"

I shrugged jerkily. "I don't know what happened. But that's my guess. Rafe has put some very bad people away. One of them must have decided to get revenge. The truck driver, before he left town. Or the warehouse worker, before Spicer and Truman went through the place."

"Or it could be the third guy," Dix said. "The one who hired the prostitute." He sat down next to me. "She's on her way."

Grimaldi, I assumed, not Little Ginger.

"If it was Hernandez, he has a place other than the house in Woodbine."

"Well, if he was planning to kidnap and torture a special agent," Dix said reasonably, "he wouldn't give his parole officer the address where he planned to do it."

No, he wouldn't.

"I'm sure Rafe will be able to tell us who it was. All the damage was to his front; he had to have seen who did it. I just didn't want to ask, with everything that was going on."

Dix shook his head. "Best let Tamara and Mr. Craig take care of it. It's their job."

We sat in silence for a minute. "I'm sorry," I said eventually.

"You didn't do anything," Dix answered.

"I got involved with him." My lips twisted as I turned to my mother, and not in a smile. "You always did tell me he was trouble, and that I should stay away from him."

She had the grace to look... if not exactly ashamed, then at least somewhat embarrassed. "Now, darling..."

"I bet you never saw this coming, did you?" I'm afraid my laughter had a slight hysterical edge. But can you blame me? I was sitting in a hospital lobby in the middle of the night—and not just any night, but what should have been my wedding night—with my mother and my brother, while the groom was being sewn back together after some sicko had been practicing his whittling skills on his chest.

"He's all right," Dix said calmly. "Everything's fine."

"Everything is *not* fine! You saw what he looked like. He's hurt. He's in pain. He escaped from someone who would have continued to hurt him, and would undoubtedly have ended up killing him. Someone who might be back, if we can't figure out who he is, and where he is, and how to stop him!"

"We'll... they'll stop him," Dix said. "It's what they do. And Collier will know who and where he is. By tomorrow night, this will all be over."

"You don't know that." I could hear my voice rising and becoming shrill, but I couldn't stop it. "You can't know that!"

"Darling," Mother said, glancing around at the empty lobby, "not in public."

"No, God forbid anyone sees that I'm upset because some psychopath with a knife went to work on my boyfriend!"

"Inside voice, dear," Mother said.

I huffed and fell silent.

Nine

I figured it would be a toss-up who we'd see first: Wendell, Grimaldi, or the doctor who worked on Rafe. I didn't know where Wendell hung his hat when he wasn't at the TBI, but I knew where Grimaldi lived—or at least I knew the neighborhood: Charlotte Park—and it was a good twenty minutes from Skyline Hospital.

But the two of them walked in together, and they got there before the doctor came back out to update us.

"Any word?"

I shook my head. "They took him in almost half an hour ago. We haven't heard anything since."

"But he was pretty damaged," Dix added. "They had a lot of patching up to do."

"What kind of patching up?" Grimaldi wanted to know, at the same time as Wendell asked, "What kind of damage?"

They looked at me. I nodded to Dix, since I was still feeling fragile, and wasn't sure I could make it through a recitation without either having hysterics again or breaking down in tears.

"Bruises and lacerations," Dix said. "Cigarette burns. Cuts. Most of them fairly shallow, but one, at least, looked like it went straight through his forearm."

My ears started ringing, and I could feel all the blood leave my head.

I hadn't noticed that. My focus had been on the extremely visible—one might even say flashy—cross-stitch patterns on his chest and stomach. He'd had a knife stuck through his arm?

"She's gonna faint," Grimaldi's voice said, from far away. "Somebody grab her."

Someone did, and shoved my head down between my knees. I'm fairly certain I recognized my brother's grip on the back of my neck. I gulped in a couple of breaths and the ringing in my ears subsided. The nausea continued to roil in my stomach, though, and being bent over made it worse, so I pushed against the hand and straightened up. "Sorry."

Nobody acknowledged the apology, so maybe they thought it was unnecessary.

"Didn't notice that?" Grimaldi asked.

I shook my head. "There were a lot of other things to look at."

Wendell handed me a can of Coke. He must have run to the nearest machine while I was doing my heavy breathing.

"Thanks," I said. It wasn't the best thing for the baby, but I could use both the sugar and the caffeine at the moment, and one can of Coke surely wouldn't hurt. I popped the top and took a sip.

Steps in the corridor behind the swinging doors brought us all around. The doors opened and a doctor came through, his scrubs stained with blood. "Collier?" he said, looking around.

We all nodded.

Wendell was the only one of us who looked anything like he might be related to Rafe, at least on the surface, so the doctor addressed him. "He's stable. Medicated. Resting. We stitched the deeper cuts and closed the others with surgical glue and bandages. Nothing much we could do about the cigarette burns, other than put salve on them and bandage them up. As for the knife that went through his forearm—"

Oh, God. I sucked on the Coke until my cheeks were hollow.

The doctor went on, his voice perfectly calm. "We cleaned it, stitched it and bandaged it. The knife missed the major arteries, which was a lucky break, but— Pardon me?"

"Nothing," Wendell said grimly. "Will he be OK?"

The doctor hesitated. "The cuts and burns will heal. There'll be some scarring. The muscles and nerves in the arm are damaged. He'll certainly get back to using it, in more or less of a normal fashion, but from now on it will always be a bit weaker than the other one. And is likely to cause him discomfort for a while."

Discomfort. *Hah!*

"When can we see him?" I asked.

The doctor looked at my face, glanced at my stomach, and moved north again. "Wife?"

"Fiancée." No need to go into the fact that if this hadn't happened to him, we would be married by now.

"I'm not sure he's awake, but you can certainly go in and see him for a bit. He's stable. Not in any danger. Healthy, other than the injuries." He looked around. "I don't have a duty to report physical abuse other than suspicions of child or elder abuse, but..."

"Police," Grimaldi said, flashing her badge.

"TBI," Wendell added, flashing his.

"Ah." The doctor looked relieved. "He's in room 210. You can go right up. But if he starts to act tired, for God's sake let him sleep. He's been through a lot."

No kidding. And we probably hadn't heard the half of it.

I looked around. Five of us. Did we need to go in shifts? Grimaldi and Wendell were certainly going to want to talk to him about what had happened, if he were awake and up for it. But that wasn't something Mother and Dix needed to hear. I wasn't sure I needed to hear it myself.

Then again, it might not hurt for Mother to learn about the things Rafe had dealt with. If nothing else, it might make her a bit less inclined to think him unworthy of me.

"I'll wait here," she offered, and Dix nodded, indicating his willingness to cede the floor to the rest of us, as well. I'm sure he thought he was being polite. Mother I'm not so sure about.

"I'd rather we all went up," I said. "You don't have to stay long."

Mother opened her mouth, met my eyes, and closed it again. "Of course, darling."

"Whatever you want, Savannah," Dix added, and extended a hand to help Mother out of the chair.

Room 210 was on the second floor, and not difficult to find. It was the middle of the night, of course, so everything was mostly quiet and the lights were low, although it's never completely dark or quiet in a hospital. Lights flashed and machines beeped from behind half-open doors, and we heard the squeak of rubber soles as the nurses moved behind the desk.

Rafe's room was a single, so once we were all inside and had closed the door, we had privacy. Not that we were going to do anything we needed privacy for, but I thought there was a chance that Wendell and Grimaldi would prefer it while they debriefed Rafe.

At first, he didn't seem to be in a state to be debriefed. When we walked in, he didn't stir. I tiptoed over to the bed and looked down at him.

He's never really pale. LaDonna was a blue-eyed blonde like me, so her fair hair and pale complexion did their part to lighten Tyrell's brown eyes and skin, but Rafe is still distinctly what people in the old days used to call 'colored.' Golden skin, almost black eyes, and espresso-colored hair he keeps so short he's practically bald. During the time he'd pretended to be Jorge Pena, he'd kept it longer and gelled, along with a trim goatee, but as soon as he could go back to being himself again, the goatee vanished, and so did most of the hair, along with the stud in his ear.

But at the moment, there was a distinct pallor to his skin. There was no warm glow, no bloom in the cheeks.

As I stood there, his eyes opened. It took him a second to focus on me, and then the corners of his mouth twitched. "Making sure I'm still breathing?" His voice was hoarse, and he had to clear his throat.

I shrugged. Not so much that he was breathing. Now that he was back, I wasn't too worried about that. It was more like I was taking inventory. Making sure he was still there, and in one piece.

"Grimaldi and Wendell are here." I took a step to the side so he could see them over by the door. "Are you up for a couple questions?"

The tip of his tongue came out to moisten his lips. "Don't imagine I have much choice."

I shook my head. "The sooner the TBI and the police know who did this to you, the sooner they can dispatch the bloodhounds. And we all want that."

Grimaldi and Wendell came closer. I stepped back as they crowded in by the bedside.

There was a moment, then— "You look like shit," Wendell said.

I didn't glance at Mother to see how she took this pronouncement, but I imagine her eyes widened.

Rafe made a noise that might have turned into a laugh had it been given the chance to grow up. And it must have hurt him— bothered his stomach—because he winced.

Wendell didn't say anything, just reached out and put a hand on Rafe's shoulder. For the two of them, it was the equivalent of a warm hug. "Huron?"

Rafe nodded.

"What?" Grimaldi said.

"Huron." Wendell turned to her. "Spanish word. Means 'the Ferret.' Eugenio Hernandez's nickname."

"He did this? Eugenio Hernandez?"

She turned back to Rafe, who said, "Yeah."

"Why?"

"He's a sick bastard?" Wendell suggested, and Rafe made another of those not-quite-a-laugh noises.

"He's a sick bastard," he agreed, his voice still rough. "And while he was serving his three to five, someone happened to mention that Hector Gonzales was in prison just over the state line in Georgia, and who put him there."

"He figured out you were an undercover agent," Grimaldi translated, and Rafe nodded. "I guess he grabbed you out of the parking lot at Gabe's night before last?"

"Blue van," Rafe said, "next to the bike when I was leaving. I didn't think nothing of it till the door opened. Losing my edge." He grimaced.

"You had other things on your mind," Grimaldi said soothingly, although Rafe didn't look particularly soothed, and Wendell looked grim.

"He hit you?"

"Knocked me out." Rafe worked a limp hand out of the blankets to touch the back of his head. It happened to be the arm with the bandage wrapped around it, and we all watched as he tucked it back under the blankets. No one commented. Rafe continued, "I woke up a couple hours later tied to a chair."

"You wanna talk about it?"

"No," Rafe said. "The fucker drove a knife through my arm and into the table. You can get the other details tomorrow. When she ain't here."

He glanced at me.

"She's going to be here," I told him. "Unless you were talking about Mother. I imagine she'll go home to Sweetwater in the morning, now that you're back. But if you were referring to me, I'll be here. Tomorrow. And the next day. And the day after that."

"Don't imagine they'll keep me here that long, darlin'."

I didn't imagine they would, either. These days, they seem to send people home as soon as there's no chance they'll die on the way there.

"I'll be here for however long you're here," I told him. "And then I'll go wherever you're going. You're not getting rid of me this easily."

It was something he'd told me once or twice, and he must have recognized the words, because his lips curved. "D'you think I'd run out on you, darlin'?"

He reached a hand out from under the blankets toward me. The other hand this time. I took it and held on. "For five seconds. Maybe ten."

He looked skeptical, and I added, "I thought about it. Wondered about it. But I didn't really believe it."

His fingers—usually warm and hard—were cold today. A combination of shock and blood loss, most likely. Or whatever medication they had put into him. He wasn't on an IV drip—I don't imagine he'd have welcomed that suggestion, especially after what he'd gone through—so whatever pain medicine they'd given him, had been oral.

"You should get some rest," I said.

"Soon as we finish talking." He turned back to Wendell and Grimaldi, but kept hold of my hand. "What else d'you need?"

"Where you were," Grimaldi said, and Wendell added, "So's we can go out there and get the bastard."

Rafe shook his head. "He ain't there no more."

"How d'you know?"

"He left," Rafe said. "Stuck my arm to the table and walked out. I don't think he was happy with my performance. Prob'ly went out to find someone more entertaining."

There was a moment's pause. Then—

"How did you...?" Grimaldi paused delicately.

"Lifted my arm up," Rafe said, like it was nothing; like he hadn't had to push up against the handle of a knife that was driven through his arm and into the wood of a table. "Took the knife out with my teeth and used it to cut the ropes. And got the hell outta there."

There was silence again. This time I'm fairly certain it was awe. I was tempted to look at Mother, to see what sort of expression was on her face, but it would have necessitated turning my head all the way around, so I refrained. I hoped she was impressed, though. It was almost unbelievable that she could be anything else, but then we were talking about my mother and my boyfriend, and it didn't do to take anything for granted.

"Where was 'there?'" Grimaldi asked after a suitable pause. "Where were you?"

"Cabin in the woods somewhere." He tried to shrug, and it, too, must have hurt, because he made a face and stopped trying. "Not sure. I followed a dirt road for a while, and then a paved road, and then I hotwired an old truck and started driving. Made my way back home finally. But it ain't really all that clear, you know?"

I wasn't surprised. He'd been hurt, and bleeding, and possibly still woozy from the knock on the head, and half naked—not that that was really a problem with the heat wave we were having, but with all the cuts and open wounds, even the warm night air must have been uncomfortable...

"Can you at least tell me which direction you were in?" Grimaldi asked, somewhat desperately. "Just to give us some idea of where to start?"

"East," Rafe said. "Past the Stone's River Dam."

"Wilson County?"

"Mighta been."

Wendell and Grimaldi exchanged a glance, and I thought I knew why. Wilson County was where the police had had a John Doe yesterday morning, one who had fit Rafe's description. Coincidence?

"The truck ran outta gas just past the airport," Rafe added. "I made it the rest of the way on foot." And he made it sound easy, although he'd walked miles. In his condition. "You can go check the registration. I found it in a driveway after twenty or thirty minutes. If the owner lives there, it'll give you a baseline."

Grimaldi and Wendell exchanged another glance. "I'm on it," Wendell said. "Then I'll go rustle the boys. Can you get a car down to Woodbine, just in case he comes back there?"

Grimaldi nodded. "Don't pull your boys off until someone else gets there."

"I've been doing this job since before you were born," Wendell informed her, and turned to Rafe. "You get some rest, boy. You look like shit. I'll be back in the morning."

Rafe nodded.

"He's right," I told him, as Wendell made his way toward the door, with a polite nod at Mother and Dix, who moved out of his way. Dix sidled closer to the bed, now that there was more room. Mother stayed where she was. "You should try to get some sleep. It's been a long day." And a long night. And a long night last night, too.

I tried to twitch my hand out of his, so he could put it under the blanket again and be warm, but he held on. "I'm sorry I missed the wedding."

"Don't be ridiculous," I said. "First of all, it's not as if you could help it. And second, compared to what happened to you, postponing the ceremony is a very small thing. It wasn't like we'd planned to have a party. We were just going to City Hall. We can get married anytime."

"You could get married right now," Dix said. He came to a stop on the other side of the bed. "Hospitals usually have chaplains. There's probably someone here who could perform the ceremony right now. And we're all present."

He looked around.

We *were* all present, except for Wendell, who had disappeared down the hall. But he'd be back tomorrow. And I didn't think Dix was talking about getting married right this second. It was the middle of the night. The chaplain was most likely asleep, and while I'm sure he was on duty for things like last rites, I wasn't about to wake him up just so he could marry us. Rafe wasn't going anywhere. Getting married tomorrow morning would be sufficient.

Although the groom shook his head. "No offense, darlin'. But I'd like to marry you standing up, not flat on my back. And with this," he raised the bandaged arm, "ain't no way I'd be able to carry you across any threshold when we got home."

"You shouldn't try to do that anyway," I told him. "I'm carrying extra weight these days. You'd throw your back out."

He looked insulted, and before he could try to assure me that he was perfectly capable of carrying me and the baby, and probably Dix and Mother as well, I added, "No offense, but at the moment, I'm pretty sure *I* could take you."

That got me a smile, anyway, even if that wasn't what I'd been going for. "Darlin', you can take me anytime you want."

OK, then.

I blushed, of course, while Rafe managed an approximation of a lascivious wink. Dix hid a grin, and so did Grimaldi. I'm sure Mother looked scandalized, but I didn't glance at her. "You must be feeling better," I said instead, half disapproving and half delighted, "if you can think about sex."

"Darlin'," Rafe drawled, "I can always think about sex."

Yes, he was definitely feeling better. A result of the pain pills, no doubt.

"Go to sleep," I told him. "If you feel better tomorrow," and if he got to go home, because there was no way I was getting it on in a hospital bed, "we can have sex then."

"I'll hold you to that."

"And we'll wait to get married until you feel better." Although I still wouldn't let him carry me—and my passenger—across the threshold.

He nodded. "Sorry to drag you out in the middle of the night," he told Grimaldi, who gave him a 'get-real' sort of look, before telling him,

"I'll be out of here in a minute, too. If Mr. Craig is handling the truck and cabin, I'll rouse Spicer and Truman and see if there's any connection to the DB in Wilson County."

"What DB?" Obviously Rafe didn't need an explanation for what a DB was.

"Dead guy whose description matched yours," I said, before Grimaldi could. "Spicer and Truman drove out there yesterday morning, to make sure it wasn't you."

He didn't say anything immediately. "Sorry."

I knew what he meant. *Sorry you had to spend time worrying it was me.*

"It's OK," I said. "I didn't actually know about it until afterwards. Grimaldi didn't tell me until they'd driven there and had confirmed that it wasn't you."

He nodded. "Thanks," he told Grimaldi.

Who told him, easily, "No sense in worrying unnecessarily. I don't suppose you have any idea who it might have been?"

Rafe shook his head. "Huron was alone the whole time I saw him."

Grimaldi nodded. "It may not be related at all. Wilson County's a big place. Plenty of people with all sorts of reasons for wanting one another dead. It's probably just a coincidence. But it won't hurt to check."

"Does this DB have a name?"

"Not so far," Grimaldi said. "Or not that I've heard. He was a John Doe this morning. I'm not sure whether they've identified him since. Since he wasn't you, I didn't worry about it."

Rafe nodded. "When you find out his name, run it by me. Just in case."

Grimaldi promised she would. She turned toward the door, and then turned back. "I'm glad you're OK."

She didn't wait for him to respond, just pushed the door open.

"I'll walk you down," Dix said—displaying good manners and maybe the desire to spend a couple of minutes alone with his... friend.

Mother didn't say a word, but she slipped out the door behind him. I'd like to chalk it up to delicate feelings, and to wanting to give Rafe and myself a few moments alone, but I'm afraid she probably just didn't want to be stuck in here alone with us. Either that, or she had her suspicions about Dix and Grimaldi, and wanted to nip anything that might happen in the bud.

Ten

It was late morning by the time Wendell and Grimaldi came back to update us—or Rafe—on where their investigations had taken them.

We were all still there, in the hospital room. Rafe had tried to talk me into going home, but I had refused to leave him. I knew it was silly, but part of me—a half-ashamed, mostly subconscious part—worried that if I let him out of my sight, he'd disappear again. I knew it wasn't likely that the hospital would allow that to happen, but I couldn't bear to leave. If I stayed by his bedside and watched him sleep, I could make sure nothing happened to him.

And while I had tried to talk Mother and Dix into leaving, they'd chosen to stay the rest of the night, too. Don't ask me why. Dix liked Rafe well enough, but there was certainly nothing he could do at the moment, and I would have expected Mother to insist on being taken back to the house immediately.

Then again, it was Rafe's house, and a house in a 'bad' neighborhood, so maybe she felt safer here.

"I guess you guys are planning to head home soon?" I asked sometime during the midmorning, after we'd all been wakened by the nurse who came in to check that Rafe was still breathing.

He was, but a bit harshly, so she asked him whether he wanted an IV drip. He said no, and she gave him another pain pill instead, but not until she had hauled him out of bed and into the adjacent bathroom so he could relieve himself.

There was—sadly—no hospital gown gaping open over his admittedly excellent rear end. Instead, he was wearing a pair of pants, the kind with a drawstring waist that the doctors and nurses wear, the bottom half of a set of scrubs, that hung low on his hips. With every step he took, it looked like the pants might give in to gravity and slide off, but it never happened. He made it to the door to the bathroom with his dignity intact. And of course he turned in the doorway to glance at me over his shoulder, and to wink when he saw me staring. The nurse gave me a jaundiced look before propelling him into the bathroom.

Dix chuckled. Mother looked pained. I shrugged unapologetically. Not only is he nice to look at, even in his current condition, but I love him. I'm supposed to look at him like I can't get enough.

He made it safely back into bed, too, although the movements looked like they pained him.

The nurse left, after promising to bring him something to eat, and I went to adjust the blankets. "How bad is it?"

"Itches," Rafe said. "I hate getting stabbed."

I tucked the blankets around him. "As many times as it's happened, you should be used to it by now."

He shook his head. "It itches just the same every time."

"Itching is good. It means the skin's healing."

"I know that," Rafe said, his voice grumpy, "but it's still irritating as hell."

No doubt. "Would you like for me to scratch it for you?"

"No," Rafe said, "cause scratching it would hurt."

Right. "I guess you'll just have to suffer the itching, then. And think about something else."

"Easy for you to say," Rafe grumbled.

And that's when I turned to my brother and mother and asked whether they were planning to drive back to Sweetwater soon, because they certainly hadn't come all this way to hear us bicker, and anyway, I didn't think it was helping Rafe's cause at all with Mother.

"We're not in a hurry," Dix told me.

I wasn't surprised. He hadn't had a chance to see Tamara Grimaldi by herself, just the two of them, for more than a minute or two since arriving in Nashville yesterday.

Not that that was likely to change. She was busy working now, and wouldn't have time to stop to canoodle.

Or maybe he just wanted to find out as much as he could about what was going on before he left. "It's still early. And I want to know whether Mr. Craig found the cabin and whether Detective Grimaldi figured out who the dead man was."

Understandable. I wanted to know those things, too. "I'm sure they'll be here soon. It's more than four hours since they left."

Dix nodded.

And indeed, there was no more than ten minutes later, that Grimaldi walked through the door with Spicer and Truman in tow.

They're your stereotypical partners, the kind you see in the movies. Lyle Spicer is middle-aged and cynical and going thin on top, with reddish hair turning gray around the edges, and what's usually called a lived-in face. George Truman, meanwhile, is as bright and shiny as a new penny: barely old enough to shave and prone to blushing if I smile at him too hard.

They're nice guys, though. They've caught me doing several things I shouldn't be doing—and I'm not just talking about kissing Rafe—and they haven't arrested me. And also, they seem to genuinely like Rafe, which scores points in my book. Now they looked honestly distressed as they moved up to the bed to greet him.

"They won't be staying long," Grimaldi told me, "but they wanted to see him."

Spicer nodded. "After all the times we've hauled your sorry ass into headquarters so the detective could talk to you, feels like we're friends." He put out a hand. "Glad you're still in one piece, man."

Rafe took it, and they shook, hopefully gently, since it was the arm with the bandage, the one the knife had gone through. My knees still felt a bit quivery every time I thought about that.

"We were a little worried," Spicer added, pumping Rafe's hand, "going out there to Wilson County yesterday morning."

Yes, indeed. If I'd know they were going, and why, I'd have been a bit worried too.

"Quite a relief, getting there and seeing the John Doe wasn't anybody we knew."

"Thanks, man." Rafe extricated himself, carefully, and tucked the arm back under the blankets again. He nodded to Truman, who said,

"I took a picture of the dude. The DB. With my phone. D'you think you might...?"

Rafe nodded, and waited while Truman fished his phone out of the pocket of his uniform pants and scrolled through the pictures.

"I guess the Wilson County sheriff hasn't identified him yet," I turned to Grimaldi.

She shook her head. "I don't know how hard they've tried, but they tell me his fingerprints aren't on record, and obviously he wasn't carrying identification when he was found, or none of this would have happened."

I nodded. Meanwhile, Truman had found the picture and handed the phone to Rafe. "D'you know him?"

I leaned closer for a glimpse of my own, but to be honest, the man just looked dead to me. He could have been almost anyone.

Rafe shook his head. "Don't think I've ever seen him before." He handed the phone to me.

"Not someone you know?" Grimaldi prompted. "Or someone you worked with at some point? Someone else you put away? It could have been a long time ago."

I looked more closely at the picture.

Yes, he was definitely dead. His eyes were closed, but with his coloring, it was a safe bet that they were as dark as the hair. The picture was just his head from the chin up, so I had to take the height and build on faith, but chances were he was somewhere over six feet tall, and muscular. His ears stuck out a bit more than Rafe's, and the nose was a little wider. The shape of the jaw was different. There was really not much resemblance at all, but the same description could apply to both of them: a light-skinned black or mixed-race male, thirty to forty, black and brown. Rafe was thirty-one. This guy looked closer to forty.

There was no chance at all that anyone had killed him thinking he was Rafe, anyway. Not unless Eugenio Hernandez had gone blind in prison. And the very precise cross-stitch pattern on Rafe's chest and stomach argued otherwise.

Rafe shook his head.

"You're sure?"

"They pay me to be sure," Rafe said. "I spent ten years undercover. You don't make it that long unless you remember everything. I remember everyone I worked with. I especially remember everyone I put away. This guy wasn't one of 'em."

Grimaldi nodded. "What about you?" she asked me.

I handed the phone back to Truman. "I've never seen him before. Are you sure it isn't just a coincidence?"

"No," Grimaldi said. "But we have to make sure." She turned back to Rafe. "Any chance he might have been at Gabe's night before last?"

"Christ." Rafe shook his head. "It was a Friday night, Detective. The place was packed. I'd have recognized Huron if I'd seen him, but this guy? Sure, he coulda been there. But if he was, I never noticed him. Didn't see him, didn't talk to him."

Grimaldi nodded. "We'll run the picture past Mr. Craig. See if he or any of the trainees noticed the man." She handed the phone back to Truman. "Send that to my phone, please, and I'll forward it."

Truman nodded and began pushing buttons.

"I'm sure they'll be here soon," I said. "They left more than four hours ago. If you stick around, you'll probably see them."

"I'm on the clock today," Grimaldi answered. "Unless they

show up in the next five minutes, I'll be gone."

OK, then. "What makes you think this dead guy in Wilson County has anything to do with Rafe? Other than that he was found on the morning after Rafe disappeared? You said yourself that Wilson County is a big place."

Grimaldi hesitated. "Wilson County *is* a big place. And there might not be a connection. But he ought to be identified, whether he's connected or not. His family, if he has one, deserves to know what happened to him. And the Wilson County sheriff seems to have run out of steam, so if we can help, we're happy to. And also—"

"And what?" Rafe said, when she ran down.

Grimaldi sighed. "His throat was cut. If he'd just been shot, I'd be less interested in him. But anything having to do with a knife gets extra priority right now."

Yes, I could quite see why. I think we all could.

"I thought this guy was a petty criminal," I said. "Why are we suddenly thinking he's running around killing people? I mean," I turned to Rafe, "I'm not doubting that he's the one who hurt you..."

"I was awake for all of it," Rafe said grimly. "You can believe I know who did it."

"But wasn't this guy just some unimportant flunky on the outskirts of Hector's organization? He didn't even go to prison over anything important. Lots of people hire prostitutes."

"Wendell fill you in?" Rafe asked.

I nodded. So did Grimaldi. Spicer and Truman faded into the woodwork, but didn't leave the room. I guess they wanted to hear the rest of the story, too.

"He prob'ly didn't tell you everything," Rafe said. "See, this girl Ginger wasn't the first hooker Huron brought home. There were two before her. But we couldn't ever find either of'em."

I nodded. "Wendell told us that."

Rafe didn't answer, just looked at me, brow arched. He can do that: arch just one eyebrow. It gives him a very patronizing, overly patient sort of look. And I admit it took me a moment—maybe more like a minute—but I finally caught on to what he wasn't saying. And I came close to choking on the idea. "You've got to be kidding," I managed finally. "You think he killed them?"

"They were gone," Rafe said. "We couldn't find'em. So we couldn't prove nothing. There were no bodies, and no live women. But yeah, I think he killed'em."

I glanced, wide-eyed, at Grimaldi, who didn't look anywhere near as surprised as I felt. Obviously she'd seen this coming. She had undoubtedly caught on as soon as Wendell told the story yesterday. "Did you know this?"

She glanced at me. "I assumed."

"Why didn't you tell me?"

"Not your job," Grimaldi said. "And I'm pretty sure he," she glanced at Rafe, "likes that you don't think that way."

"Makes for a nice change. Somebody who just talks about food and clothes."

I sniffed. I do not just talk about food and clothes! "So you think this guy Hernandez killed two prostitutes four years ago. And when you saw him with a third, you called Wendell."

Rafe nodded. "If he hadn't agreed to call the cops, I woulda busted in and started a fight or something. But the cops came, and the girl turned out to be seventeen, and we got Huron off the street for a couple years. It was the best we could do."

And it made a lot more sense than the scenario had made so far. If Hernandez had killed two women and Rafe thought he planned to kill a third, then going to prison must have really messed with his mojo. He'd been on a roll, and suddenly he'd had to stop, cold turkey. No prostitutes in prison.

"So this guy is a serial killer."

"Pretty much," Rafe said.

"A serial killer who liked to pick up and murder prostitutes."

And probably do other things to them before he killed them. At least if Rafe's injuries were anything to go by.

He nodded. "Not that we could prove it."

"We'll prove it this time," Grimaldi said, her face grim. "You got away. You can identify him. I should put a guard on your door."

Rafe looked insulted. "I can take care of myself. Just make sure I get a gun."

"You have only one functioning arm," Grimaldi pointed out.

"I can shoot with either hand. And anyway, I don't think he's stupid enough to come after me again. When he got back to the cabin and saw that I was gone, he prob'ly got in his car and started driving."

"To Montana."

Rafe glanced at me. "They don't like people like him in Montana, darlin'. He's more likely to go to Miami."

"Or maybe Wendell and the boys found him." I smiled optimistically. "Maybe they traced the truck and found the cabin and he was still there. Maybe they've got him."

"Don't hold your breath," Rafe advised.

And indeed, when Wendell and the rookies walked in thirty minutes later, they had not found Hernandez.

Grimaldi, Spicer and Truman had left by then, to continue trying to figure out who the John Doe in Wilson County was, and whether he had any connection to Rafe or to Eugenio Hernandez. Grimaldi seemed reasonably certain that Hernandez had killed the guy—that cut throat seemed to have decided it for her once and for all—but proving it was likely to be a difficult matter. Especially if we—she—had no idea who the victim was.

"Could he be a fellow criminal?" I'd suggested at one point. "An accomplice? Maybe someone Hernandez met in prison?"

"Not if his fingerprints aren't on file," Grimaldi said. "And if they were, we'd know who he was."

Of course.

So she took Spicer and Truman with her, and they went back to work. Dix did not try to walk her out this time. I guessed they'd most likely chat by phone later. And then Wendell and the boys showed up, and gathered around Rafe's bed, chattering.

I removed myself to the corner, where Dix and Mother were waiting. "Are you sure you don't want to leave? It can't be any fun for you, sitting around here." And now that Dix had seen Tamara Grimaldi, maybe he was ready to get outta Dodge and back to his girls.

Wendell must have heard us talking, or maybe he just wanted to give Jamal, Clayton, and José a chance to talk to Rafe before he butted in. Either way, he joined us over in the corner. "Thinking of leaving?"

"Dix and Mother just came up for the wedding," I explained. "And there won't be a wedding this weekend. Rafe wants to wait until he's back on his feet."

Wendell nodded. "Thanks for coming up, and for sticking around while everything went sideways." He offered his hand to Dix, who shook. Then he took Mother's hand and kissed it. Old-fashioned courtesy, which Mother would normally appreciate, but it was Wendell, so it was hard to know for sure. She was polite, anyway.

"It was a pleasure to meet you, Mr. Craig."

"Likewise, Mrs. Martin." Wendell made a half-bow. "Once your daughter marries my boy, we'll almost be family."

Mother blinked. I hid a grin and changed the conversation. "Before we go, did you discover anything? Like the cabin?"

Wendell's face changed from jovial to grim. "Found the cabin. Empty, of course. No sign of Huron. But there was plenty of blood, so no doubt it was the right place. Door stood wide open. No way to know whether he came back and found the boy gone, or whether he never came back at all. I posted a guard up on the road, just in case. And our CSI team's going over everything."

A CSI team? Why?

"It's a crime scene," Wendell said when I asked. "We'll be confirming that it's Rafe's blood. And we're looking for proof of who was there with him. Fingerprints, hair, fibers."

"But he told you who was there."

"Proof's always helpful," Wendell said. "We also have to try to figure out who the place belongs to. Tomorrow, when the Wilson County courthouse opens and we can get access to the records."

"I might be able to help you with that today," I told him. "I have access to real estate records of various sorts. If you give me the address, I can try to dig up that information today, so you don't have to wait."

He shook his head. "I wish it were that easy, darlin'. But the cabin's in the middle of nowhere. No street name, no street number. No mailbox. It's like the place don't exist."

"It has to exist. Somewhere."

"I'll draw you a map," Wendell said. "Maybe you can figure it out. But I swear to God, if there was a street name or a number, the boys and I didn't see it."

"I can at least try. It's better than doing nothing. And maybe I'll get lucky."

Wendell nodded. "Why don't the three of you head home and get cleaned up. It's been a long night. The boys and I'll hold down the fort for a while."

I hesitated. I didn't want to leave Rafe, but a shower and clean clothes—not to mention the thought of brushing my teeth— sounded really good. And if Wendell and the boys would make sure nothing happened to him... "You won't leave him alone, will you?"

"Not until you get back," Wendell said. "I need to take his statement, anyway. In a lot more detail than what we got last night. I don't imagine you're gonna wanna stick around for that."

He imagined right. The details I'd already heard had been

quite enough. I didn't need any more food for nightmares.

"Maybe we'll just go home for a bit," I said. "And get cleaned up." Take a shower, change, brush my teeth. "Dix needs to get his jacket, too." And Mother had left her purse at the house, it seemed. At least she didn't have it with her. Although I suppose it might be in Dix's car. "Then they can drive home to Sweetwater, and I can come back in my own car."

"Sounds like a plan," Wendell said. "I'll keep the boy occupied."

"And safe."

He nodded. "That, too."

I glanced at the bed, but Rafe was deep in conversation with José, while Jamal and Clayton leaned in to listen. "I don't want to disturb him." He looked happy. "Just tell him where I went, OK? And that I'll be back in a couple hours."

Wendell said he would, and Mother, Dix and I walked out the door, down the hall, and out into the sunshine and heat of another June day.

Eleven

We piled into Dix's SUV and headed out of the lot. And I think we were all tired, because no one spoke for several minutes, other than, "Which way at the light?" and "Take a left at the bottom of the hill." We passed the Stor-All facility where Rafe and I had broken into Brenda Puckett's storage unit almost a year ago, and then the Congress Inn, where Jorge Pena, hitman, had stayed during his trip to Nashville, and where Rafe had spent a night turning himself into Jorge before leaving. That was where I had told him about David's existence for the first time, just before he headed out of town to take down Hector Gonzales.

"I have to call David," I said. "And let him know that Rafe is back, and OK." Or mostly OK.

Dix glanced at me in the rearview mirror. "Probably a good idea."

"I'm sure he'll want to see his father," Mother added, quite nicely. I chalked it up to a mostly sleepless night and an overload of stimulation, and kept my mouth shut.

"I'm sure he will," I agreed instead. "I'm not sure he should, though. Or that he'll be able to. I think he's spending another week at camp. Ginny might not want to take him out just so he can go to the hospital and see his father carved up like a Thanksgiving Day turkey. It might be better for him not to know exactly what happened."

Dix shrugged.

"And anyway, I'm not sure Rafe would want him to come."

Mother looked scandalized, and I added, since she obviously hadn't thought about it, "Hernandez is still out there. He might be watching. And David looks enough like Rafe that Hernandez could probably guess who he is. Just imagine if he kidnaps

David."

There was a moment of silence while we all imagined it, and shuddered.

"I think I'll just call Ginny," I said. "Tell her Rafe's back and doing all right, but that it would be better for David to stay where he is. He can see Rafe after camp is over. By then, hopefully they'll have caught Hernandez." And Rafe would have had a week to heal.

Mother nodded. "That makes sense," she said.

She was being so nice that I continued the conversation. "I'm sorry all this happened. I know you just came up for a nice, simple wedding ceremony."

"Stop apologizing," Dix ordered. "You didn't want this any more than the rest of us. I'm just glad Collier's back, and in one piece."

Me, too. Mother, of course, didn't concur, but then I didn't expect miracles. And anyway, I'm sure she did agree. She doesn't want him—or anyone else—to suffer. She just doesn't want him for a son-in-law.

"You need to call Catherine," I told Dix. "Take a right at the corner up here. Tell her you're coming home. She'd probably like to know that Rafe is back, too."

"When we get back to the house," Dix said, taking the right at the next corner, onto Potsdam. "And yes, I'm sure she'll be happy to hear that."

"I appreciate the two of you staying. It made things easier." Amazing as it sounded, having had to deal with them had given me something to focus on other than the fact that Rafe was missing. And when he came back, having someone else in the house, and someone else to drive to the hospital, had been a big help. I'm not even sure I could have gotten him off the floor and out to the car on my own.

Of course, I could have called for help—Wendell or Grimaldi, or 911—but it would have taken more time. Time I didn't necessarily want to spend. Time when Rafe would have been in pain.

"You're welcome," Dix said, "but you're my sister. And your fiancé disappeared. Anyone would have done the same."

"I guess maybe I've lived on my own too long," I admitted. "I'm not used to having family around."

"We're only an hour away, sis." He turned on his signal before I could respond, and added, "This is it, right?"

I nodded. Mrs. Jenkins's house sat at the apex of the circular driveway, windows blinking in the bright sun.

"You have a very nice house, Savannah," Mother said primly. My mouth fell open, and she added, "I'm not so sure about the neighborhood, but the house itself is lovely."

"Thank you." I couldn't resist adding, "Rafe did a good job on the renovations."

Mother didn't answer, and Dix rolled his eyes at me in the mirror. We pulled to a stop behind the Volvo in the driveway, and he cut the engine.

"I can't wait to get out of these clothes and in the shower," I told him, and opened the car door and swung my legs out. The dress I was wearing was the same one I had worn yesterday. Now it had Rafe's blood on it, in addition to being wrinkled and sweaty, and I felt sticky and gross.

"I believe I'll wait until we get home," Mother told me, exiting the front seat.

"Are you sure? I'm sure I can find something that'll fit you."

She shook her head. "It's just an hour's drive. And I'd like to soak in my own tub when I get there."

I could understand that. Getting naked in someone else's bathroom, no matter how nice, is never as relaxing as getting naked in your own.

"We'll just grab our things and get out of your hair," Dix said, following me up the steps to the porch.

I nodded. "Thanks again for staying. I really do appreciate it."

But he must be eager to get back to his girls, and Mother to her bathroom.

I had already dug the key out of my bag, and now I inserted it in the lock.

"Don't mention it," Dix began, and then wrinkled his brows. "What's wrong?"

"The door's unlocked." I withdrew the key and dropped it back in my purse while I reflected that this was uncannily like the first time I'd been here, the first Saturday in August. The door had been unlocked then, too. And Brenda Puckett had been dead inside.

Mother cleared her throat. "I think we may have forgotten to lock it," she said. "In the middle of the night. The two of you were busy getting Rafael into the car, and darling," this was addressed to me, "I don't recall that you locked the door, or that you asked me to do it."

Now that she mentioned it, I didn't recall doing it, or asking her to do it, either. Too concerned about getting Rafe in the car and to the hospital ASAP. "Oops."

"Let me guess," Dix said. "The place will be a mess and everything of value gone."

I shook my head. "I don't think so. Most of the neighbors know that Rafe works for the TBI. His being here means that there's a bit less crime in the neighborhood. They're all happy about that, so they tend to leave us alone."

"We should still take a look around before we go," Dix said, and since I was a little jumpy—shades of finding Brenda Puckett in front of the fireplace with her throat slit last year—I told him, sincerely, that I hoped he would, even though I didn't expect us to find anything at all.

We walked through the house as a group, just as we had yesterday, when I'd shown everyone around. There was no body in front of the fireplace in the library, and nothing whatsoever wrong in the dining room. The TV was still in the parlor, and since it's one of those manly flat-screens of oversized proportions, that seemed to me to be definite proof that no one had been in the house. Anyone looking for stuff to fence would have grabbed that.

The kitchen looked just as it had when we went to bed last night, and Rafe's sink full of red water was still in the half bath, ice cold now. I pulled the plug, and watched the water swirl down the drain, leaving a pink ring behind. "I'll have to clean this up."

There was plenty of blood on the floor, too. Anyone who walked into the half bath without knowing the situation would probably suspect that someone had committed a crime here. Or had had one hell—heck—of a nosebleed.

"There's blood on the floor in the hallway, too," Dix said, pointing to a trail leading from the door of the bathroom to the front door. As well as in front of the staircase to the second floor. And... up the stairs?

"I didn't realize Collier went upstairs last night," Dix said.

I hadn't, either. I hadn't heard him come up the stairs. He hadn't woken me.

Or maybe he had. Maybe that's what I'd heard when I wasn't sure I'd heard anything. "Maybe he came up looking for help. But when he saw I was asleep, he didn't want to wake me. He knows I get tired because of the baby."

Or maybe he had tried to wake me, and I hadn't roused.

God, what if he'd come upstairs looking for help, and I'd been dead asleep so he'd had to go back downstairs alone to take care of his injuries...?

"I'm sure it's something like that," Dix said, without realizing that he'd just confirmed such a horrible possibility. He headed up the stairs, careful not to step in the blood that was spattered on every other step or so all the way up to the second floor.

The trail led over to the door to my room—or Rafe's room. The master bedroom.

"I don't remember seeing that last night," I said, turning to Mother. "We were up here together. Can you remember?"

She shook her head. "Sorry, darling. I had other things on my mind."

Sure. I had, too. Like the fact that my fiancé was bleeding to death—or looked like he was—on the floor downstairs.

"I don't remember closing the door, either. I mean, I could have. With other people in the house, I might have thought it would be more private." And Mother had trained me to always make my bed in the morning. An unmade bed is a sign of a slovenly housewife. The fact that it had been the middle of the night would have made no difference as far as my upbringing was concerned.

So it was very possible I had closed the door behind me when I came out into the hallway and saw Mother coming toward me.

Nonetheless, my heart was beating faster when I walked over to the door and grabbed the handle. And twisted and pulled. And stumbled back, a scream caught in my throat.

Dix rushed up beside me, and stopped as if he'd run into a wall. "Dear Lord."

Mother peered over his shoulder into the room, and turned pale. She, too, stepped back and fanned herself with her hand. "Dear me."

"Take Mother somewhere and make her sit down," I told Dix. Normally I'd be the one having the vapors, but I was either becoming inured, or the fact that someone else was close to passing out was bucking me up.

Dix grabbed Mother's arm, but told me, "We have to call—"

"I will." My voice was, if I do say so myself, amazingly steady for the circumstances. "I just want to look at her first."

Dix nodded and drew Mother away. "Let me know if there's anything I can do."

"I don't think there's anything anyone can do," I said, "but I will."

I waited for them to move across the hallway to Mother's room, and then I took a few delicate steps into my own, and stopped by the bedside, steeling myself to look at the dead girl.

Oh, yes. She was definitely dead. Her eyes were wide open, staring up at the ceiling fan that was revolving slowly, and her chest didn't move at all.

She was sprawled across my bed, on top of the sheets and the comforter I hadn't bothered to pull up when I rushed downstairs and out in the middle of the night. A natural redhead, with eyes the same blue as the sky outside, and pale, almost transparent skin. It was hard to be sure how much of that was due to natural coloring and how much due to blood loss. There was a lot of blood, streaked on her arms and legs, dried in rivulets on her torso.

I backed out into the hallway and closed the door. And fumbled the phone out of my bag and dialed Grimaldi's number. "We need you," I told her when she answered. By then, reaction had set in, so my teeth were chattering. I plopped my butt down on the top step of the staircase as the conversation continued.

"At the hospital?"

I shook my head, even though I knew she couldn't see me. "The house."

"What happened?"

"Dead girl," I said. "In my bed."

She muttered something. I couldn't hear it, but I'm sure it was a curse. "Stay there. Don't move. Don't touch anything. I'll be there in ten minutes."

She hung up before I could assure her that we weren't planning to go anywhere at all, and we certainly weren't about to touch anything. Mother would just have to wait on her bath, and so would I.

"Is she coming?" Dix wanted to know. He came back out of Mrs. Jenkins's room with Mother in tow. She glanced at the closed door to my room.

I nodded. "She said she'd be here in ten minutes."

"Who?" Mother asked.

"Tamara," Dix told her. "Detective Grimaldi. This is her job. Homicide."

Mother nodded. "I remember. She worked on Sheila's case."

"We should go downstairs and meet her. But first..." I went back to the door to the master bedroom and opened it. The dead girl was still there, on the bed. Not that I had expected otherwise, but it would have been nice if she'd been a figment of my imagination.

"Darling..." Mother protested delicately when I raised my phone and snapped a picture of her. And then another, just of her face.

I glanced at her. "She doesn't care." And if she was who I thought she was, she hadn't cared about people seeing her naked while she'd been alive.

I sent the pictures to Wendell's cell phone with the caption, *Is this Ginger?*

And then I closed the door gently behind me and descended the stairs to the first floor, hanging onto the banister the whole way.

Grimaldi did indeed show up within ten minutes. When she knocked on the door, we were all sitting around the kitchen table swilling glasses of extra-sugared sweet tea, for the shock.

"I'll go," Dix said when the doorbell rang. "You two stay here."

He got to his feet. I wanted to argue—it was my home, so I should be the one to let visitors in—but to be honest, I didn't feel up for it. And besides, he'd had little enough time alone with Grimaldi since he came to town.

Not that there was anything romantic about taking her upstairs to see a dead body, but he offered. I decided I might as well take him up on it.

"Be careful, darling," Mother told him. "Make sure it's the detective before you answer the door."

Yes, indeed. I nodded. "Good advice."

Mother looked gratified. Dix headed down the hallway. After a few seconds we heard the front door open, and then Grimaldi's voice. The door closed, and footsteps headed up the stairs to the second floor.

I made to get to my feet, but Mother shook her head. "Let Dixon handle it," she said. For a second I thought maybe she'd sensed something going on between them, and wanted to give them a few moments together, too. But then she added, "While Rafael isn't here, he's the man of the house."

I rolled my eyes, but stayed seated. I couldn't keep my mouth shut, though. "It's my house, Mother. My bed. My dead body."

Mother shuddered. "Not *your* dead body, darling. Thank the Lord. Someone else's dead body."

"Ginger," I said. "Poor girl." If she was seventeen four years ago, she was barely twenty-one now. And honestly, looked younger. "She probably has a family somewhere. A mother and a father. Maybe brothers or sisters."

"She was a prostitute," Mother began.

"That doesn't mean she deserved to die. She certainly didn't deserve to die like that!"

"That's not what I meant," Mother told me. "But individuals who engage in risky behavior often become victims of crime."

"That doesn't change the fact that she was a twenty-year-old woman—just a girl!—who was carved up and dumped in my bed for Rafe to find!"

Mother had no answer to that. And at any rate, the footsteps were now coming back down the stairs and down the hall to the kitchen. "It's Ginger," I told Grimaldi as soon as she walked in. "The prostitute from four years ago. Hernandez must have found her again and finished the job Rafe stopped him from finishing back then. And then dumped her here. In Rafe's bed.

As a message."

Grimaldi shook her head. "Unlikely. The girl straightened up and moved away. She's in a different state. Hernandez wouldn't have had time to go find her between the time he left your boyfriend and this morning."

"Maybe he had her already."

She hesitated. "Possible. But it's more likely it's just someone who looks like her. Ginger is twenty-one. The girl upstairs looks no more than seventeen."

"I took a picture of her," I said, "and sent it to Wendell. He hasn't responded yet. But he'd be able to tell us whether it's her." She. "He'd recognize her."

Grimaldi nodded and took a seat at the table. "We'll figure it out. For now, tell me what happened."

I told her what had happened. It didn't take long. We'd left the hospital. We'd driven home. The front door had been open. We'd realized we'd left it open last night, but we had decided to walk through the house anyway. We'd noticed the blood, and we'd found her in my—in Rafe's—bed.

And God, I could just imagine how he'd react to this news. It was insult on top of injury, quite literally.

"Did you check the rest of the house?" Grimaldi asked, and brought me back to myself.

"After we found her, you mean? No. We came down here to wait for you."

Grimaldi nodded. "Excuse me." She got up from the table and put a hand on her gun.

"Oh." Mother turned pale, and I'm sure I did, too. "You mean... he could still be here?"

"I'm sure he isn't," Grimaldi said, "but why take chances?" She pulled the gun from the holster and checked the clip. "Did you walk through the entire downstairs? Where did you stop looking?"

"When we got upstairs and saw the blood leading to the

master bedroom," I said. "Dix and Mother went into Mother's bedroom after that. Although I doubt they checked the closet or under the bed."

Mother shook her head, looking ashen.

"And you didn't go up to the third floor?"

I told her we hadn't. "Do you want me to come with you?"

"No," Grimaldi said, with another of those 'get-real' looks. "Your boyfriend would have my head if he found out I'd let you walk through the house looking for a serial killer."

"We don't have to tell him."

"He'd know," Grimaldi said darkly. "Stay here." She turned to Dix, who had also gotten to his feet. "You, too."

"You need backup," Dix said.

"You don't have a weapon."

Dix looked stubborn. "If you won't let Savannah go with you, I'm coming. You're not going up there alone."

Grimaldi hesitated for a second, then shrugged. "Stay behind me. And if he shoots me, go for my gun."

"Not funny," Dix told her.

"I wasn't joking."

"I thought you said he wasn't likely to be here," I said. "And anyway, what makes you think he has a gun? So far, he's cut everyone's throat."

Except Rafe's, although he'd probably planned to get to that point eventually.

Grimaldi sent me a look. "You always expect criminals to be armed and dangerous," she told me. "You'll stay safer that way."

Right. "Be careful."

She nodded. "Come on," she told Dix. "Let's go."

"Just a second." He turned to me. "If something happens to me, will you take my girls?"

"Yes. But that's not funny, either."

"I'm sure Catherine will be happy to keep the girls, Dixon," Mother added, and then seemed to realize what he'd asked.

"What...?"

"Nothing's going to happen," Grimaldi said firmly. "Let's go. Before I change my mind and leave you down here."

She set off down the hallway without waiting for him, her strides long. Dix gave me a wink and scurried after. Their footsteps receded up the stairs, and then we could hear them walking around above our heads. There was the sound of doors opening and closing, but nothing more sinister than that. Certainly no gunshots. After a couple of minutes, I guess they had checked the entire second level, and we heard them head up the next flight of stairs to the ballroom on the top floor.

We sat in silence, straining our ears, until there was the sound of footsteps on the stairs again, descending this time. We hadn't heard the sounds of an altercation, so it didn't come as a surprise when Dix and Grimaldi walked back into the kitchen, safe, sound, and whole.

"Nothing?" I asked.

Dix shook his head. "No sign anyone had been up there. He must have just dumped the girl and left."

Grimaldi holstered her gun and dug out her phone. "I'm still going to get a crime scene crew out here. And the van from the morgue."

Of course. That poor girl was still up there, sprawled across my bed. The second hooker to die in one of my beds in a month's time. I hoped it wasn't going to become a regular occurrence.

Except Ginger—or whoever she was, although I still leaned toward it being Ginger—hadn't died there. There wasn't enough blood for that. On the body, sure. But not on the sheets. Hernandez—and I don't think there was much doubt in anyone's mind that he was the guilty party—must have killed her somewhere else, and brought her here afterwards.

"Rafe isn't going to be happy about this," I said.

Grimaldi shook her head.

"He'll take it personally."

"I'm fairly certain it *is* personal," Grimaldi said.

"'You saved her once, but you couldn't save her this time'?"

"I was thinking more like, 'I know where you live and I can get to you anytime I want to,'" Grimaldi said. And added, "'And your little girlfriend, too.'"

I wasn't the only one who turned pale. Dix muttered a curse, and Mother looked ready to faint.

"I didn't think about that," I said.

"Maybe you should think about it now."

Maybe I should. I'd really rather not, of course, because it wasn't much fun to contemplate. But yes, I should.

And then, as I thought about it—as we all thought about it— came the sound of the front door bursting open, and heavy footsteps in the hallway. Grimaldi pulled out her gun and pointed it at the kitchen door. I held my breath.

Twelve

Rafe burst through the door at as much of a run as he was capable of. It wasn't very impressive, frankly. At the moment, he moved both slowly and stiffly, but he *was* moving. Up, out of bed, still dressed in just the drawstring pants the hospital had given him. The white bandages around his torso and arm stood out in stark contract to the dusky skin.

He lurched to a stop behind Mother's chair and braced himself, breathing hard. Mother stiffened her spine, looking uncomfortable.

"You can put the gun down," I told Grimaldi. "I don't think he's going to hurt anyone."

He scowled at me. "I wouldn't be so sure."

"Why are you mad at me? I didn't do anything!"

"You left without saying goodbye," Rafe growled. "I looked up and you were gone. And then the phone signals and you've found another effing dead body!"

Mother blanched.

"You're scaring my mother," I told him. And then, because I knew he wasn't really upset with me, he was upset about the situation, and about the fact that I had left and was alone and had to deal with this on my own, without him, I got up from the table and went to put my arms around him. "I'm sorry I didn't tell you we were going. But you were talking to the boys. I was just going to go home and take a shower and change my clothes and then come back. It wasn't going to take very long. I didn't expect this to happen."

His arms came around me, too, and he stood for a second, breathing into my hair. "I got scared," he told me, his voice low.

"I know." I petted him. Gently, because of the bandages.

There were tremors running through his body. "But it's OK. There's nobody here. It's safe."

"For now." He shook his head. "You have to leave."

I straightened, to where I could look in his face. "Have you lost your mind? I'm not leaving!"

"He knows where we live," Rafe said.

"And your solution is that I should run away? And leave you here? In your condition?"

"He likes to hurt women," Rafe said. "With me it was personal, but he prefers to hurt women. It's a sexual thing."

Great. Just what I wanted to hear.

Not that I hadn't already known that, subconsciously. When a guy tortures and kills prostitutes, sex usually plays a part in it somewhere.

"Be that as it may," I said, happy to hear that my voice was steady, "I'm sure he'd be happy to finish the job he started on you, too. And don't tell me you can take care of yourself. He caught you once. He can catch you again. Especially in your current condition."

He scowled. "Stop talking about my condition. I can still aim and pull a trigger. And I want you somewhere safe."

"I'm safe here. With you."

Since there was nothing he could say to that—not without admitting that he wasn't in any kind of shape to protect me—he didn't try. "I'd feel better if you'd go somewhere else for a couple days."

"I suppose you want me to go to Sweetwater?"

Everyone was watching the show, their heads swiveling from him to me and back. Mother looked apprehensive, Dix looked concerned, and Grimaldi and Wendell—leaning in the doorway—looked amused.

"It's a start," Rafe said.

"I don't think so. What if he follows me to Sweetwater? It's only an hour away. I'd put Mother at risk. And Catherine. And the girls. They're just children, but who knows where this sick bastard draws the line?"

Nobody looked amused anymore. Mother looked nauseous and Dix terrified. Both Grimaldi and Wendell looked grim.

"No," I said again, shaking my head. "I love you. I don't want you to have to worry about me. But I'm not going to Sweetwater. Although Mother and Dix should go. Now."

Dix didn't waste any time in getting to his feet. "If you don't need us," he told Grimaldi.

She shook her head. "Go home. Take care of your girls. I can get any information I need from Savannah."

Dix nodded and extended a hand to Mother, who took it and let him help her up.

Wendell stepped out of the doorway with a polite nod to let them pass.

"I should go wave goodbye," I told Rafe. "And you ought to sit down before you fall down."

"Sounds familiar. Didn't I tell you that once?" But he sat. Or more accurately, fell onto the nearest chair; the one that had most recently held Mother's posterior. Wendell wandered over to the table and grabbed Dix's chair.

"I'll be right back." I headed down the hallway and out on the front porch, just in time to see Dix close the passenger side door of the SUV with Mother behind it. "Sorry," I told him.

He shook his head. "Not your fault." But he didn't stop, just continued around the car to the driver's side door. Couldn't get away from me quickly enough.

Not his fault, I reminded myself. He was worried about his girls. And who could blame him?

"I'm sure the girls are safe," I called after him. "He doesn't know who they are or where to find them. He probably doesn't even know who you are. They're fine."

Dix nodded and opened his door. "I just want to see them. I'll call you."

He didn't wait for me to answer, just got in the car and closed the door. A second later, the engine cranked over.

"He's worried," Grimaldi's voice said next to me, trying to excuse Dix's rudeness.

I glanced at her. "I know. I don't blame him. I should have thought before I spoke. I just couldn't believe that Rafe would suggest that I should leave him alone here with this nutcase gunning for him!"

"He's worried, too," Grimaldi said, as the car crunched down the gravel driveway. "He knows better than anyone what Hernandez is capable of. And not only are you his girlfriend, you're carrying his child. That's two nightmares rolled in one."

The SUV slowed to turn onto Potsdam, and she lifted a hand to wave. I have no idea whether Dix or Mother waved back, or whether they were even looking at us, but I flopped my hand in the air, too.

"He wants you to be safe," Grimaldi added. "That's his main concern. Much more than his own safety. Or anyone else's."

I knew that, too. But I still wasn't going. Wasn't risking drawing Hernandez's attention to Sweetwater and everyone there, and wasn't leaving Rafe.

The SUV had disappeared down the street. I turned to go inside. "He'll have to lump it."

"I figure he knows that," Grimaldi told me as she followed me through the door. "But you can't blame him for trying."

I suppose. In his shoes I might have done the same thing. Although he really should have known better.

"I'm sorry you didn't get to spend any time with Dix," I told Grimaldi as we headed down the hallway together, taking care not to step on any of the blood spots. At least I took care; I'm not so sure about the detective.

As always when I brought up her relationship with my brother, Grimaldi looked blank. "Finding your boyfriend was more important."

"Of course." No argument here. Not that anyone had found him; he'd found his way home on his own. "But I'm sure Dix was hoping to spend time with you. And then Mother insisted on staying." I shook my head.

"I was gonna ask you about that," Rafe told me, catching the last sentence as Grimaldi and I walked into the kitchen. "Your mama drove up from Sweetwater to watch you marry me?"

I nodded.

"Why'd she wanna do that?"

"I don't know," I said. "I assume it's because I'm her daughter, and it was an important day for me." Or would have been, if the groom had been present.

"Or maybe she woulda objected when the preacher said, 'If anyone knows of a reason...?'"

"Maybe. Do they say that in civil ceremonies?"

"Dunno," Rafe said. "I've never been married before."

I had, but not in a civil ceremony. And the preacher at the church in Sweetwater had said, 'If anyone knows of a reason why this man and this woman should not be joined in holy matrimony, speak now or forever hold your peace.' Or something very like it.

I doubted Mother would have drawn attention to herself by speaking up at that moment, though, no matter how happy it would have made her if I didn't marry Rafe. Although who knew?

"Whatever her reason," I said, "she was here. Catherine was, too, but she went home after lunch, so she could take care of the kids. Her own, and Dix's. I thought for sure Mother would go with her, but no. She wanted to stay. And that was after seeing the house and the neighborhood."

"No accounting for taste," Rafe said.

"You know I don't mean that. I like it here. But it's not exactly Mother's style. Although she did say it was a nice house."

"No kidding."

I shook my head. "She seemed to like David, too."

Rafe's brows lowered. "When did your mama see David?"

"We drove out to Peaceful Pines yesterday afternoon," I said. "That was when we still thought you might have left of your own free will. We thought you might have told him something." Like goodbye. "But he said he hadn't seen you since last week."

And that reminded me—again—that I had to call David and tell him Rafe was back, and safe. I'd forgotten in the excitement of finding Ginger.

Or maybe I should just have Rafe call him. It would make him feel better to hear Rafe's voice.

But first we should get Ginger squared away.

I turned to Wendell. "You obviously got my message."

He nodded.

"Is it Ginger?"

He shook his head.

"Are you sure?"

He nodded. "Too young. Someone else he picked up."

"Another hooker?"

"They're easy to find," Rafe said. "And they get into your car with no fuss."

Not like abducting a kicking and screaming civilian. "You don't know her, I suppose?"

"Not from the picture," Rafe said, putting his hands on the table and pushing himself to his feet. It took effort, and we could all see it, but nobody commented. "I'll go look at the real thing. And put on some clothes while I'm up there. Before the crime scene crew starts crawling all over my bedroom."

He took a second to find his balance before tottering off across the kitchen toward the door. He was moving like an old man, stiff and slightly hunched.

"Do you want help?" I threw after him.

"I got it."

Sure. Because it's so easy to bend from the waist to pull on a pair of pants when your torso's bandaged almost from hips to armpits.

But I didn't say so. Instead I just told him, "Holler if you change your mind."

He didn't answer, just moved down the hallway to the stairs. After a moment—I figured he stopped at the bottom to gauge how far away the last step was, and I'm sure it looked like the top of Mount Le Conte—he began dragging himself up.

"Like a mule," Wendell said.

I nodded. "Did you go upstairs and look at her?"

He shook his head.

"Maybe you should. That way you can help him with his pants."

"I don't think he'd like that," Wendell said. "I'm damn sure I wouldn't."

"Just wait for him to ask," Grimaldi advised. "Give him a chance to realize he needs help. If you force it on him, he'll keep telling himself he could have done it on his own."

He probably would, at that. Like all men, he's nothing if not stubborn.

"So what happens now?" I looked from one to the other of them.

"I called in a crime scene team," Grimaldi said. "I'm waiting for them to get here. Once they're working, I'll have to try to figure out who the girl is."

"We're going back out to Wilson County," Wendell added. "Now that the sun's up and folks are awake, we're gonna start going door to door in the area around the cabin. Just in case he has another hole out there, or somebody knows something. He musta chosen that area for a reason. I doubt it was luck that he found an empty cabin."

I nodded. "I should get busy trying to find out who owns it. I forgot all about that, with everything that's happened since we left the hospital."

The sound of crunching gravel from outside reached our ears.

"That must be the crime scene team," Grimaldi said, getting to her feet. "I'll go let them in. You—" She glanced at me, "had better go upstairs and help your boyfriend get dressed before you do anything else. I'm sure he won't want to be caught with his pants down and a dead woman sprawled across the bed."

My face twisted at the image. "No. I'm sure he won't." *Gah.* "Do people really...?"

They both looked at me, two pairs of flat cop eyes that had seen a lot more than I had, and I shook my head. "Never mind."

"Lots of sick people in the world," Wendell said, and Grimaldi nodded.

"Come on. Let's go."

She headed for the door, and I got to my feet and followed. In the foyer, Grimaldi went to the front door and out on the porch, where I'm sure she'd brief the CSI team to give me time to get Rafe dressed and ready. I hustled up the stairs and into the bedroom, where he was leaning against the wall, breathing hard, as naked as the day he was born and with a pair of jeans pooled around his ankles.

Normally, the sight of my butt-naked boyfriend would have gotten my blood pumping. At the moment, I was too concerned with the fact that his face was ashen with what had to be pain, and that a couple of new, bright red spots of blood decorated the hitherto pristine white of the bandages.

Yelling wouldn't do any good, though, and would just make him feel worse. So I didn't say anything, but simply crossed the room, edging around the bottom of the bed—making sure to keep my eyes off the body sprawled there—and crouched in front of him.

He looked like he couldn't lift his head, but his lips curved. "If I was feeling better, that'd look promising."

"If I thought it would help," I told him, "I'd consider it. But you'd probably fall flat on your face."

He nodded. "Prob'ly."

"So I'm just going to help you get these on." I grabbed the pants and tugged. "I guess you decided that underwear was too much trouble?"

"Pants are too much trouble," Rafe muttered, but let me pull them up and close the zipper. Gently.

"I'm sorry," I told him. "I wish you could just go to bed and stay there. But Grimaldi's crime scene crew is downstairs. We figured you wouldn't want to be caught with your pants down, standing over the body." I turned to the bureau and then hesitated. "A shirt with buttons might be easier to deal with than a T-shirt."

"Whatever," Rafe said. "No, that wouldn't be good."

"You're bleeding again. I guess we'll have to go back to the hospital." I pulled out a long sleeved shirt. Under normal circumstances it would be much too warm for June, but he was shivering. And very docile when I helped him slip his arms through the sleeves. I didn't bother with the buttons.

Downstairs the door opened, and we could hear voices. Grimaldi was explaining about the different trails of blood: one going down the hall to the half bath—Rafe's—and one going up the stairs to the bedroom.

"Just another minute. You keep holding up the wall."

I pulled the sundress over my head, dropped it in the laundry basket, and pulled another out of the closet and yanked it over my head. New underwear would just have to wait. I could already hear footsteps on the stairs.

"Let's go." I put my arm around him and guided him around the bed. His feet dragged. "Did you look at her?"

"Yeah."

"It's not Ginger, is it?"

He shook his head. "Don't look much like her, really. Except for the hair."

We walked a few steps before he added, "Seen her before,

though."

"You have?"

"Friday night. Outside Gabe's."

"Really?"

He shrugged, so maybe he wasn't entirely sure. Or maybe he just needed his breath for walking.

"We can talk about it when we get downstairs," I said, as we passed over the threshold and into the upstairs hallway. The crime scene crew—two women and a man—were on their way up, followed by Grimaldi, and we stood aside to let them pass. Both of the women gave Rafe curious glances on their way past, but nobody commented.

Once they were past us and inside the bedroom, I added, "Can you make it down the stairs on your own if you hold onto the banister? I'll walk in front of you in case you fall."

"You'll walk behind me," Rafe corrected, grabbing the railing hard enough that his knuckles turned white, "so I don't take you out if I do."

"That doesn't make any sense—"

"You're pregnant, darlin'." He took the first step down. I held my breath. "Falling down a staircase wouldn't do you or the baby any good."

No arguing with that. I walked behind him instead, and wrapped my hand in the waistband of his jeans. If he stumbled, maybe I would be able to keep him standing.

But he kept on his feet, and we made it safely to the first floor. Back in the kitchen, Rafe dropped down onto the chair with a grunt, and drooped like a wilted lily. "Shit." He had a hard time catching his breath.

Wendell looked sympathetic, but said bracingly, "At least you're wearing real clothes."

"We have to go back to the hospital," I told him, taking my own seat on the other side of the table. "He's bleeding again." I turned to Rafe. "And this time I'm going to make sure they handcuff you to the bed!"

"Darlin'..." Rafe muttered. I rolled my eyes.

"I should have just put you to bed in one of the other bedrooms upstairs. The crime scene crew would have left you alone."

"No offense, darlin'," Rafe told me, "but I managed to stay outta Marquita's bed when she was alive. I ain't going there now. And sleeping in my grandma's bed is just weird. Specially after your mama spent the night there."

"We may not have a choice," I told him. "Because I don't feel real good about sleeping in our bed tonight. Even after the body's gone."

"I'll get the boys over here to haul away the mattress," Wendell offered. He looked at Rafe. "And don't you give me no lip about moving it yourself, boy. You can barely keep on your feet. Ain't no way you're moving nothing."

Rafe shook his head. At least he seemed aware that some things were beyond his abilities at the moment. "You going back out to Wilson County?"

Wendell nodded. "We could use you, if you think you're up for sitting in a car for a couple hours. The boys'd be happy to have you."

"I dunno..." Rafe said, glancing at me. "With Huron on the loose, I don't feel so good about leaving Savannah on her own."

"It's broad daylight," I told him. "I have a house full of cops. I don't think he'll try to do anything to me."

He looked doubtful.

"Unless you don't think you're up for it. If you just want to go to sleep. Or back to the hospital. You should, so they can look at—"

"No," Rafe said. "I feel all right. I just tried to do too much."

No kidding.

"But I can sit in a car for a couple hours and watch other people work. And I wanna be there when they take him down."

"I don't think we'll be taking him down today," Wendell said. "I dunno..." He glanced at me. "Maybe she's right. Maybe you need to go back to the hospital."

Rafe looked mutinous. I threw my hands up, literally and metaphorically. "Take him. Just make sure he takes it easy. If he's bleeding when you bring him back here, I'm going to be angry."

"I'll be good," Rafe promised.

"That'll be a first."

"That ain't what you usually tell me."

While I sputtered, he added, "I'm gonna need a pair of socks. I ain't walking around barefoot. And tell Tammy she'll have to stick with you till I get back."

Rafe is the only person in the world who calls Tamara Grimaldi Tammy and gets away with it. She told me once her own mother didn't even call her Tammy.

"I'm sure she'll be thrilled to do that," I answered dryly. "You can't just dump me on her, Rafe. She's working. She's got a fresh homicide to deal with. She's not going to want to babysit me."

"And I don't want nothing happening to you."

I didn't want anything happening to me, either. So I got to my feet. "I'll go talk to her. And get you a pair of socks. I'll be right back."

I left the two of them sitting there while I headed back upstairs. If Grimaldi didn't feel good about being stuck with me for the rest of the afternoon, I guess I could just stay in the house for as long as the crime scene crew was here, and then lock and bolt all the doors when they left.

Thirteen

"Rafe wants to go to Wilson County with Wendell," I told Grimaldi, after I'd dug a pair of socks out of Rafe's underwear drawer. The crime scene crew was surrounding the bed, as well, so between the five of us, there was standing room only in the bedroom. "He wants me to stay here with you."

"I'm not staying here." She didn't take her eyes off the techs who were circling the bed and the dead girl. "I have a homicide to solve."

"He thinks he's seen her before," I told her. "At Gabe's—or outside Gabe's—on Friday night."

She glanced at me. "Is that the truth? Or is he trying to give me incentive to babysit you?"

"Maybe a little of both?" I shrugged. "If he says he thinks he saw her, I'm sure he thinks he did. I'm not sure how reliable it is, since he only thinks so, and since it might have been just before Hernandez hit him, and so his memory might be a bit wonky."

Grimaldi nodded. "Are they still downstairs?"

"As far as I know. I don't think they'd leave before they know for sure that I'm safe."

"Then let's go," Grimaldi said, and shooed me out the door and down the stairs ahead of her. "You can't babysit your own girlfriend?" she added when we walked into the kitchen.

Rafe broke off in the middle of a sentence to turn to her. "First," he said coldly, "I gotta go to Wilson County. I figure she'd rather stay here where it's cool, instead of sitting in a car in the middle of the woods in the heat."

He had a point. Then again, not necessarily. I mean, it was cool in the house and hot outside, but there was a dead woman in my bed. A dead woman who had gotten the same treatment

Rafe had gotten last night, with—I assumed—some additional sexual thrills thrown in for good measure. I didn't necessarily want to sit around down here while the crime scene crew and the ME were messing around upstairs.

"And second," Rafe continued, "let's just say I'm not in the best shape I've ever been. There's a chance we'll run into Huron out there. I'd feel safer if Savannah was here with you."

It was the closest he'd probably ever come to admitting he wasn't sure he could protect me, and it almost broke my heart.

But since he hadn't actually come out and said so, not straight out, for me to tell him I'd trust him with my life—any day, any time—would only make him feel worse. So I didn't.

Grimaldi huffed. "Fine."

"You both make me feel all warm and fuzzy inside," I said, scowling. "If neither of you wants to be saddled with me, I can stay here with the crime scene crew. Or go to the nearest mattress warehouse, so we'll have something to sleep on tonight."

They both shook their heads. "You're going with Tammy," Rafe said.

"You're coming with me," Grimaldi said at the same time.

She shot him a look, and continued, "I'll make sure you stay in one piece."

"We'll take care of the mattress," Wendell added. "Let us know when the CSI crew is gone, and the boys and I'll haul out the old mattress and bring in a new."

Grimaldi nodded. "Stay in touch. Let us know what happens on your end."

"You do the same," Wendell said, and Grimaldi promised she would, before turning to Rafe.

"Savannah said you might know her?"

There was no question who 'she' was.

Rafe shook his head. "Not to say 'know.' I mighta seen her on Friday night. Outside Gabe's."

"When was this? Before or after Hernandez clubbed you?"

He gave her a look. "Before. After, I was rolling around the back of the van. I didn't see nothing but the insides of my eyelids. And anyway, it was earlier. When we got there. Seven o'clock, maybe. Seven-thirty."

Grimaldi had pulled out her notebook and was scribbling. I couldn't imagine why, since this information wasn't exactly hard to remember. But maybe she had to keep notes for the file. "What was she doing?"

"Walking," Rafe said. "Through the parking lot."

"To the bar? Or away?"

"Neither," Rafe said. "There's a sleezy motel back there, behind the fence and down the hill. I figured they came from that."

"They?"

"There were two of 'em. The redhead and a brunette. They took a right outta the parking lot and started walking down the side of the road." He shrugged. "I figured they were headed for the truck stop."

"Hooker?" Grimaldi asked.

"That's what I thought. She," he glanced at the ceiling, "asked me if I wanted to get lucky."

I sniffed, and he chuckled. "Don't worry, darlin'. Sixteen-year-old redheads don't do it for me no more."

Grimaldi and Wendell looked at him, and then at me.

"He slept with a girl named Yvonne McCoy back in high school," I explained. "She was a redhead."

"Still is," Rafe added.

I scowled—yes, she was, and wasn't above flirting with him whenever she saw him, either. "But she isn't sixteen anymore."

"That she ain't." He grinned before turning back to Grimaldi. "Regular women sometimes ask if I wanna get lucky, too. But she looked like she was hooking. Tiny shorts, skimpy top, lotsa makeup. A little desperate."

Grimaldi nodded. "What about the other girl?"

"Fluffy brown hair," Rafe said. "Short skirt, pink backpack. Less comfortable with the whole thing."

"And you think they were headed for the truck stop."

"That was just a thought I had," Rafe said. "I didn't watch'em or nothing. But they were going that way, and that's where I figured they were headed."

Grimaldi nodded. "We'll go check if anyone at the truck stop knows her. It might be her usual place of business."

"She wasn't very old," Rafe said. "Prob'ly younger than Ginger was back then. Might be a runaway."

"I'll check with missing persons." She hesitated. "This guy Hernandez... did he have a thing for redheads?"

Rafe shook his head. "Liked'em young, though. But I don't think he cared if they had red or black or brown hair."

"The other two women you said you saw him with, four years ago..."

Rafe nodded.

"Were they as young?"

"Older than Ginger. But not by much. No more'n twenty."

"You looked for them, right?"

"Yeah," Rafe said, with heavy patience. "We couldn't find'em. Alive or dead."

"Did you check missing persons reports?"

Rafe shook his head. "I was deep undercover. I couldn't go to the police station to look at pictures of runaways. I had to keep doing my job, and keep the focus off me as much as possible. Wendell did some looking—" he glanced at Wendell, who nodded, "but he hadn't seen'em, so there wasn't much he could do."

"I spent a couple nights driving around," Wendell said, "talking to working girls. Never found anyone who admitted being picked up by Huron, or knew anyone who was. I asked about girls going missing, but there's always someone. Hookers disappear all the time, especially if they're runaways. They show up in other neighborhoods and other towns. They go home. They leave the life. Sometimes they die, although we never did find any bodies."

"We found this one," Grimaldi said.

"And this time we'll get him for it. Now'd be a good time to tie in the other girls, too. He wasn't tried for murder last time. Not enough evidence. And double jeopardy."

Grimaldi nodded. "If you don't have the evidence, it's much better to wait until you do."

"Hopefully this time we will." Wendell glanced at Rafe, and got to his feet. "Ready?"

"Socks," I said, crouching next to his chair to help him get them on. I'm not sure he could have bent over if his life depended on it. "Want a hand getting up?"

"I can do it." He put his hands flat against the tabletop.

"Knock it off," I told him. "There are stitches in that arm." There had to be. Top and bottom, if the knife had gone straight through. "You'll pop them, doing that."

He scowled, but didn't object when I grabbed one of his arms and nodded to Grimaldi to grab the other. Between us, we managed to get him to his feet.

"Weak as a baby," he muttered, disgusted.

I shook my head, but it was Grimaldi who told him, "Most people would be in the hospital. Hell, most people wouldn't have made it home at all."

And then she capped it off by adding, "So stop whining."

Rafe's lips curled. "Yes, ma'am."

"Take care of yourself," I told him. "Please don't overdo. I don't want to spend another night at the hospital."

"They prob'ly wouldn't take me back anyway. Not after the way I tore outta there earlier."

Perhaps not. I hadn't been there to see his departure, but I could imagine, based on the way he'd come into the house, what it might have been like. "Did they at least give you a prescription for painkillers before you left? You're not going to be able to get through this on aspirin."

Rafe shook his head, but Wendell nodded. "I was the one had to stop at the desk to sign him out. I told'em to call something in to the pharmacy. We'll stop on the way to Wilson County and pick it up. And stop for a new mattress on the way back."

"Thank you," I said. Sincerely.

He smiled. "No problem. Me and the boys'll get him back to you in one piece."

"I'll hold you to that."

I turned to Grimaldi, who said, "Unless you want to kiss your boyfriend goodbye, we're ready to go."

I did want to kiss my boyfriend goodbye. But he was unsteady on his feet as it was, so it was safer not to take any chances.

"I'll help you out to the car," I told him instead, and slipped my arm around his waist. Partly, it was because I wanted to be close, but partly, it was also because I figured he could use the support and wasn't the type to ask. The arm he draped over my shoulders was heavy, and our progress out of the kitchen and along the hallway was slow. I rubbed my head against his shoulder. "Be careful out there."

He nodded. "Always."

As if. "Keep us updated on how things go. If you find him. Or even if you don't."

"If we do," Rafe said, as we passed through the front door and onto the porch, "you'll be the first to hear about it. Trust me."

We started down the stairs, one careful step at a time. He gave a grunt with each one. I guess the impact jarred his torso, and more than it normally would because he wasn't exactly his usual graceful self. He's a big guy—six-three and muscular—but under most circumstances, he moves quickly and silently. Now, I felt like I was guiding a lumbering bear.

He was a shade paler by the time we got to the bottom of the steps, too. "I'm sorry," I muttered, feeling wretched. "You really should be flat on your back in bed, not walking around chasing bad guys."

"Getting Huron back behind bars so he's not out there will do me more good than being flat on my back," Rafe told me, although I could hear the strain in his voice. "Not that bed doesn't sound good..."

I bet. Bed sounded good to me, too—or would have, if it hadn't been for the dead body currently occupying it. Rafe had had a much worse night than I had—obviously—but between the worry yesterday and the trip to the hospital in the middle of the night, I wasn't feeling my best, either. Under normal circumstances, on a Sunday morning, we'd both be taking it easy.

"Tonight," I told him. "When you get back from Wilson County, and the boys have brought in the new mattress and we have clean sheets, we'll lock and bolt all the doors and crawl in and sleep."

He nodded.

By now, we'd reached Wendell's car, and I opened the passenger door and steadied Rafe while he maneuvered inside. It took a lot longer than usual, and when he was finally inside, he relaxed against the seat with another grunt and a grimace. "Shit."

I twisted my hands together. "Are you going to be OK?"

He smiled, but it lacked some of its usual energy. "Long as I don't have to move."

"No." I shook my head. "Please don't. Just sit there. Rest. Let Wendell and the boys do the heavy lifting."

He nodded, putting his head back against the seat. "Gonna need a painkiller soon, I think."

God. Another sign, if I needed one, that he was feeling terrible.

"Wendell will stop at the drugstore," I told him, my heart knocking hard against my ribs. I hardly ever hear him admit to weakness. "Five minutes from now, you'll be doped to the gills."

"Sounds good." The smile was tired, and his eyes half closed.

"Maybe you can take a nap on the way to Wilson County." I reached over him to buckle the seatbelt so he wouldn't rattle around. He hadn't done it himself, which might just mean that he couldn't. "It would do you good."

"Maybe." He sounded like he was already half asleep, although when Wendell opened the driver's side door, his eyes flicked open and in that direction. "Ready?"

Wendell nodded.

"Just one more second," Grimaldi said, coming to a stop next to me. "The two girls from four years ago..."

Rafe nodded.

"Can you give me a description?"

"I only saw'em for a minute." And it was four years later, which he didn't bother to point out. "One was white. Blond hair to her shoulders, blue eyes. Five-six, one-thirty. The other looked Hispanic. Shorter. Black and brown. Five-three, maybe one-ten. Long hair."

"And young," Grimaldi said.

"Nineteen. Give or take."

Grimaldi nodded, and took a step back. "Keep your phone on. We might be sending you pictures."

"Don't have a phone," Rafe said.

"Did Hernandez take it?"

He shrugged, sounding groggier by the minute. "Dunno. I didn't stop to look for it. Wallet's gone, too."

"If it's in the cabin, the crime scene crew will have found it," Wendell said, putting the car in gear. "We'll check with them. Meanwhile, send anything you find to me."

Grimaldi nodded. "Come on, Ms.... Savannah. Let's go."

She headed for her sedan. "Take care," I told Rafe, and closed the door. Wendell backed up a couple of feet and cut onto the grass to move around Grimaldi's car. They crunched down the driveway while I got into the sedan. Grimaldi cranked the engine over, and we followed. At the bottom of the driveway, they went one way and we went the other.

"So how does this work?" I asked. "Is everybody working the same case?"

She shot me a look. "Not exactly. They're looking for the guy who abducted and tortured one of their agents. I'm looking for the guy who killed a prostitute and dumped her in your bed."

"But it's the same guy. Doesn't that make it the same case?"

"Two different crimes," Grimaldi said. "You and I'll focus on the murder investigation. They'll focus on the abduction and torture. And we'll cooperate on finding the suspect."

The way she kept repeating 'torture' made me feel queasy. I realized that that's what it was—what it had been—but it's a disturbing word. I put a hand on my stomach, where the baby felt like it was doing cartwheels. Most of the morning sickness was gone now that I was a couple of weeks into my second trimester, but something like this could easily bring it back to the forefront again.

I swallowed hard. "D'you think the truck stop sells ginger ale?"

"I'm sure they do," Grimaldi said, taking a right onto Dickerson Road. "Feeling sick?"

"It's the way you keep saying 'torture.'"

"Sorry." She glanced at me. "You're not going to boot in my car, are you?"

"Hopefully not. Maybe we could talk about something else for a while?"

"Sure," Grimaldi said. "After we go to the truck stop, we'll go downtown. You'll be spending most of the afternoon in a nice air-conditioned office looking at pictures of runaways. There's a soda machine just around the corner. I'm not sure there's ginger ale, but I know we have plenty of Coke."

"That'll work, too." I could also use something to eat. Queasiness notwithstanding, the baby demanded sustenance. Hopefully, the truck stop would have something edible, as well. "So while the guys are trying to figure out where this guy Hernandez might be holed up, we're trying to find the girls Rafe thought he killed four years ago?"

"It's a long shot," Grimaldi admitted. "If they couldn't find them then, our chances of finding them now are slim."

"But they couldn't really look for them back then. Rafe was still working the case, and Wendell was backing him up."

Grimaldi nodded. "That's why we're going to try to identify them, and then match the identifications to any Jane Does we can find. Maybe we'll get lucky."

Maybe. "I won't have to look at crime scene photos, will I?"

Grimaldi glanced at me. "What's the matter? You handled the real crime scene well enough. You even went back upstairs to get your boyfriend a pair of socks."

"Only because I didn't want him to attempt the stairs again himself," I said. "He was in bad shape the first time. I'm amazed he isn't flat on his back in bed. I would be."

Grimaldi nodded. "Most people would. But he's trained himself to focus on the job. It was the same thing when he was shot last fall. Most people would have taken a day off. He let the doctors patch him up and went into cramming so he could take on the persona of Jorge Pena."

I glanced at her. "Have you ever been shot?"

"I haven't had that pleasure. Most of us go through our careers without shooting anyone, and without being shot ourselves. But I hear it hurts."

"It does." I had had the pleasure. A week or so after losing Rafe's baby last fall, I'd managed to put myself in the crosshairs of the person who killed my sister-in-law, Sheila. Rafe and I had matching bullet wounds. "I certainly wasn't up and running the next day."

Grimaldi shook her head. "No sane person is."

My lips curved. "You're telling me my boyfriend is crazy?"

"In a good way," Grimaldi said. "Sooner or later he's going to crash, though. If not sooner, then when he comes home tonight. Has anyone taught you to shoot a gun?"

I blinked. "No. Don't you just aim and pull the trigger?"

"Squeeze," Grimaldi said. "Squeeze the trigger. Although if Hernandez took your boyfriend's wallet and phone, chances are he took the weapon, too."

"There are other weapons." And if Wendell had any sense, he'd make sure Rafe got one. Rafe might not think about it—I had a feeling he might already be asleep—but Wendell had been in the business of protecting Rafe for a long time; he'd take care of things. "I can tell you right now, I'm not going to be able to stay awake all night to be on guard. I didn't sleep more than a couple of hours last night, and it's been a rough couple of days."

Grimaldi nodded. "We'll get you some protection," she told me, as she took a left onto Trinity Lane. "Your boyfriend's rookies will probably fight it out for the privilege of spending the night on your sofa, clutching a gun."

I smiled. Probably.

The underpass for Interstate 65 was at the bottom of the hill in front of us. Gabe's was on the other side. And the truck stop was coming up on our left. Grimaldi signaled, and we pulled into the parking lot.

Fourteen

I'd driven by on the road before, but I'd never made the turn around the building and into the lot. Now I looked around curiously while Detective Grimaldi slotted the car into an empty parking space and turned off the engine.

A half dozen big rigs were parked under roofs, their engines turned off, like sleeping giants. Several more were rumbling, filling the air with noise and exhaust. Burly men in jeans and ball caps stood in clusters talking, while three women with big hair and small clothes had their heads together on the other side of the parking lot.

Grimaldi headed for them. After a second, I scurried after.

Not too long ago, I had watched Grimaldi walk into a bar where a table of men scattered like cockroaches when she passed. Rafe had told me it was because she smelled like cop.

Obviously, that was a figure of speech, since as far as I could tell, she smelled more like Ivory soap and shampoo. But she had that flat-eyed cop look to her. The women saw her coming, and the youngest of the three looked like she was thinking of bolting. It took one of the others holding her back to keep her in place.

The oldest of the three raised her voice. "Something we can help you with, Officer?" She sounded like Harvey Fierstein, like her vocal chords had been exfoliated with sandpaper.

"Detective," Grimaldi said, flashing her badge. I slid to a stop next to her and gave the trio a more thorough look.

One was around my age, or maybe a few years younger, but hardened by the life she lived. Dishwater blond hair, faded blue eyes, too much makeup, and lips that were already a lot tighter than mine. I might have looked something like that if I hadn't grown up with the privileges I'd had, and it was a sobering thought.

One was older: a buxom fake redhead who must have been pushing forty, unless she, too, looked years older than she was. Which wasn't unlikely. She had brown eyes and the roots of the burgundy hair were a faded brownish gray. No longer svelte, she had a roll of fat hanging over the waistband of the cutoff jeans she was wearing, and her breasts threatened to spill out of a flaming red halter top. It clashed horribly with the hair.

The last girl—the one who had tried to bolt—was really just that: a girl. She had soft, brown hair and round cheeks, and was dressed in a short skirt and flip-flops. She even had a backpack in lieu of a purse, and looked like she might have been on her way home from high school, instead of selling herself at a truck stop off the interstate.

She also looked like the girl Rafe had described; the one who had been walking through the parking lot at Gabe's on Friday night with our dead redhead.

Grimaldi gave her a thorough look. "How old are you?"

The girl swallowed. "Eighteen."

"Can you prove that?"

She dug into the backpack, and even I could see that her hands were shaking. While she was searching for her—probably fake—ID, Grimaldi addressed the other two. "I'm looking for information about a girl. Around five-five, one-twenty. Maybe eighteen years old, but probably not. Red hair, blue eyes. She was seen walking in this direction on Friday night."

The two of them exchanged a look. The girl was still bent over her backpack, but I noticed her cheeks turning pink.

"Why d'you want to know?" the older of the women asked. I guess maybe she was—or saw herself as—the mother figure.

Grimaldi didn't pull any punches. "Because she's dead, and I need to know who she was, so I can notify her family."

There was a moment of shocked silence. Nobody spoke, but everyone blinked. The girl with the brown hair straightened, her face pale now. "Dead?"

Her voice was hardly even a whisper.

Grimaldi nodded. The girl had no ID in her hand, and I'm sure Grimaldi noticed, but she didn't say anything more about it. "I need to know who she was, and I need to know anything any of you know about what happened to her." She glanced around the parking lot, with the rumbling rigs and the clusters of men. "Why don't we go inside and get a table? This could take a while."

It wasn't a suggestion, and everyone complied. We moved across the parking lot to the door into the restaurant. Grimaldi showed her badge to the hostess, and asked for a big table out of the way. We ended up in the back corner, away from most of the hustle and bustle. When the waitress appeared with five glasses of water, I ordered a ginger ale and a turkey sandwich.

"Anyone else?" She glanced around the table.

Everyone else shook their heads, although the girl looked tempted. I smiled at her. "Why don't you have something, too? That way I don't have to eat alone."

She hesitated, just long enough for Grimaldi to say, "Make it two, please. And a pot of coffee."

The waitress nodded and withdrew. Grimaldi turned back to the rest of us. Or them, I guess I should say. "Do you know who I'm talking about, or would you like to see a picture?"

"A picture?" The girl squeaked the words out. "Of the *body*?"

Grimaldi nodded. "I should warn you, it isn't pretty. She was tortured before her throat was cut."

There was that word 'tortured' again. I lifted my glass and gulped some water, while the other three women processed the news.

"Her name was Kelly," older redhead said eventually. "She said she was nineteen, but I think she was lying."

The blonde nodded. "She said she was from Chicago, but it sounded more like Minnesota or Wisconsin to me."

"Any of you know a last name?" Grimaldi had pulled out her notebook and was writing things down.

They both shook their heads. "We don't stand on formality around here," the redhead informed her.

"What about you?" Grimaldi turned to the young brunette. She was closer to the dead girl in age—Kelly, I told myself; the dead girl's name was Kelly—so of all the prostitutes, it was most likely that the two of them had been confidantes.

The brunette looked like Bambi in the headlights, with small, white teeth sunk into her bottom lip and her eyes enormous, fringed by soft, curved lashes. She wasn't even wearing any makeup, in stark contrast to the other two, whose faces were so thickly painted I was surprised I didn't see cracks.

"I have to notify her family that she's dead," Grimaldi added.

"Her mother kicked her out," Bambi said.

Grimaldi's brows rose. "She tell you this?"

Bambi nodded. "Kelly said her mother's boyfriend came on to her. The mother blamed Kelly."

Grimaldi scribbled.

"I don't know whether it was true or not." She looked miserable. "She said it was, but..."

"Doesn't matter," Grimaldi said. "She's dead. Whatever it was, happened in the past. Did she tell you where she came from? Was she a local girl?"

Bambi hesitated, and into the pause came the waitress, with a pot of coffee and three mugs looped through her fingers. "Sandwiches coming right up," she told me as she spread the cups around and filled them up. "Ginger ale, too."

"Thank you."

"You expecting?"

I nodded.

"Must be tough being a pregnant cop."

"Oh," I said, "I'm not..."

And then I caught Grimaldi's eye and closed my mouth. She

probably wasn't supposed to take a civilian with her when she interviewed possible witnesses.

Then again, she probably wasn't supposed to stand by while I claimed—or didn't disclaim—being a cop, either.

"Milwaukee," Bambi said.

"Did either of you see her yesterday?" Grimaldi wanted to know, as the waitress came back and put a thick, white plate with a sandwich and a handful of chips on the table in front of me and in front of Bambi. I thanked her, and Bambi looked like she'd died and gone to heaven.

"Go ahead," Grimaldi told her, "eat."

She turned to the other two, who were both sipping coffee out of thick mugs of the same white stoneware. Along with the sandwiches and drinks, the question was still on the table, so when Grimaldi arched her brows, the two looked at one another.

"I saw her last night," the blonde said, as I took a bite of sandwich and chewed. Not bad, but the turkey was the packaged kind from the refrigerator section of the grocery store. Then again, it was a truck stop, so the clientele probably wasn't all that picky. Bambi certainly didn't seem to mind that it wasn't haute cuisine. "She was alive then. But I got busy, and I didn't see her again after that."

Grimaldi nodded. "You?" she asked the redhead.

She shook her head. "It was a Saturday. Busy night. I didn't see her at all."

"You?" Grimaldi asked Bambi.

Bambi swallowed. "I saw her. It was late. After midnight. We were standing there talking when this guy came up to us."

I felt a sort of buzz shiver up my spine, and I think Grimaldi must have, too, because her eyes sharpened. "I imagine a lot of guys must come up to you. What was different about this one?"

"He was creepy," Bambi said, with a shimmy. I think Grimaldi may have been tempted to roll her eyes, but if so, she resisted.

"Are you sure you're not just saying that because you know she's dead?"

Bambi shrugged.

"Can you describe him?" I asked, taking the role of good cop, since we obviously needed one.

"Old," Bambi said. "At least thirty-five. Really short hair. Brown eyes. Brown skin."

"African-American?" Grimaldi asked. She was scribbling again.

Bambi shook her head. "Not that brown."

"Tall? Short? Fat? Skinny?"

Bambi said he'd been of medium height and on the thin side, with short, dark hair and brown eyes. The description could fit fifty percent of the male population.

"I need you to come downtown with me," Grimaldi said, and corrected, with a glance at me, "with *us*, to look at some mugshots."

Bambi's eyes widened and her voice quavered. "Are you arresting me?"

This time Grimaldi did roll her eyes. "Did I say I was arresting you? I need you to look at mugshots, so we can find this guy."

Since we already knew who the guy was, I figured the detective must have some ulterior motive for wanting Bambi to go downtown. Or maybe it was procedure: we knew Hernandez was involved, but if Bambi could pick out his picture, it would be additional, and independent, proof.

"Do I have to?" She glanced at her friends.

"When the police ask you to do something," I said, "it's usually a good idea to do it."

Bambi swallowed noisily, but she nodded. Grimaldi turned to the other two. "Neither of you saw Kelly leave with anyone?"

They both shook their heads.

"Either of you work here four years ago?"

They exchanged a glance, but neither tried to deny that they were working. I kept an eye on the blonde, because I thought she might fit Rafe's description of one of the girls he'd seen with Hernandez back then. Older, yes, but it had been four years, and in the kind of life she led, I'm sure she aged more than a year every twelve months.

But she shook her head.

"I did," the redhead said.

Grimaldi focused on her. "I'm trying to track down two girls from back then, who were also in the commercial company business."

Was that what they called prostitution these days? Commercial company?

"A blonde," Grimaldi said, "and a Hispanic girl. They would have been eighteen to twenty at the time, give or take." She described them the way Rafe had, which wasn't very much help at all, considering that the descriptions could have fit any number of women. "They went off with a customer and may not have come back."

The redhead shook her head. "Can't think of anyone like that. People come and go, you know. But if a trucker took a girl with him, we woulda noticed. This is a good place to work. People care about each other here."

Bambi and the blonde both nodded. I wasn't sure whether to laugh or cry.

"There was a Hispanic girl, though," the redhead added. "Maria. But she didn't go off with a trucker. A guy in a car came and picked her up. He looked like he was Spanish, too. I figured he was her pimp. Or maybe her daddy." She shrugged. Her assets jiggled under the halter top.

"Did she come back?" Grimaldi asked. "Didn't you think that was cause for concern?"

"Listen." The redhead leaned forward across the table. "We get all kinds here. Kids who get kicked outta home, like Kelly.

Runaways, like Naomi here."

Bambi flushed. Grimaldi glanced at her, but didn't speak. The redhead continued. "Lot lizards, who've been here for years. That's their business. But I see any pimps beating on their girls, or any small kids working the trade, I tell the folks in the diner, and they call the cops."

Grimaldi nodded. "We appreciate the heads up."

"Yes'm. I don't want none of that here. This is a nice place. We take care of each other here."

"So about Maria," I said, and she turned to me.

"Like I said. This guy came and picked her up. I figured pimp, or family. I figured he took her somewhere else to work, or he took her home. Either way, it was none of my business. She didn't look like she was afraid of him."

She wouldn't have known any better, I imagined.

"But she didn't come back," Grimaldi said, and the redhead shook her head. "Any idea what her last name might have been?"

"Sorry. Like I said, we don't stand on formality around here."

"Know anything else that might pertain?"

They both shook their heads.

"Then you're free to go," Grimaldi said. She pushed away from the table, and threw a couple of bills down, enough to cover the food and coffee. And my ginger ale. "Let's move it out, ladies."

I put the rest of my sandwich down and wiped my fingertips with the paper napkin. "You couldn't wait until I've finished eating?"

"Places to go, people to see," Grimaldi said briskly. "Murders to solve."

"Yeah, yeah." I pushed back from the table.

"You can take it with you," Grimaldi said, nodding to the sandwich.

"That's OK. It wasn't all that good. And my stomach has

settled some." Although who knew how long that would last?

"Then let's get this show on the road." She stuck her hands in her pockets and looked pointedly at Bambi—Naomi—who stuffed the last of her sandwich in her mouth. Her cheek bulged like a chipmunk's.

"Nice to meet you ladies." Grimaldi put two business cards on the table for the two older prostitutes. "If you think of anything else, contact me. And if you see the guy again, the one Kelly left with last night, or the one Maria left with four years ago, don't go anywhere with him."

They both shook their heads.

"Come on." She shooed me and Naomi ahead of her toward the door to the outside. Naomi looked close to tears, and kept glancing over her shoulder to see if her friends would stop Grimaldi from taking her. Of course, neither said a word.

And then we were outside in the fresh, if hot, air, and on our way to the sedan.

"Do you have anything other than that?" Grimaldi wanted to know, nodding to the backpack slung over Naomi's shoulder. "Suitcase? Change of clothes?"

Naomi shook her head.

Grimaldi opened the door to the back seat and gestured her in. Naomi looked like she was thinking of bolting, but Grimaldi's raised brows must have convinced her otherwise. She crawled into the sedan and pulled the backpack in behind her. Grimaldi closed the door, and opened the passenger door. "Come on, Ms.... Savannah."

"Thank you, Detective." I got in and closed my door while Grimaldi walked around the car to the driver's side. In the back, Naomi had just figured out that there was no way out of a police car, unless the police opened the door for you from the outside.

"Don't worry," Grimaldi said, eyes on the rearview mirror as she reversed out of the parking space. Or maybe she was looking at Naomi. Her next words indicated that she was. "You're not in any trouble. I just want to know if you can pick out the guy you saw."

Naomi nodded, but sniffed. Grimaldi turned to me. "Feeling better?"

"Yes, thank you. Although it wasn't necessary for you to pay for my sandwich and ginger ale."

"I'll put it on the expense account," Grimaldi said and swung the car into traffic. "Consider it payment for taking you back there."

"Back where? The house?"

"The crime scene," Grimaldi corrected.

"We have to go back there?"

"We need positive identification of the victim. I figure she's still there. Easier to take Naomi there than wait for the body to be transported to the ME's office."

I guess. Although it struck me as somewhat cold, walking a young girl into that scene.

Then again, Grimaldi was the detective and I wasn't, so she probably knew what she was doing. I settled back against the seat and tried not to think about how little I, personally, wanted to see the body again.

Fifteen

Detective Grimaldi's brilliance didn't become clear to me until we'd been in the bedroom at 101 Potsdam and Naomi had positively identified the victim as her friend Kelly. She was—to use a phrase—as white as a ghost when we walked back down the stairs, and shivering as though she'd encountered one. Grimaldi had to take her arm to steady her, and help her into the car, where she dissolved into hysterical sobbing in the back seat. I looked at Grimaldi, feeling like this had been a very bad idea, and she told me, "Give it a minute."

Sure. I sat back and prepared to wait.

By the time we reached police headquarters in downtown, not very many minutes at all from the Potsdam area, Naomi had cried herself out, and was limp and flushed like one of Dix's kids after a temper tantrum. She didn't say a word when Grimaldi extricated her from the back seat and walked her into the building. She didn't say a word when we walked into Grimaldi's office and she put Naomi in one of the chairs in front of the desk and handed her a box of tissues, either.

"I'll go get Savannah settled," she told Naomi, "with the computer next door."

I nodded.

"But before we do that, I want you to understand something." She waited for Naomi to look up before continuing. "That could have been you back there. I'm sure you realize that."

Naomi's eyes overflowed, and she nodded rapidly.

"For reasons of his own, he wanted a redhead last night. If he hadn't, he might have picked you. You're just his type. His likes young women. And he likes doing what he did to your friend."

Naomi nodded, sobbing again.

"I don't want to go to work tomorrow morning and have to ask one of your friends at the truck stop to identify *your* body."

Naomi shook her head. Tears spattered.

"I want you to stay here and think about that," Grimaldi said, "while I go next door with Savannah. When I come back, we're going to have a talk. About where you came from and what you're doing here and what made you leave. And whether there's a reason you can't go back, or whether I just need to buy you a one-way ticket home." She paused for long enough to let that sink in before she added, "But one thing I'm not doing, is sending you back out there for this nut-job to find. Not only are you just the type he likes, he knows you saw him yesterday. I wouldn't be surprised at all if he came back for you tonight."

She didn't wait for Naomi to answer, just turned to me. "Let's go."

We went. Out of the room and into the corridor with the sound of Naomi's terrified sniffles in our ears.

"She's lucky," I said.

Grimaldi nodded. "I don't know whether she has any idea how lucky, but I think showing her the body went some way toward driving that point home."

Yes, indeed. "I hope she has somewhere safe to go. That she isn't from an abusive home or anything. Or that she wasn't kicked out, like she said Kelly was."

Grimaldi nodded. "There are places I can put her if she doesn't have a home to return to. But I hope so, too."

She opened the door to the computer room. I'd spent some time there before, looking through mugshots. It had been last fall, with Rafe in the wind and another scary Hispanic man hanging around, looking for him. A few hours of searching had helped me pinpoint Jorge Pena. Now I guess I'd get to do it again.

"First thing I want you to find me," Grimaldi said, showing me to a work station, "is a mugshot of Eugenio Hernandez, and mugshots for at least five other men that look similar. It doesn't matter who they are or what they did; they're just there to make sure she can pick out Hernandez."

I nodded and took a seat. "What if she can't?"

"Let's hope it doesn't come to that." Grimaldi leaned in to get the computer set up for me. "We can make the connection between your boyfriend and Hernandez without it, but I'd appreciate a positive ID." She straightened. "The printer is over there in the corner. When you have your six or eight printed out, bring them to my office so she can look at them."

I nodded.

"After that, you'll start looking at runaways and Jane Does."

Lucky me.

"I'm on it," I said, flapping a hand. "Go. Deal with her."

"Don't take too long." Grimaldi headed for the hallway. I stuck out my tongue, but didn't say anything. She closed the door, and I turned to the computer.

Finding a picture of Eugenio Hernandez was a simple task. He was in the system from when he was arrested four years ago. There was even an updated photo from just a month ago, before he was released.

In both, a set of hooded, dark eyes peered out at me from under heavy brows. He'd had very little hair even before he was arrested: just dark fuzz covering his skull. The nose was long and appeared hooked, and the mouth was wide but the lips thin. It wasn't a handsome face, and I thought I could see cruelty in it, although that could have been my imagination, and based on what I knew about him. He certainly wasn't someone I'd want to get involved with, and if I'd been forced to sell my body at truck stops, his wasn't a car I'd have wanted to get into. But I guess when you're in that position, you can't be picky.

I printed out both pictures, and then went to work finding others I could put with them. That didn't take long, either, since there were a lot of Hispanic or Hispanic-looking men in their thirties in the database. I even came across Jorge Pena, and decided I might as well add him to the mix. He was dead, but Naomi didn't know that, and he fit the general description of the guy who had driven off with Kelly last night. I knew from experience that he was taller than medium height—if an inch or two shorter than Rafe—but that wasn't part of the mugshot, either.

Ten minutes might have passed before I walked back into Grimaldi's office with my stack of photos. "Here you... Oops. Sorry."

The detective was on the phone, and put up a finger to tell me to wait. I tiptoed past the desk and took a seat in the chair next to Naomi. The girl was still clutching a soggy tissue, her eyes rimmed with red and her nose swollen, but she'd stopped crying and was watching Grimaldi intently, her expression halfway between hopeful and scared.

I must have come in just after the detective dialed, because the first thing that happened was that she introduced herself. "This is Detective Tamara Grimaldi with the Nashville PD."

There was a slight pause, and quacking from the phone. Grimaldi nodded. "Yes, ma'am. Nashville, Tennessee. I'm looking for Mr. or Mrs. Bradford."

The phone quacked again, more frantically.

"Yes, Mrs. Bradford," Grimaldi said. "It's concerning Naomi."

Quack, quack.

"No, ma'am. She's not in any trouble."

Quack. Quack, quack, quack-quack-quack.

"Homicide," Grimaldi said. And waited.

The phone was silent.

"As I was saying, your daughter is not in any trouble." I don't think I imagined the slight emphasis on the possessive pronoun. "Another girl her age was murdered last night."

She didn't say it, but the implication was that another family would be getting this same phone call, but their daughter wouldn't be all right.

"Naomi saw the killer, and is helping us identify him."

The phone quacked again, more subdued this time.

"Yes, Mrs. Bradford," Grimaldi said. "Your daughter wants to come home."

Next to me, Naomi nodded vigorously.

"Is there any reason she wouldn't be welcome?"

Quack. Quack-quack-quack!

"That's good to know," Grimaldi said. "I'll be putting her on a bus leaving Nashville this afternoon. I don't know how long it will take her to reach you, but I'll call you back when she's on her way, and you can call your local bus station and check with them on arrival times."

Mrs. Bradford went off on a long speech, and from Grimaldi's grimacing, I rather thought it was a whole heap of gratitude. "Yes, ma'am," she said when she could get a word in edgewise. "I'll have her contact you when she's free. Yes, ma'am. Yes. Thank you."

She didn't heave a sigh of relief when she got Mrs. Bradford off the phone, but I could tell she wanted to. "Your parents have been worried about you," she told Naomi, who had tears rolling down her cheeks again now. "You shouldn't do this to people who love you."

Naomi shook her head. And I guess Grimaldi must have decided she'd torn the girl down far enough, because she didn't push any farther, just gestured for the pictures. I handed them over, and she looked through them. "Very nice. Naomi."

Naomi nodded, and Grimaldi spread the pictures out across the desk. "I want you to look at these and tell me if any of them look like the man who left with Kelly last night."

It only took a second. "Him," Naomi said.

"You're sure?"

Naomi nodded. "He drove a blue van. The kind with no windows in the back."

Further corroboration, had we needed it.

"Thank you." Grimaldi shuffled the pictures back together and put them on a corner of her desk. I put the older picture of Hernandez, the one I had held back, on top.

"I thought that might come in handy if you go back to the truck stop to see if the woman with the red hair can identify the man who left with Maria."

Grimaldi nodded. "Good. Thank you. You know what to do now?"

I did. "Look up Jane Does and runaways from four years ago. Cull the blondes and the girls who might be Maria."

"Thank you," Grimaldi said, and went back to Naomi. "What I'm going to do, is type up a statement of everything you've told me. When it's finished, I'll print it out and you'll read it and, if you agree with it, sign it. Then I'll take you to the bus station."

Naomi nodded. And that's all I saw and heard, because I closed the office door behind me and headed back to the computer room and my search.

The next hour was a quiet one, interrupted only by the humming of the computers, the clicking of the printer when I used it, and occasional muted voices from outside the door. I don't think the police ever really shut down, but they must be operating with a diminished crew on Sundays, because the computer room was empty aside from me.

The first thing I did, even before starting Grimaldi's search for runaways and Jane Does Hernandez may have killed four years ago, was to access the property databases I had promised Wendell I'd check, to see if I could track down the owner of the cabin in Wilson County for him.

It didn't take long. All I had to do was access the courthouse records system for Wilson County, engage the mapping function, and then pick my way over the terrain and the directions Wendell had provided, until I had pinpointed the location of the cabin itself.

Once that was done, I switched from graphic to satellite image, and then to street view. There were a lot of trees in the way, but I was able to catch a glimpse of a shadowed one-story building with deep-set windows and a low-slung roof.

It looked sinister, as hooded and evil as Hernandez himself, although that, too, could just be my imagination.

The owner of record was a man named Judd Lincoln. And since his name was highlighted in blue, indicating he owned other property, I clicked it. And lo and behold, I discovered that he also owned a house in Nashville. By clicking on that record and going to street view, I was able to determine that Judd Lincoln owned the house in Woodbine that Eugenio Hernandez had told his parole officer was his address in Nashville.

Since I'd gone this far, I figured I might as well run Judd Lincoln's name through the mugshot database. Maybe I'd get lucky, and he was a jailhouse buddy of Hernandez's.

But there I struck out. There was no Judd Lincoln with a criminal record in the state of Tennessee. Plenty of other Lincolns, but when I cross referenced, none had either the house in Woodbine or the cabin in Wilson County as their address of record.

Still, it was a nice coincidence, and I called Wendell and presented it to him like a Siamese cat with a dead mouse. He gave me the requisite pat on the head. "Good work."

"Thank you," I said. "I looked him up in the database—I'm downtown in Detective Grimaldi's computer room—but he didn't show up as ever having been arrested."

"It's good work anyway," Wendell told me.

"Thank you. We found a girl who saw the dead girl—her name was Kelly—leave with Hernandez last night. She identified him from his mugshot."

"That'll help when we go to court. We all know he did it, but someone who can put him with the girl will be helpful."

"And we have a lead on one of the missing girls from four

years ago. One of the other hookers said that a Hispanic girl named Maria got into a car with a Hispanic man and never came back. That doesn't mean she's dead—"

"No," Wendell agreed.

"But I'm going to start looking through the database for missing persons and Jane Does, to see if I can find her."

"Good," Wendell said.

"How's Rafe?"

"Asleep," Wendell said. "He dropped off on the way out here. No point in waking him up yet."

No. The more rest he got, the better. "He's safe, right?"

"I'm looking at him. He's sleeping like a baby."

"No chance that Hernandez will sneak up on him and finish the job?"

"No," Wendell said. "We're keeping him covered. And I don't think Huron's out here anymore. But we gotta check."

"Where do you think he is?"

"Dunno," Wendell said, "but I think he used the cabin Friday night and Saturday. He might even have come back last night. But I think once he saw that Rafe was gone, he woulda left and he wouldna come back again."

I nodded, not that he could see me.

"If he had sense," Wendell added, "he'd be halfway to Miami by now."

"I hope he is," I confessed. "He's scary. I'd really like to believe he's gone, and that he won't be coming after Rafe again." Or after me.

"We'd all like that," Wendell said, but without trying to reassure me that it was so.

"You don't think he is," I said, "do you?" And clarified, "Halfway to Miami?"

"I'd like to think so," Wendell said, "but no. I think he's here, looking to finish the job he started."

"So he'll be coming after Rafe again."

"Or you," Wendell said. "Harder on the boy if it's you. Always harder when it's someone you care about. We'd all rather take the hit ourselves."

Yes, but if Hernandez got his hands on Rafe again, he'd kill him. And I certainly didn't want that.

Not that I wanted him to get at me, either. Or anyone else that Rafe cared about.

That was very few people, in the scheme of things. Me. His grandmother. David. Whom I still hadn't contacted to tell him that Rafe was back.

"I need to get off the phone and call Ginny Flannery," I told Wendell. "Rafe has only known about David since last fall, long after Hernandez went to prison. Hopefully Hernandez doesn't even know that David exists. But it depends on how long he was following Rafe around before he grabbed him. Rafe and David went to a ballgame together week before last. If Hernandez was following them then, he would have seen David. And while he might not have realized Rafe is David's father—he might think they're brothers, or something—he'd have been able to tell that they're related."

"Go," Wendell said. "Call. I'll keep an eye on your boyfriend. And I'll call the nursing home and put them on alert, too, in case he tries for Miz Jenkins."

"Thank you." The idea of Hernandez getting hold of Mrs. Jenkins was abhorrent. The idea of him getting hold of anyone was abhorrent, but she was a sweet, confused, old lady. She wouldn't understand what was happening, and how dangerous he was, until it was much too late.

David probably wouldn't stand much of a chance either, against a full-grown man, but he was a smart kid, and good at taking care of himself. He'd sense the danger and might be able to get away.

"Let me know what else you find out," Wendell said.

I told him I would, and hung up. And this time I really did

dial Ginny Flannery's number

By now, we were halfway through the day on Sunday. I figured that was enough time for Ginny and Sam, devout church-goers, to do their Sunday morning thing, including brunch. At the very least, I wouldn't be interrupting the sermon.

I figured Ginny would answer the phone. She didn't. It went straight to voicemail. And under any other circumstances, I don't think I would have thought twice about that. The circumstances being what they were, I admit it worried me, even if I told myself, and mostly managed to convince myself, that Eugenio Hernandez had no way of even knowing who Sam and Ginny Flannery were, let alone where to find them.

The longer this was going on, the more people I realized were in danger.

"Hi, Ginny," I told the phone, taking care not to sound too tense, but unable to sound entirely breezy, either, "this is Savannah. I just wanted to give you an update. Rafe's back. A bit worse for wear, but he'll be OK. The hospital patched him up and sent him home."

No sense in mentioning that he had sent himself home, most likely against doctor's orders.

"So you can tell David not to worry. And... um... there's something going on, so it wouldn't be a bad idea to keep everyone at the camp on alert. It isn't Rafe they have to worry about, and I honestly don't know that this guy even knows who David is... anyway, it won't hurt to tell everyone to be extra careful."

Hard to know how much to tell her over the phone. Hard to decide how much was too much, and whether telling her more rather than less would make her more or less likely to worry.

"Call me if you have any questions," I finished, turning to the door as the handle turned. "Hope you're OK. Talk to you soon."

I hung up, just as Grimaldi poked her head through. "We're done."

"I'm just getting started," I said. "But I've tracked down the name of the owner of the cabin in Wilson County, which happens to be the same as the owner of the house in Woodbine."

"That's quite a coincidence."

"Or no coincidence at all. I called Wendell and told him. And I called Ginny Flannery and left a message telling her that Rafe's back, but that she should continue to keep a close eye on David."

Grimaldi nodded. "I'm going to run Naomi down to the bus station and put her on the bus. There's a departure for Milwaukee in forty minutes. Once I know she's safely onboard where Hernandez can't get to her, I'll be back."

"You want me to stay here?" By myself?

"You may as well," Grimaldi said. "No chance he'll get at you here."

I guess not. "Are you afraid he's after Naomi?"

"She can identify him," Grimaldi said. "She *did* identify him. And she's just his type. I wouldn't be surprised if he came back for her. And we have no idea where he is. He could have been watching the house all morning. He could have followed us to the truck stop and watched us pick her up. He could follow us to the bus station."

He could. "I'll stay here," I said. Grimaldi would have her hands full protecting Naomi. No sense in giving her—or Hernandez—another target she had to keep an eye on.

She nodded. "I'll be back within the hour. Try to get me something good."

She withdrew before I could respond. "Yes, ma'am," I grumbled, but the door had already closed. I turned my attention to the computer and the database of missing teenagers and young women.

Sixteen

Thirty minutes later, I had a list of blond and Hispanic runaways and missing persons as long as my arm. Several of the Hispanic girls were named Maria, and one of the blondes was, too. I printed out the Hispanic Marias, and since the blonde fit Rafe's description, I printed her out, as well, along with a handful of other blondes I thought might have been the girl he'd seen. Plus a few Hispanic girls who weren't named Maria, but who had long hair and the right height and weight. Then I got to work looking at Jane Does, from now back to four years ago. There were fewer of those, but still too many. By the time Grimaldi walked back through the door, I was up to my elbows—metaphorically speaking—in dead girls.

When I first heard them, the footsteps in the hallway startled me. So far, it had been quiet out there, and I'd been deep into reading about young women and all the bad things that can happen to them. One Jane Doe was bludgeoned to death, her face unrecognizable, even after the forensic anthropologist from the Body Farm at UT Knoxville had had a go at piecing the skull together. There were just too many tiny fragments to recreate her face accurately. Another had had gasoline poured over her and most of her face had burned away, while a third had suffered a shotgun blast to the face that had rendered her impossible to ID. And then there were the two who were too badly decomposed—one reduced to just bones—by the time anyone found them.

I was jittery. And then I heard footsteps outside. Slow footsteps. Footsteps that stopped outside the door. A second passed, and the doorknob started to turn. By the time the door opened, I was staring at it like a rabbit does a snake; wide-eyed and ready to bolt.

Grimaldi's hand went immediately to her gun, and she looked around the room. "What's wrong?"

"Nothing." I took a breath. And then another. "Just jumpy. This is unpleasant reading."

Grimaldi holstered the gun again and hiked a hip up on the edge of the desk. "Have you found anything?"

"Too many things." I blew out a breath and turned back to the task at hand now that my heart had settled back into rhythm. "There's a stack of pictures on the printer of runaways and missing persons who fit the descriptions of the girls Rafe saw. Three of them are named Maria. Two Hispanics and one blonde."

"The girl the prostitute told us about was Hispanic," Grimaldi said, taking her hip off the desk to walk over to the printer.

"But we don't know that the girl the hooker saw and the girl Rafe saw were the same."

"True." She started flipping through sheets of paper.

I leaned back on my chair. "Naomi get off OK?"

Grimaldi nodded. "She's on the bus bound for Milwaukee. Whether she gets there or not is up to her. I can't stop her from getting off somewhere between here and there. But she's as safe as I could make her. There was no sign of Hernandez."

"Do you think she'll get off the bus between here and Milwaukee?"

"Depends," Grimaldi said, her attention still on the print-outs. "If she told the truth and there's no reason why she can't go home, she'll probably just go home. If she lied, then she might not get there."

"Do you think she lied?"

Grimaldi shrugged. "She sounded truthful. But kids who have grown up with abuse get very good at lying. She had a reason for leaving. She might just have been going with her friend Kelly when Kelly's mother kicked her out of the house, but there might be more to it."

"Maybe Naomi's the one whose mother kicked her out of the house, and Kelly went with her."

Grimaldi nodded. "Maybe. When I spoke to the mother, I didn't get the feeling that anything was going on at home, but abused wives get good at lying, too. I'm going to put in a call to Milwaukee PD, just in case."

"That sounds like a good idea," I said. "In addition to the runaways and missing persons you're looking at, I've been checking out unidentified dead women."

Grimaldi lowered the papers and came to look over my shoulders. "Anything?"

"Not much. Two in the past four years. One in Cheatham County, one in Wilson."

"Wilson," Grimaldi said.

I nodded. "The woman from Rutherford County isn't someone we're looking for. She was black, thirty to thirty-five. That doesn't mean Hernandez couldn't have killed her, but she was also killed during the time he was in prison. Body discovered eight months ago, killed within three days of being found."

"What about the Wilson County woman?"

"Found three years and two months ago. Skeletonized." So killed long enough ago that her body had decomposed completely. "No clothes found with her, so she was naked when she was killed."

"Or when she was dumped," Grimaldi said.

I nodded. "She was found in a wooded area not too far from Highway 70, by a man walking a dog."

And the less I thought about the details of that, the better it would be.

"That could be her," Grimaldi said. "Do we know cause of death?"

I shook my head. "If it was Hernandez, and he used a knife, he didn't nick any of her bones."

Grimaldi nodded.

"The Body Farm at UT Knoxville did a facial reconstruction. This is what they think she looked like." I pulled the reconstruction up on the screen. A pretty face with blue eyes and high cheekbones looked back at me. "They gave her blue eyes because they say her hair was blond, but they don't know that she actually had blue eyes. Apparently there wasn't enough left for that."

And again, eewww.

"But we could have Rafe look at it, to see if he recognizes her."

"Can't hurt," Grimaldi said. "Let's see if we can narrow it down first, though. Go ahead and print her out."

I did.

"We'll take all of them back to the truck stop and see if we can get an identification on Maria, at least. And the thing is that just because your boyfriend only saw Hernandez with two—plus Ginger—doesn't mean there weren't more."

"I didn't think about that," I said.

"Think about it now." Grimaldi headed for the printer and then the door. "Let's go."

I scrambled to my feet and followed.

Five minutes later we were in the car. Ten minutes later, just as we were making the turn onto Trinity Lane and could see the truck stop ahead, my phone rang.

"Savannah." Ginny Flannery's voice was tense.

I smiled at the phone, since it's supposed to convey. "Hi, Ginny. Everything OK?"

"No," Ginny said. "David's gone."

That wiped the smile right off my face, of course. "What do you mean, he's gone?"

Grimaldi glanced at me, but kept driving.

"He's gone," Ginny said, her voice creeping toward

hysterical. "He went to bed last night, and when the others woke up this morning, he was gone."

I glanced at the clock on Grimaldi's dashboard. "It's almost two. Why are you just telling me this now?"

"I've been busy," Ginny said, with a heavy dose of 'duh' in her voice. "I didn't think about it."

"You didn't think Rafe might like to know that his son's missing?"

Grimaldi shot me another look, this one with arched brows.

There was a pause on the other end of the line. Then— "*My* son," Ginny said.

I rolled my eyes. "Of course he's your son. Nobody's disputing that. That's why you're out there and we're only hearing about this now. But Rafe's his biological father. You might have considered letting him know."

"Until you called," Ginny said, "I had no idea he was back."

She had a point. "Sorry," I said. "I should have called you earlier. He came back in the middle of the night, and then we had to go to the hospital, and when we got home—"

There'd been the dead body in my bed. Although now wasn't the time to bring that up. Ginny had enough on her mind. "Where is he?" I asked instead. "David?"

"If we knew that," Ginny told me, "he wouldn't be gone, would he?"

I took a breath while I pinched the bridge of my nose. And then I took another. *She's a mother whose child is missing. Be patient.* "Have you called in the local police?"

Ginny said they had. "The local firemen are combing the woods for him. In case he walked in his sleep and left the cabin and got lost. He used to do that sometimes when he was little." Her voice cracked. "Once, he fell down the stairs."

As long as he hadn't walked into the lake and drowned. Although the cool water would have woken him up if he'd tried, wouldn't it?

More likely, if he'd been sleep-walking, that he'd wandered away and had either gotten lost, or had fallen into a ravine or something and hurt himself, so he couldn't make it back.

And then there was the third option, which was that Hernandez had him. But that was also something Ginny didn't need to hear right now.

"We'll be there as soon as we can," I said, as Grimaldi pulled the car to a stop behind the diner. "I'm not sure how much help we'll be—" Me in my summer dress and sandals and Grimaldi in her dark suit; it wasn't like we could walk through the woods in an area we didn't know dressed like that, "but maybe there's something we can do."

"Sam's out looking," Ginny said, and now I could hear the exhaustion in her voice. "I'm waiting here, in case he comes back."

"Nobody heard or saw anything?"

"Nothing. They're saying one of the bikes is missing, but they're not sure."

David had run away once before, the day after Dix and I had gone to Ginny and Sam's house to tell them that David was Elspeth's heir. He'd been eavesdropping, and had gotten an earful, some of which must have come as a shock to him. That was the first time he heard that he was adopted, and wasn't Sam and Ginny's biological son.

The next afternoon after school, he'd taken off instead of going to sports practice. He'd made it to the bus station in downtown Nashville, and from there had made it to Columbia, and to Damascus, where Elspeth had grown up. He'd crept into her house—his house by then, I guess—through a basement window, and had looked around. And then he'd 'borrowed' her bicycle to make his way to Sweetwater and the Bog, the trailer park where Rafe had grown up. That's where we'd found him, sleeping on the floor in Rafe's room, before dawn the next morning.

The missing bicycle sounded familiar.

"Sounds like maybe he just took off," I said, wishing I dared believe it. "Maybe I scared him when I told him Rafe was missing, and he wanted to come home and see what he could do to help."

It was a nicer scenario than either of the other two: stuck in a ravine with a broken leg, or tied to a chair with Eugenio Hernandez making holes in him.

"Maybe." But Ginny didn't sound encouraged. And I knew why. Even if David had taken off on his own, on a borrowed bicycle, he'd started out hours from home, two counties away, in the dark. It was anyone's guess what might have happened to him between Peaceful Pines and Nashville. Someone could have grabbed him, someone entirely unrelated to Eugenio Hernandez; just another creep who happened to like young boys. Or a car could have hit him and he could be lying dead in a ditch somewhere. Or in a hospital bed, on life support.

Or maybe he'd simply gotten lost.

It must have been twelve hours since he left camp. Probably more. Would a trip that took an hour and a half by car, take more than half a day by bike?

For a twelve-year-old boy, one who had to stick to the secondary roads because bicycles aren't allowed on the interstates, it might. Then again, in the middle of the night, he might risk the interstate, since it would be faster and nobody was likely to see him anyway.

"Let me call Rafe," I said. "He and four other TBI agents are out in Wilson County. They're closer to you than we are. Maybe they can help search."

Ginny didn't say anything. Maybe she was nodding, maybe not.

"And let me know what you find out."

She said she would, and we hung up.

"Missing?" Grimaldi said.

I nodded. "It sounds like he left in the middle of the night on a bike. But there's a chance someone took him. Or the bike could be a red herring, and he could be lost in the wood." Or dead, in the woods or elsewhere.

"The police are involved?"

"That's what she said. And the local fire department is out looking for him. I need to call Rafe."

"Are you sure that's a good idea?"

I looked at her, and she added, "He's injured. The last thing you want him to do, is crash through the woods in his condition. And you know he's going to want to do just that."

She was right about that. However— "David's his son," I said. "He's going to want to know. If I don't tell him, he'll be very upset with me."

Grimaldi nodded and reached for her door handle. "You go ahead and update them. I'll go talk to our friend over there, and see if she can identify anyone."

"I'll be right there," I said, dialing, while Grimaldi opened the door and took her ream of paper outside.

"Take your time."

She closed the car door. I watched her in the rearview mirror, making her way across the parking lot to where the redheaded prostitute was standing, while I listened to Wendell's phone ring in my ear.

"Craig."

"It's me," I said. "David's gone."

"Who?"

"Rafe's son. Ginny and Sam Flannery's kid." I explained where David was—or rather, where he had been, up until the middle of the night—and what had happened since then. There was no need to lay out the possibilities of what might have happened to him. Wendell knew them, better than I did. "They're combing the woods for him," I said. "The local police and the fire department are out there. I'm sure the camp counselors and the other kids are helping, too."

"Sounds like they got it covered."

"If you can convince him of that," I said, not bothering to specify who 'he' was, "I'd appreciate it."

"Dunno about that, darlin', but I'll give it a try. You said there's a bike missing?"

"They think there is. I think maybe he borrowed it and set out for home, because he was worried about Rafe and wanted to help look for him. How is he?"

"Still asleep," Wendell said. "Those are some strong drugs they gave him. I'll call the boys in, and then we'll wake him up and head out to this place and see what we can do."

"We'll probably do the same." Unless I could convince Grimaldi to drive the back roads of Wilson and Smith counties, on the off-chance that we'd run into him. "We're back at the truck stop with some pictures that we'll be running by the woman who's been working here for the past four year. After that, we'll be headed out your way, too."

"Keep me posted," Wendell said, and hung up. I did the same and exited the car.

By the time I reached them, Grimaldi and the redhead were already busy looking at pictures. Grimaldi kept showing them, and the redhead kept shaking her head. "No. Never saw her. No. No. Wait."

Grimaldi moved the page back. I craned my neck and saw that it was one of the Hispanic Marias. The redhead nodded. "That's her."

"Maria?"

The redhead nodded.

"The same Maria you saw getting into a car with an unidentified Hispanic male four years ago."

"That's right."

"You're sure?"

"Positive." The redhead tapped a finger on the paper. The nail had once been painted coral, but was mostly chipped now. "See this scar right here?" It was at the corner of one eye. "She said she got it when she fell off a bike when she was eight. Her eyebrow's a touch higher on that side, see?"

Grimaldi nodded. So did I.

"Good," Grimaldi said. "Anyone else you recognize?"

She flipped through the rest of the pictures, but the redhead didn't pick anyone else out. Grimaldi shuffled them to the bottom of the stack and began spreading the pictures of the men across the hood of the nearest car. "Do any of these guys look like the man you saw her leaving with?"

This time she kept the older picture of Hernandez in the mix, and left the new one out.

The redhead pondered. I held my breath until I couldn't hold it anymore, and then tried to let it out as unobtrusively as possible. It wasn't unobtrusive enough, because Grimaldi gave me a look.

"Sorry," I said.

She shook her head and went back to watching the redhead examine the pictures.

It must have taken close to two minutes, which doesn't sound like a long time, but which felt like an eternity. Finally she lifted a finger. "Him."

"You sure?"

"Looks like him. Don't look like any of the others."

"Thank you," Grimaldi said, and gathered the pictures.

The redhead folded her arms, pushing already impressive breasts up to impossible heights. "That the same guy that killed Kelly?"

"We believe so," Grimaldi said. "If you see him, please let me know. And don't get in the car with him."

"Can I keep that?" The redhead nodded to the papers in Grimaldi's hand. "And share it with the others?"

Grimaldi hesitated, but in the end, I guess she couldn't see a downside to putting the women Hernandez would be stalking on alert. It wasn't like we couldn't get another picture of him if we wanted one, or like he thought we didn't know who he was. "Take this. It's more recent."

She handed over the release photo. The redhead looked at it. "I'll post it inside," she said. "Make sure everyone sees it. The waitresses and the truckers, too. If he comes back here, we'll get him."

"You mean, you'll detain him and call me."

The redhead looked at her for a second before she spoke. "Yeah. That's what I mean. We'll call you. After we detain him."

Grimaldi nodded, satisfied. I think she knew as well as I did that if Hernandez showed up here, the redhead's way of detaining him would be beating him with her purse until he was unable to walk away, but it seemed fair. "Just keep him alive. I need to ask him some questions."

The redhead nodded. "Yes, ma'am. We'll keep him alive. We'll just make him wish he was dead."

No doubt.

Seventeen

"I need to get to Peaceful Pines," I told Grimaldi when we were back in the car. "If you don't want to go, you can drop me off at home and I'll drive myself out there."

Grimaldi nodded. "It isn't that I don't want to go, but I have a homicide to deal with. The brass doesn't like me to put off solving it."

I wasn't surprised.

"And I haven't notified next of kin yet, because I prioritized getting the information Naomi had, and then making sure she was safe. I need to do that."

Yes, she did. Kelly's mother deserved to know that her daughter was dead, even if she had kicked her out of the house.

"I can't believe a mother would do that," I said. "I mean, here's Ginny Flannery, who isn't even David's biological mother, losing her mind because he's missing." And Rafe, who hadn't known David existed a year ago, doing the same. Not to mention me, who was neither biological nor adopted mother, going crazy, as well. "And there's Kelly's mother, throwing her daughter out of the house. And over a man!"

A man who, whether he'd come on to Kelly or she had come on to him, was slime either way, if he'd touched her.

Grimaldi shrugged. "It takes all kinds."

Yes, it did. And I should know better. As I've matured, and grown out of the insular bubble I was raised in, I've realized I'm one of the lucky ones. Not everyone grew up as privileged as me—and I'm not using the word 'privileged' in the economic sense, although I was that, too. My mother might be a bit of a pill, especially when it came to my boyfriend, but she'd never kick me out of the house. I've never doubted that she loves me, even if she shows that love in mysterious ways sometimes.

"Sorry," I said. "I just... Mother irritates me, and I forget how lucky I am to have had parents who loved me and took care of me."

Grimaldi nodded, but a shadow crossed her face, and I remembered, a second too late, that she was one of the unlucky ones, as well. She hadn't been neglected or unloved, not that I knew about, but her mother had died when she was young, so her childhood after that might not have been a bed of roses, either.

But apologizing, or saying anything about it, would just make it worse, so I simply told her, "Yes, please. You can drop me off at home and I'll drive myself to Peaceful Pines. That way you can get busy on your case."

Grimaldi nodded, but kept niggling at it. "If you think there's something I can do..."

"I don't." I shook my head. "I don't think there's anything I can do, either. I think everything anyone can do, is being done. I just have to be there."

To give moral support. And to keep Rafe from deciding to take matters into his own hands. The last thing I wanted was for him to get it into his head that he could find David when no one else could. He was in no condition to go hiking across the Cumberland Plateau.

And anyway, I suspected they wouldn't find David by searching the woods. I knew they had to try; I just didn't think he was there.

"Would you mind if I work this out while we drive?" I asked Grimaldi, who shook her head. "Whatever happened to David—or whatever David did—happened in the middle of the night. Ginny said they went to bed, and when they woke up, he was gone."

Grimaldi nodded.

"They're children between ten and sixteen—at least that's

what they looked like when I was at Peaceful Pines yesterday—so chances are they had a curfew no later than midnight."

Grimaldi nodded.

"Naomi said it was after midnight when Hernandez came to the truck stop and picked up Kelly. At midnight, he might still have been working on Rafe."

Grimaldi glanced at me. I continued. "Although he probably wasn't. The cabin would be at least thirty minutes away, wouldn't you think?"

She nodded. "Most likely. Not much less. Could be more."

"It would have taken Rafe at least a few minutes to get free and out of there after Hernandez left him. I imagine that knife was driven pretty hard into the table, and it must have hurt pulling it up. I don't think it would have been a matter of seconds."

Grimaldi shook her head.

"And then he had to pull it out of his arm—" With his teeth. *Gah!* "—and use it to cut the ropes on his other arm, and probably his feet. That would have taken more time. And then he said he walked twenty or thirty minutes before he found the truck."

Grimaldi nodded.

"It would have taken a minute or two to hotwire it, I imagine, since one of his hands must have been fairly useless by then."

"I'd think so," Grimaldi said.

"Then he drove toward Nashville. Say another thirty minutes before the car broke down on the side of the road. That's at least an hour from the time Hernandez left; maybe more like an hour and a half."

Grimaldi nodded. She turned on her signal and put her foot on the brake. We made the turn onto Potsdam Street.

"It must have taken him another hour to walk home after that. Maybe more."

Grimaldi nodded.

"It was two-fifteen when I woke up, and I didn't get the impression he'd been there very long. That would mean Hernandez left him sometime around midnight."

"Sounds reasonable," Grimaldi said.

I thought so, too. "He must have followed Rafe to Gabe's earlier in the evening, to know where to find him. Because I don't think it was a coincidence that he was outside Gabe's the night Rafe happened to be there."

Grimaldi shook her head.

"He probably saw Kelly and Naomi cross the parking lot. And that means he saw Kelly proposition Rafe, and noticed how much she looked like Ginger. He would have known exactly where to go to find her the next day. If the drive from the cabin is somewhere between twenty and forty minutes, that would put him at the truck stop sometime between twelve-twenty and twelve-forty. Give or take."

Grimaldi nodded.

"That's the same time Naomi said he was there. After midnight."

Grimaldi nodded.

"At that point, if we're right, David was still in bed at Peaceful Pines. They probably stayed awake for a while, the way kids do, and talked, but staying up late isn't anything new to them by now. They've been at camp for a week. And he wouldn't have waited too long after everyone else was asleep, since he might have been afraid he'd fall asleep himself before he could make his getaway."

Grimaldi nodded.

"So he was most likely out of there by one o'clock. Hernandez might have had time to grab him. If he drove there directly from the cabin in Wilson County. But he wouldn't have made it to the truck stop by twelve-thirty if he did."

"No," Grimaldi agreed.

"Unless our timeline is off. If it took Rafe another hour to walk home after the truck broke down, or if Naomi was wrong about the time when Hernandez got there. All she said was that it was after midnight. That could have meant two o'clock. Or three."

Grimaldi nodded.

"But if he had David, why would he bother going after Kelly?"

David would have made a much more satisfying statement. Kelly was an instance of thumbing his nose at Rafe—*you stopped me last time, but you couldn't stop this!*—but David would have been personal. And devastating.

I imagined walking into my bedroom to find David's body on the bed, and shuddered.

"He wouldn't," Grimaldi said. And changed it to, "Probably wouldn't."

"So chances are Hernandez doesn't have him. That's good. But if he left the camp more than thirteen hours ago, shouldn't he be here by now?"

"He should," Grimaldi said. "If he decided to come to Nashville, where would he have gone once he got here?"

"To the house," I said, "if he was coming home because he wanted to help look for Rafe. And I can't think of any other reason he'd run away the same evening I told him Rafe was gone."

Unless something was going on at camp that we didn't know about, but surely that was too much of a coincidence to even contemplate.

"The crime scene crew is still there," Grimaldi said. "Or at least they haven't called to tell me they're done. We can check with them and see if they've seen him. If not your house, where else would he go?"

"Home, to the house in West Meade?"

"I can have someone check there," Grimaldi said.

"I don't really know much about his day-to-day life. His

friends, who he hangs out with. I'm sure Ginny would have checked with them, though."

Grimaldi nodded. "Anywhere else?"

"The nursing home where Mrs. J lives. Although he doesn't know her very well, so it's much more likely he'd come here. Or he might have gone to the Bog. That's where he went last time he ran away. He might have reasoned that if Rafe had changed his mind and didn't want to marry me, that's where he'd go." To the place where he'd grown up. I added, "David's twelve. He wouldn't realize that Sweetwater is the last place on earth Rafe would go if he left me."

"Makes sense," Grimaldi said. "I can call the sheriff. Or if you don't want to get him involved, you can call your brother and ask him to swing by the Bog to see if David's there."

I suppose it couldn't hurt to do that. Sweetwater's a small town. Everything's a hop, skip, and jump from everywhere else. And I wasn't really interested in getting into a conversation with Sheriff Satterfield at the moment.

Grimaldi crunched over the gravel up to the front door while I dialed. "The thing is," I said, while I waited for Dix to pick up on the other end of the line, "David has no idea that the Bog is gone. I mean, it's still there. The land. But all the trailers and shacks are gone. Ronnie Burke had them hauled away when he started laying out the plats for Mallard Meadows. Before—"

"Savannah?" Dix's voice said in my ear, and I broke off my conversation with Grimaldi.

"Dix. I need a favor."

"Sure," my brother said.

"Where are you? It sounds like you're still in the car. Aren't you home by now?"

"We went out for lunch," Dix said. "Mom and I drove to Catherine's house to pick up the girls, and then we all went out for something to eat while we updated Catherine and Jonathan on everything. We're just coming back now. I'm about to drop

Mother off at the house."

"The mansion."

"Yes," Dix said, "but that sounds so pretentious, doesn't it?"

It did. My lips curved. "Rafe calls it the mausoleum on the hill."

"I'm sure he does," Dix said dryly. "How is he?"

"Worried. David's gone."

There was a moment. I pictured Dix glancing into the back seat at his own daughters, just to make sure they were still there. Of course he knew they would be, but it would be any parent's first inclination. "Gone?"

"Went to sleep with the other campers last night. Gone by this morning. I think he ran away so he could help look for Rafe. We probably worried him when we came out to talk to him yesterday afternoon."

"What can I do?" Dix asked.

I took a breath. "I think there's a chance he might have gone to the Bog."

I laid out my reasoning, with Grimaldi nodding in the seat next to me, especially as I managed to make it a bit more succinct this time.

"So you want me to go to the Bog to look for him."

"If you don't mind," I said, while in the background, I could hear Mother murmur something.

"No," Dix said. "I don't mind at all."

"Thank you. And tell Mother thanks."

"No problem," Dix said. "What do you want me to do with him if we find him?"

"Sit on him. Put him in the car and take him home with you. Or take him to the mansion. And then call me so I can come pick him up. And so I can call everyone else and let them know he's safe."

"Consider it done," Dix said. "We're turning around right now. I'll call you when we get there."

He hung up before I had the chance to thank him.

"They're going to look for him," I told Grimaldi. "They'll call me if they find him."

She nodded.

"In the meantime, I guess I should get in my car and get going. Either way, I'll have to drive somewhere." Either to Sweetwater or, if David wasn't there, to Peaceful Pines.

"I'm going to go inside and check with the CSI team," Grimaldi said, "and then go back to the office and get busy on the reports and the notification. Keep me updated."

"Of course." I opened the car door and swung my legs out. "If Dix doesn't find him in Sweetwater, I think I'll drive out to West Meade myself, and make sure he isn't at his house before I head to Peaceful Pines." Ginny and Sam would have gotten the call that he was missing, and would have left home before David had time to get there.

"I'd be happy to send a car," Grimaldi began, but I shook my head.

"I'm sure Spicer and Truman have better things to do. And if he's at home, he's not in any danger. I'll just drive over there and make sure while I wait to hear from Dix."

"Whatever you want," Grimaldi said with a shrug, and turned toward the porch steps. "Let me know what happens."

"You do the same."

She headed up the steps, and I walked across the gravel to the Volvo and got behind the wheel. Only to realize, when I cranked the engine over, that the gas gauge was hovering perilously close to the big E.

The last thing I wanted to do, was take time out to fill gas. But if I didn't, I'd make it no more than ten miles down the road before I'd be stranded, and that wouldn't help anyone.

Luckily, there was a gas station on the way to the interstate. I drove down Potsdam to Dresden, stuck my tongue out at the Milton House on my way past, and headed out Dresden to

Dickerson Road, where I pulled in beside a pump. And because I could use some fuel, too, I went inside to pay for my gas and pick up a snack. And found myself face to face with Malcolm, the kid from two houses up, across the counter.

"Savannah!" He gave me a big, white grin. "Everything OK?"

"Not so much," I admitted, digging for my wallet to pay for the candy and gas. "Someone dumped a dead girl in my house."

That statement very effectively wiped the grin off Malcolm's face. "No shit?"

I shook my head. "None. I spent most of the night in the hospital with Rafe, and when we came back this morning, there she was."

"Shit."

Like a true Southerner, Malcolm drew the four-letter word out until it had at least three syllables. He took my debit card and swiped it through the machine.

"Thirty dollars on number two," I told him, "and the candy bar."

He started hitting buttons on the cash register, but without paying much attention. I might end up overpaying for this visit. "Who's the girl?"

"Just a random girl," I said. "Cute redhead. Sixteen. A runaway from Milwaukee turning tricks at the truck stop on Trinity Lane."

"Shit."

"I don't suppose you happened to see anything around my house this morning? Or in the middle of the night?"

"I was sleeping in the middle of the night," Malcolm said, handing me my debit card back. "Didn't see nothing."

"That's too bad. I thought maybe you'd worked late, or something."

He shook his head. "Got home before midnight last night. Didn't see nothing."

"When did you start work this morning?"

Malcolm said he'd started at seven. "Thirty more minutes." He glanced at the clock on the wall.

I did, too. It was just past two-thirty. Twelve hours since I'd found Rafe washing blood off his chest in the bathroom.

Ten minutes since I'd called Dix. Shouldn't he have called me back by now?

"Rafe's son's missing," I told Malcolm. "He was at a camp on the Cumberland Plateau, and it seems like he snuck away in the middle of the night. I don't suppose you've seen him? He looks like Rafe, but smaller. He's twelve."

Malcolm shook his head. "Ain't seen nobody. The lady down on the corner was walking her rat-dog when I went out this morning." A white Chihuahua, and silently, I agreed with Malcolm that it did bear an unfortunate resemblance to a long-legged rat. "And the Kings were headed out to church." The Kings lived on the other side of Malcolm; an elderly black couple, very active in their congregation. "Somebody working across the street."

The house across from Malcolm was a renovation object. Someone had bought it and was in the process of fixing it up, prior to moving in. I wouldn't have thought they'd be doing it before seven on a Sunday morning, however.

"That's a funny time to be doing work. Are you sure?"

"Van in the driveway," Malcolm said.

I felt a squiggle of ice down my spine. "What color?"

He squinted at me. "Blue, I think."

My heart started beating harder against my ribs. "Did you see anybody? A person?"

"Mexican guy," Malcolm said. "He was just sitting in the car when I saw him. Smoking. I guess maybe he was taking a break. Or waiting for his boss to come open the door."

It was a logical assumption. Except I didn't think this particular Mexican guy—if Hernandez was Mexican—was waiting for his boss. It was more likely he was waiting for us to come home, so he could see what happened.

I hadn't noticed the blue van there when we got home, but that didn't mean it hadn't been there. I wouldn't have thought to look for it.

Or maybe he hadn't been there by the time we came home. Maybe, in the hours between seven, when Malcolm went to work, and nineish, when we got back from the hospital, David had pedaled down the street and into the driveway.

I had made a good case for why Hernandez hadn't been able to snatch David out of bed at the church camp in the middle of the night. But there was no reason at all why he couldn't have been hanging out outside Mrs. J's house when David arrived, and why he couldn't have taken the opportunity to snatch him then. He had lost Rafe, and Kelly was dead. At that point, he must have been thrilled to find another victim.

"Thank you," I told Malcolm and grabbed my receipt. "I appreciate it."

"Sure thing, sugar."

He turned to the next customer as I hustled out of the store and over to the Volvo.

Dix still hadn't called, and while the car was filling up with gas, I defied all the posted warnings and used my cell phone to call Grimaldi to tell her what I'd just learned. "What do you think? Could David have made it here by seven in the morning? Could Hernandez have grabbed him?"

Grimaldi hesitated. "I don't know," she told me. "It seems tight. It's a long way to pedal. But maybe. If he got a ride."

"A ride?"

"There are people in this world," Grimaldi said, "who'd give a twelve-year-old on a bike a ride out of the goodness of their hearts. Just like there are people who'd grab that same twelve-year-old and hurt him. If someone picked him up—along with the bike—and shaved some time off his ride, then yes. He might have gotten there before seven. And if Hernandez was lurking, he might have taken the opportunity to snatch him."

Damn. I mean—darn.

Not that I hadn't expected it. I just didn't want it to be true. "Should I call Rafe?"

"No," Grimaldi said. "Nothing's changed. We don't know that he was here or that Hernandez grabbed him. No sense in upsetting your boyfriend unnecessarily. Any word from your brother?"

"Not yet. But I should get off the phone. In case he calls."

"Let me know what he says," Grimaldi said and hung up.

I finished filling the tank, and then headed for West Meade, where the Flannerys live.

Mrs. Jenkins's house is in East Nashville, which are the urban neighborhoods just east of downtown. West Meade, obviously, is on the other side of town, just beyond Hillwood.

I was halfway there when my phone rang. I snatched it, and pushed the button with a shaking finger. "Dix!"

"Sorry, Savannah," my brother's voice said. "He isn't here."

My heart sank. "Are you sure?"

Dix sounded about halfway between sympathetic and annoyed. "There's nowhere for him to hide, sis. All the houses are gone. It's just bare dirt and some stakes and string. We got out of the car and called his name, just in case he heard us coming and went into the trees, but he didn't respond. And since I assume he'd remember us from yesterday, and he'd realize we're not there to hurt him, he wouldn't have a reason to keep hiding."

No, he wouldn't.

"Damn," I said. "I mean... darn."

"Sorry."

I shook my head, even though he couldn't see me. "It's not your fault. I was just hoping it would be easy. My neighbor Malcolm told me he'd seen a blue van parked in a driveway across the street early this morning. If David happened to come by...”

I didn't finish the sentence. I didn't have to.

“Let's hope that didn't happen,” Dix said firmly. “What are you going to do now?”

I told him I was on my way to West Meade. “Just in case he went home.”

“Let me know when you find him.”

I promised I would, and secretly felt cheered by the 'when,' not 'if.' “Thanks for checking the Bog.”

Dix nodded. I couldn't see him, but I knew he did. “We're on our way to drop Mother at home. Then we're going back to the house for the rest of the day. Let me know if there's anything else I can do.”

I told him I would, and then I put the phone down and concentrated on driving. If David wasn't in Sweetwater, it was even more imperative that I find him, healthy and in one piece, at home.

Eighteen

West Meade is an affluent neighborhood full of large mid-century ranches and custom-designed, hug-the-hillsides contemporaries. I don't spend much time there, although I've sat the occasional open house for one of my colleagues, and shown the occasional house to clients, as well. And of course I've been to the Flannerys' before.

They live in a 1960s ranch on a road called Pennywell. The lots are all oversized, with the houses sitting back from the road, and there are a lot of trees everywhere. I couldn't see the Flannerys' house at all until I'd stepped on the gas and gunned the car up the steep driveway.

There was no sign of life. Not surprisingly, since Ginny and Sam were two hours away, at Peaceful Pines.

I looked around for a bicycle, but couldn't see one. And I had a hard time believing that David, if he had biked all night and half the day from the Cumberland Plateau, wouldn't have just tossed the bike into the nearest bush and hobbled up to the door. He wouldn't have taken the time to put it away neatly in the garage.

Still, I went up to the front door and knocked. Then I went around to the back door and knocked there, too. I called David's name. I pressed my nose to the windows, but without seeing any sign of life inside.

He might be dead asleep in his room, worn out from the long ride. But surely he wouldn't have gone to bed without first calling his parents to tell them he'd made it home safely? He was twelve, but he was neither stupid nor thoughtless. And he knew how they'd worried last time he'd run away.

I was just about to start hunting under the doormat and above the door for a key, when a voice came from somewhere to the left.

"Can I help you?"

Narrow escape. Another ten seconds, and she would have seen attempt to break and enter.

I looked in the direction of the voice, and saw a tall woman of the type usually called handsome peering at me over a hedgerow. She had short, gray hair cut close to her head, and was holding a pair of garden shears in gloved hands.

"Hi." I gave her my best smile as I made my way closer. "I'm Savannah Martin."

I dug one of my real estate business cards out of my bag and handed it over.

She looked at it. "Ginny and Sam are selling their house?"

"Oh, no. Not at all. I'm just looking for David."

Her eyes narrowed. "Why?"

I hesitated. This was a dilemma. Had Ginny and Sam told the neighbors that David was adopted?

Likely not, I figured, since they hadn't mentioned it to David himself until they'd had no other choice.

Hell—heck—as far as I knew, they hadn't even told Ginny's mother the truth. At least that's what Ginny had told me last fall. She hadn't been thrilled when Ginny married Sam—shades of my own mother and her racial prejudices—but once David was born—or adopted—she'd fallen in love with him, and had forgiven Sam the crime of being black.

I wondered whether Mother was likely to forgive Rafe for being who he was once the baby was born. It didn't seem very likely, unfortunately. Even if she had seemed rather taken with David yesterday, when they met.

Anyway, telling the suspicious lady that I was David's biological father's fiancée probably wasn't the best thing to do.

I tried another bright smile. "I'm one of his teachers."

"This says that you're a real estate agent," the neighbor said, lifting the card.

Oops. "Um..." I thought fast. "Part time job."

She didn't even bother to look like she believed me.

"Have you seen him today?" I added.

"No," the neighbor said. She didn't add, 'and I wouldn't tell you if I had,' but it was implied.

"What about Ginny and Sam? Have you seen them?"

"This morning," the neighbor said. "They went to church."

"But not David?"

"David's away at camp."

I wish. "So you haven't seen him today?"

"No," the neighbor said firmly.

"How about someone else? Has anyone else been here? Like... maybe someone in a blue van?"

She looked like she suspected me of being a few bricks shy of a load. "No one's been here. Not between the time Ginny and Sam left this morning and now. Not David. Not someone in a blue van. No one but you."

Good. "Thank you," I said. "If you should happen to see David, please have him call me. Or call me yourself."

"He's at camp, Ms. Martin."

I nodded. "I know. You said that. But if you see him, please tell him to call me. Or his mother. Or call one of us yourself."

She didn't roll her eyes, but I got the feeling she wanted to. She did not continue arguing, however. Just said, "Of course," and watched me as I walked back to my car and got in. She watched as I executed a neat eight-point turn and headed down the driveway, and she was still watching as I turned left out of the driveway and onto Pennywell. I have no doubt she continued to watch until I stopped at the stop sign at the bottom of the hill and took a right, too.

And then I was on my way back to the interstate and to Peaceful Pines, since I couldn't think of anything else I could do in Nashville, or anywhere else David might have gone, that I should check.

It had been quite disappointing to find out that he wasn't in Sweetwater. I'd been so sure I'd been right, that he'd done what he did last time he ran away, and had gone there. His reasoning had made sense, from a twelve-year-old perspective, and for someone who didn't realize that all the dwellings in the Bog were gone, courtesy of Ronnie Burke, the real estate developer who had bought the land with the intent of building an affordable housing development called Mallard Meadows there.

Was there a chance Dix may have missed him?

But no. David might have gotten out of sight when he'd heard the car. He was a smart kid. But once they started calling his name, and once he realized they were my family, the same people he'd seen with me yesterday, I didn't think he'd have continued hiding.

So he wasn't in Sweetwater.

He wasn't at camp.

Maybe Ginny was right and he really had just walked in his sleep and gotten lost. Maybe they'd find him in the woods.

But wouldn't they have found him by now? They must have been looking for four or five hours. Surely, walking in his sleep wouldn't have taken him that far from camp?

So I was back to his having stolen a bike and left. And something having happened to him on the way. A traffic accident, hit-and-run, or someone grabbing him. Hernandez or some other sick bastard.

Maybe instead of taking the direct route to Peaceful Pines, I should figure out the route David would have taken, and drive that. I didn't relish the idea of finding him dead in a ditch along the way, but horrible as it sounded, at least we'd know something.

I tried to picture the landscape in my mind, from Nashville east to the Cumberland Plateau, but there were just too many roads. So I pulled over at the next exit, and into a Cracker Barrel parking lot, where I manipulated buttons on my phone until I had found the location of Peaceful Pines. From there, I put myself in David's shoes and tried to figure out the route he would have taken back to Nashville, if he hadn't decided to risk the interstate.

Looked like maybe US Highway 70 through Watertown to Lebanon, and then state route 24 into town.

That was if he'd been going to Nashville, of course. If he'd been headed for Sweetwater, it was more likely to be SR 53 to US 70 to SR 231 to 373 through Lewisburg... and my head was already spinning. Was it even possible for a twelve-year-old to manage that? In the dark, on a bicycle?

And anyway, I was in Nashville, going to Peaceful Pines. What made sense, was for me to take Highway 70 to Lebanon and Watertown, and keep a sharp eye out along the way, for a twelve-year-old boy or an abandoned bicycle.

I was about halfway there—to Lebanon Road, Highway 70; not Peaceful Pines—when my phone rang again. Less than ten minutes had passed since I left the Flannerys' house, in other words. And when I saw that it was my mother, I was tempted to let it go to voicemail. I had a lot on my mind, and the last thing I needed—and granted, I had said that a lot today, about a lot of things—but the last thing I needed, at least at the moment, was to hear my mother's opinion of the situation and how we could all have been so amiss as to let David run away.

She wouldn't include herself in 'we all,' of course.

Not that she should. She hadn't been there. Then again, neither had I.

But if I didn't pick up now, I'd just have to call her back later, and come up with some sort of excuse for why I hadn't answered the first time. And she had cared enough to spend the night with me in scary East Nashville to provide moral support when Rafe was missing. And as I'd told Grimaldi, although I sometimes forget, I do realize how lucky I am to have a mother who loves me.

I answered the phone. "Mother." I even managed to force my lips into a smile.

"Darling," my mother said, and I could already hear the faint whiff of accusation in her voice. So I decided to nip it in the bud.

"I'm sorry. It's not that I'm not happy to hear from you and learn that you got home safe, but I'm a bit busy up here..."

"That's all right," Mother said. "This won't take long. About the child..."

"David." She had always had a problem uttering Rafe's name. Usually, she referred to him as 'your boyfriend.' In rare instances, when she couldn't avoid his name, she called him Rafael. Looked like maybe she was transferring her feelings for Rafe onto David, and was going to be giving him the same treatment. Poor kid. He couldn't help who his father was, and the fact that my mother doesn't like him.

"Yes," Mother said. "David."

"He's still missing. I'm on my way out to Peaceful Pines now. Along the route I think he must have taken if he bicycled to Nashville. I'm hoping I'll get lucky, but to be honest, I'm afraid Hernandez may have gotten him. Did Dix tell you that one of my neighbors saw Hernandez's van parked across the street this morning?"

"Yes, darling," Mother said. "About David..."

"If he got there while Hernandez was sitting outside, there's no way Hernandez wouldn't have tried to grab him. The house was empty, and nobody else was around. He wouldn't even have to force David into the van. All he'd have to do, would be to say he works with Rafe at the TBI. That he was doing surveillance from the other side of the street. That Rafe was back and in the hospital and that if David got in the car, he'd drive him there."

"Yes," Mother said, "but..."

"He's just a boy. He wouldn't know any better. And once he was in the car, Hernandez could take him wherever he wanted."

"Darling," Mother said.

I took a steadying breath. "Yes. I know. I should look on the bright side. Maybe it didn't happen that way. Maybe he just had a flat tire. Or drove off the road, or got lost, or something. Maybe he'll turn up."

"He did," Mother said.

"Maybe... what?"

My foot accidentally slipped off the gas pedal, and the car behind me came close to engaging my tailpipe. The driver gave me an angry toot of the horn, and a raised middle finger when she zipped out and zoomed past on the left.

"He's here," Mother said.

"David? But Dix went to the Bog and he wasn't there."

"He isn't in the Bog," Mother said. "He's here at the house."

"The mansion?"

"He was asleep on the porch when I came home." Her voice sounded almost jubilant. "Dix didn't see him. I didn't see him immediately, either. Not until I got up to the door and was trying to get my keys out. That's when I noticed someone sleeping on the porch swing."

"And it was David?"

"Yes, dear," Mother said. "Out cold."

"But he's safe?"

"Sitting at the kitchen table drinking milk and eating a sandwich."

"Oh, my God." I could feel the tears starting to prickle behind my eyes. "Thank you!"

There was a moment's pause. Then— "Did you think I would leave him on the porch?" Mother asked, with that patented mix of hurt feelings and accusation only a mother can manage.

If it had been Rafe...

But I decided not to go there. She'd brought David inside. She was feeding him. He was safe. I could afford to give my mother the benefit of the doubt. Or a break. Or whatever you'd call it.

"Of course not. I'm just excited that he's safe. And found. And there."

"He's fine," Mother said. "Worn out from riding his bike all night. Hungry and thirsty, since he didn't have anything to eat or drink. But relieved to get here, and to hear that Rafael is back."

Right. Um... "You didn't tell him... what did you tell him, exactly?"

Hopefully none of the gory details. Because he didn't need to hear those.

"Just the essentials," Mother said calmly. "That Rafael came back in the middle of the night and spent what was left of it in the hospital. But that he's fine now, and that he's at Peaceful Pines helping to look for David."

"Thank you."

"Of course, dear." She sounded a touch miffed. Probably annoyed that I'd felt the need to question her. "I assume you'll want to come pick him up?"

"Unless you want to drive back to Nashville today," I said, and immediately regretted it. She was being nice; I didn't need to be snarky. "Yes, Mother. I want to come pick him up. I can get there and back almost before Ginny and Sam can make it back to Nashville." Especially if Sam was tramping through the wilderness, and had to be brought back to camp before the two of them could leave. And as for Rafe and the TBI bunch, they may not even have made it to Peaceful Pines yet. "I have to call Rafe. And Ginny and Sam."

"Of course, dear. David and I will stay here and wait for you. He might want to take another nap. It was a long night."

For all of us. "Just sit on him," I said. "Make him stay there. Don't let him leave again."

"Of course not."

"I'm on my way. Thank you, Mother."

"Of course," Mother said. "Goodness, darling. The way you talk, one might think you'd expect me to keep him on the porch."

She hung up without giving me a chance to answer. I took just a second to shake my head, and then I dialed Rafe's number. Only to realize after a second that he didn't have his phone, that he hadn't had it since last night, and that I had to call Wendell instead. I'd remembered all day long, but now, in the excitement, it had blown straight out of my head.

I dialed again, steering the car with one hand and pushing buttons with the other, with one eye on the road and the other on the phone. Dangerous, but it was a Sunday afternoon, and the roads headed south out of town were, if not deserted, at least fairly quiet. There were several car lengths between me and the car in front of me, and no one in the next lane. And with David waiting in Sweetwater, there was no way I wanted to take the time to pull over to make my phone calls.

After the phone rang once, and then twice, Wendell answered. "Craig."

"Savannah," I said. "I've got him."

There was a moment, I assume for him to sort out the various male pronouns. Then— "David?"

"Yes. And I shouldn't have said that. I don't have him. My mother does. But I'm on my way to get him."

"Talk to Rafe," Wendell said, and I heard the sounds of the phone being handed over. Then Rafe's voice.

"Darlin'?"

"My mother has David," I told him. "He made it all the way to Sweetwater. She found him on the front porch, asleep, when she got home from lunch."

For a moment he said nothing, then I could hear him exhale. "Thank God."

"I know," I said. "I was afraid Hernandez had gotten him. Malcolm—you know, the kid from up the street?—said he saw a blue van with a Hispanic guy in it, sitting in the driveway across the street this morning."

There was another pause, and when his voice came back, it had turned dangerous. "No kidding."

"No. He seemed sincere. And it sounded like it was Hernandez."

I heard Wendell's voice murmur something in the background, and Rafe's answering, "Uh-huh."

"What?" I said.

"Prob'ly sitting there, waiting to see what'd happen when you found the body."

"That's what I figured," I said. Wendell murmured something else, and I added, "What?"

"Nothing. You wanna call Ginny, or you want me to?"

"You can," I said, thinking that it might give him a bonus point or two with David's mother. She liked him well enough, I thought, or at least she didn't dislike him. But she seemed a bit leery of him—afraid he was trying to take her kid away—and also too quick to jump to conclusions, like when she decided to have the local police arrest him on sight if he showed up at Peaceful Pines. It was just as well he hadn't ended up there.

Unless he had.

"Where are you? You didn't make it all the way to Peaceful Pines, did you?"

"Just passed Watertown," Rafe said. So no, they hadn't. "We're turning around."

"You might as well. He isn't there. I'll drive down to Sweetwater and get him, and bring him back to Nashville. Ginny and Sam can just go home. I'll be there almost as quickly as they will."

"I'll tell her. Drive carefully, darlin'."

"You, too," I told him. "Any news on Hernandez? Did you find anyone who knew him, or had some idea where he might be?"

But they hadn't. "A couple people noticed the van coming

and going. He was there for a couple days. But he didn't talk to nobody, and nobody talked to him."

He hadn't come across as the kind of person you'd want to chit-chat with, I guess.

"What about the owner?" I asked. "Mr. Lincoln?"

"Nobody's seen him for a couple days," Rafe said. "We finally figured out why."

"Why? Did Hernandez kill him, too?"

"Looks that way. Remember the John Doe the Wilson County cops found? The one Spicer and Truman went to make sure wasn't me?"

"Don't tell me," I said, although he sort of already had, "that was Judd Lincoln?"

"That's what it's maybe looking like. One of the neighbors said he was a tall, light-skinned black guy."

"Then that makes a lot of sense. I guess Hernandez hooked up with him somehow, after he got out of prison. Knew him from before, or maybe he just answered an ad for a rental house in Woodbine. And when they got to talking and Lincoln told him he lived in a cabin in Wilson County, Hernandez decided he'd rather do his torturing and killing there."

"Uh-huh," Rafe said.

"But then Lincoln either realized what Hernandez was planning to do and didn't like it, or Hernandez just decided to get rid of him. Maybe he figured he could use the practice after spending four years in prison."

"Could be."

Outside the car, the southern end of Davidson County flashed by. I crossed the invisible border into Williamson, marked only by a sign on the side of the interstate. "I'm in Williamson County," I said.

"Good for you," Rafe answered. "We'll try to dig up a picture of Lincoln, see if we can get a positive ID. If not, I guess we'll have to track down a relative, match DNA."

"If Judd Lincoln's missing and this guy who matches his description turned up dead at the same time—after associating with someone we know is a killer—that's pretty conclusive, don't you think?"

"To you and me," Rafe said, "but you go to court with it, you ain't gonna get beyond a reasonable doubt."

Maybe not. "Anyway, it's good to know."

Rafe agreed that it was.

"I should get off the phone. Concentrate on driving." And on getting to Sweetwater ASAP, so I could put David in the car and bring him home. "You need to call Ginny."

Rafe said he would, and we hung up. I put the phone down and focused on driving.

Nineteen

Sweetwater is a typical small Southern town, located about halfway between Columbia and Pulaski, and a bit east of both.

It started out as a Native American hangout. They called it *Cullee Oke*, which means Sweet Water in their native dialect.

Middle Tennessee became officially settled in 1779, with Fort Nashborough on the banks of the Cumberland River in what's now downtown Nashville. (A wooden replica of the fort is still there, if you're interested in seeing how the pioneers lived. I usually drive by it and shudder.) Over the next fifty years, progress crept south along the Antebellum Trail to Natchez and to Atlanta.

The Martins came to the Sweetwater area around 1830, and grabbed up a bunch of land for tobacco farming. The mansion was finished in 1839. It sits on a knoll outside Sweetwater proper, on the Columbia Road. At one time, it was surrounded by Martin land, but these days, there are only a few acres left. A thick band of trees, protecting the house—and Mother—from the indignities of McMansion subdivision living beyond, and a big lawn around the house itself, and around the few outbuildings that have been preserved: one of the slave cabins, a smokehouse, and a carriage house. There's a small private cemetery, too, tucked away in the woods, and a couple of times a year, local school children come out to gawk at the slave cabin and the graves.

The mansion itself is big and square: red brick, two stories, with tall, white pillars out front, a porch on the first floor, and a balcony that runs across the front face of the building. As I'd already mentioned to Dix, Rafe calls it 'the mausoleum on the hill,' and I have to admit there's a resemblance. I think he may have been referring equally to the stuffiness of my mother when he said it, though.

At any rate, I got there just over an hour after I left Nashville. Traffic had been light, and I'd been driving a few miles above the speed limit the whole way. Eager to see David, to make sure that he was indeed all right—not that I thought my mother would have lied about it—but also somewhat concerned about what might have happened in the last hour with the two of them alone together. Mother had seemed strangely taken with David at the camp yesterday, and had sounded almost mellow—maybe even a bit indulgent—when she'd called me to say he was there. But he *was* Rafe's son, and twelve years old, so I didn't want to expect miracles. There was a good chance he'd worn her nerves very thin by now.

Everything looked quiet when I crunched up the gravel drive to the front door. The mansion has one of those broad, shallow staircases up to the front porch: three steps, with a big concrete urn on either side. The front of the house faces south-east, and gets full sun until late afternoon, so at this time of year, the urns were filled with a mixture of daylilies and coneflowers. Each one comes up to my waist, and weighs at least three times what I do.

I parked in front of the steps, and walked up to the double front doors. David's bicycle—blue—was leaning against the wall next to the door, beside another planter full of phlox.

I twisted the door knob and pushed the door open, and raised my voice only about halfway. "Mother?"

I didn't want to yell, since I thought there was a chance David might be asleep again. If the poor kid had been awake all night, pedaling his bike across half of Middle Tennessee, he must be exhausted.

There was no answer. I closed the door behind me and headed across the foyer. There's a staircase on either side, going up to the second floor, and a long central hallway running all the way to the back of house. In the old days, before air conditioning, they'd keep both doors open in the summer, to get cross ventilation going. These days, thankfully, we have artificial cold air to help us survive. A blast of it hit my ankles as I passed one of the vents in the old, wide-plank floor.

Like in Mrs. Jenkins's Victorian, the first floor is made up of common rooms. Parlors, dining room, kitchen, guest bath, butler's pantry... Upstairs, there are bedrooms and more bathrooms. If mother wasn't down here, I'd check there, since I figured there was a good chance she was exhausted, too. She hadn't been pedaling, but the stress of Rafe being gone—if she'd felt stress over that; I knew I had—combined with the hours in the hospital and then the dead body, must have wiped her out, as well. It wouldn't be surprising if she'd decided to lie down while she waited for me to get here, especially if David was napping.

They weren't downstairs. The parlors, bathroom, and dining room were all empty. So was the kitchen, although it showed evidence of recent occupation. There was a plate with crumbs on it on the kitchen island, next to an empty glass with milk residue on the bottom. I took a minute to load both into the dishwasher, and to brush the crumbs off the counter into my hand and from there into the sink, before I headed into the butler's pantry and up the servants' stairs to the second floor.

They're a bit narrower than the front stairs, and a lot more enclosed. And when I say 'a bit,' I mean that it's almost impossible to turn around. I know people were smaller two hundred years ago, but I imagine it would have been a tight squeeze for a normal human being even then. If you got in with a tray full of cups and a teapot, you could forget about changing your mind and going back for sugar. You'd just have to keep going until you could go no farther, and then go back down for what you'd forgotten.

The servant stairs let out at the very rear of the second floor. I stopped in the hallway to catch my breath. Climbing stairs has become a bit harder lately, what with the extra weight I carry up front, and also because the stairwell is so narrow and tunnel-like that it's hard to breathe. I know that sounds ridiculous, but you can take my word for it. Also, there's no AC vent. So while the stairwell is surrounded by thick plaster walls, and stays halfway cool as a result, it's still considerably warmer and more stuffy than anywhere else in the house.

The upstairs was quiet. I took a couple of breaths of the nice, cool air, and then made my way down the middle of the hallway, stepping on the fluffy Oriental runner, to my mother's bedroom door.

I tapped lightly, and then, when there was no sound from inside, a bit harder. There was no answer. I turned the knob and pushed the door open.

The room was empty, with no sign that Mother had even been up here since she left home yesterday morning. The bed was neatly made, the tasteful coral and off-white comforter pulled up and unwrinkled, with Mother's armful of pillows artfully arranged. There were no dirty clothes on the floor, no wet towel hanging on the door knob, no steam coming out of the bathroom.

I wrinkled my brows and stepped across the hall to what had been my brother Dix's room growing up.

It still looked a bit boyish, although it had been restored to most of its old glory in the years since Dix left. But the bedspread and curtains were blue, and so was the rag rug. I would have expected Mother to have put David to bed here, if he was going to sleep somewhere, since my old room is all frilly and girly and white. But the bed was empty and the blue bedspread as pristine as in Mother's room.

So maybe he was sleeping in my bed. Mother may have thought it would make him feel more comfortable to be told, "This is Savannah's old room," than "This is Savannah's brother's old room." I didn't really think David would have cared one way or the other, but Mother might have supposed he did.

I grew up in the room next to Dix, while Catherine's room was across the hall. I opened my door first. The bed was empty. And then, with my heart thudding hard in my chest, I pushed open Catherine's door, praying that somehow, they'd both be there.

Catherine's bed was empty, as well.

"Mother?" I called, my voice panicked. "David?"

There was no answer, just the echo of my own voice coming back to me from the high ceiling.

Heart thudding, I raced back through the house. I checked all the beds and all the bathrooms. I checked the parlors, the dining room, the butler's pantry, the kitchen again. I checked the closets. I even steeled myself to go down into the basement, a place I haven't been in at least ten years.

It's old. A dirt basement dating from almost two hundred years ago, when the house was built. There's nothing at all down there anymore, except for spiders and maybe mice, but it was part of the house, so I had to check.

The hinges screamed like a wounded animal when I pulled the door open. A cobweb the size of Utah covered the upper half of the opening. I brushed it away with a shudder, wiping my hand on the side of my thigh afterwards. *Gross.*

I stuck my head through the opening, breathing in the dank, musty smell. "Mother?"

My voice disappeared into the dark, and I cleared my throat and tried again, louder. "Is anyone down here? Mother? David?"

No one answered. No one even made a sound. I decided to spare myself the trip down the rickety wooden steps, and closed the door again.

At that point there wasn't much more I could do. The house was empty, and my mother and David were gone. Vanished into thin air, basically. Now I had to decide whether it was time to panic yet.

Could they be somewhere else on the property? David was twelve and curious. Maybe he'd asked to see the slave cabin or the old cemetery. Maybe Mother had walked him out there and they hadn't heard me drive up...?

I scrambled out of the house and across the lawn to the cabin. It was empty. The bed where Dix used to tuck away his dirty magazines was empty too, and didn't look like it had been slept in. And no wonder. It was as stuffy and uncomfortable in here as in the servants' staircase in the house, with the added aroma of sweaty logs. It was also somewhere around a hundred and ten degrees. No wonder David had opted to go to sleep on the front porch swing instead. It was almost as hot, but a lot more airy.

The smoke house was empty, if equally hot, and so was the garage AKA the old carriage house. Mother's car was there, though. So if they'd gone anywhere, it had been on foot.

I followed the path through the trees to the old cemetery, feeling my blouse become stickier with each step. Summer in the South is awful, and made worse by the fact that I was pregnant and had hormones pinging through my body. I have no idea how they did it in the old days, with their layers of petticoats and voluminous skirts.

I'd gotten married in a hoop skirt. It had been so wide that I'd practically knocked the flower decorations off the edges of the pews as I walked down the aisle. It had been June then, too. Five years ago. Two years of marriage—almost—before Bradley told me he wanted a divorce so he could marry his mistress, and then three more of being divorced. And now I was looking at getting married again.

But without the hoop skirt and the rosy outlook this time. I knew that marriage to Rafe wouldn't be easy. There were too many creeps from his past ready to come crawling out of the woodwork at any moment. I loved him too much not to want to try, though. It may not be easy, but it would be worth it.

The cemetery was empty. Of anyone living, anyway. I stood

for a second looking at the lopsided gravestones behind their knee-high iron fence before the thought penetrated.

The cemetery was empty. Mother and David weren't here.

So where were they?

I turned in a circle. It was a touch cooler here, under the green canopy of the trees. A slight breeze rustled the leaves over my head. I raised my voice. "David? Mother? Are you out here?"

There was no answer. A few birds took flight, but that was the only sign of life.

I turned around and headed back through the woods. The lawn was still empty. Mother's car was still in the garage. There was no answer when I pushed open the door into the mansion and called their names.

I was reaching for my phone to call Dix when it started ringing. I dug it out of my purse and looked at it. And felt my heart skip when I saw Rafe's number. Just the person I wanted to talk to! Not because there was anything he could do from an hour away, but because he always manages to say the right thing.

This time I didn't have to focus to put a smile on my face. It was just there. "Rafe! Thank God you called. There's something really weird going on down here. I can't find Mother or David anywhere—"

And that's how long it took me to remember that Rafe didn't have his phone.

That Rafe hadn't had his phone since Friday night.

That if someone was calling me on Rafe's phone, it wasn't Rafe.

The person on the other end chuckled. It was an evil chuckle, or maybe that was just because I knew what I knew about Eugenio Hernandez. "Hello, Savannah," he said.

That sounded evil, too. Not threatening, but oily and overly familiar. Creepily chummy. I almost asked him how he knew my name, but it was obvious once I thought about it. Rafe's speed-dial.

And to be honest, my heart was beating too hard for me to talk, anyway.

Into the silence, Eugenio Hernandez added, "You have a lovely home."

I forced my vocal chords to respond. "Thank you." To my relief, my voice wasn't shaking too badly. I certainly didn't want this creep to know that just talking to him on the phone had the tiny hairs on the back of my neck standing up. "Rafe will be pleased to hear you say that. He worked hard on that house."

He chuckled again, and the back of my neck prickled. "It's a shame you'll never get the chance to tell him," he said.

His voice came to me in weird stereo, and when I swung around, I saw why. He was standing at the top of the stairs looking down at me.

I took a couple of running steps toward the front door. It was pure instinct. *Danger! Flee!* And I only made it those couple of steps before a bullet buried itself in the hardwood floors in front of me and brought me to a quivering stop. Through the ringing in my ears, I heard Hernandez say calmly, "I wouldn't do that if I were you."

I swung back around, breathing hard, as he moved to the top of one of the staircases and started down. "I can probably make it to the car before you can kill me."

This time my voice did shake, and I could tell from his expression—that excited light in his eyes—that he liked it.

He nodded cordially. "Maybe so. But then what would happen to your mother and the brat?"

He had Mother and David?

But of course he did. Why else would he be here? He hadn't followed me. Or if he had, I hadn't noticed.

"You followed them this morning, didn't you?" I hadn't thought it through until now, but suddenly the words came spilling out as if I'd known all along. "One of the neighbors saw you, sitting in a driveway up the street just before seven. You waited for us to come home, and then you followed Mother and Dix when they left."

He smiled, pleased, as if I were a grade school student getting a tricky answer right. "It was easy."

No doubt. Dix wouldn't have thought to look for a tail. His only concern would have been to get home to his daughters as quickly as possible. And in doing so, he'd done exactly what I'd been afraid of doing: leading Hernandez to Sweetwater.

Where I'd made the mistake, was thinking he wanted me, and as long as I stayed in Nashville, everyone in Sweetwater would be safe. It hadn't even crossed my mind that he might have followed Dix and Mother.

She and David must be upstairs. God only knew where he'd kept them while I ransacked the house earlier.

"You'd kill them," I said, trying to sound calm, as I walked backwards to the other staircase. He had made it about halfway down the one on his side of the foyer, and as he started down the second half, I started up mine. "The same way you killed Kelly. And Maria. And the other girl. The blonde, four years ago. And Judd Lincoln."

"You figured all that out?"

I thought about telling him it hadn't been hard, that he'd left a trail of breadcrumbs the size of Pluto, at least recently. But I thought that might make him angry. So instead I said, "Rafe did. That's why he had you arrested back then. So you wouldn't kill Ginger."

His face darkened at the reminder, so maybe that hadn't been the best thing to say, either.

But even so, I decided to goad him a little farther. Angry people sometimes make mistakes. And the longer I kept him talking, the more likely I—or someone else, like David or Mother—would think of something to do to end the standoff. I didn't know where they were, but they weren't in the foyer with us. The more time I could give them by themselves, the better the chances were that they'd be able to escape.

So I told him, "You must have been angry when you got back to the cabin and discovered he'd left. You probably didn't think he'd be able to do that."

He snarled something. It was in Spanish—or at least it wasn't in English—and I didn't know what it meant. I didn't ask him to translate, however, since I was sure it was the kind of word a lady wasn't supposed to acknowledge anyway.

Instead I smirked. "You didn't really think he was going to sit quietly in your cabin and wait for you to come back, did you?"

He didn't answer immediately—it looked like he was chewing on his tongue—so I decided to give the metaphorical knife another twist. "I mean, you know he took down Hector Gonzales's entire network. Someone you met in prison told you that, right? That while you were sitting in a cell for soliciting an under-aged prostitute, Rafe blew Hector Gonzales's whole organization sky high. Did you really think you could just pin him to the table like a beetle —" My stomach revolted at the thought, and I had to swallow hard, "—and walk away, and he'd still be there when you got back?"

I managed a condescending chuckle. "He's a lot better at what he does than you give him credit for. He stopped you last time. He'll stop you this time, too."

"Not before I gut you like a fish," Hernandez told me, as he stepped onto the floor of the foyer.

It was an unlovely simile, and I had to swallow again. "Maybe not. But you only got four years last time because they couldn't prove you had killed anyone. Rafe knew you had, but he had to maintain his cover. He couldn't go out and find the girls you murdered. So you only got four years."

He was crossing the foyer by now. I scrambled a couple more steps up the staircase, getting closer to the top, while I kept talking. "This time we have Kelly's body. You left DNA on her, you know. On Kelly and in the bedroom. We have a witness who saw you outside the house this morning. And Rafe's alive to talk about what you did to him."

I got to the top of the staircase as Hernandez reached the bottom. "And this time he isn't a small-time crook working for Hector Gonzales's organization. He's a respected TBI agent. One who busted open the biggest South American Theft Gang in the Southeast. He doesn't have to hide, and he doesn't have to maintain his cover. He can stand up in court and tell the judge and the jury exactly what you did. And then you'll go away for the rest of your life."

Something shifted in his eyes at that. Maybe it was the realization that he was going back to prison. I can't imagine that it wouldn't have occurred to him already, but maybe he'd just been too caught up in the moment, in his quest for revenge, to think everything through that coldly.

At any rate, it registered. Something flipped over in his brain, and...

You know that saying, 'he had murder in his eye?'

That's what it was like. He was looking up at me, and the words I said penetrated. I could see his eyes change, turn feral, and then he started up the stairs, with that look in his eyes that said that he planned to catch me, and I wouldn't like what happened when he did.

I turned on my heel and ran.

Twenty

I don't know that I really thought about what I was doing. I think maybe I was headed for the servants' staircase, to run back downstairs.

It wasn't a conscious plan, though. Consciously, I wasn't thinking at all. It was all just a refrain of words running through my head. *Run! Move! Get away!*

I legged it down the hallway toward the back of the mansion, my only thought to put as much distance between myself and Eugenio Hernandez as I could. I could hear his feet pounding up the staircase behind me. Any moment, I expected to hear him gain the top of the stairs, and then it was anyone's guess what would happen. He might continue to chase me—he was the type who got off on that—or he might shoot me in the back and drop me like a stone.

I scrambled along the Oriental runner, my blood rushing in my ears. And I probably would have gone for the staircase had the door to Mother's room not been open, and had I not seen her through the opening.

At the last second, I veered off, just as Hernandez burst off the staircase. The gunshot whined down the hallway and buried itself in the old plaster wall with a slap and a trickle of dust. It might have hit me, had I not launched myself through the door and into the master bedroom. Hernandez's feet pounded down the hallway as I spun around and threw myself at the door, slamming it in his face. My hands shook as I twisted the lock. A second later, Hernandez's body hit the outside of the door with a smash and a grunt.

I whirled around to take in the room.

Mother was on the bed, and under other circumstances, it

might have struck me that she looked damned good for her age.

That thought lingered only a second, before my brain recognized that this was my mother, naked, and how that was totally squicky. Yes, I'm twenty-eight, but some things never change. A child never wants to see his or her mother naked.

Or his or her grandmother, or pseudo step-grandmother, either.

A muffled sob came from my right, and I spun in that direction as Hernandez hit the door again. It vibrated, but the lock held.

David was sitting on my mother's boudoir chair, bound hand and foot and gagged with what looked like a Hermès scarf. Tears were trickling down his cheeks and into the silk, and the expression in his eyes was terrified.

I was terrified, too, and more so as Hernandez changed his tactics out in the hallway, and instead of throwing his entire weight at the door, began kicking it.

"Get him," my mother said. Meaning David, I guess.

I yanked the Hermès scarf down, and David immediately sucked in a breath and told me, "No! Get her!"

I hesitated. And in the second it took me to do so, Hernandez must have gotten sick of hitting his head against the wall—or his boot against the door—and decided to employ stronger measures.

There was a bang, and another bang, and another, and another. David screamed, and I did, too. The door quivered under the onslaught. Then the lock splintered as Hernandez kicked it open and strode in.

He must have emptied the gun into the lock, because he flung it aside. It sailed through the air and hit the plaster wall with a crack. It might have left a dent, although I wasn't paying attention. Time enough to repair the damage later. If we survived the next few minutes.

But at least the gun really did seem to be empty, because the impact didn't cause it to discharge and another bullet to fly. So that was one thing to be grateful for, in the midst of the chaos.

Hernandez stopped inside the door and looked around. He fumbled at his belt, and for a second I thought he was unbuckling. My heart did a weird sort of shimmy. But then I saw that he was only—*only!*—changing weapons. The bright afternoon sunlight pouring through Mother's sheer curtains glanced off the steel of the knife he flicked open.

"C'mere, bitch."

This was me, obviously. I would have known it even without the gesture, since none of the others were capable of moving. Mother was stretched out across the bed—and Lord, was that a sight I would have to burn out of my brain if we survived this— while David was trussed to the chair. He'd have to bleach his eyeballs too, poor kid, and was likely to need therapy.

And that possibility was a lot more pleasant than the alternative, which was that we didn't get out of this with our lives.

"No," I said.

Hernandez blinked. I guess he wasn't used to anyone saying no. But really, without the gun, there wasn't much he could to me. As long as I stayed at a distance, I was safe.

Or so I thought, until he turned toward the bed. And Mother.

"Fine." I moved a step closer. Just far enough to get his attention away from Mother.

"Gonna gut you like a fish," he told me.

I nodded, even as my heart started knocking against my ribs so hard it hurt. "I know. You said that downstairs."

"Gonna slice you open and make you bleed."

It was a wonder this guy was walking around free. With that kind of obsession, I was surprised someone hadn't had him committed years ago. Like, when he was ripping the wings off butterflies in grade school.

Or at the very least, someone should have examined him

while he was in prison, and decided he was a menace to society, one that couldn't possibly be released on an unsuspecting public. Then we wouldn't be in this situation.

Those dead, black eyes dropped to my stomach. "Gonna cut the bastard right outta there," he grunted.

I felt myself turn hot, and then cold. And I'm not sure where the words came from, or how I was able to say them, but my voice was steady and ice cold even as my nails dug into my palms hard enough to hurt. "You do that, and you may as well kill yourself while you're at it. He won't let you live after that. He'll hunt you down and put a bullet in your brain like the animal you are. So you better enjoy life while you can, because you won't be long for this world."

There was no point in specifying who 'he' was. We all knew.

Hernandez's eyes came back to mine, dead and black and crazy.

He lunged.

I stumbled back. My heel got caught in a loop of Mother's overly fluffy bedroom rug, and I went down, flat on my back. I hit the back of my head on the hardwood floor, and for a second I saw stars. My back slammed against the floor, and knocked the breath out of me. Worse, it jarred my stomach. I thought I felt something give, and that isn't a good thing for someone who's four months pregnant and prone to miscarriages.

But I had no time to worry about it. Hernandez followed me down, his fetid breath in my face. That, combined with the weight on my diaphragm, almost made me gag.

I didn't have time for that, either. I had lives to save. Mine, the baby's. David's. Mother's. Because if he killed me, the next thing he'd do, would be to kill them.

So I fought like a mad-woman, kicking and hissing and squirming under him. David helped by yelling and kicking out at Hernandez with both bound feet. The impact was likely no more painful than a mosquito bite—not at all, in other words—

but I can imagine it was also distracting. And while Mother was still stuck on the bed, she was screaming, the kinds of words I never thought I'd hear from that quarter.

Somehow—and I think it was luck as much as design—one of my knees managed to connect with Hernandez's crown jewels.

I can only assume he wasn't used to someone who fought back. I mean, look at Mother. Bound hand and foot: there was no way she would have been able to defend herself. And he'd probably done the same thing to Kelly, and Maria, and the blonde we still hadn't identified.

But my legs were free, and flailing around. I kneed Hernandez in the groin. I could feel my kneecap connect with the squishy parts between his legs—some of them less squishy than others, and that was totally gross, too. I mean, here I was, fighting for my life, and he was getting turned on by the idea of killing me.

Until my knee pushed his balls up into his intestines, and then for a second, everything hung in the balance.

He made a weird sound, like he was being squeezed, and his eyes rolled up. For just a moment, he didn't move. And again I wasn't thinking consciously, but I think I knew that once this tiny reprieve was over, he was going to be more angry and more determined to kill me. I had to act *now*.

I grabbed for the knife. He held on. Not with the same strength as earlier, but I figured it was just a matter of time—and chances were not very much time—before he was fully recovered.

I held on, too.

I held on as his color returned and his lips curled back from his teeth.

I held on as the knife descended toward my stomach and pierced cloth and skin.

The shock was like a splash of cold water in my face.

I screamed, more in anger than in pain, even as I felt the first warm trickle of blood start.

Mother screamed too, and David somehow managed to launch himself and the boudoir chair forward.

I saw him coming, and tried to get out of the way, but with Hernandez on top of me, I couldn't squirm very far.

David, still with the chair tied to his rear, slammed into Hernandez.

Hernandez dropped onto me.

We were still fighting over the knife, and both our hands were on it. But since I could see David coming, and Hernandez, on top of me, couldn't, I had warning, and at the last second, managed to twist the point of the knife away from me.

Things would have gotten ugly if I hadn't. It was a sharp knife, and it was aimed directly at my stomach. When I twisted it, it penetrated Hernandez's gut instead.

And then David landed on top of him and pushed him down on the blade.

He stiffened, and jerked.

I was still hanging on to the handle of the knife, and for a second I almost let go. But then Hernandez's eyes met mine, and they were still crazy, and I held on.

He made a feeble attempt to throw David off. In doing so, he lifted himself halfway off the knife. Blood gushed out of the wound, warm and wet, and coated my hands. Hernandez groaned and dropped back down.

"Get off," I told David. I felt like I said it calmly, but I think my voice was pretty shrill. Hernandez's blood was soaking through my clothes, sticky against my skin, and he was breathing sort of funny, with this weird rattle in his throat. The combined weights of him and David—three hundred pounds, give or take—pressed against my diaphragm and made it hard for me to breathe. I started to feel claustrophobic and panicky. "Get off!"

David tried, but with the weight of the chair keeping him

down, it wasn't easy. My ears started ringing, like I was about to pass out.

Faintly, I heard noises downstairs. The slamming of the front door, then footsteps on the stairs.

Someone's voice called my name. "Savannah!"

I could hear the fear laced through it even in my current predicament.

"Rafe," I whispered.

It was the best I could do. I didn't have enough breath to shout.

Hernandez heard me, though. He stirred feebly, and made another attempt to get rid of the weight on his back. This time, he managed to shift David far enough that the boy—and chair—tumbled to the floor. David grunted. More blood gushed out of the wound in Hernandez's stomach and onto mine as he tried to lever himself up. In looking down at myself, I saw that my stomach—gently rounded under the dress—was colored red.

The footsteps came down the hall. As they came closer, Hernandez pushed himself to his knees. And somehow—God only knows—he managed to pull the knife out of his abdomen. As a result, when Rafe came to a stop in the doorway, Hernandez was on his knees, leaning over me, the knife in his hand dripping blood onto my already red stomach.

A roar filled the room. There was a rush of feet across the floor, and then Hernandez flew, like a rag doll, across the room. He smacked against the wall, slid down, and stayed there. Rafe dropped to his knees beside me.

"Savannah." He fumbled for my hand.

"Get David," I whispered.

Downstairs, there were more footsteps, and voices. I recognized Wendell's, and Jamal's. Rafe must have brought the whole crew with him.

"My mother," I told him. "Cover my mother. Please. Before they get up here."

He looked at me for a second before he got to his feet. I watched as he took the couple of steps over to the bed.

Once upon a time, almost a year ago, it had been me tied to a bed. Rafe had burst through the door to save me then, too. That encounter had ended with another man stabbed, and bleeding to death on the floor. I wondered whether Hernandez was headed that way too, and then I realized I didn't much care.

When it was me on the bed, Rafe hadn't been above doing a bit of flirting. With Mother, he simply grabbed a blanket and draped it over her.

"Thank you." Her voice was hoarse, most likely from screaming. And although I couldn't see her from down here on the floor, I'm sure she was mortified, and holding on to the shreds of her dignity with everything she had.

Rafe nodded, and turned away to lift David and the chair upright. Once that was done, he pulled a knife out of his pocket and began to cut the ropes. David was sobbing, and the exertion it had taken for Rafe to get here, had taken its toll on him too, I saw. I wasn't the only one sporting bloodstains. The bandage around Rafe's arm was spotted with new patches of bright red, as well.

Once David was free, Rafe put a hand on his head for a second. They looked at one another, but neither spoke. David got busy rubbing circulation back into his hands, while Rafe walked back to the bed and began cutting the ropes holding Mother to the bedposts. By the time Wendell and crew arrived in the doorway, she was sitting up, with the blanket wrapped around her, also rubbing her hands.

Rafe was back on his knees next to me. "Don't move."

"I'm fine," I told him. "Just shaken up, and got the wind knocked out of me."

Although when he put an arm around me to help me to sit up, I winced at the pain in my stomach.

"We have to get her to a hospital," Rafe told Wendell, his

voice tight. "She's hurt."

"It's mostly his blood," I told them both, which was certainly the truth. Nonetheless, I did feel a little worse for wear. And I was a bit worried about that wrenching sensation I'd felt in my stomach. A trip to the hospital—just to make sure everything was all right—didn't sound like a bad idea.

For any of us.

Wendell looked over at Hernandez, slumped against the wall, still unconscious. "What happened there?"

"He stabbed himself," I said, leaning back against Rafe's arm. "Pretty much."

They both raised their brows at me.

"It's true," David said. He was sitting on the floor with his back against the bed, still rubbing his wrists. "He was trying to hurt Savannah. He was on top of her, with the knife. He said..." He swallowed. "He said he was going to cut the baby out of her stomach."

Nobody spoke, but the look Rafe gave the unconscious Hernandez was everything I had warned Hernandez about, and more.

"He gonna survive?" Wendell asked, with more clinical curiosity than caring.

Rafe shook his head.

"How do you know?" I asked. "You haven't looked at him."

He glanced at me. "Cause if he does, I'm gonna kill him. So he'll be dead one way or the other."

Wendell shook his head. "Call an ambulance," he told the three rookies, who were crowded into the doorway, looking at the carnage with wide eyes. "And then go downstairs and meet the paramedics. Tell'em we've got a man bleeding to death from a stab wound, and some minor injuries."

All three of them nodded, and they withdrew. We could hear them start to talk as they scrambled down the staircase to the first floor.

"Excuse me, please," Mother said. It was faint, but dignified. She didn't look at any of us as she rose from the bed, wrapped the blanket more securely around herself, and padded into the bathroom with her head held high. The door closed with a definite snick of the latch and, a second later, a click of the lock.

"She's embarrassed," I said apologetically. Softly, so she wouldn't hear me.

Rafe arched a brow.

"She's naked," David told Wendell, also in a whisper. Mother has bat-ears, and was probably pressing one of them to the keyhole as we were speaking, but he might as well give it his best shot. "He made her take her clothes off, and then he tied her to the bed. And he tied me to the chair. And then we waited for Savannah to come back."

Wendell nodded. "He's done for. Can't hurt you anymore."

He moved over to where Hernandez was slumped, and put a hand to Hernandez's throat. Hernandez didn't stir.

"If he makes it through this," Wendell added, sitting back on his heels, "he'll spend the rest of his life in prison."

"Good. I want him to pay." David glanced from me to the locked bathroom door and back to Wendell. "He hurt us."

"We hurt him, too," I told him. "Worse than he hurt us."

Not that he hadn't planned to do worse than he did.

Breathing was easier now, so I endeavored to get to my feet. Rafe's arm tightened around me. "Careful."

"I'm all right. I told you. It's mostly his blood."

"Mostly."

"He graced me with the knife," I said. "Nothing like what he did to you, so don't go all macho on me. It's just a scratch."

At least I thought it was. It was hard to be sure, with the way the entire front of my dress was soaked with blood.

"I'd like to change into something else," I said, and Rafe nodded.

"I'd like that, too." He lifted me to my feet, with no concern for his bandaged arm, and made sure was standing on my own before he let go. "You sure you're all right?"

I assured him I was, and he nodded and reached out a hand to David. "C'mon, kid. Let's you and me get outta here and give these women some privacy."

David let himself be hauled to his feet, like a cork out of a bottle.

When he was upright, Rafe continued, "We gotta call your mama, anyway. She's on her way back to your house, and we better tell her that maybe she oughta come here instead. This hospital thing could take a while."

David nodded and followed him out of the room. "Is she mad?" he wanted to know.

I have no idea what Rafe's answer was, but I could imagine it fell along the lines of 'if you ever run away again, someone will tan your hide.'

It wouldn't be him, of course. He wouldn't raise a hand to David, not after the way Old Jim used to knock him around when he was small. But someone had to put the fear of God into the boy, because the way he was carrying on was likely to turn us all gray before our time.

I turned to Wendell, with a glance at Hernandez. "Is he... will he make it?"

"It don't look good," Wendell said. "It depends on how soon the ambulance gets here."

I nodded. "I feel..." Not bad, exactly. I hadn't killed him on purpose. It had been self-defense, and not my fault. If I hadn't managed to twist the knife, I'd be the one bleeding out from a stomach puncture. But it had still been my hands on the knife.

"It wasn't your fault," Wendell told me. "He'd have done it to you if he could have. And to your mother. And David."

I nodded. I knew that. Still, it was strange to know I might have taken a life. Even if I'd been defending my own.

"Will you be OK here on your own until the ambulance

comes?"

Wendell looked at me strangely, and I guess maybe it was a strange question.

"I want to give my mother something she can wear," I said. "And then I want to find something of hers that I can wear, and take it to another bathroom where I can wash all this blood off."

Wendell nodded. "Sure. I'll stay with him. But you don't hafta worry he's gonna come out of it. He might survive till the ambulance gets here, or he might not, but he ain't gonna get up and start walking around. You're all safe."

"Thank you." I gestured to the closet. "I'll just..."

He nodded, and turned back to Hernandez, whose breath was becoming more and more thready. I went to the closet and started rooting through Mother's things for something that would fit me.

Twenty-One

Hernandez was still breathing when the paramedics carried the stretcher out of the mansion to the ambulance, although he wasn't breathing well. They put an oxygen mask on him—how that was supposed to help a man bleeding to death from a stab wound I have no idea—and started an IV as soon as he was inside the ambulance. But the consensus seemed to be that he'd lost so much blood that recovery was unlikely.

"Why didn't anyone compress the wound?" one of the paramedics wanted to know, righteous indignation all over her face as she looked from Rafe to Wendell and back.

"Multiple murderer," Wendell told her. "If he survives, he'll be spending the rest of his life in prison. It didn't seem worth the trouble."

"Oh." She looked taken aback. Her colleague just shook his head and kept packing Hernandez's wound with bandages.

"Just get him to the ER," Wendell told them. "Alive or dead don't really matter. We'll be right behind you. I gotta stick with him until we know one way or the other whether we're arresting him or burying him."

He shooed the rookies over to the SUV. "You all right?" he asked Rafe, who nodded.

"We're right behind you, too. I want somebody to look at Savannah. Make sure she's all right."

"And I want someone to look at him," I added, nodding to Rafe. "From the way those bandages look, you've popped at least half your stitches. At the very least, you need new bandages."

Rafe glanced down at this arm and grimaced. I don't think it was pain, or even anticipated pain. Probably more the coming agony of having to sit still while the doctor removed the old stitches and made new ones.

"David's coming with us," he told Wendell. "His folks are gonna come to the hospital and pick him up."

Wendell nodded. "We'll see you there."

He headed for the SUV.

"What are they doing?" David wanted to know.

I followed his gaze... not to the ambulance and the paramedics laboring over Hernandez, but to the three rookies standing outside the SUV. I wrinkled my brows. "It looks like they're playing rock, paper, scissors."

"Why?"

He looked at Rafe, who grinned. "Figuring out who gets to ride shotgun."

"But they're adults!"

"You should never get too old to play, my man." He ruffled David's hair. "You wanna ride shotgun in Savannah's car?"

David hesitated. He glanced at me. "It's fine," I said. "I think I'll be more comfortable in the back anyway."

He nodded.

"C'mon." Rafe led the way over to the car and opened the door for me. I crawled in. Then he opened the door for David, who did the same. Then he walked around the car and opened the other back door. "Miz Martin?"

Mother hesitated. I held my breath. Eventually she moved past him with a regal nod.

He closed the door—not on her foot—and got in the front seat. "Buckle up," he told David, "this is gonna be fast."

It was. We kept pace with the ambulance and Wendell's SUV the whole way to the Maury County Regional Hospital. It's usually about a fifteen minute drive, but we made it in eight. Both cars had lights and sirens going, and the Volvo just slid through the intersections in their wake.

When we pulled in to the emergency room entrance, a team was ready and waiting to whisk Hernandez into surgery. I guess they had to do that. It was their job to try to save lives, even lives that perhaps would be better unsaved.

Of course, I realize that's not my call to make. Life and death are above my pay grade. But Hernandez would be spending the rest of his life in prison if he survived. Maybe it would be kinder to just let him die.

Not that I was feeling particularly kind. He had planned to torture and kill me, and my unborn baby. He had tortured and would happily have killed Rafe. Chances are he would have killed Mother and David, too. And he had tortured and killed several other people. He deserved prison. But if he died on the operating table, I could be satisfied with that.

The team disappeared through the doors with the gurney, and with Clayton and José flanking them on either side. The SUV rolled away. Wendell and Jamal looking for a parking space before joining the others, no doubt. They'd all be hovering over Hernandez until he either breathed his last, or recovered.

Rafe pulled up in front of the double doors and stopped the car.

"We can't stay here," I told him.

"I know, darlin'. I'll move the car as soon as I know you're taken care of."

This time he didn't bother with Mother's door, just came around the car and opened mine. And when he'd pulled me out of the back seat, he scooped me up in his arms.

"I can walk," I told him, a little breathlessly, as always when I'm pressed against him. It's a nice feeling. I hope it never goes away.

"You're bleeding. You shouldn't walk."

"You're bleeding, too," I pointed out. "You shouldn't be carrying me."

"It don't hurt."

He carried me toward the doors as if it didn't, but surely he couldn't be telling the truth. The bandage around his arm was soaked through with blood, and there were patches of it on his chest, too.

I guess maybe ten years undercover had made him so good at sidelining his own feelings—pain, anger, worry—that it was second nature by now.

"You'll have someone look at you," I asked as we passed into the lobby, "right?"

He nodded. "After I know you're OK."

Since it was the best I was likely to get, I settled for it.

Thirty minutes later I was in a hospital bed with a weird belt strapped around my waist—or around my belly, rather, since my waist was a thing of the past—and some sort of monitor perched just above my belly button. The baby's heartbeat thundered through the room, as rapid as the pitter-patter of rain.

I wasn't alone. In fact, I was anything but alone. My room was filled with people. Mother was there, of course, and she had called the sheriff to tell him what had happened, so Bob Satterfield was there too, hovering over her as she perched on a chair in the corner.

Dix had arrived with Catherine: I assumed they'd dumped all five kids on Jonathan again. That poor man deserved a medal, although knowing him, I'm sure he thought being married to my sister was reward enough.

David was there, naturally. Ginny and Sam hadn't made it down here to pick him up yet. A nurse had taken a quick look at him, and at Mother, and declared them both good to go. Aside from abrasions around their wrists and ankles from the ropes, and David's bruises, both from rolling around on the floor in Mother's bedroom and bicycling all night, they were both unharmed. I thought David might end up needing some kind of counseling—it isn't every twelve-year-old who can go through what he had and not have some residual anxiety—but for now, he seemed both happy and calm, nibbling on a pastry someone had unearthed.

With the exception of Todd and the addition of David, it was almost exactly the same crew who had shown up at the hospital in Nashville after I'd had my miscarriage last fall.

That didn't seem to be a danger this time. I'd jarred my back when I fell, and the doctor recommended a trip to either a chiropractor or a masseuse if I didn't start to feel better in a day or two, but other than a bump on the back of my head, there didn't seem to be anything seriously wrong with me. The baby's heartbeat sounded fine to him—insanely fast in my ears, but they all assured me it was normal—and I wasn't in labor, and was in no danger of losing the baby. The knife hadn't gone deeply enough to do any damage. I hadn't even needed stitches. Just a thin stripe of surgical glue and three butterfly bandages along the side of my stomach.

So for the time being I was flat on my back being monitored, and in a short while, once all the more seriously injured had been taken care of, someone would be by to do an ultrasound, just to make sure everything was as it should be inside me.

Hernandez was still on the operating table. Wendell had left the rookies in charge of keeping watch and had stopped by to tell us that the knife had done some damage to Hernandez's internal organs, and that he'd lost a lot of blood. It was still touch and go as to whether he'd survive.

At one point, even Grimaldi walked in and up to the bed. "Can't leave you alone for a minute," she asked me, "can I?"

I smiled. "Sorry, Detective. But I caught him for you."

She grimaced. "I can do without that kind of help, thank you."

I could have done without the experience myself. Although I was glad Hernandez was in custody and off the streets, where he couldn't hurt anyone else. "You didn't have to come all this way to see me. I'm fine."

"I didn't," Grimaldi said, and added, "Not that I'm not happy to know you're fine. But I have to stick around to see what happens to Hernandez. Just in case he'd like to make a deathbed confession about where he put the bodies."

She looked around the room. "Where's your boyfriend?"

"They took him away to be re-stitched," I said. "He tore open the stitches in his arm, and a few in his chest and stomach, too. They have to put him back together and rewrap him."

"When he comes back, tell him to come find me. I want to show him the pictures of the girls you found and see if he can identify anyone."

"I'll let him know," I said.

"I have to go hover over Hernandez." She glanced sideways at the belt and monitor strapped around my stomach. "You sure you're OK?"

"I'm fine. The baby's fine. Listen to the heartbeat. Doesn't it sound fine?"

She shrugged.

"They're doing an ultrasound later. It may be late enough by now that they can see whether it's a boy or a girl."

"Do you care whether it's a boy or a girl, Savannah?" my sister wanted to know from over by the wall.

I shook my head. "As long as it's healthy, I don't care. I probably don't even care then. Although I hope it's healthy."

Just between you and me, a girl might be nice, though. Rafe already had a boy, and I'm not sure I'd know what to do with one. With a girl you can buy pretty dresses and little hair barrettes and shiny shoes with bows, but a boy is going to get dirty a lot and bring worms and frogs into the house. Girls sound like they'd be easier. And I've had more practice with girls. Not only am I one, but I've spent more time with Dix's daughters than with Catherine and Jonathan's sons. It isn't that I don't like Cole and Robert—of course I do—but they feel sort of foreign to me. I suspect they feel the same way about me.

"Do you have a name picked out?"

"We haven't talked about it. And I guess we didn't want to get too invested until we knew for sure that everything was all right." Since I'd lost a baby last year, and another three years ago.

Catherine nodded. "I have some good ideas, if you have a hard time coming up with something."

I didn't think that was going to be a problem, but I told her I'd keep it in mind. But between my family and Rafe's, there were plenty of options. We couldn't use Robert, after my father, since Catherine had already done that. But there was Calvert, after Mother's family. Dix's middle name. We could call him Cal for short. Cal Collier. Or name him after one of the longer-ago relatives, like great-grandfather William. Or maybe Tyrell, after Rafe's father. I could only imagine Mother's reaction to that.

It might be worth doing, just for the expression on her face.

Or maybe we should just call him Martin, my maiden name. Martin Collier had a nice ring to it.

And if it was a girl, she could be Margaret Jean, after my mother and Rafe's. Or LaDonna Anne, ditto. Or Tondalia, after his grandmother, although Mother wasn't likely to approve of that, either.

She could be Sheila, after Dix's late wife.

Then again, maybe none of us needed that reminder every day.

Or maybe Lila, after my friend Lila Vaughn. It was Lila's murderer who had tied me to the bed in his McMansion that time when Rafe came and rescued me. And while none of us needed to live with the reminder that Sheila was gone, it might be nice to remember Lila that way.

I had a few other ideas too, but the conversation had started up again.

"I'm sorry I'm going to miss that," Grimaldi said politely, but with an expression that said clearly that she was thrilled she didn't have to sit through my ultrasound, "but I should go find Hernandez and see how things are going. If he dies on the table, we've lost our only chance to find those bodies."

I nodded. "Go." The missing women's families deserved closure, if we could give it to them. Maria's family had cared enough about her to file a missing person's report. They'd waited for more than four years for her to come back. I'd waited less than twenty-four hours for Rafe, and they'd been the longest twenty-four hours of my life. If he hadn't come back when he did—if he hadn't come back at all—I don't know how I could have stood it. So while we couldn't give Maria's family their relative back, we could give them the knowledge of what had happened to her, and the assurance that her killer was behind bars—or dead, if things turned out that way. Maybe we'd even be able to give them a body, or what was left of one.

If Rafe hadn't come back, I would have wanted to know what happened to him. Even if he'd left me. Even if he didn't want to be with me—or with the baby. Even if he was dead. I would want to know what happened.

And if there was a body, I would have wanted it. Bodies bring closure. So if Grimaldi could get the location of Maria's remains out of Hernandez before he died, it would help Maria's parents. They'd still grieve, but they'd have their daughter back.

What was left of her, after four years.

So Grimaldi left on her grisly errand, and after a few seconds, so did Bob Satterfield. "Y'all don't mind if I go see what's going on, do you? My county and all?"

None of us did, not that it would have mattered if we had. He was right: it was his county and technically speaking his job. If Mother had begged, he might have stayed with her, but of course she didn't. So he walked out of the room, and the rest of us settled back down to our small-talk while we waited for the ultrasound technician. For a couple of minutes, anyway, until we heard rapid footsteps in the hallway outside.

Virginia Flannery burst through the door. "David!"

She's short and plump and blonde, with pale blue eyes. A bustling sort of woman in her forties, no taller than her son. David takes after his father. Both of them. Sam stopped in the doorway a moment later, tall and skinny, bald and black.

"Mom!" David launched himself off the chair and into Ginny's arms. Sam wrapped them both in long arms, his nose buried equally in Ginny's blond curls and David's short crop of black.

It was a lovely family moment, broken only when Ginny took David by the shoulders to shake him. "Don't you *ever* do that again!"

"I just wanted to help," David said.

"And you did," I told him. He had. If he hadn't launched himself on top of Hernandez, we might all be dead. I would certainly be. "But your mom's right. We were all worried sick about you. You can't keep running away. If you do, we'll all have heart attacks, and then where will you be, with nobody left to take care of you?"

"I can take care of myself," David said, even as he leaned into his father. Ginny turned to me, her eyes wet.

"Thank you for finding him."

"I didn't," I told her. "He found my mother, all on his own." I glanced at her, and she got up from the chair in the corner and came to shake Ginny's hand.

"Margaret Anne Martin."

"Virginia Flannery," Ginny said, and no doubt shocked the daylights out of Mother by wrapping her in a hug. "Thank you for helping my son!"

"He's a lovely boy," Mother said uncomfortably, "and as Savannah said, he found me."

"You still haven't told me about that," I told David, just as much because I was curious as to give Mother a hand. Ginny let her go, and turned to her son.

"I'd like to hear it, too."

Sam nodded.

"I wanted to help," David said. "So I waited until everyone was asleep, and then I left. I was going to go to the Bog, because I thought he might be there—" Again, no one bothered to ask who 'he' was, "but when I got there, everything was gone."

I nodded. "A company called Cornerstone bought the land last summer, to develop. It took them until this spring to have all the trailers and shacks removed. But then the owner got himself in trouble," of his own making, although there was no sense in mentioning that, "and now everything's on hold again. But the Bog's just a patch of dirt right now."

"I didn't know what to do," David said. "I'd been cycling all night. I was tired. I wanted to sleep. But there was nowhere to go."

Not unless he wanted to curl up under a tree. But maybe he'd had enough of that during the week he'd spent at camp.

"But then I remembered that you grew up here, too. I didn't know where to find your brother—" His gaze glanced off Dix, "—but my dad... my other dad... Rafe told me that you'd grown up in this big mansion on the other side of town from where he grew up. So I went that way. And when I saw it, I figured that had to be it." He shrugged. "He said it looked sort of like a funeral home."

I suppressed a smile. Dix didn't bother, since Mother wasn't looking at him.

"But nobody was there," David said, "so I sat down to wait. And then I guess I fell asleep."

And so he reduced the whole night, all his effort and all our worrying, to just a few sentences.

"I found him curled up on the porch swing when I came home from lunch," Mother told Ginny and Sam. "I took him inside and fed him." Her face darkened. "And then that monster showed up."

"Monster?" Ginny said blankly. I guess Rafe hadn't bothered to go into that aspect of things on the phone.

And just as well. The less she knew, the less she'd worry.

"An old acquaintance of Rafe's," I explained, downplaying things as much as I could. "He was just released from prison, and decided to come after Rafe, since Rafe was the one who put him there."

Sam nodded. I guess maybe he'd done some research on Rafe before letting him spend time with David. I wouldn't blame him. If David were my child, I'd do the same.

"And when he lost Rafe," I continued, "he started going after the people in Rafe's life. It was pure bad luck that David was here. He was aiming for Mother." And eventually me, although he couldn't have known, when he followed her and Dix home this morning, that I'd be showing up in Sweetwater by late afternoon.

"He tied us up," David said, his voice smaller now, less cocky and self-assured, "and marched us down to the basement. It was dark, and it smelled bad. Savannah opened the door once. I could hear her voice. But she didn't come down the stairs. And then we waited until she went outside before he took us back upstairs. And he tied me to the chair and made Savannah's mother take all her clothes off, and he put her on the bed..."

His eyes were full of tears and remembered horror.

"Where is he now?" Sam wanted to know, his voice grim.

"On his way to the morgue." The answer came from behind him, from the doorway. Rafe slipped back into the room, the bandages around his arm and chest once again sparkling white, even if his shirt still sported blood stains. This time, the wounded arm was in a sling.

"He didn't make it through surgery?" I asked.

He shook his head. "Died on the table."

"Did he tell Grimaldi where the bodies are buried?"

That sounded sort of flippant, and I added, "Of the women you think he killed four years ago, I mean. Did you see her? Did she show you the pictures?"

He nodded. "She did, yeah. And no, he didn't."

"Damn." I shot a guilty look at Mother. "I mean, darn."

"We'll find'em." He extended a hand to Sam, and they shook. "Good to see you, man."

"You, too," Sam told him, with a nod to Rafe's arm. "What happened there?"

"Spent some time with an old friend. Long story." And one he clearly didn't want to talk about right now. "I'll tell you over a beer sometime. They stitched it back up. I've just gotta take it easy for a couple days."

Sam nodded. "I'm sorry the man died. I would have liked to have seen him go back to prison."

We all would. But that's life. Sometimes you win, and sometimes you lose.

He and Ginny left a couple of minutes later, taking David with them. He was headed back to camp to finish out his two weeks. I'm sure Ginny would have liked to have kept him at home, where she could hug and squeeze him as much as she wanted, and assure herself that he was whole and safe, but she sucked it up and said yes when he asked if he was going back to camp.

"You made a commitment, son," Sam added. "You gotta see it through."

David grinned. "Good. We're watching *Young Frankenstein* on the big screen tomorrow, and I don't wanna miss it."

So that was that. They walked out, and left the rest of us—the family—alone together again.

There was a moment of silence, broken only by the thump-thump-thump of the baby's heartbeat from the monitors. Rafe tilted his head to listen, and his lips curved.

"What a lovely family," Mother murmured. I glanced at her,

startled, but of course she wasn't talking about us.

"Ginny and Sam? Yes, they're great. David got lucky when he ended up with them." I turned to Rafe. "I'm sorry, but..."

He chuckled and sat down on the edge of the bed. "Don't worry about hurting my feelings, darlin'. I woulda made a lousy father back then. And Elspeth woulda made a lousy mother. Besides, I was in prison."

I nodded.

"I'll do better now." He put a hand on my belly, next to the monitor, his skin dark against the fish-belly whiteness of mine. A Southern Belle avoids the sun at all costs. It promotes wrinkles and premature aging.

"You'll do great," I told him, breathlessly, as the warmth of his palm seeped into my skin. The belly was cool, exposed like this in the air conditioning. "You're great with David. He adores you. And you'll be great with the baby, too."

"Just gotta make sure I stay alive."

"Yes," I said, "I think it would be really great if you could do that."

Twenty-Two

As it turned out, it was a few weeks too soon to be able to determine the baby's gender. The ultrasound tech did her best, and said it looked like it might be a girl, because she couldn't see a little wee-wee—her word—but she warned us that the absence of the wee-wee at this point wasn't conclusive, since it was still early in the pregnancy.

"Another three to four weeks," she said, "and you should be able to get a better idea."

"But everything's normal?"

She smiled. "Everything's fine. The heartbeat is healthy and everything looks good. You're seeing an OB, aren't you?"

I nodded. Growing up, my gynecologist had been Dr. Seaver in Columbia, but she wasn't practicing anymore, and besides, I lived in Nashville now. I had found myself an obstetrician closer to home, and was getting regular checkups. Not frequent ones yet, but I had a monthly appointment in two weeks, and we were supposed to talk about scheduling an ultrasound then.

"Then I'm sure everything will be just fine." She gathered up her equipment and headed for the door.

"So I'm good to go?" I called after her. "I don't have to stay here any longer?"

She shook her head. "No reason that I can see why you should." She disappeared into the hallway. I turned to the family.

"Sorry about that."

"There's nothing to be sorry about," Mother said firmly. "The baby is healthy. That's all that matters."

Very nice of her to say that. And a bit surprising, since I'd been fairly certain that she was not excited at the prospect of being a grandmother to Rafe's child.

"When I had the three of you," she added, "we had to wait until after you were born to know whether you were boy or girl."

"The bad old days."

"Surprises can be nice," Mother said primly.

"Much easier to pick a paint color if you know what you're having, though," Catherine told her. I wasn't surprised. My sister has always been the pragmatic one of the three of us. It comes from being the eldest, I assume.

She got to her feet. "If the excitement's over, I think I'll go home to my own kids. They've probably turned the house upside down by now. I hope Jonathan's all right."

"I'll go with you," Dix said, and got up, too, "and get my two."

"You'd better," Catherine told him. "You drove me here."

"Right." He turned to me. "You all right, Savannah?"

"Fine," I said. "I'll just wait for someone to come and take this monitor off my stomach, and then Rafe and I'll drive home."

To our house in East Nashville where the sheets were still bloody because Wendell and the rookies had been busy here and hadn't had the time or opportunity to get us a new mattress.

"I think you should stay the night," Mother said, and we all turned to her. She ignored the variously shocked and aghast expressions. "Not in the hospital. At the house."

I opened my mouth, and closed it again without speaking. I didn't know what to say. I never thought I'd see the day when my mother volunteered to have Rafe stay at her house. And not just volunteered, but actively encouraged.

"You're still in pain," she told me, which was certainly true, "and I'm sure Rafael could use a good night's sleep before driving back to Nashville."

He probably could. As good a night's sleep as he could expect under my mother's roof, with her disapproving presence just down the hall.

"If you're worried about privacy," Mother added, which was as close as she'd ever come to acknowledging that Rafe and I were having sex, sometimes even under her roof, "I plan to find Bob and spend the night with him."

As close as she would probably ever come to acknowledging that she was having sex with the sheriff, too.

Catherine and Dix sported matching expressions of mingled shock and horrified fascination. Rafe looked like he had a hard time keeping a straight face. I wasn't sure what to think, let alone what to say. "Thank you," I managed eventually. "That's... um... good to know."

Mother nodded. It was a very dignified nod, even if she had flags of high color on each cheek. "I'll see you both tomorrow morning." She sailed past Catherine and Dix and out of the room with her head held high.

Hopefully the sheriff was still around, conversing with Grimaldi or Wendell and the rookies. If not, she might be coming back up here for a ride in a few minutes.

For a moment or two after she walked out, no one spoke. We all just stared straight into the air, avoiding one another's eyes. Then—

"I didn't see that coming," Dix said.

Catherine shook her head. "I'm not sure whether to applaud or go hide somewhere."

Rafe chuckled. It was easy for him; he didn't have a mother to embarrass him.

Then again, he'd surely been embarrassed plenty growing up.

"It's the adrenaline," he said. "Going through a traumatic experience like your mother did, makes some people wanna reaffirm life by banging like hammers."

He gave me an exaggerated leer. My face twisted. "Oh, eewww. If there's one thing I don't need, it's a mental picture of my mother and the sheriff banging like hammers. Eewww."

"And on that note," Catherine said, shaking her head as if to dislodge the image, "I think I've had all I can stand. Ready to go?"

She looked at Dix. He nodded. "Let's get out of here before something else happens." He turned to me. "Call me if you need anything. If not, drive safe tomorrow."

We promised we would, and Dix and Catherine vanished through the door and into the hallway. I turned back to Rafe. "You know, Mother isn't the only one who went through a traumatic experience today."

The amusement dropped off his face. "You all right, darlin'?"

"I'm fine," I said. And then qualified it. "Or maybe not exactly fine. I killed someone."

He didn't answer, just looked at me. But at least he didn't deny it, to try to make me feel better. And he didn't make light of it.

"I didn't mean to kill him. It wasn't even that I thought, consciously, 'if I turn this knife around, I can stab him with it.' We were just rolling around on the floor, fighting—"

Rafe's expression turned to stone.

"—and he was trying to stab me, and I was trying to protect myself and the baby, and then I saw David coming—he threw himself on top of Hernandez, chair and all—and I knew the knife would go into me if I couldn't turn it away, so I did... but it wasn't like I was trying to kill him."

Rafe shook his head.

"It was him or me, you know?" I shook my head. "I know that sounds like a cliché. It *is* a cliché. But it's the truth. He was trying to hurt me. And the knife was going to go into somebody. I just made sure it wasn't me."

Rafe nodded.

"But I wasn't trying to kill him. I didn't want to kill him. I just didn't want him to kill me. Or Mother. Or David."

Rafe nodded.

"You've killed people. Does it ever get easier?"

His mouth twisted. "Killing people?"

"Of course not." Although if you did it enough, surely even that became commonplace after a while. "Living with it. The knowledge that you ended someone's life. Does it ever go away?"

He shook his head. "If you care that you took their lives, you carry'em with you. I figure it's better that way than if you don't care."

I nodded. "Anyway, that's actually not what I was talking about."

He glanced at me, and I added, "When I said that Mother wasn't the only one who'd gone through a traumatic experience today. I didn't mean that I was upset about Hernandez. Although I am, a little. But I meant that Mother isn't the only one needing to reaffirm life."

He arched a brow.

"I promised you sex after the hospital." We had been in a different hospital when I made that promise, with him in the bed instead of me, but it came to the same thing, didn't it? "Want to go back to the mansion and bang like hammers?"

There was a scuffing sound over by the door. I looked up, and Rafe turned around. A blushing junior nurse stood there, looking mortified. "I'm sorry. I'm so sorry."

She wouldn't even look at either of us, and her cheeks were as red as apples.

Rafe turned back to me. "Soon as we get outta here," he said, with a wink.

But of course it wasn't that easy. The belt and monitor had to come off, and after being hooked up to it for an hour or more, I had gotten used to hearing the rapid pitter-patter of the baby's heartbeat. The silence once it was gone, was deafening.

Then before we could leave, we had to track down Grimaldi,

Wendell, and the rookies, and confer with them.

We found them in the lobby, discussing what their next moves should be. Hernandez was dead, and couldn't pay for his crimes beyond what he'd already paid, but Grimaldi wanted to find the women Rafe suspected he'd killed. And without Hernandez's input, that was going to be tricky. As far as anyone knew, Hernandez was the only person who knew what he'd done with the bodies. And that was if Rafe was right and there were bodies. He could be wrong, and the women could be alive and maybe even well somewhere.

Talk about finding a couple of needles in a haystack.

"I might could help you with that," Rafe said, after we'd stood and listened for a minute.

Grimaldi turned to him. "How could you do that?"

"I know where he lived back then. We could start there."

Grimaldi thought about it. "You think he might have buried them under the floorboards?"

"No," Rafe said. And qualified it by adding, "Prob'ly not. But it's worth checking."

Grimaldi shrugged. "Sure."

"Here's the address." He recited it. Wendell nodded. Obviously he remembered the place. The address sounded vaguely familiar to me too, although I don't know how I would have known where Eugenio Hernandez lived four years ago, so it must just be my imagination.

"Savannah and I are gonna stay the night down here," Rafe added. "We could meet you in Nashville in the morning."

"Ten o'clock," Grimaldi said. "If you think you can drag yourselves out of bed by then. And let's keep this between the..." She counted heads, "seven of us for the time being."

Wendell nodded. "No sense in bringing out the backhoe until we know something for sure. You boys up for some digging?"

The rookies exchanged a glance. "Whatever you need, boss-man," Jamal said. Clayton and José nodded.

"Let's go." Wendell nodded to the doors, and the rookies filed in that direction, with nods to the rest of us, and gentle punches in the shoulder for Rafe.

"Take care, man." Jamal grinned. "When're you coming back to the mat? I might could take you now."

"If you can only take him when he's got one arm in a sling," Wendell told him, "we gotta work on your hand-to-hand some more. Move it, boy."

He shooed Jamal ahead of him toward the sliding doors. Jamal grinned and went.

"They seem like nice boys," I told Rafe when the doors had closed behind them.

He nodded. "Not somebody you'd wanna meet in a dark alley, but yeah. They're good kids."

"They chose the TBI over a life of crime. That has to count for something."

"It ain't a tough choice," Rafe told me, and I guess he ought to know, since he'd been asked to make it. "They tell you they can get you out in two weeks if you'll just do'em a little favor, or you're staying in for three more years. It don't take much brains to know which one to pick."

"Were they all in prison?" Grimaldi wanted to know, starting to make her own way toward the sliding door. We fell into step with her, and Rafe shook his head.

"Just Clayton. Stupid kid got caught working in a chop shop. He told somebody he had information about a statewide system for moving stolen cars, so he got tossed to us. Jamal's kid brother went down to gang violence, so he wants to do something about the Bloods and the Crips, and José just wanted to be in law enforcement. Kid's fluent in Spanish, so he'll be useful. You never know when someone might set up another SATG." He grinned.

If someone did, then José could deal with it. I looked at Grimaldi as we passed through the door and into the sticky humidity of the parking lot. "I guess you're headed back to Nashville."

She nodded. "I thought I might stop by your brother's house on my way."

Sure. Never mind the fact that Dix's house is almost thirty minutes in the opposite direction of the one she was going.

"I'm sure he'd like that," I said. "You two barely had time to say a word to each other all weekend."

She shrugged. "You two going back to your mother's house?"

I said we were. "She informed us she's spending the night with Bob Satterfield."

"She came and got him," Grimaldi said. "Determined lady, your mother."

"It's the Southern Belle thing. We always get our way." In a very polite and ladylike fashion, but we get it nonetheless. Just as I was about to get mine with Rafe, once we got back to the mansion.

"Enjoy your visit with Dix," I told Grimaldi. "We'll see you tomorrow morning."

"See you then." She headed for her car. We turned in the other direction for mine.

"Do you want me to drive?" I asked when we got there. "That arm must be hurting." After being stitched up twice in twelve or fifteen hours.

"I ain't proud." He walked around to the passenger side. "You sure you're all right?" he added when he'd gotten in.

"I'm fine." I turned the key in the ignition, and the Volvo purred to life. "I've still got some lower back pain from when I hit the floor, and a low-grade headache, but just knowing that the baby's all right and that no damage was done, makes me feel better."

He nodded. "When I walked into that room and saw you on the floor, with blood all over your stomach..."

He had thought the worst had happened. Of course.

"It was his blood," I said, heading out of the parking lot. Ahead of me, I could see Grimaldi's police issue sedan. It took a left out of the hospital entrance and zoomed south on the Pulaski Highway. "Hernandez's. But I'm sure it looked awful."

"I thought he did what he said he was gonna do, and cut you open."

"He tried. He didn't succeed." We pulled up to the stop sign and looked both ways before following Grimaldi. "I'm all right. The baby's all right. David and Mother are all right. You're even sort of all right."

"I'm fine," Rafe said, apparently thinking nothing of the Death of a Thousand Cuts.

"Sure."

He slid me a narrow glance. "Ain't nothing wrong with the part of me you're interested in."

"I'm interested in every part of you," I said, "although I admit at the moment, one part interests me more than the others."

His lips curved. "Uh-huh."

"I thought I lost you. When you weren't there in the morning on our wedding day, I thought you wouldn't be coming back."

He didn't respond to that.

"We should be married by now. We should have been on our honeymoon this weekend. And instead we've had to deal with this... this... this!"

"Sorry, darlin'."

"I'm not blaming you," I said. "God, Rafe. It's not your fault that some nutcase comes after you. Or after me. You did your job. You saved a woman's life four years ago. Little Ginger got herself straightened out and went away to college. Grimaldi told me."

"Good for Ginger," Rafe said.

"But Mother isn't the only one who needs to reaffirm life. I was afraid I'd lost you. I thought we'd never be together again. I need to get you naked and horizontal and have my way with you."

Those curved lips turned into a grin. "I'm always up for that."

"I don't doubt it," I told him, and stepped on the gas.

The mansion was empty and dark when we got there. Mother, as she'd told us, was nowhere to be found. Reaffirming things with Bob, no doubt. In broad daylight, too. It wasn't even six o'clock yet. I wondered what Todd thought of the proceedings. He lived with his dad, and if Mother and Bob weren't here, then they were there. The only other option was a room in a cheap motel out by the interstate, and that was something I couldn't imagine Mother doing.

But maybe Todd was busy elsewhere. He'd been conspicuously absent from the hospital. And the last time I'd had any contact with him, he had seemed like maybe he had started to look beyond me for love.

I don't mind telling you it had been a relief. Having him show up at the hospital this afternoon would have been beyond awkward.

Anyway, the house was empty. We walked up the stairs hand in hand, but hesitated in the hallway outside my door.

"That bloody rug is still on the floor in my mother's room," I said.

Rafe nodded.

"Do you think we should move it?"

"You sure you're up for that?"

I was more concerned that he wasn't up for it, with his arm, although he was right: I shouldn't lift anything too heavy, either.

"It's a fairly small rug. There are two of us. And I think she'd probably appreciate if it were gone the next time she walks into the room."

"Anything I can do to please your mama," Rafe said

So we went into the master bedroom and rolled up the fluffy rug and staggered down the stairs with it. Or at least I staggered, with the roll of carpet on my shoulder and one hand on the banister. Rafe sauntered, with the roll of carpet tucked under his good arm. He wasn't even breathing hard. "Where d'you wanna take it?"

"Out," I panted.

"You all right?"

"Fine." We hit the bottom of the stairs and started moving across the foyer. "Let's just put it in the trunk of the car. We can throw it away when we get home."

"No problem."

We headed that way, and two minutes later, the rug was wedged into the trunk of the Volvo. Rafe slammed the lid and turned to me. "Everything OK in there?" He put a hand on my stomach.

"Everything's fine. There and everywhere else." The rug really hadn't been that heavy. Just big and unwieldy. "Is your arm all right?"

He twisted it back and forth inside the sling. "Fine."

"You should get some rest." Flat on his back, with me on top of him.

His lips curved. "Prob'ly."

I took his hand again, and we made the trek upstairs a second time. This time, there was no hesitation in the hallway, and no rug to remove. Nothing else to do, either. We just went into my room, closed the door, and turned to each other.

He reached out a hand and slipped it around my neck and into my hair. And then he tilted my head back so he could lean down and fit his lips over mine.

I got a bit emotional. I hadn't been sure I'd ever get the chance to kiss him again. And when I wrapped my arms around his waist, I must have held on a little too tight, because he murmured against my lips, "Careful, darlin'."

"Oh, God." I'd forgotten that he was injured. "I'm so sorry!"

The corners of his mouth twitched. "You could kiss it and

make it better."

"I could." I definitely could. "Maybe you should just get on the bed," I suggested. "By yourself. Carefully. And once you're there, I'll come over and make you feel better." Maybe that way I wouldn't hurt him.

And in fact, there didn't seem to be much wrong with him at all when he sauntered over to the bed and made himself comfortable, with his ankles crossed and one arm folded behind his head. If it hadn't been for the sling and bandages, visible through the open shirt, I wouldn't have known there was anything wrong with him at all.

"How about some music?" he suggested.

"Music?" It took me a second to catch on. Maybe more than one. "You're not asking me to strip, are you?"

"You said you'd do anything I wanted."

"Yes, but..." Take my clothes off to music? In daylight? "I'm fat."

"You're not fat," Rafe said. "You're pregnant. And hot." He looked me over from top to bottom. "But I can do without the music. I like that shirt."

His eyes zeroed in on my breasts. The blouse was one of Mother's, raw silk and a bit smaller on me than on her. It was snug across my chest. Snug everywhere else, too.

In fact, it might feel good to get out of it. I was having difficulty breathing.

Although in all honesty, that might not be the fault of the blouse. That could just be from the way he was looking at me.

I lifted my hands to the top button.

"Keep going," Rafe said, his eyes turning darker as he watched me flip open the buttons, one after the other. When I shrugged out of the blouse and let it drop to the floor, he smiled. "Now the skirt."

It was tight, too, and pulling the zipper down definitely felt good. I shimmied the skirt down to my ankles, and stepped out of it.

"C'mere." He crooked a finger at me.

"What about the shoes? And the rest of it?" Bra and panties. Mine. Not Mother's.

"The shoes are hot," Rafe said. "They can stay. And I'll deal with the rest of it."

"I thought this was supposed to be about me having my way with you."

But I obeyed that beckoning finger and headed for the bed. Slowly, since I could tell that although I felt self-conscious, he was enjoying the view.

He reached out for me as soon as I got close enough. "C'mon up here."

No problem. I crawled onto the bed, and for good measure onto Rafe, as well. And if I had needed proof that he still found me desirable, that proof was now nestled between my thighs.

He made a small sound—halfway groan, halfway sigh—when I moved against him. Maybe a bit of laughter, too. "You trying to kill me, darlin'? I'm already weak, remember."

"You don't feel weak to me," I informed him. "But you're right. None of that yet. I was supposed to kiss it and make it better."

"No..." But when I leaned down and put my lips to a patch of his chest that wasn't covered by bandages, he dropped back on the pillow, this time with an arm covering his eyes. "You're gonna kill me. I know it."

"No, I won't." I found another patch of skin and kissed it. "Not yet." And then another. And another. By the time I had dropped kisses all the way down his stomach to the waistband of his jeans, his body was quivering like a plucked guitar string.

When I flicked open the button in his jeans, he lifted his head. "You just better not be thinking that I can last if you do anything like that down there."

"Really? You usually like it when I do things like that down here."

"Not today," Rafe said. "I dunno if it's the pain pills or just the pain, but I ain't got that much control at the moment."

"Really?" That was disappointing. Pushing Rafe to the limits of his (considerable) control is something I enjoy doing, but only if he has control to spare. If he wasn't even going to present a challenge, what was the point?

And besides, he'd mentioned pain. That isn't something that happens often.

I pulled the zipper down, very carefully, and just as carefully slipped my hand underneath. "Maybe I just need to be very gentle with you."

"Yeah," Rafe said, his voice hoarse. "Very... damn... gentle."

I was gentle for a minute, and then I managed to the jeans down to his knees. Getting them the rest of the way necessitated getting off the bed, so I did. And while I was standing up, I shimmied out of the panties I still had on, as well as unhooked my bra.

"Keep the shoes on," Rafe said, watching from under his arm.

"Don't you have enough scars?" But I kept them on as I climbed back on the bed. "Now you just stay there and let me do everything. Don't move unless I tell you to."

"You got a little bit of dominatrix in you, darlin'?" He was grinning, eyes lit with laughter, but they turned to liquid black when I sank down on him. "Christ..."

"Like I said." I wiggled, just to get more comfortable, and because it made his eyes roll back in his head. "You just lie back and enjoy."

"Yes, ma'am."

But of course he didn't. It started out slow and gentle, but then his hands found my hips, and slow and gentle gave way to a driving pace that ended with us side by side on the bed, gasping for breath. I only remembered at the very last second that I couldn't collapse on his chest the way I normally do, and

I'm afraid I may have hurt him when I rolled to the side and plopped on my back next to him. He grunted, anyway, and then just lay there, struggling to catch his breath.

"I didn't hurt you," I managed when I could talk again, "did I?"

He rolled his head to look at me. "I was hurt already, darlin'."

Oh, God. "I'm sorry," I said wretchedly. "It was supposed to be gentle."

His lips curved. "It started out gentle."

"It didn't end there."

The smile turned to a grin. "No."

"You're incorrigible," I told him and rolled to a sitting position. "When was the last time you took a pain pill?"

"They gave me something at the hospital when they stitched me up."

That didn't answer my question. "Not a pill, though. Right? A shot?"

He nodded. "Yeah."

"I'll get you one." I got to my feet and—after finally kicking off the shoes—padded over to where his jeans had landed. The pill bottle was in the pocket. I'd felt it earlier. "Here you go." I shook one out and put it on the bedside table. "Let me get you some water to take it with."

I didn't wait for him to answer, just walked out of the room and up the hall to the bathroom. When I came back into the bedroom a minute later, the pill was gone and Rafe was asleep. His eyelashes fluttered when I put my hand on his cheek and said his name, but he didn't stir. I put the water down and walked around the bed to where I could curl up next to him, and then I pulled the blankets up over both of us and went to sleep, too.

Twenty-Three

Rafe slept all the way through the night, and woke up in the morning looking a lot better.

I didn't—sleep all the way through the night, I mean. I was up a couple of times, hyper-alert for any noise or movement, however slight. But every time I opened my eyes, everything was as it should be. Rafe was there, next to me, and we were both safe.

When I opened my eyes for the third or fourth time—into daylight—he was already awake, lying on his side looking at me.

"Morning, darlin'."

"Good morning," I said. "You look like you feel better." The dark pain from yesterday was gone from his eyes, and the shadows were gone from under them. He was, perhaps, just a touch pale still, but otherwise he seemed OK. And the bandages around his arm and chest were still pristine, still white. No fresh bloodstains.

"Amazing what sex can do for a guy." He grinned.

For a girl, too. I felt good, as well. When I stretched, experimentally, the pain in my lower back and stomach seemed to be gone.

It was still early—before seven-thirty by the clock on the bureau across the room—but I could smell coffee.

"I think Mother's back."

Rafe nodded. "Smells that way."

"And we have places to go, people to see."

He nodded.

"If possible, I'd like to stop at home first, before we go to meet Grimaldi, to change clothes. Everything of Mother's is tight, especially now that I'm pregnant."

"I kinda like the tight clothes on you," Rafe said, and grinned unrepentantly when I looked at him. "Sorry, darlin'. I'm a guy. We like women in tight dresses."

"But I'm fat."

He shook his head. "No, darlin'. You're pregnant. They're different."

"I don't look pregnant," I said. "I just look fat. I don't have that front-heavy figure yet. So it just looks like I've gotten thick around the middle."

His hand was back on my stomach, moving in circles. "You're not thick around the middle. You're making a baby in there. My baby."

"Easy for you to say," I grumbled. "You're perfect."

Hard muscles, smooth skin, 3% body fat.

"Oh, yeah. Those scars are gonna look great when they heal. I'm gonna be walking around with this fucker's name carved into my stomach for the rest of my life."

I sat up, fast enough that my head spun. "What?"

He stayed where he was, looking up at me. "I guess you didn't look at'em close enough to see that, huh?"

I shook my head. I hadn't looked closely at the damage done to him at all. One quick glimpse had been enough. More than enough.

"Yeah. He carved his name in there. Called it signing his work."

My stomach flipped. "That's grotesque." And stupid. How had he expected to be able to get away with murder if his name was carved into the victims' skin, for God's sake?

"I don't imagine he thought I'd leave," Rafe said.

"No. But still. That's not very smart."

He shrugged.

"Did he 'sign his work'—" I made quotation marks in the air, "when he killed Kelly, too? The girl in our bedroom?"

Rafe nodded.

"I didn't notice that, either," I admitted.

"I don't blame you. It ain't pretty to look at."

No, it wasn't. "He might have 'signed' the other women he killed too, then. If there's enough left of them when we find them..."

Rafe nodded and rolled away from me. "Let's get outta here. Get this thing done."

I nodded. I'd been thinking that another quickie might be nice before we got up, but this conversation had effectively made me lose my appetite, so to speak. "Do you want to take a shower?"

He shook his head. "Not for a couple days. Can't get the bandages wet."

"I took one yesterday afternoon," I said. "I think I'm good, too. Let's just brush and go."

"We'll have to stop and talk to your mama."

We did. Much as I just wanted to sneak out of the house without facing her—and the fact that she'd spent the night with Bob Satterfield—it would be rude not to thank her for her hospitality.

"You can have the bathroom first," I told him.

He nodded. "I'll be quick."

"Don't worry about it. Just take the time you need." I stayed where I was and watched him pad across the floor to the door, naked except for the bandages circling his torso and arm. As he passed through the door and into the hallway, I giggled. Hopefully Mother was downstairs, where the coffee smell came from, and not up here. I could just imagine my mother coming face to face with my naked boyfriend in the hallway.

Then again, maybe it would explain a few things to her.

Not that the way he looks and the size of his equipment is all that attracted me to him. Far from it. But the fact that he makes me go dry-mouthed every time I see him naked isn't exactly a bad thing.

And anyway, he'd seen Mother naked yesterday. It seemed

fair. As he'd told me once, 'tit for tat.'

But there was no scream of outrage from the hallway. Just the sound of the bathroom door closing. Mother must be in the kitchen.

I rolled out of bed and dragged on used underwear and the same clothes I'd worn yesterday. I will not raid my mother's underwear drawer—there are limits—and if we were going home anyway, I might as well just wear the same clothes I'd borrowed yesterday. No sense dirtying anything else. Both blouse and skirt were wrinkled from spending the night crumpled on the floor, but I shook the wrinkles out the best I could, and put them on. By the time Rafe padded back into the bedroom, his body somewhat less alert than when he'd left, I was already dressed. "Do you need help with your clothes?"

He grimaced. "Prob'ly."

Hard to bend, no doubt. I helped him with the things he couldn't do himself, and left him to handle what he could while I went to the bathroom and brushed my teeth. When I came back into the bedroom, he was buttoned up and ready to go. We walked down the stairs together, along the hallway and into the kitchen.

Mother was there, of course, also wearing the same clothes she'd worn last night. They also looked worse for wear, like she'd left them crumpled on the floor, too.

"Good morning," I said brightly.

She turned to me, and looked me up and down. "Good morning, darling." Usually she would have mentioned something about the rumpled way I looked, and would have been justified in doing so, but she refrained. I was grateful.

Then she moved her attention to Rafe. Her eyes lingered for a second on his shirt, and the bloodstains, and her mouth compressed.

"We're going home to change," I said defensively. "We didn't realize we'd be spending the night here. If we had, I would have brought a change of clothes."

"Of course, darling." She turned to the coffee machine. "Coffee?"

"Not for me. It isn't good for the baby." I headed to the refrigerator for the orange juice instead. And I was just about to ask Rafe whether he'd like coffee, since Mother doesn't address him directly, when—

"Rafael? Coffee?"

I blinked. So did Rafe.

"Yeah," he said after a second. "Thanks."

Mother poured coffee for him with her own hands. "Sugar? Milk?"

"Just black. Thanks."

She handed the cup to him with her own hands, too, instead of setting it on the counter in front of him. I watched, so intently that I almost over-poured the juice, and I think it's possible their fingers may have touched when they transferred the cup from hand to hand.

"Darling," Mother said.

"What?"

She nodded to my glass, about to overflow.

"Oh. Sorry," I tilted the rest of the juice into the carton and put it back in the fridge. Rafe sipped his coffee. I sincerely hoped it wasn't poisoned. But Mother already had a cup, it seemed, so unless she'd brewed his separately, I didn't think so.

"What are the two of you up to today?" She sipped from her cup.

"We're going to meet Detective Grimaldi and Wendell and the rookies to see if we can find the bodies of the women Rafe thinks Hernandez murdered four years ago," I said.

Mother swallowed wrong and coughed. I patted her on the back until she stopped. "*You're* going to do that?"

"I know it isn't particularly ladylike." And might be unpleasant. Being outside would be hot and sticky, and human remains are gross. "But I feel sort of invested now. I'd like to see the case through to the end. And we may not find anything."

I glanced at Rafe. He shook his head. And he was still breathing—and still drinking—so that was a good thing.

"And after that?" Mother asked.

I glanced at Rafe again. "I guess we'll go home and clean up. Get a new mattress and sheets for the bed. Wendell and the boys will help us with that, since we can't really haul anything too heavy ourselves." And since that reminded me, I added, "We took the rug out of your room. We'll throw it away once we get home." There was a dumpster up the street across from Malcolm's house, in the driveway where Hernandez had been biding his time yesterday morning. We could toss it in there.

Mother blinked. "Thank you."

"It was no problem," I told her. "It just took a few minutes. And we didn't want you to have to deal with it when you came home."

"That was thoughtful."

"We were happy to do it." I glanced at Rafe, who nodded. Whether he'd been happy to do it or not last night, he made it look sincere now, anyway.

"Will you reschedule the ceremony?" Mother asked, and for a second, I couldn't think what ceremony she was talking about. Then I remembered: the wedding. The one we should have had two days ago, when she'd driven up to Nashville to see me marry Rafe.

"I assume." I looked at him. "You still want to get married, right?"

He nodded. "Yeah."

"Then we'll reschedule. We'll let you know for where and when."

Or maybe we'd just elope. Get in the car and drive the four hours to the Smoky Mountains, and go to one of the wedding chapels. We could have Elvis sing me down the aisle, and spend our wedding night in a mountain chalet with a heart-shaped tub. And we wouldn't have to deal with any of our friends or family.

Mother cleared her throat. "You could get married here," she said.

I stared at her.

"At the mansion."

I blinked. And looked at Rafe. Mother did, too.

"Rafael," she said. And although it sounded like she had a slight problem getting the word out, she did.

Rafe looked at her.

"Would you consider..." She gave her head a little shake. "Would you consent to..."

But apparently that one didn't pass muster, either. "I would consider it an honor if you would marry my daughter here. In Sweetwater."

There was silence. I think we were both too shocked to speak. I know I was.

I looked at Mother. I looked at Rafe. I looked back at Mother.

I opened my mouth to ask who she was and what she'd done with my real mother, but closed it again, since the levity was misplaced. The thought did cross my mind, though.

Through it all Rafe didn't say a word. Just looked at her. I don't know what he was looking for, but he must have found it, because finally he nodded.

It wasn't a 'yes, I'll do that' nod. It was more of an 'I see what you're trying to do' nod.

"Savannah," he said, without looking at me.

"Yes?" My heart started beating faster.

"You wanna get married in Sweetwater?"

I hesitated, weighing my options. The honest answer was yes, I did. I had married Bradley here, in front of everyone in town. How could I do less for Rafe?

He'd been the black sheep of our hometown for as long as I could remember. LaDonna Collier's good-for-nothing colored boy. While I'd been the town princess: Margaret Anne Martin's perfect younger daughter. I wanted to stand up in front of God and everyone and promise to love and honor him for as long as we both were alive.

But I'd never kidded myself that that's what he wanted. He didn't like to come back to Sweetwater. He didn't have good memories from living here.

"It ain't a hard question," he told me. "Just say yes or no."

"If I say yes, you'll do it because you'll want to give me what I want."

"So you'll say no cause you think it's what I want you to say?"

"Isn't it?"

He didn't answer. Just turned to my mother. "Yeah. I'll marry your daughter here."

Mother's face relaxed. It was infinitesimal, but I could see it. I guess she'd been afraid he'd refuse.

As for me, I was jumping up and down inside, although I stayed as calm as I could on the outside. "Are you sure?" I asked him. "I know this isn't your favorite place in the world."

He shook his head. "I don't care about any of that. I just wanna marry you. I'll marry you anywhere you want to. You never asked if we could get married here."

"I didn't think you'd want to," I said. "It's your wedding day, too. I want you to be comfortable." And I'd been certain Mother would have a hissy fit if I made the suggestion, so I hadn't even considered it. In fact, I was still taken aback that she'd suggested it.

I turned to ask her if she, too, was sure, but before I could, she spoke. "I'll take care of all the details. The ceremony will take place next Saturday at eleven."

"This coming Saturday?"

Five days from now? That was a hell—excuse me, heck—of a lot of details in a very short time.

"Haven't you waited long enough?" Mother wanted to know.

When I didn't know what to say to that—because yes, I had—she nodded briskly. "Just leave everything to me. I'll get started right now. Excuse me, please." She walked out of the kitchen, down the hall, and into the parlor with the desk. After a moment, we could hear her voice on the phone.

I turned to Rafe, speechless.

"Go?" he asked.

I nodded. The sooner we got out of this alternate reality and away from my very alarming mother, the better I'd like it.

"That was weird."

It was five minutes later, and we had escaped the mansion and were in the car on our way to Nashville.

Rafe grinned. "Amazing what a night of good sex can do for a woman."

My nose wrinkled. "Oh, eewww. Gross."

He chuckled. "You know they were doing it."

"Yes, but she's my mother. I'm not supposed to think about that."

"Just cause she's your mother don't mean she can't have sex," Rafe said. "She ain't old. She's a good-looking woman for her age. And your daddy's dead. You should be glad she ain't alone, and that she's happy."

"I am glad she's happy. I just don't want to think about her and the sheriff doing it."

He shrugged. "Some people change when something big happens to them. She prob'ly thought she was gonna die yesterday. And that you and David were gonna die, too."

Probably. I had thought we were going to die. I had no doubt she'd thought the same. "She did offer to let us get married in the mansion, didn't she? I didn't imagine it?"

He shook his head. "She's pulling it together right now. Whaddaya wanna bet she's gonna put me in a monkey suit?"

A tuxedo? "I'm sure she will," I said. "You can't have a proper wedding without the tuxedo." And wouldn't he look absolutely gorgeous in one?

"That mean she's gonna put you in a gown, too?"

I hoped not. I was already voluminous. I didn't need a puffy gown making me look bigger. "I doubt it. Wearing the white gown for a second wedding is tacky. Especially when the bride is pregnant." And my mother is never tacky. "Besides, I doubt there's time to have a gown made." And I wouldn't fit into the one I'd worn last time. Not that Mother would suggest it. Wearing the same dress to marry Rafe that I'd worn to marry Bradley went beyond tacky and into supreme bad taste.

"You think we oughta worry about this?"

"I think she's trying to make amends," I said. "Or maybe she's just trying to make you forget you saw her naked yesterday. If she's nice to you, there's less chance you'll make a big deal out of it."

He rolled his eyes.

"You're marrying her daughter," I said. "And you saw her at her most vulnerable. You're lucky she's talking to you at all."

"I'm not sure," Rafe told me, "but I think maybe I liked it better when she didn't."

I wasn't sure either, but I thought maybe I agreed. Having Mother suddenly arranging my wedding to Rafe—in the mansion in Sweetwater—was disconcerting, to say the least.

Twenty-Four

"I remember this place," I said two hours later.

We'd driven to the house on Potsdam and changed clothes, and then we'd gone back out to meet Grimaldi, Wendell, and the rookies at the address Rafe had provided yesterday. And now that we were here, I knew why it had sounded familiar.

Some five months ago, another old acquaintance of Rafe's had walked away from a work-release program in Montgomery County, and had shown up in Nashville. Desmond Johnson hadn't been looking for Rafe; he'd been after his girlfriend and child, a toddler named Justin whom I had mistakenly believed to be Rafe's. Justin and Tanya—AKA Lantana DuBois, exotic dancer—had been living here, incognito, in a rental held in Rafe's name.

It was a brick duplex in a neighborhood south of town, the kind of place where nobody cared overmuch what anyone else did. The perfect kind of place for someone who wanted to keep a low profile and go unnoticed, and for much of his career, that had been exactly what Rafe had needed.

"I lived on one side," he told me. "Huron lived on the other."

Grimaldi arched her brows. "Wouldn't you have noticed if he'd left bodies rotting under the floorboards?"

We were all standing in the parking area in the rear of the building: she, I, Rafe, Wendell, and the three rookies.

Rafe sent her a look. "Depends," he said.

"On what? Once you've smelled a dead body, it isn't the kind of thing you forget."

No, it isn't. There was no way Rafe could have lived here while bodies were rotting in the apartment next door. Anyone with a nose would have noticed.

"I didn't stick around long after Huron was busted," he said. "People got worried about what he was telling the cops, and what kinds of deals he was trying to make to get himself outta jail."

An understandable concern when you were involved in breaking the law.

"He didn't get busted for anything we were doing, but he knew everything that was going on. We had a big job planned in about three weeks."

He glanced at Wendell. "You were getting ready to bust the whole thing open. And instead we pulled up stakes and went somewhere else. Jackson, I think."

"I remember that," Wendell nodded. "More than a year of preparation down the drain. And all because Hernandez couldn't keep his pants zipped."

A little more than that, surely. But I saw his point.

"Anyway," Rafe added, "I was outta here within a couple days. I kept up the rent on the place, but it wasn't till last summer that I came back. If there are bodies, they wouldn't smell no more by then."

No, they wouldn't.

"And it don't need to be in the house." He turned to look at the backyard, and we all turned with him. "There's a couple acres of trees back there, before you get to Murfreesboro Road. Plenty of room to dump a couple bodies. And there ain't no tracks or nothing, so nobody much goes in there."

"We have to search all of that?" José looked dismayed.

"We'll check the house first," Grimaldi said. "But if we don't find anything inside, it might come to that."

The boys exchanged a glance. "Let's go," Jamal said.

"I lived on the left," Rafe told us. That was the same unit where Tanya and Justin had stayed earlier in the year. "Huron was on the right."

"You have keys to them both?"

He shook his head. "But it'll only take me a second to open the door."

A slight exaggeration, but not by much. It took less than a minute, while Jamal, Clayton and José leaned over him, admiring his handiwork.

"When you gonna teach us to do that?" Jamal wanted to know.

Rafe glanced up at him. "I wasn't gonna for a while yet, but since there's some other things we can't do till I heal up, maybe I'll make it sooner. Tomorrow?"

"All right!" They exchanged high fives all around. I made a mental note to ask him to teach me how to pick a lock, too. You never know when a skill like that might come in handy.

Although surely the TBI wasn't expecting him back to work in the morning? He'd been injured. Didn't he get a couple of days off, at least, to recuperate?

Rafe straightened and pushed the door open. "Ladies first," he told Grimaldi, who gave him a stony stare.

She went through the door first, though. The rookies followed, after a glance at Wendell that gave them permission. He followed them inside, and Rafe turned to me. "You sure you wanna do this?"

"I doubt he has them stacked against the walls," I said. "I don't think there's anything to see in there."

He shook his head. "Prob'ly not. More likely he took'em out there." He glanced at the woods. "Or loaded'em in the trunk of the car when I wasn't looking, and took'em somewhere else."

"So no reason why I can't go inside."

"I guess not." He gestured. I walked through the door in front of him, into Hernandez's share of the duplex.

It looked like rentals all over Nashville. Not too different from the one I had occupied for a few years, if in slightly worse shape. There were the ubiquitous off-white walls, and the ever-present tan carpets everywhere except in the kitchen and bathroom, where there was seen-better-days vinyl. The kitchen cabinets were cheap particleboard, the counters fake butcher-block, and the appliances at least fifteen years out of date.

I glanced at Rafe. "Does the other side look like this, too?"

He nodded. "I know it ain't much. But I've lived in worse."

Yes, he had. I had seen the inside of the Colliers' trailer in the Bog before it was removed, and it had looked considerably worse than this. And then there were the two years he'd spent in Riverbend Penitentiary. I was reminded, not for the first time, how different our lives had been, and how lucky I was to have had mine.

The apartment wasn't very big: just the living room and small kitchen, bedroom and bath. It didn't take but a minute to determine that it was empty. Of life, and of death.

"Nothing," Jamal announced when he bounced back into the living room after checking the other rooms. Everyone else followed at a more leisurely pace. Meanwhile, Jamal looked around. "This place have a basement?"

Rafe shook his head. "Crawlspace."

"Outside?"

Rafe nodded.

"How about an attic?"

"Crawlspace," Rafe said again. "The access is in the closet on the other side. It's prob'ly in the closet on this side, too."

It was. A square panel outlined with planks in the ceiling of the closet, and pieces of wood nailed to the wall to create a makeshift ladder.

Jamal looked at it and shook his head. "Somebody else is gonna have to go up there. That ain't made for somebody my size."

Clayton and José sized each other up. Clayton was taller, but skinnier, while José was short but buff. I personally didn't think his shoulders would fit through the hole. Before I had the chance to say so, Wendell had already decided. "You," he told Clayton.

Clayton nodded. The other two gave him a boost, and he shimmied up the wall like a monkey. It took him a few seconds to lever the piece of wood out of the opening, hanging onto the wall by his other hand, but it was only a minute or so before he could wiggle through the opening and into the upper crawlspace.

It wasn't a tall space. We could see that from below. The underside of the roof was close to the floor of the crawlspace, with the spiky ends of nails poking through every so often, where the roofers had driven them through the shingles and decking into the attic.

"Your tetanus shot up to date, boy?" Wendell called up to Clayton. "We've spent enough time in the hospital this week."

"I'll be careful, boss."

Clayton crawled out of sight. We heard him moving around, and occasionally a muttered, "Shit," but nothing that would indicate he'd found Hernandez's graveyard.

After a couple of minutes he came back, his head gray with cobwebs. "Nothin'."

"C'mon down," Wendell told him, and Clayton swung back through the hole. His hands and the knees of his pants were black with dirt, and he stopped off in the bathroom to wash some of it off while the rest of us headed out to look for the entrance to the underside of the house.

It was another wooden panel, barely bigger than the one in the closet, inserted into the cinderblock foundation. Jamal levered it off and crouched to peer inside the dark hole. "Anybody got a flashlight?"

"Car," Wendell said, and José set off at a jog. He handed the flashlight to Jamal, who took it and squeezed through the opening into the underside of the house.

His voice came back to us as he crawled around, no doubt getting just as dirty as Clayton, who bounced out of the house to join us in crowding around the crawlspace door. "Got some trash here. Candy wrappers and soda cans. A beer bottle. Half a PVC pipe."

His voice faded as he moved farther away from the opening. The crawlspace wasn't likely to be divided as the upstairs was; it would be just one long area under the entire structure. Once Jamal reached the underside of Rafe's half of the duplex, we could no longer hear him.

It took a lot longer for him to come back than it had Clayton, but eventually he slithered back through the hole, in even worse shape than Clayton had been. "You gotta plumbing leak," he told Rafe when he'd shaken off the worst of the dirt. "No bodies, though. The only bones I saw looked like they mighta been a raccoon or something."

He lifted his hands to his nose and sniffed, and his face twisted. "I smell like shit." It probably wasn't intended to be a pun, so I suppressed my giggle. "I gotta go wash."

He set off for the house, holding his hands as far away from his nose as possible.

José, the only one of the three who still looked pristine, glanced at the woods behind the house. "So we gotta go in there."

Grimaldi nodded. "Come over to the car."

She grabbed a file folder from the front seat and opened it on the hood of the car while we circled around. "I didn't get a chance to update you yesterday," she glanced at me, "but these are the women we're looking for. Mr. Collier—" she nodded to Rafe, "identified the pictures yesterday afternoon. "This is Maria Elena Figueroa," one of the Hispanic Marias I had found, "and this is Krystal Ellison." A young blonde with an oversized nose and shoulder-length hair. "Krystal left home five years ago; most likely willingly. She was seventeen, and from Pittsburg. Not the one in Pennsylvania; the one about two hours south of here, just before Chattanooga."

We nodded.

"Her mother reported her missing. There was no father. She had a boyfriend, and left with him. I tracked him down last night. He's still in Nashville. He said he didn't make Krystal sell herself, but at this point, there's no way to know whether he's telling the truth or not. His story is they got here and had a fight. Krystal said she was going home. She walked away, and he never saw her again. Could be the truth, could be a lie."

"But he's not a suspect," José said, "since we know who killed her."

"Correct. But I'd still nail him for trafficking if I could." She moved on. "Maria Elena grew up in El Salvador. The family came to Oklahoma when she was fourteen. At sixteen, still in high school, she vanished."

"From Oklahoma?"

Grimaldi nodded. "In Maria's case, we suspect a violation of the Mann Act."

She had mentioned the Mann Act once before, so I knew what it was. Born during the 'white slavery' hysteria of the early 20th century, the Mann Act makes it a crime to transport someone across state lines for immoral purposes. Taking Maria from Oklahoma to Tennessee to make her a truck stop prostitute was definitely a violation. Not that there was any chance at all of finding who was responsible after all this time.

"They won't look like this now." Grimaldi tapped the photographs. "More than likely, we're looking for bones. We probably won't find clothes, and we have no idea what they were wearing when Hernandez grabbed them, anyway. That happened months after each girl disappeared from home. They could have been wearing anything."

We nodded.

"Maria had a chain with a gold crucifix around her neck when she left home. She might still have been wearing it when she died. We didn't find it among the things in Hernandez's van. She also had pierced ears, so there might be earrings. Krystal had pierced ears, as well, and favored big hoops. It isn't likely we'll find anything like that, but keep an eye out for anything shiny."

We nodded.

"I don't expect a thorough search," Grimaldi said. "We'll most likely have to bring in the K-9 unit to get results. But we're here. We may as well have a look around."

We nodded. Jamal had joined us now, so he nodded, too. "Let's do this," he said, chivvying his fellow rookies toward the tree line.

"Spread out about twelve feet apart," Wendell called after them. "Holler if you find anything."

They nodded, scampering off into the woods like three puppies let off the leash.

Wendell turned to the rest of us. "They make me tired."

Rafe's mouth twisted. "How d'you think I feel?"

"You're gonna heal and get better, boy. Ain't no fixing old age." He nodded to the woods. "Shall we?"

We should. I'd even put on halfway-sensible shoes, just in case. By which I mean low heels. Although pushing through the brush wasn't going to do my exposed calves any good.

"You can stay here with the cars," Rafe said. "I don't want you overdoing in the heat."

I didn't want him overdoing in the heat, either. "If you're going, I'm going." We'd just take it slow. As Grimaldi had said, we weren't likely to find anything anyway.

But for once, we got lucky. If you can call it luck when you're looking for a couple of dead women. Only about ten minutes had passed when José's voice rang out between the trees. "I think I got something!"

We all turned in his direction. He was on the far end of the line, with Jamal between him and Clayton, then Wendell, and finally Grimaldi. Rafe and I were together, both of us no doubt thinking we'd help the other across the rough spots. He was moving easier today than yesterday, but 'slow' and 'careful' were still watchwords.

When José called, we all waded through the brush toward him, still keeping a sharp eye out for anything that might be bone instead of twig.

Rafe and I got there last, and by then, everyone else was crowded around José's find.

At first glance it looked like another branch. Stripped of bark and bleached by sun and rain. But— "Femur," Grimaldi said.

The back of my neck prickled. "Thigh bone, right? Are you sure it's human?"

Wendell nodded and raised his head. "Spread out from here. Look for anything else that might relate."

It was Jamal who found the next clue. "Gotta pink rubber band over here," he called out. "And... shit!"

He took a step back.

We all converged on Jamal's location. He was standing there shaking, not over the dirty pink elastic band—the kind a girl (or boy) with long hair might use—but over the skull sitting a foot away, staring at us through empty eye sockets.

Even I couldn't mistake that for a twig. Or think it was anything but human.

"Maria had long hair," I said. My voice was hushed, and sounded weird in the silence under the trees.

Grimaldi nodded. "Time to call in the dogs. And the crime scene crew." She reached for her phone.

"Can we keep looking until they get here?" Clayton asked when she'd finished her call. He hadn't found anything, so maybe he was feeling like he needed to prove himself. Or maybe he just wanted to help. "If she's here," he glanced at the skull, "maybe the other girl's here somewhere, too."

"It's been four years," Wendell said to Grimaldi. "Not like they can compromise the crime scene. Rain and snow and animals already did that."

"And it isn't like we don't already know who the killer is," I added.

Grimaldi nodded. "Keep looking. For now, we'll assume this is Maria. Let's see if we can find Krystal." She took a handkerchief out of her pocket and tied it to a branch above Maria's head. Above the skull.

We fanned out again.

Several more bones were found within a minute or two. Pieces of Maria, we assumed, since they were within six or eight feet of her head.

"He didn't cut up the body," I whispered to Rafe, "did he?"

He shook his head. "She's been here four years. Water may have moved some of the bones around. And animals prob'ly got at her and took some of the bones away."

"What kinds of animals?" We don't have anything too scary around here. No bears, no wolves, no cougars.

"Could be dogs," Rafe said with a shrug as he examined the ground. He must have sensed my horrified expression—*dogs?*—because he looked up. "They don't know no better, darlin'. To them it's just a bone. They don't know that it used to be a person."

"I suppose."

"Or it could be raccoons or maybe coyotes. We get those around here sometimes."

We did. "It's horrible," I said, shuffling through the brush. "Those poor girls. First they're tortured and then they're killed and then they're tossed out here like so much garbage. And then dogs and coyotes rummage through their bones."

Rafe had his eyes fastened on the ground. "We'll find 'em. And then they can go home to their families and go in the ground with some dignity. There."

He stopped.

"Where?"

He pointed. I looked. "Oh, God."

It was an almost entirely intact skeleton, laid out in the brush as if in a coffin. Legs straight, hands on its chest. A glimmer of gold nestled among the vertebrae of the neck, just below the grinning skull.

"This is Maria," Rafe said. "That back there must have been Krystal."

Or someone else, someone we didn't know about.

But yes, this was Maria. A slender crucifix on a thin gold chain circled what had been her neck. And another hair elastic, this one green, rested in the vicinity of her third rib, curled three times. Maybe she'd had her hair in a braid that day, with the green elastic at the bottom. I thought about asking Rafe if he remembered a braid, but I decided I didn't really need to know. This was Maria. The crucifix proved it.

Grimaldi agreed. "That's both of them. If there are any more, the crime scene crew can find them. We're done. Good work, y'all." She marked the location of Maria's body the same way she'd marked Krystal's, and we turned back to the duplex, still visible in the distance, between the trees.

"He didn't carry'em far," Jamal remarked.

No, he hadn't. Although in the middle of the night—which was when I would have gone out to dispose of a body—and carrying dead weight through brush and trees, concerned that the noise he was making would wake up the guy sleeping in the apartment next door, maybe it wasn't such a surprise.

"Far enough that nobody found'em till now," Clayton answered, which was certainly also true.

José didn't say anything, and when I turned to look for him, I saw that he was still standing over Maria's body. His head was bent and his hands clasped in front of him.

Jamal opened his mouth, but Wendell shook his head. "He ain't doing nothing wrong. Leave him be."

We trudged out of the woods and back to the house in silence.

Grimaldi immediately got busy on the phone. José joined the rest of us after a minute—nobody gave him a hard time about praying, at least not in my hearing—and the three rookies piled into the SUV with Wendell and took off, leaving the rest of the body detail to Grimaldi and the MNPD crime scene crew. Rafe, it seemed, had the rest of the day off to rest and recuperate.

"Gee," I said, "a whole day. Are you sure you won't be bored, being idle so long?"

He grinned. "I'm sure we can think of something to do."

"I was being sarcastic," I told him. "After being kidnapped and tortured and almost killed, and had your girlfriend and son and future mother-in-law held hostage and almost killed, I would have thought they'd give you more than twenty-four hours off."

He shrugged. "There's stuff I can do there that'll keep me off my feet. Like teaching Jamal to pick locks."

Sure. "Maybe we can go buy a new mattress, since you don't have anything to do today." And since the one at the house still had Kelly's blood on it.

"I think we might could do that," Rafe said. "And then maybe we can break it in later." He winked.

"I think we might could do that," I answered, and made him grin.

Twenty-Five

Mother called on Friday morning to inform me that everything was ready to go for Saturday. "The tent is arriving this afternoon, along with the chairs. The caterer will be here tomorrow morning. So will the flowers. When are you coming?"

I blinked. Part of me had suspected the whole get-married-at-the-mansion/leave-everything-to-me bit had been a joke, suggested in the heat of the moment and forgotten by now. "I don't know. Rafe's at work until five."

Mother wrinkled her brows. I could hear it. "Perhaps you can drive down by yourself. I don't think the dress will need alteration, but just in case."

"I'm not leaving him here," I said.

"You can't spend the night together in any case, darling. It's bad luck for the groom to see the bride before the wedding."

"I'm not leaving my boyfriend in Nashville and driving to Sweetwater by myself," I informed her. "Last time we didn't spend the evening before the wedding together, he didn't show up the next morning. I'm not taking any chances."

Mother huffed. At least it sounded like a huff. "I suppose Rafael can spend the night with your brother. Dixon has a large house."

He did. And he liked Rafe well enough that dumping my boyfriend on him, unexpectedly, for the evening, might not be a big deal. Maybe the two of them could have their own bachelor party—minus the strippers—in Dix's kitchen tonight. Or the treat-my-sister-right-or-else talk, since I didn't have a father to set my boyfriend straight.

"That would probably be acceptable," I said.

"I'm glad to hear it," Mother answered dryly. "You'll be

staying here, of course. Audrey, Catherine, and I will be on hand to help you get ready in the morning."

Audrey, Catherine, and Mother had been on hand to help me get ready for my wedding to Bradley, too. This was going to bring back memories.

"What do I need to bring?" I asked.

"Just yourself," Mother told me. "The groom. And the rings."

"You've done everything else? Dress for me? Suit for Rafe? Wedding bouquet?"

"The groom brings the wedding bouquet," Mother said. "But it's been ordered. I'll have it delivered to Dixon's house later today."

I'm almost certain I heard the scribbling of a pen as she wrote a note to herself.

"Guests?" Maybe that was the joke. Rafe and I would get married at the mansion, but nobody would be there to see it.

"It will be a fairly small and intimate gathering," Mother said.

Hah!

"Only thirty or forty people."

I blinked. "That's not intimate." The ceremony we'd planned at the courthouse, with Wendell, Grimaldi, Dix and Catherine, had been intimate. Thirty or forty people was not intimate.

"We entertained almost three hundred for Dixon and Sheila's wedding," Mother informed me, and tacked on a, "rest her soul."

"Who did you invite?" Did Rafe and I even have forty friends between us? "David and the Flannerys? Wendell? Detective Grimaldi?"

"Of course," Mother said. "And the family will be there."

"So this is actually happening."

"Yes, Savannah," Mother said. "You will marry Rafael tomorrow morning. Unless you've changed your mind?" She sounded sort of hopeful. "If so, you should tell me now, while I can still cancel the flowers and the caterer."

"I haven't changed my mind," I said. "I'm having his baby.

My baby deserves a father. I love him. I haven't changed my mind." *Sheesh.*

"Then I will expect you this evening," Mother said and hung up in my ear.

"She's serious about this," I told Rafe two minutes later. I'd had to call him, of course. "She has actually put together a whole wedding." And in just five days. "With flowers and catered food and a tent and a wedding dress and guests. This is real!"

There was silence on the other end of the line.

"Hello?" I said. "Rafe?"

"I'm here. You thinking maybe you don't wanna do this?"

"What? No! Of course not. I just didn't think she'd actually go through with it."

Although that wasn't entirely true, either. When my mother said she was going to do something, she generally did it. After my father died, she'd said she was going to turn the mansion into an event venue. Weddings and music videos and photo shoots for magazines. And she had.

No, I hadn't really thought she'd say it and not do it. I just hadn't thought it would really happen.

"She's invited guests," I said. "Wendell. Grimaldi. David and his parents. I don't know if they're coming, but she invited them. She said there'll be thirty or forty people."

"I didn't think we knew thirty or forty people," Rafe said. "Not people who are gonna wanna watch you marry me."

I hadn't thought so either, but it didn't seem like a good idea to tell him that. "I guess we'll find out tomorrow who's there. You'll be spending the night with Dix."

There was silence.

"It's bad luck for the groom to see the bride before the wedding," I added.

"It's a good thing I like your brother," Rafe told me. "And that he tolerates me."

"I think he does more than tolerate you. And it could be

worse. She could have stuck you with Bob Satterfield."

Rafe snorted. "Between him and his son, they could kill me and nobody'd ever find the body."

"You're safer with Dix."

"Damn straight," Rafe said, and hung up, too.

He came home just before six. I had packed an overnight bag for myself, and Rafe always keeps a go-bag ready: left over from those years when he never knew where he might be headed on a moment's notice. Then we locked up the house, got in the Volvo, and headed to Sweetwater. I dropped Rafe at Dix's house—Mother must have warned my brother to expect us, because he opened the door with a, "The beer's cold and the pizza's on order,"—and then I drove to the mansion.

To be honest, I don't remember much about the evening. Too preoccupied with what was going to happen tomorrow to pay much attention to what was happening tonight. Mother took me outside and showed me the rows of chairs set up on the lawn, and the tent. She also made me try on the gown that was hanging in a garment bag in my room, just in case it needed a nip or a tuck by tomorrow morning.

I admit I'd been worried. The hoop-skirt gown I'd worn for my wedding to Bradley had been Mother's idea. I was concerned about the kind of monstrosity she might try to foist off on me now. But cooler heads—Catherine's, or maybe Audrey's—had prevailed. The dress was gorgeous. Off-white silk, with a delicately sequined bodice, empire waist, and a flowing chiffon skirt to my ankles. No train. No veil, either. "You had that the first time," Mother said. "You don't need it again."

No, I didn't. The dress came with a sequined headband, and once my hair was curled and shaped and twisted and sprayed in place, I'd look great. With the cut of the dress, I didn't even look all that pregnant.

My wedding day dawned warm and sunny. I woke up alone,

and for a second, I felt a stab of fear when I realized that Rafe wasn't next to me in bed. But then I opened my eyes and realized where I was, and I felt better. Dix had him. Dix wouldn't let anything happen to him.

"Dixon called," were the first words out of Mother's mouth when I padded into the kitchen in my bathrobe. "Everything is fine."

The last weight fell off my mind. Nothing had happened to him, and he hadn't decided to run away during the night. This was really happening.

Catherine showed up in a lovely blue dress, and a few minutes later, Audrey walked in, leggy in purple. She's my mother's best friend, and they look as different as night and day. Where Mother is soft, genteel, and ladylike, Audrey is tall and angular. She has thick, black hair in a dramatic wedge that somehow manages to emphasize both cheekbones and jaw, and she stands almost a head taller than Mother in her shiny patent-leather peek-a-boo pumps with platform soles. She runs Audrey's on the Square, the only designer boutique in the county, and I had no doubt whatsoever that my dress had come from her shop.

Between them, they spent the next two hours tweezing and painting and curling and spritzing me with various substances. The last thing that happened, was that the dress dropped over my head, covering the elegant satin-and-lace bra and panties that Audrey had also supplied. The idea that my mother and her best friend had picked out the underwear my husband would be peeling off me on our wedding night was a little disconcerting, but it was beautiful underwear, so I tried not to think about it.

They adjusted the dress, and adjusted the headband and hair, and blotted my lipstick one last time. When I was ready to scream, Mother finally stepped back. "All right, darling. What do you think?"

She turned me toward the mirror.

I looked at myself.

Catherine chuckled. "He's going to die when he sees you."

"I sincerely hope not," Mother said, "since this will all have been wasted effort."

Oh, sure. Because that was the biggest concern by far. That the preparations—the food, the flowers, the tent, and the dress—would be wasted because the groom was dead.

I tuned them out and focused on the mirror. The dress was gorgeous. My hair looked good. The makeup made me look dewy-fresh and glowing. Or maybe that was just the pregnancy.

Or the occasion.

"I look good," I said, unable to keep a hint of surprise out of my voice.

Everyone nodded.

"And I don't look like I'm wearing a tent." The chiffon draped over the baby bump without adding extra volume, and the detail on the bodice drew the eye up and away.

Audrey sniffed. "Certainly not."

"You're pregnant," Catherine added, "not fat."

I looked at myself in the mirror again. "I'm getting married."

All three of them smiled. Mother's may have been a bit strained, but only a bit. "If you're ready," she told me, "it's time to go."

Was it? I checked the clock on the bureau. Yes, it was.

Tamara Grimaldi was waiting in the foyer, in a dark blue dress similar to mine. Satin bodice with blue sequins, blue chiffon overskirt. Hers only came to the knees, though.

I blinked. Grimaldi was my bridesmaid? Not Mother or Catherine?

She handed me a spray of flowers: simple and stunning. White gardenias and baby's breath surrounded by glossy, dark green magnolia leaves, and finished off with trailing ivory ribbons. I lifted them to my nose, and was practically knocked back a step by the scent.

"You look stunning, Savannah," Audrey told me, with a kiss on the cheek.

Mother kissed the other one. "Good luck, darling."

I guess she still, in spite of practically begging Rafe to marry me, thought I might need it.

"Go knock him dead," Catherine added with a grin. She didn't bother kissing me, just herded Mother and Audrey ahead of her through the double doors and down the steps.

Grimaldi lifted a smaller gardenia bouquet from the foyer table. "Ready?"

I hesitated. "He's here, right?"

"Who? Your boyfriend?"

I nodded.

"Of course he's here," Grimaldi said. "Your brother babysat him all last night to make sure nothing happened."

"How does he look?" Nervous? Ready to bolt? Ready to throw up?

"Good," Grimaldi said, with a grin. "Wait until you see him."

"Did Mother make him wear a tuxedo?"

The grin widened. "Oh, yeah."

Oh... wow. I'd seen Rafe in a tailored suit before, and he'd looked great. Of course, if you ask me, I think he looks great in anything. And best wearing nothing at all. But there's just something about a good-looking man in a tuxedo.

Especially if that man's waiting for you at the altar.

"Ready?" Grimaldi asked again. "It's almost eleven. They'll start the wedding march any moment."

"There are musicians?"

"Of course," Grimaldi said. "Do you really think your mother would arrange a wedding with canned music?"

When she put it like that... "I guess not."

"We should go. Or he might start to worry that you've changed your mind."

And we certainly wouldn't want him thinking that. "I'm

ready," I said.

Grimaldi nodded and opened the door. I passed through, and she closed it behind me.

While I'd been upstairs getting painted and spritzed, someone had decorated the front of the mansion with more gardenias and magnolia leaves, and thick, white ribbons. A white runner started at the bottom of the steps and led off across the grass. Grimaldi and I stepped on it, and made our way toward the chairs and the tent.

Just outside the flaps, Grimaldi stopped. "I'll walk down the aisle first," she told me. "When I get to the front, they'll start the wedding march. Then you'll walk down."

"Alone?"

"Your brother can walk you if you want. But we thought you might want to walk on your own."

I blinked. That was different. My father had still been alive when I married Bradley, so he had walked me down the aisle and given me away. But I guess I didn't mind doing it on my own. I had given myself to Rafe long ago: body, soul, and heart. This was just a formality. "Sure."

Grimaldi nodded. "You've done this before, so you know what to expect. Try not to trip and fall on the way there."

She ducked through the flaps before I could respond to that tidbit of advice.

The music changed, and I guess what was the bridesmaid's processional began. I put one eye to the space between the flaps and squinted until she'd reached what I thought was the front of the tent. The music stopped, and a sort of breathless, anticipatory hush spread as everyone turned on their chairs to peer at the opening.

My heart was thudding so hard in my chest I had difficulty drawing a breath, and my hand was shaking when I pushed the tent flap open and stepped through.

I heard oohs and aahs from the audience.

The music started, but I couldn't move. I was too busy looking around. At the rows of chairs, decorated with gardenias and magnolia leaves. At the petals strewn across the aisle—the white silk runner—all the way to the front of the tent.

At the people.

There was my family, in the front. Mother and Dix, Catherine and Jonathan, and all five children, decked out in their Sunday best. Little Hannah had a huge, lopsided bow drooping over one ear.

Charlotte, my best friend from high school, was behind them. Somehow, Mother had gotten her here from North Carolina in time for this, and her parents, too, even if they'd only come from across town.

Darcy, the receptionist at Dix and Jonathan's law firm, was sitting with Audrey and the sheriff, next to my Aunt Regina, my father's sister and also the society reporter for the local newspaper.

Good Lord, would Rafe and I find ourselves in the society column of the Sweetwater Recorder next week?

Had Mother actually instructed my Aunt Regina to announce my nuptials to Sweetwater's prodigal bad-boy in the town paper?

And on the other side of the aisle...

Wendell sat beside Mrs. Jenkins, Rafe's grandmother, whom he must have liberated from the nursing home and brought with him. She was grinning toothlessly, her gray hair neatly tamed and her ubiquitous housecoat exchanged for a summer dress in pale blue. It was anyone's guess whether she understood what was going on, and had any clue who was marrying whom, but she was here, and looked happy to be.

Jamal, Clayton, and José were here, too, José with a young woman who looked a bit like the missing persons photo of Maria Figueroa. No wonder he'd needed an extra minute with Maria's remains.

Behind them, Ginny and Sam Flannery sat side by side, with Alexandra and Austin Puckett next to them. I had met Brenda's son and daughter last year, at her funeral, and Alexandra and I had struck up a sort of friendship. She was only sixteen—well, seventeen now—so we didn't spend much time together, but she liked me. She liked Rafe, too. And Austin and David went to school together, so David must have told them about the wedding and convinced Mother that she should invite them. Maybe Austin had been at Peaceful Pines with David these past two weeks.

David himself was standing up at the front of the tent, across from Grimaldi and next to his father. He looked proud and a bit nervous. They were both wearing tuxedos, with bowties and cummerbunds and gardenia boutonnières, and David looked like a miniature version of Rafe.

Rafe...

Well, he didn't look nervous. And of course he was stunning.

Yes, he looks good naked. But the tuxedo ran a close second. And later I could take him from one to the other and get to enjoy both.

Where I'd been a bit concerned that he'd be uncomfortable—with the monkey suit, the mansion, the whole big production number in front of everyone in our old hometown—he looked perfectly at ease.

I was the one who couldn't get my feet to move, while the wedding march reached the end and started for a second time.

Audrey leaned across the sheriff to Aunt Regina and whispered something.

Rafe raised his voice. "Don't dawdle, darlin'. Let's get this over with so I can get outta this suit."

The audience tittered. I could practically see Mother's brows wrinkle through the back of her head.

I grinned and headed up the aisle to claim the man I adored, the man who was everything I'd ever wanted, even if he was nothing I'd been told I should have. In front of God and Mother and everyone in Sweetwater.

# # #

About the Author

New York Times and *USA Today* bestselling author Jenna Bennett (Jennie Bentley) writes the Do It Yourself home renovation mysteries for Berkley Prime Crime and the Savannah Martin real estate mysteries for her own gratification. She also writes a variety of romance for a change of pace. Originally from Norway, she has spent more than twenty five years in the US, and still hasn't been able to kick her native accent.

For more information, please visit Jenna's website:
www.JennaBennett.com